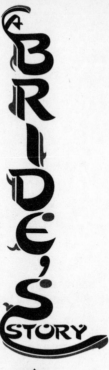

A BRIDE'S STORY

7

Kaoru Mori

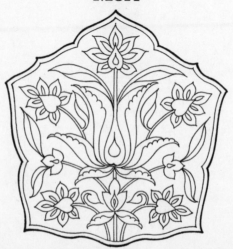

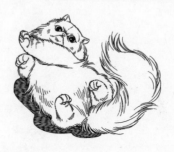

TABLE OF CONTENTS

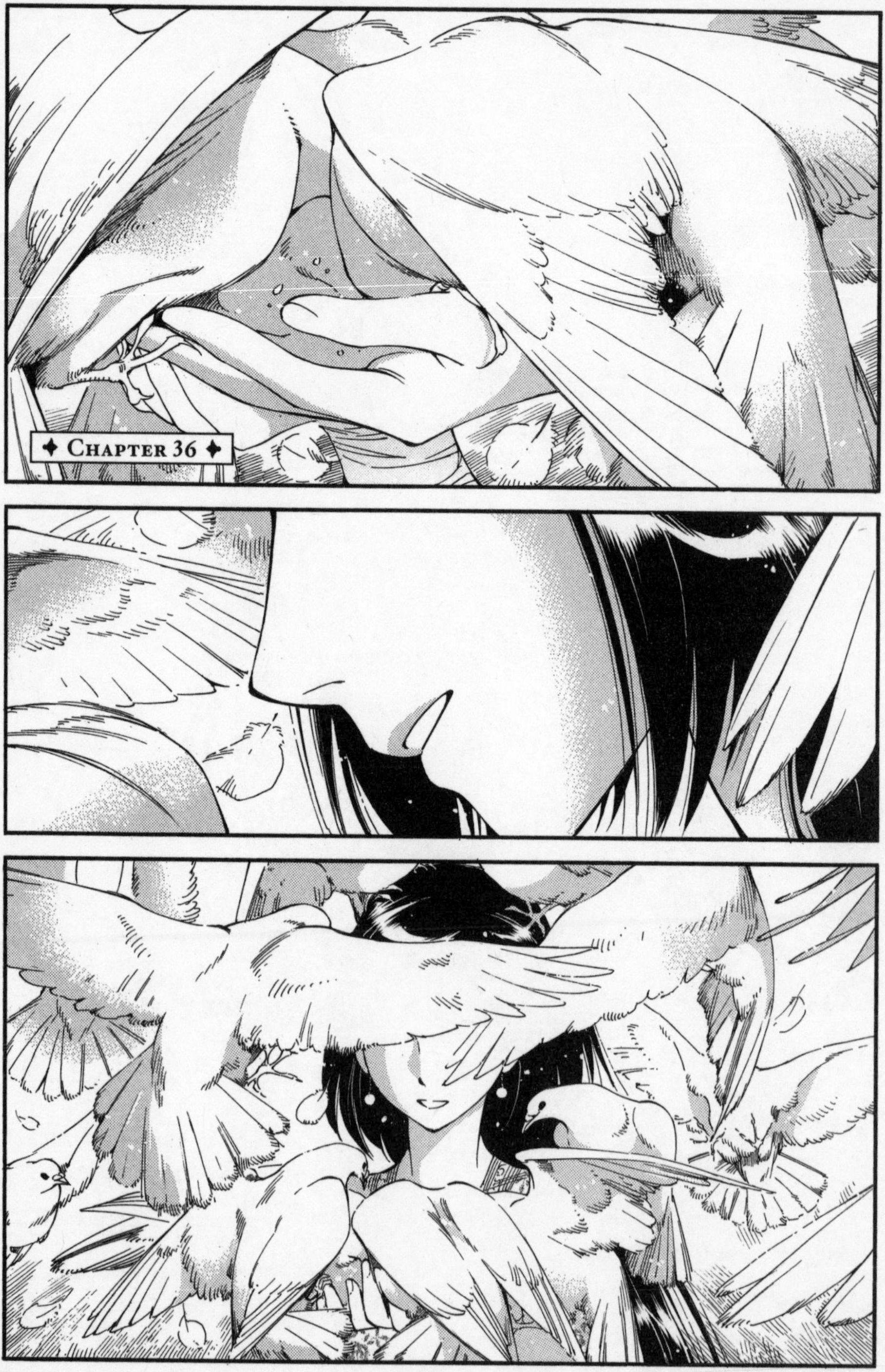
✦ Chapter 36 ✦

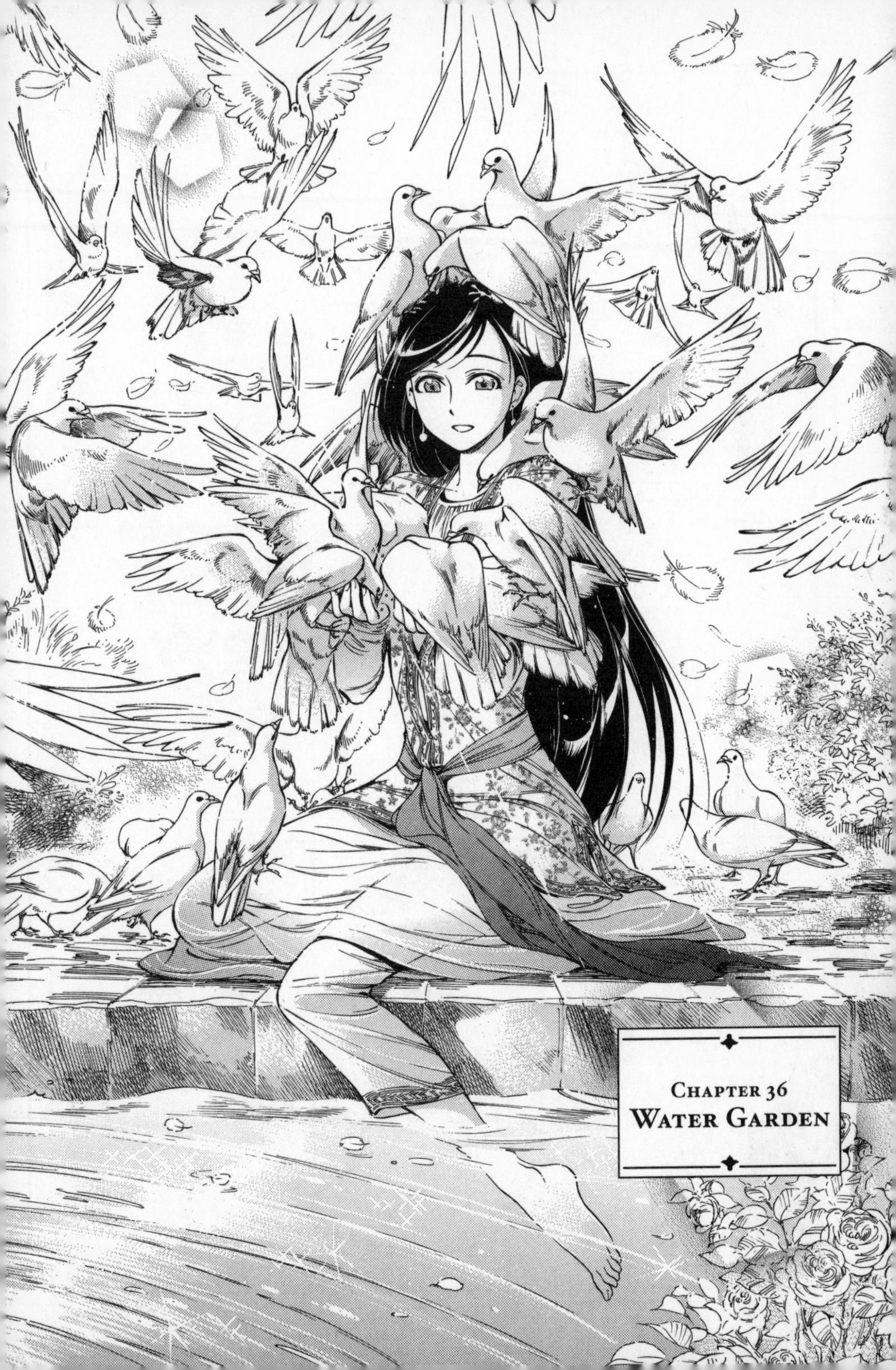

Chapter 36
Water Garden

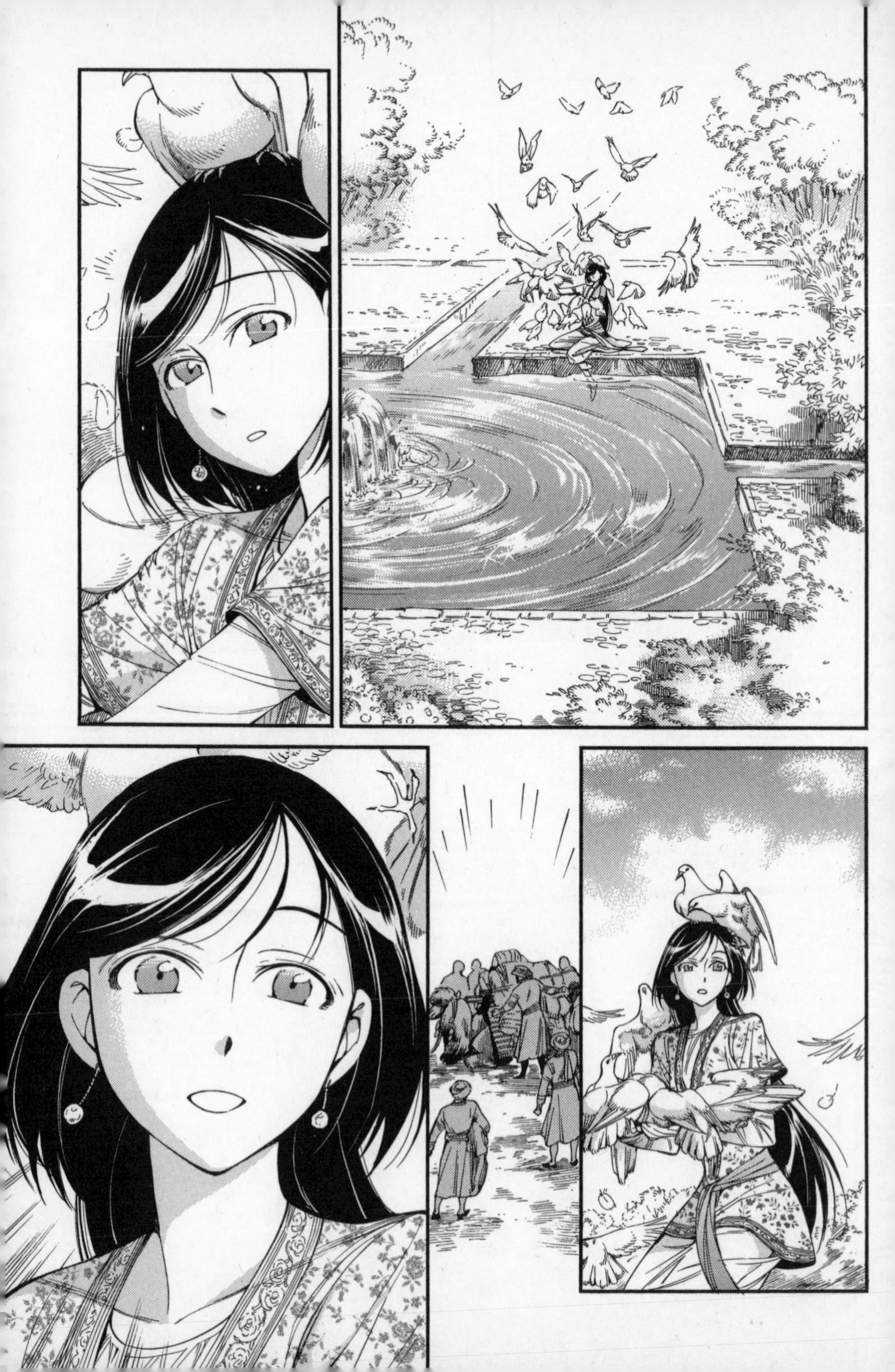

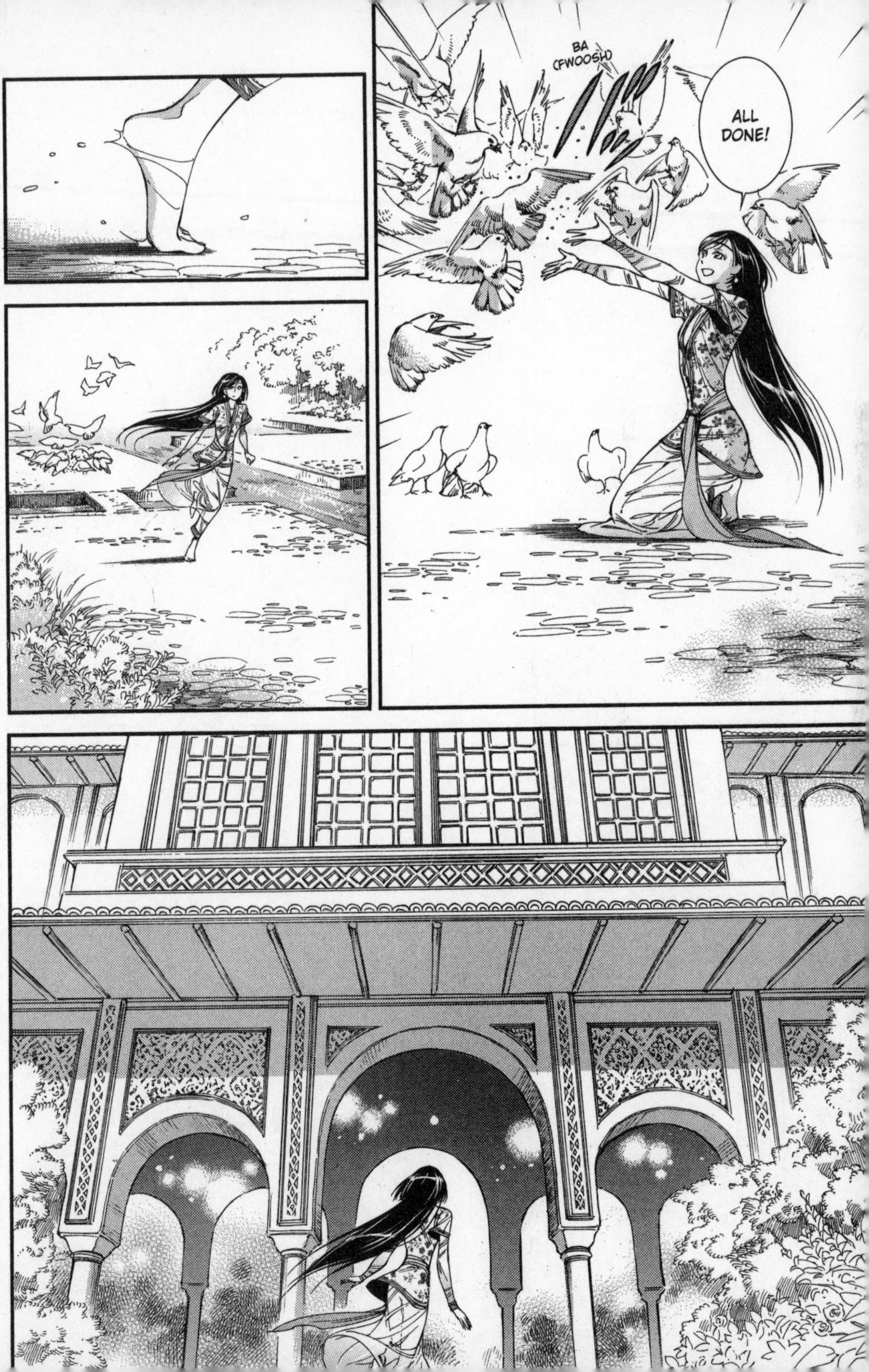
ALL DONE!
BA (FWOOSH)

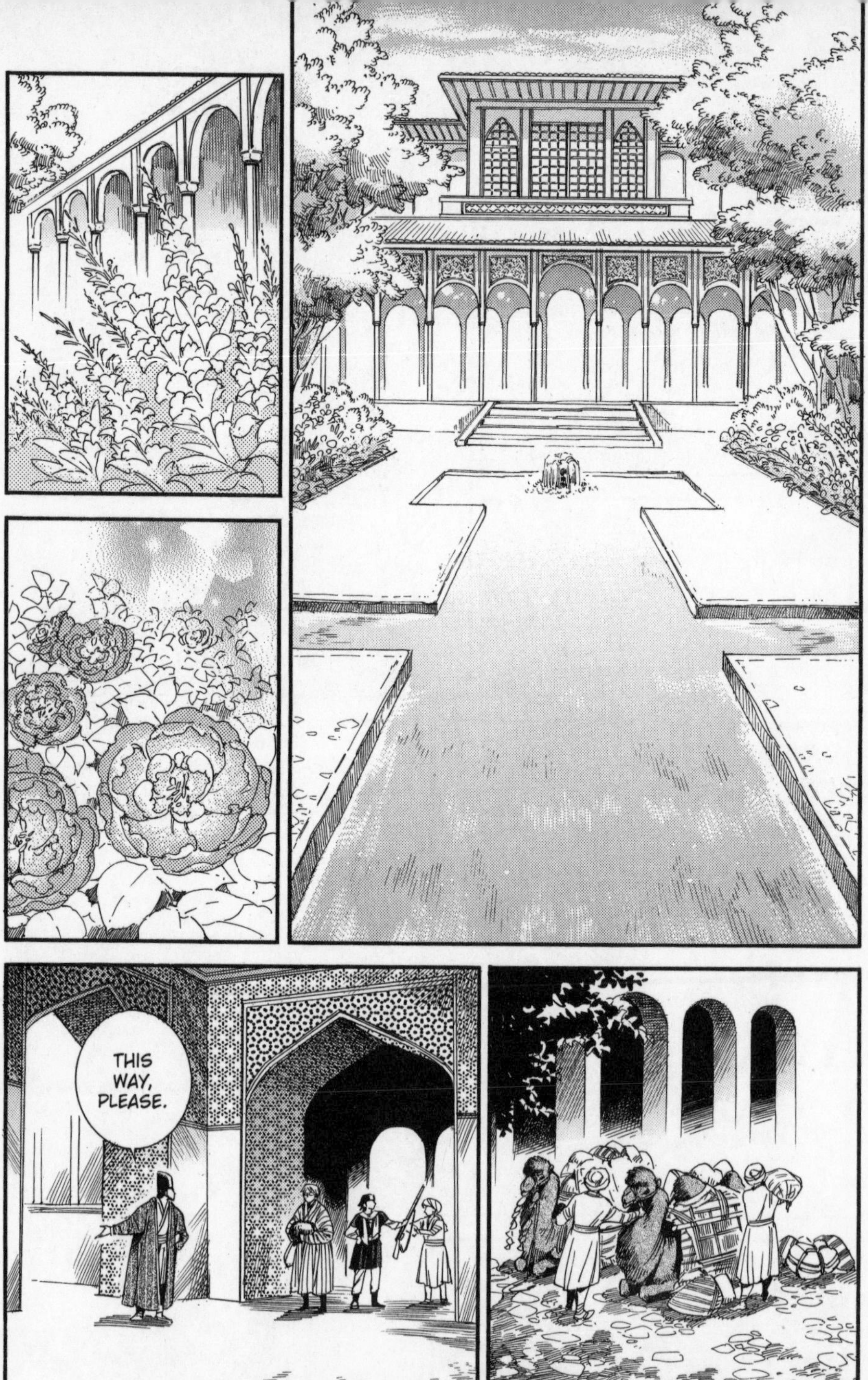
THIS WAY, PLEASE.

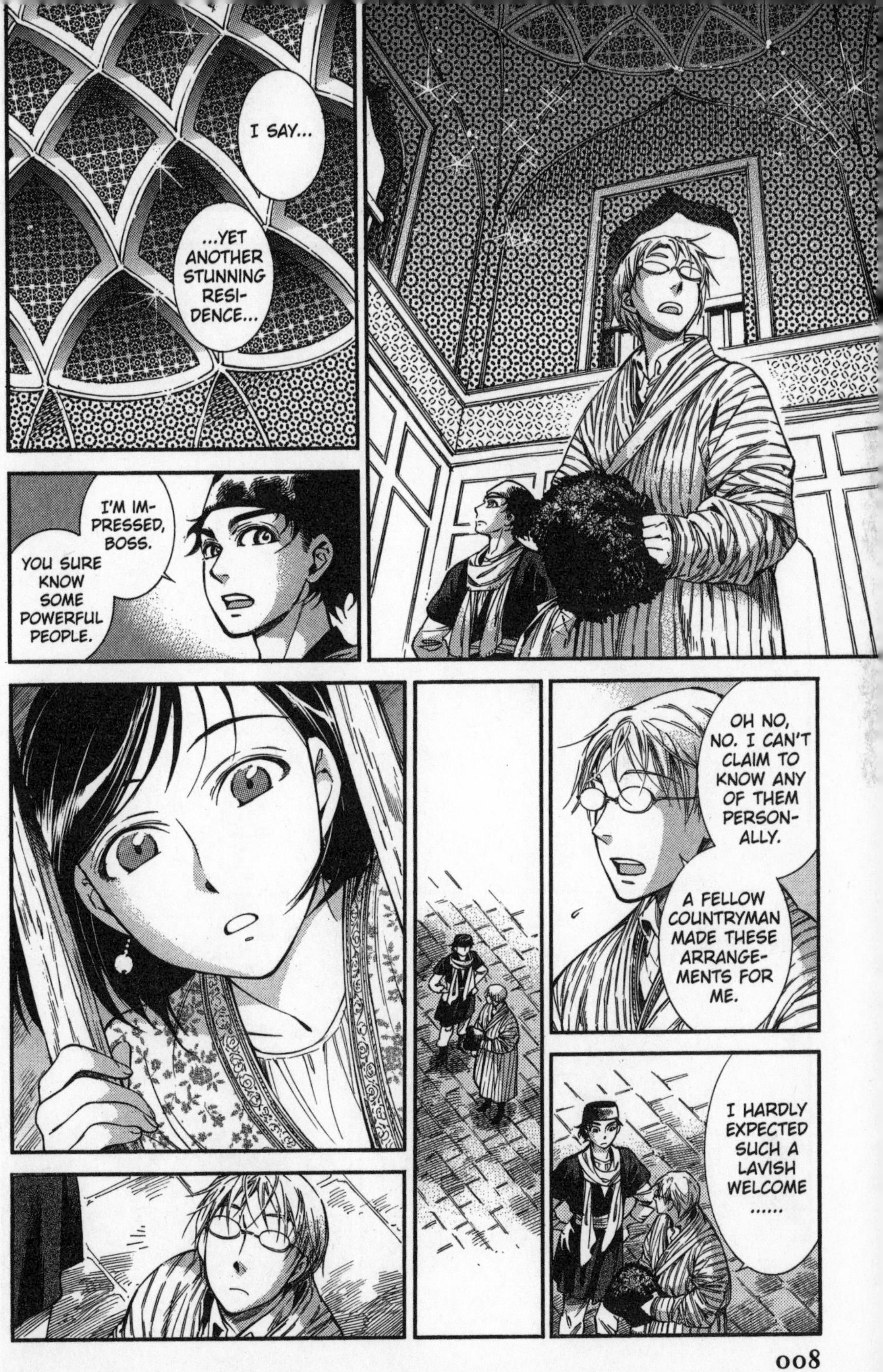
I SAY...
...YET ANOTHER STUNNING RESIDENCE...
I'M IMPRESSED, BOSS.
YOU SURE KNOW SOME POWERFUL PEOPLE.
OH NO, NO. I CAN'T CLAIM TO KNOW ANY OF THEM PERSONALLY.
A FELLOW COUNTRYMAN MADE THESE ARRANGEMENTS FOR ME.
I HARDLY EXPECTED SUCH A LAVISH WELCOME ......

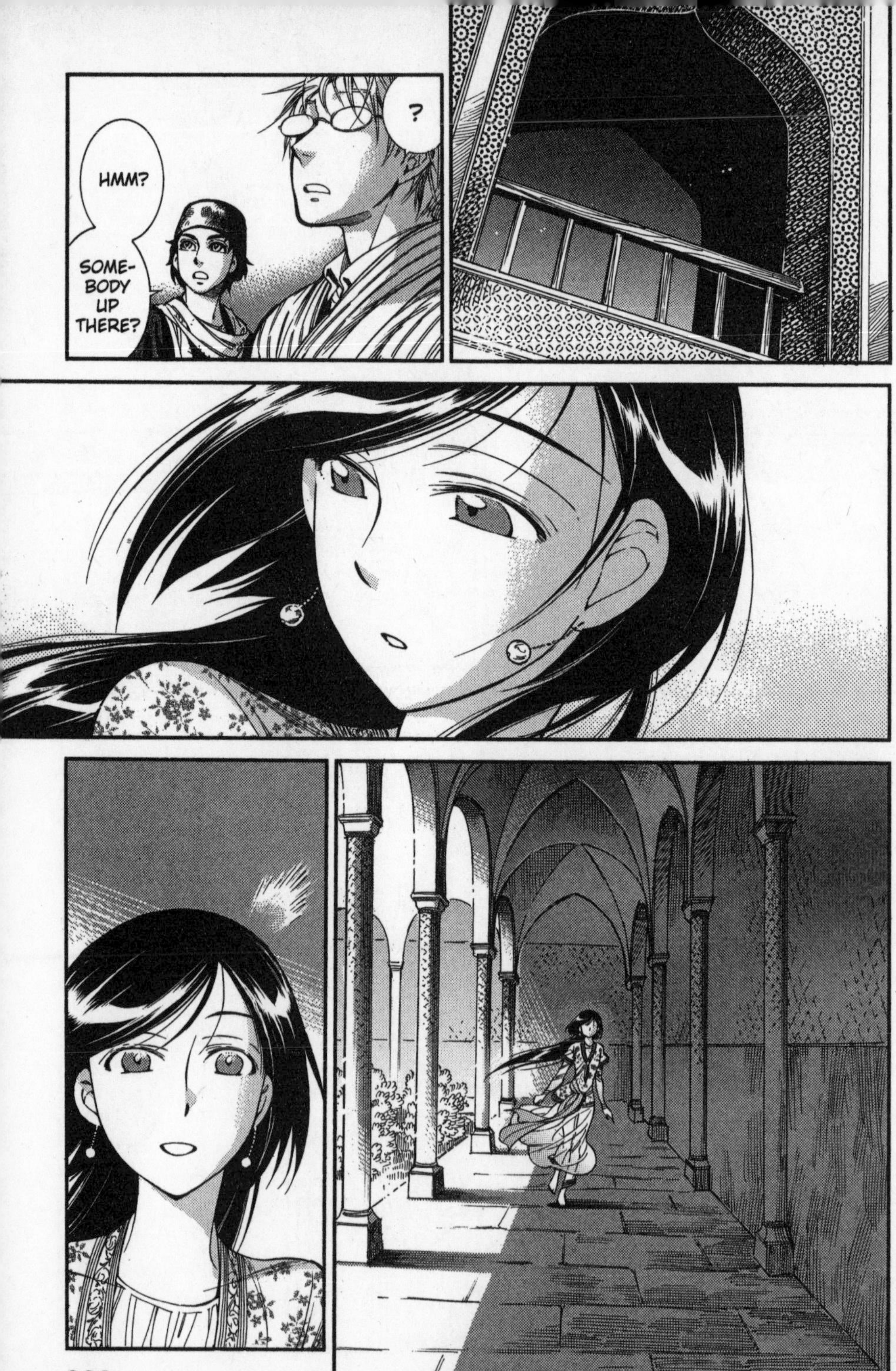
?
HMM?
SOME-BODY UP THERE?

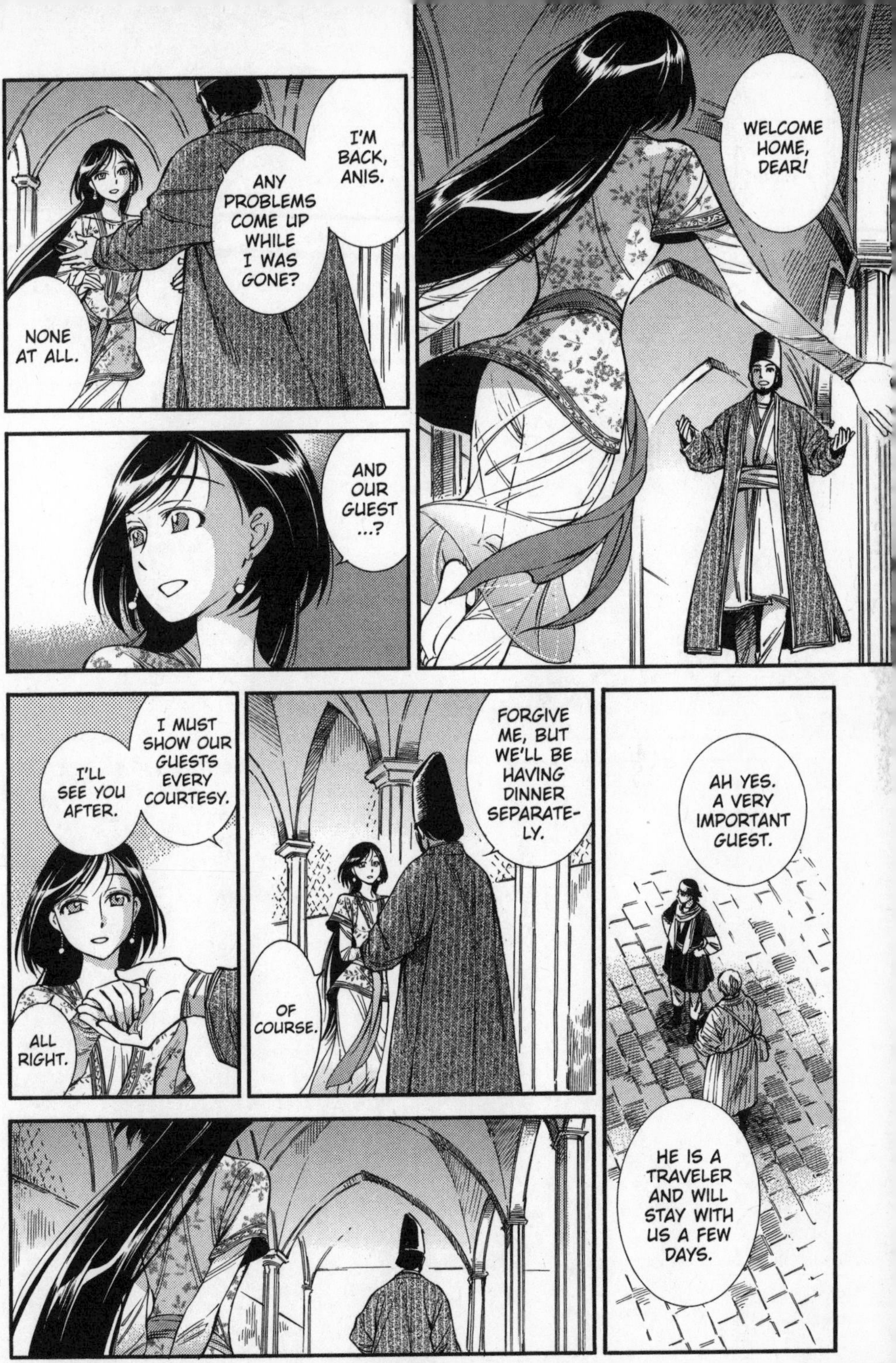
WELCOME HOME, DEAR!
I'M BACK, ANIS.
ANY PROBLEMS COME UP WHILE I WAS GONE?
NONE AT ALL.
AND OUR GUEST ...?
AH YES. A VERY IMPORTANT GUEST.
HE IS A TRAVELER AND WILL STAY WITH US A FEW DAYS.
FORGIVE ME, BUT WE'LL BE HAVING DINNER SEPARATE-LY.
OF COURSE.
I MUST SHOW OUR GUESTS EVERY COURTESY.
I'LL SEE YOU AFTER.
ALL RIGHT.

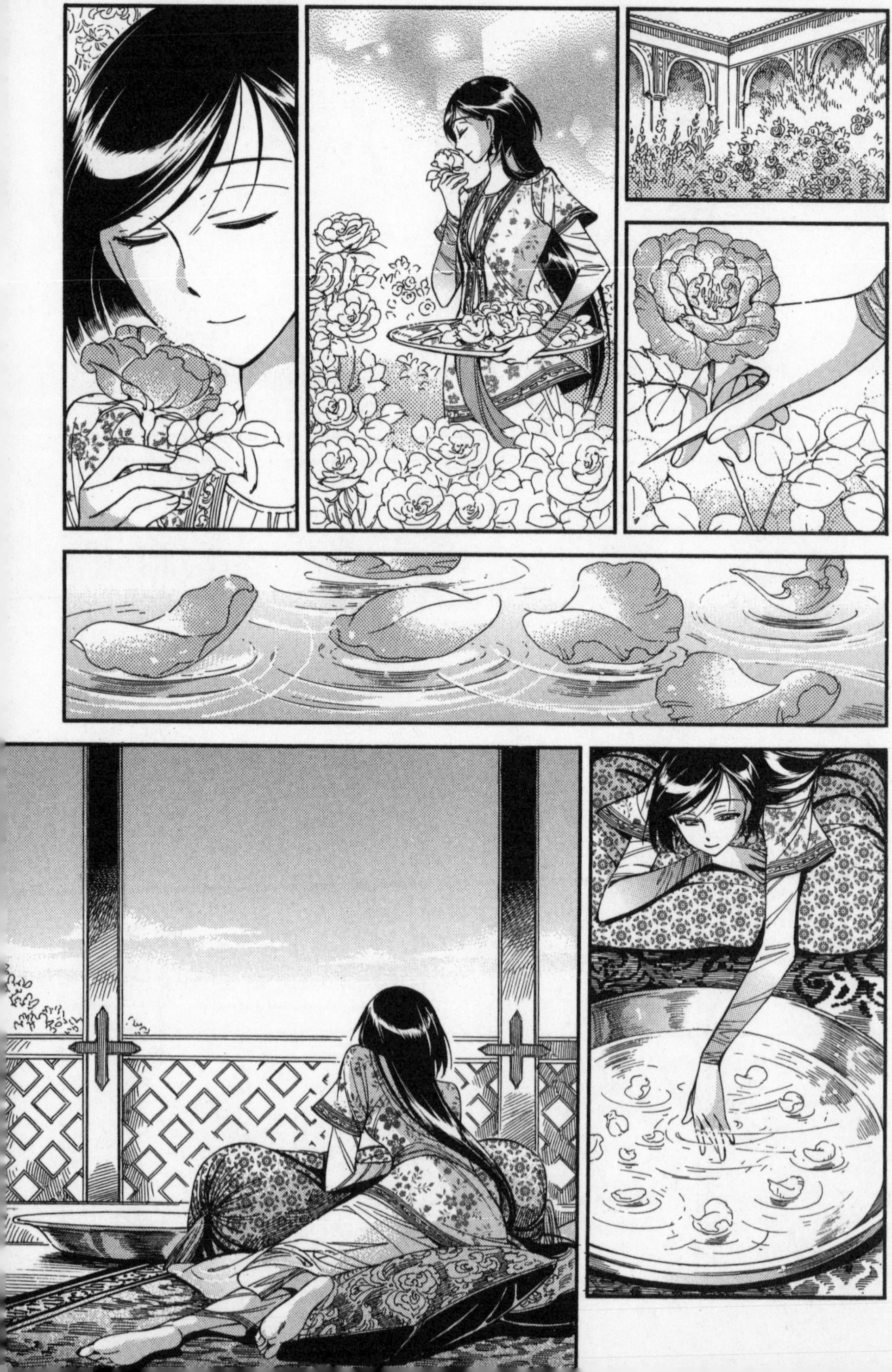

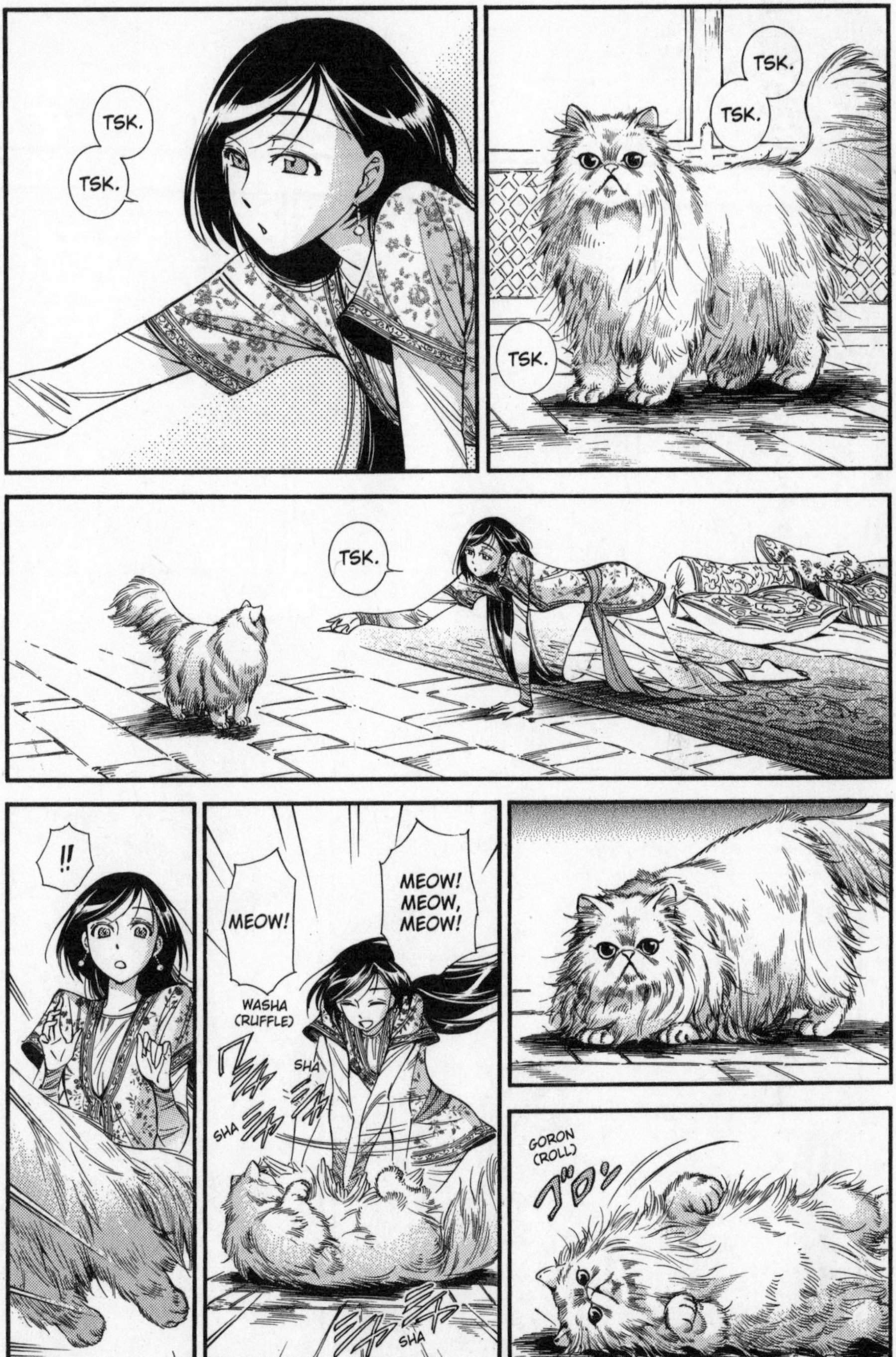
TSK.
TSK.
TSK.
TSK.
TSK.
TSK.
GORON (ROLL)
MEOW! MEOW, MEOW!
MEOW!
WASHA (RUFFLE)
SHA
SHA
SHA
SHA
!!

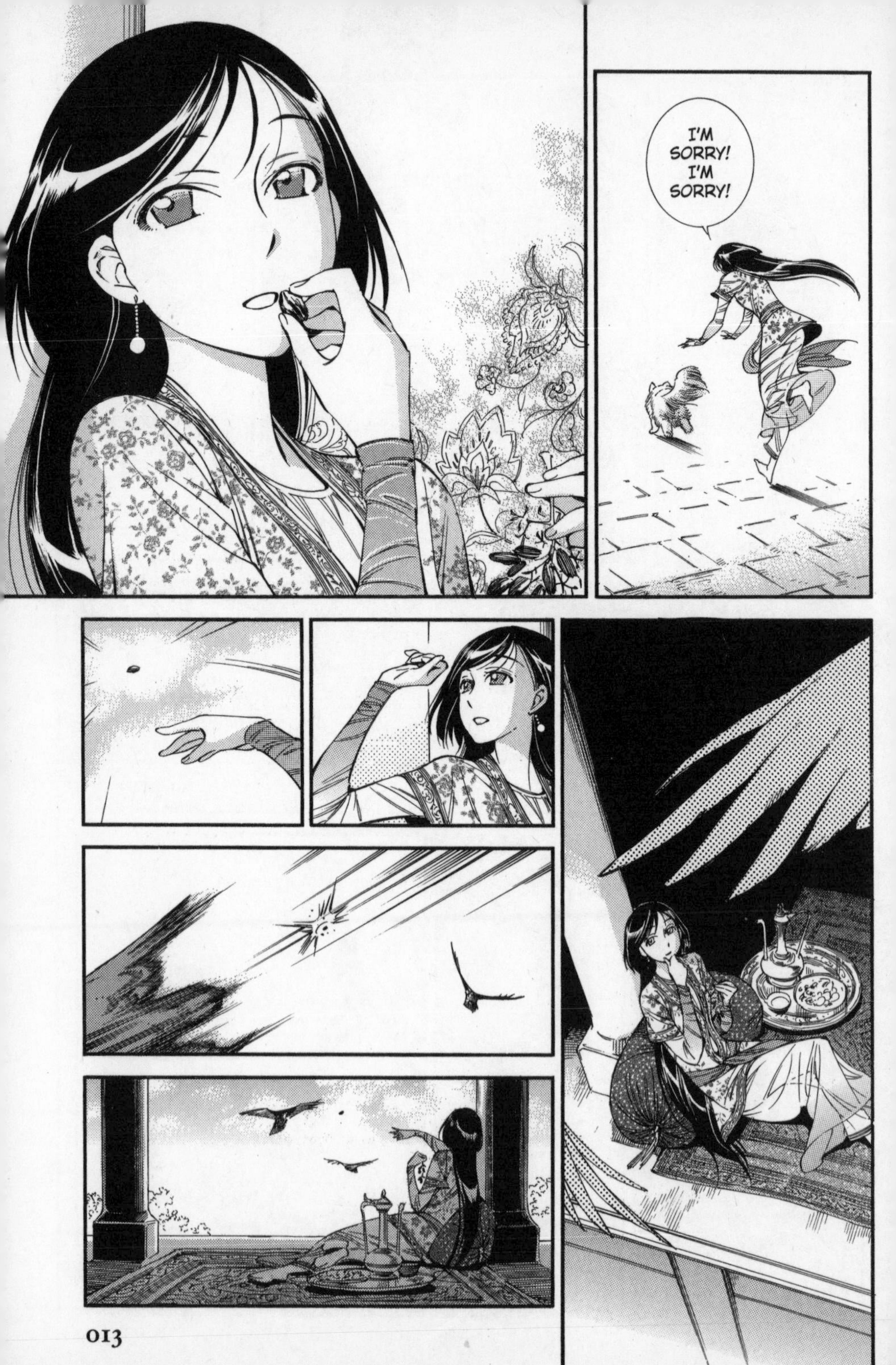
I'M SORRY! I'M SORRY!

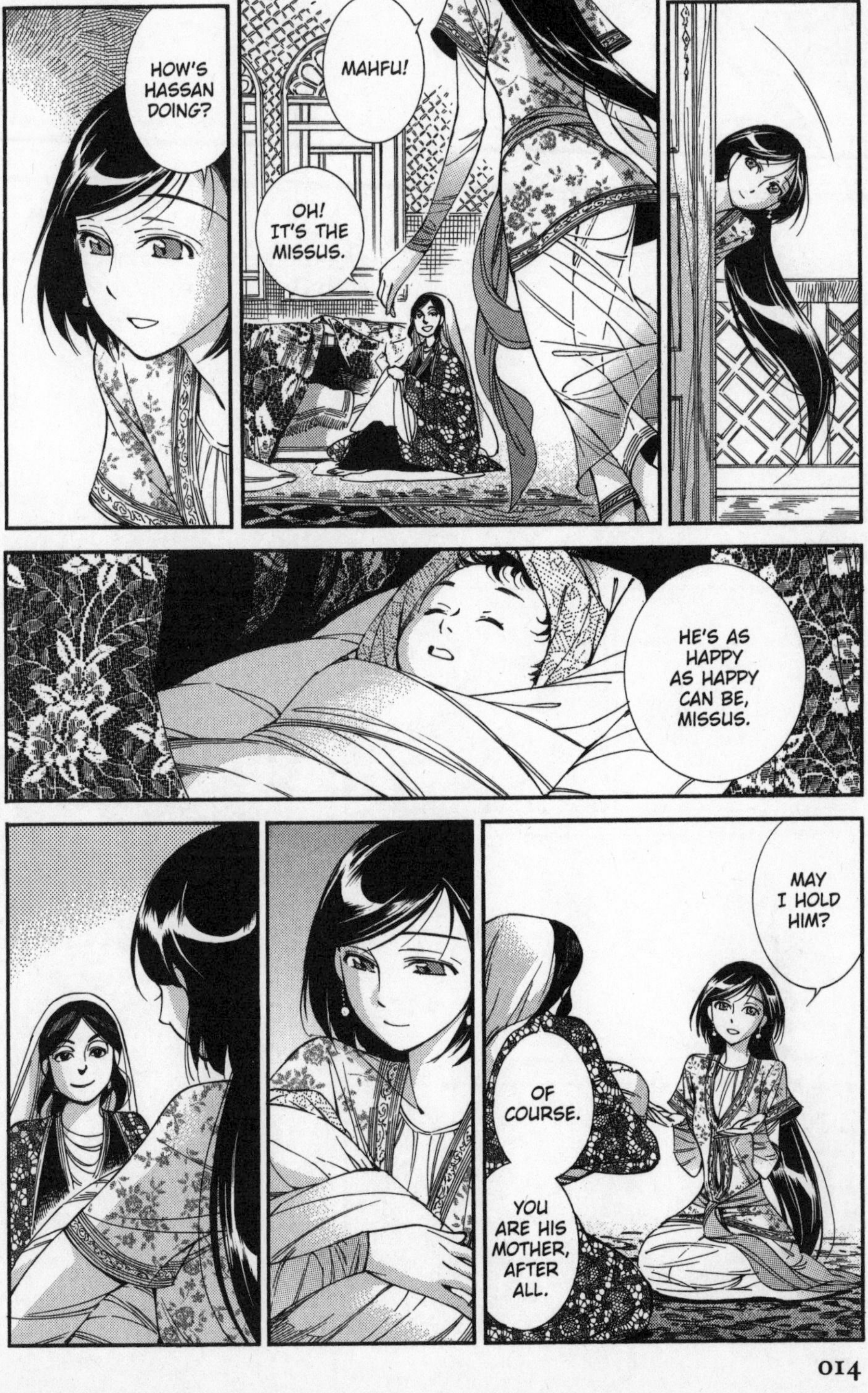
MAHFU!
OH! IT'S THE MISSUS.
HOW'S HASSAN DOING?
HE'S AS HAPPY AS HAPPY CAN BE, MISSUS.
MAY I HOLD HIM?
OF COURSE.
YOU ARE HIS MOTHER, AFTER ALL.

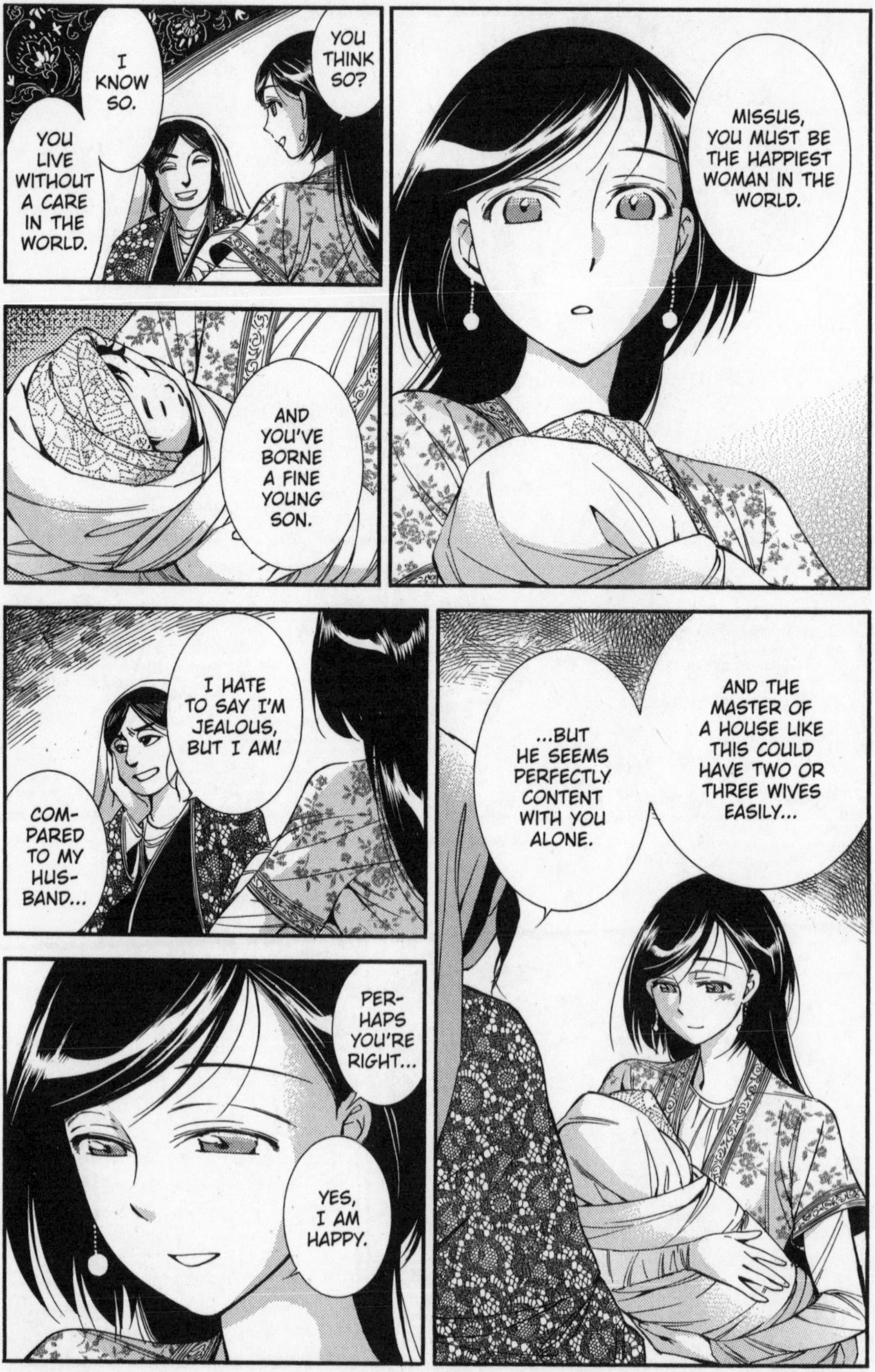
MISSUS, YOU MUST BE THE HAPPIEST WOMAN IN THE WORLD.
YOU THINK SO?
I KNOW SO.
YOU LIVE WITHOUT A CARE IN THE WORLD.
AND YOU'VE BORNE A FINE YOUNG SON.
AND THE MASTER OF A HOUSE LIKE THIS COULD HAVE TWO OR THREE WIVES EASILY...
...BUT HE SEEMS PERFECTLY CONTENT WITH YOU ALONE.
I HATE TO SAY I'M JEALOUS, BUT I AM!
COM-PARED TO MY HUS-BAND...
PER-HAPS YOU'RE RIGHT...
YES, I AM HAPPY.

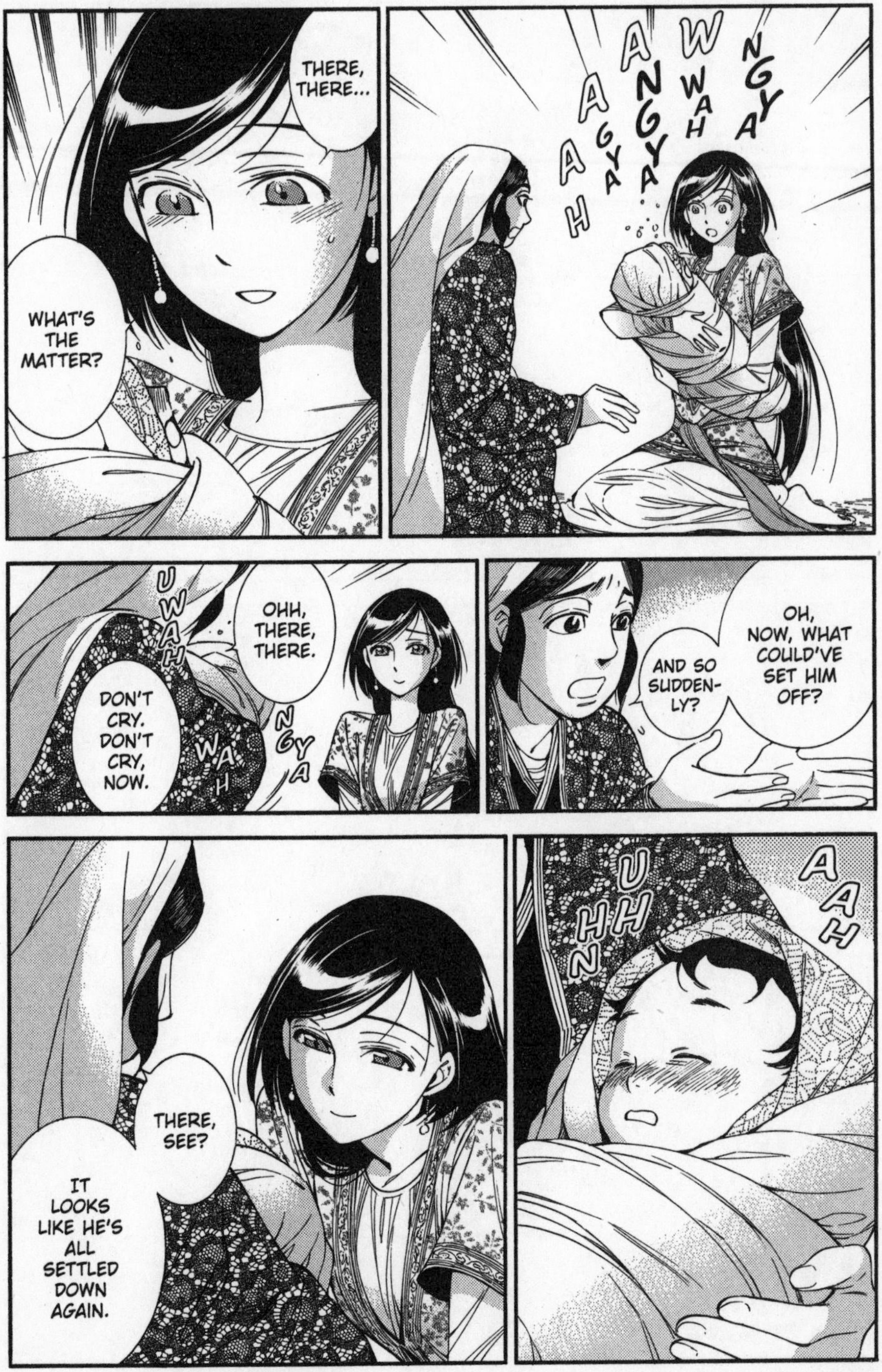
NGYAA
WWAH
ANGYAA
GYA
AAAH
THERE, THERE...
WHAT'S THE MATTER?
OH, NOW, WHAT COULD'VE SET HIM OFF?
AND SO SUDDEN-LY?
OHH, THERE, THERE.
UWAH
DON'T CRY. DON'T CRY, NOW.
NGYA
WAH
AAH
UHHN
THERE, SEE?
IT LOOKS LIKE HE'S ALL SETTLED DOWN AGAIN.

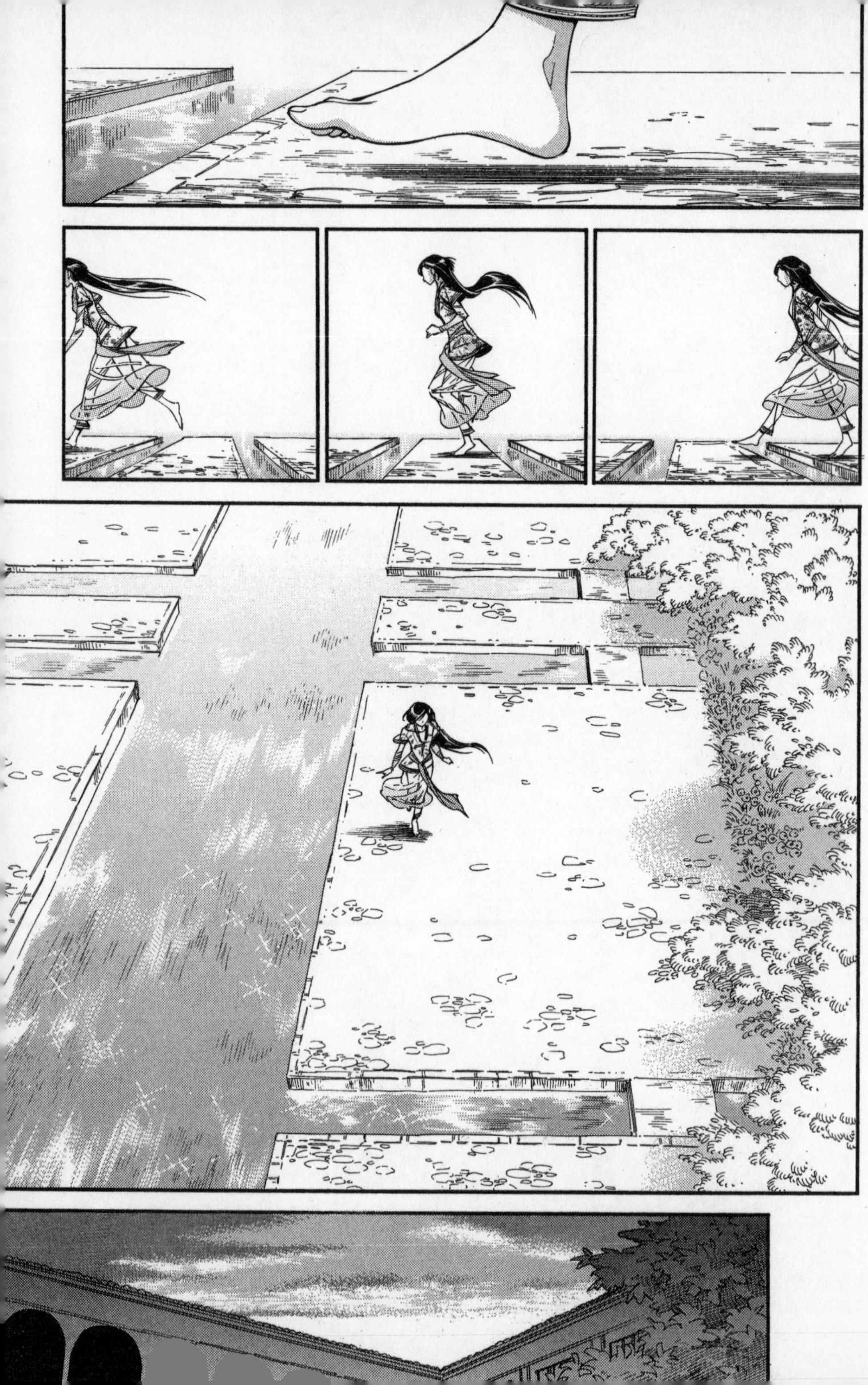

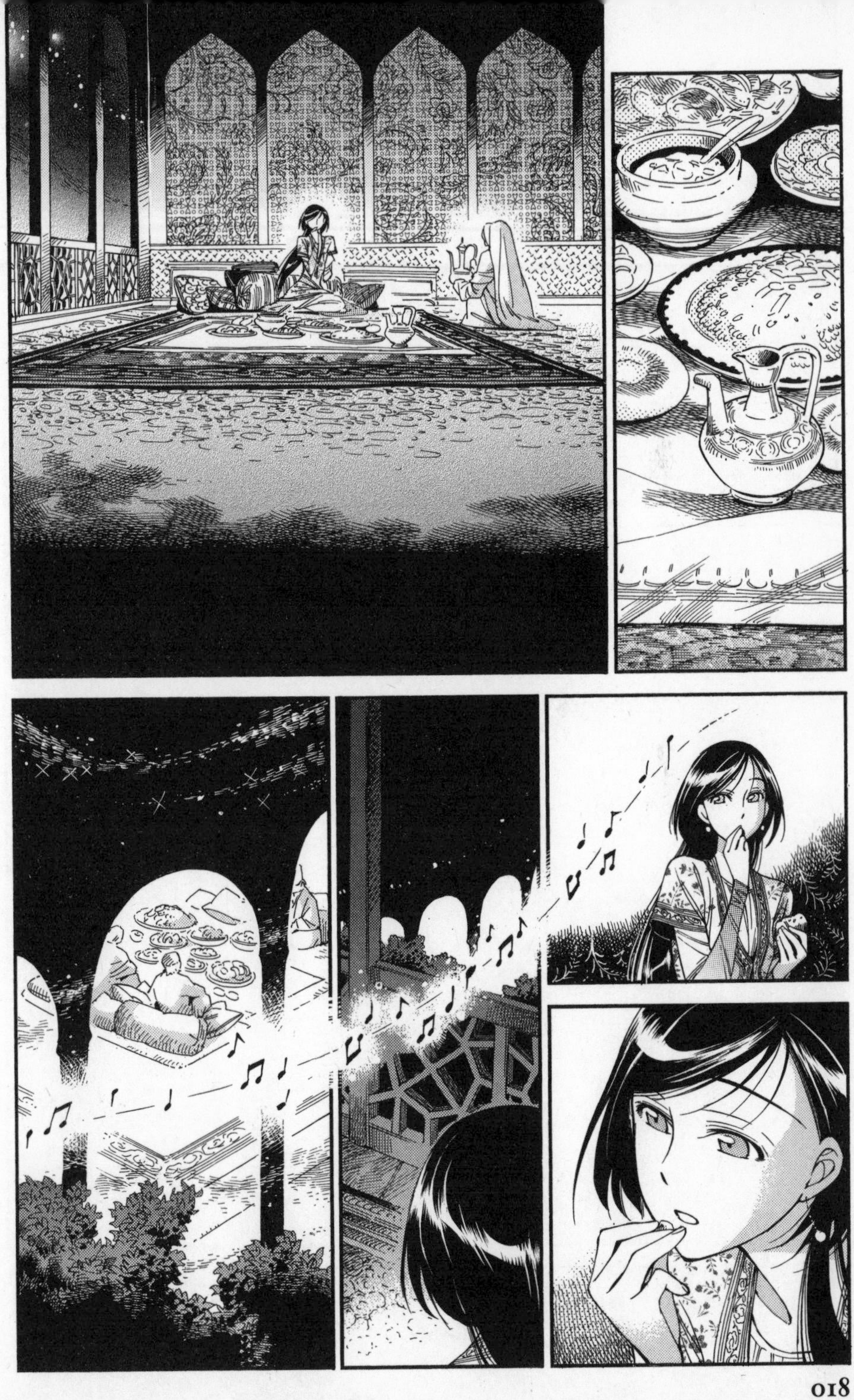

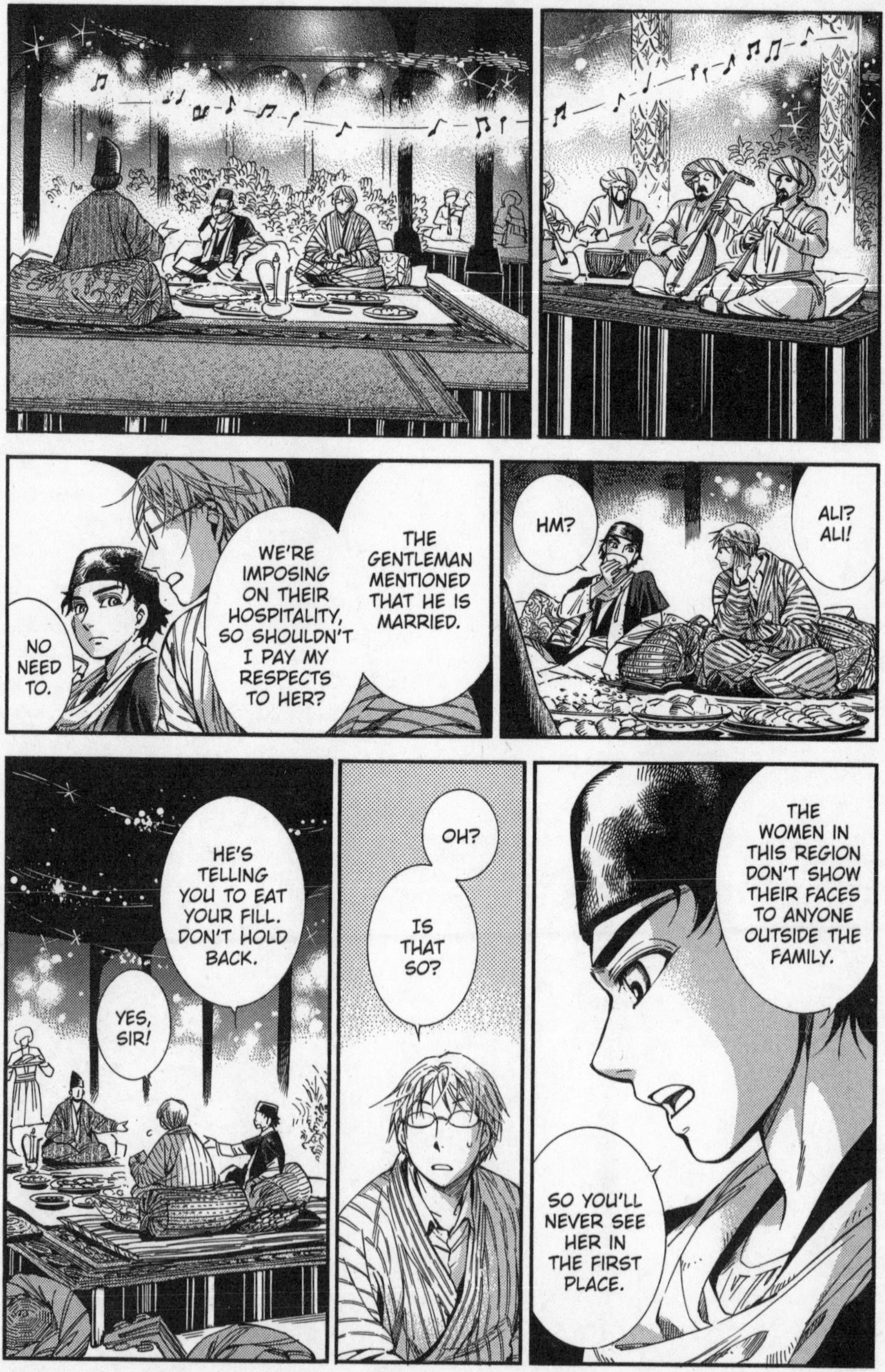
ALI? ALI!
HM?
THE GENTLEMAN MENTIONED THAT HE IS MARRIED.
WE'RE IMPOSING ON THEIR HOSPITALITY, SO SHOULDN'T I PAY MY RESPECTS TO HER?
NO NEED TO.
THE WOMEN IN THIS REGION DON'T SHOW THEIR FACES TO ANYONE OUTSIDE THE FAMILY.
SO YOU'LL NEVER SEE HER IN THE FIRST PLACE.
OH?
IS THAT SO?
HE'S TELLING YOU TO EAT YOUR FILL. DON'T HOLD BACK.
YES, SIR!

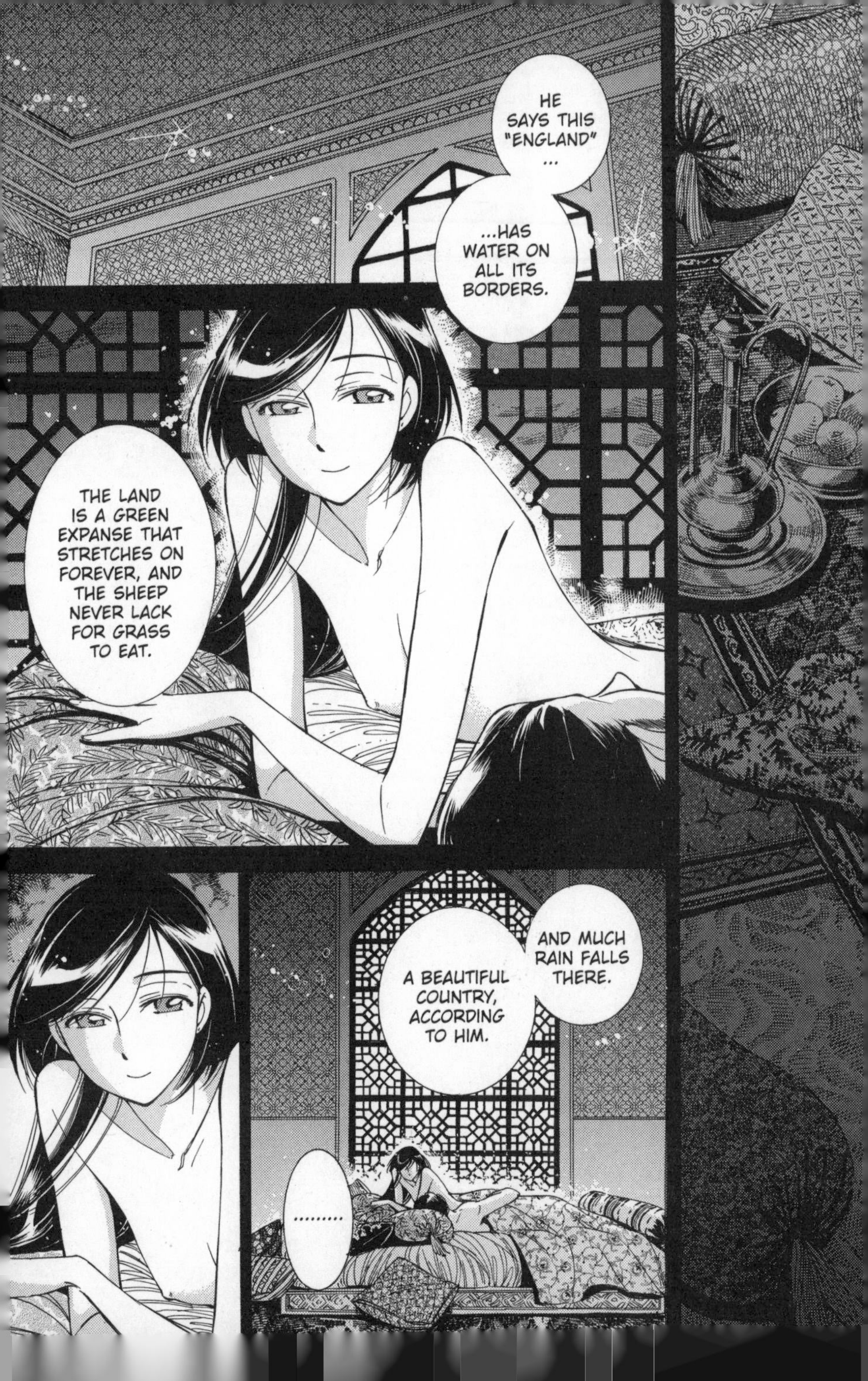
HE SAYS THIS "ENGLAND" ...
...HAS WATER ON ALL ITS BORDERS.
THE LAND IS A GREEN EXPANSE THAT STRETCHES ON FOREVER, AND THE SHEEP NEVER LACK FOR GRASS TO EAT.
AND MUCH RAIN FALLS THERE.
A BEAUTIFUL COUNTRY, ACCORDING TO HIM.
....

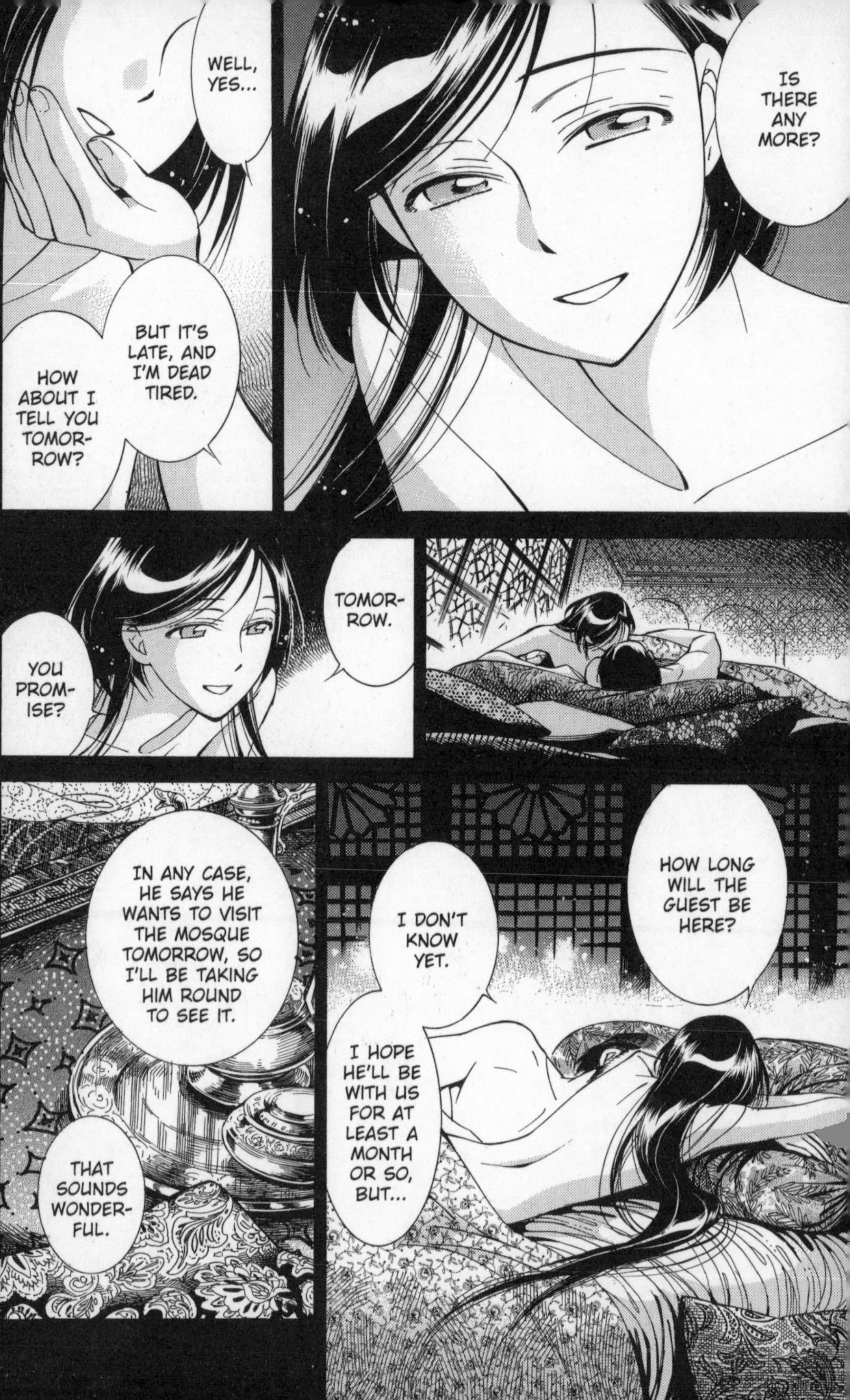
IS THERE ANY MORE?
WELL, YES...
BUT IT'S LATE, AND I'M DEAD TIRED.
HOW ABOUT I TELL YOU TOMORROW?
TOMORROW.
YOU PROMISE?
HOW LONG WILL THE GUEST BE HERE?
I DON'T KNOW YET.
I HOPE HE'LL BE WITH US FOR AT LEAST A MONTH OR SO, BUT...
IN ANY CASE, HE SAYS HE WANTS TO VISIT THE MOSQUE TOMORROW, SO I'LL BE TAKING HIM ROUND TO SEE IT.
THAT SOUNDS WONDERFUL.

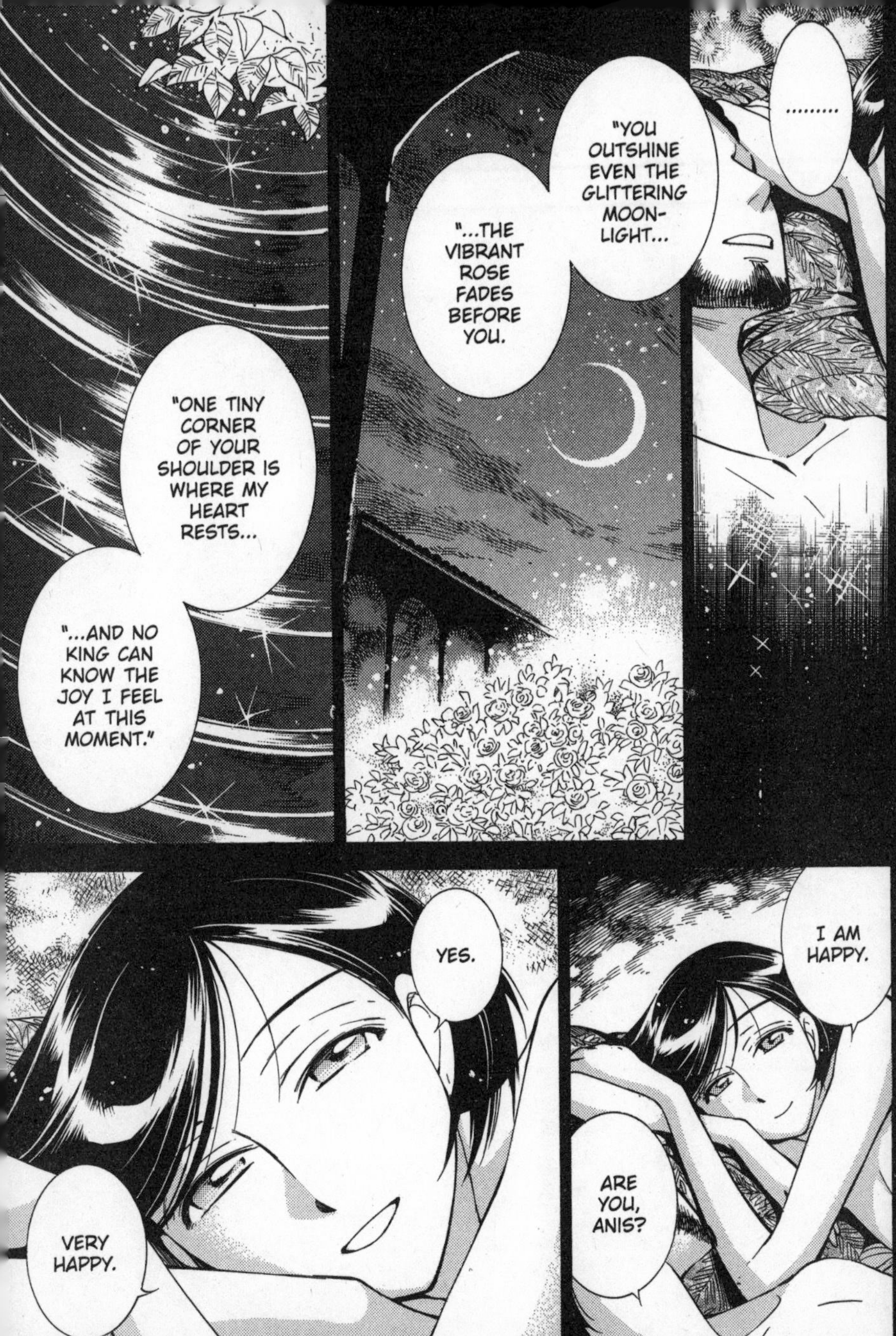
....
"YOU OUTSHINE EVEN THE GLITTERING MOON-LIGHT...
"...THE VIBRANT ROSE FADES BEFORE YOU.
"ONE TINY CORNER OF YOUR SHOULDER IS WHERE MY HEART RESTS...
"...AND NO KING CAN KNOW THE JOY I FEEL AT THIS MOMENT."
I AM HAPPY.
ARE YOU, ANIS?
YES.
VERY HAPPY.

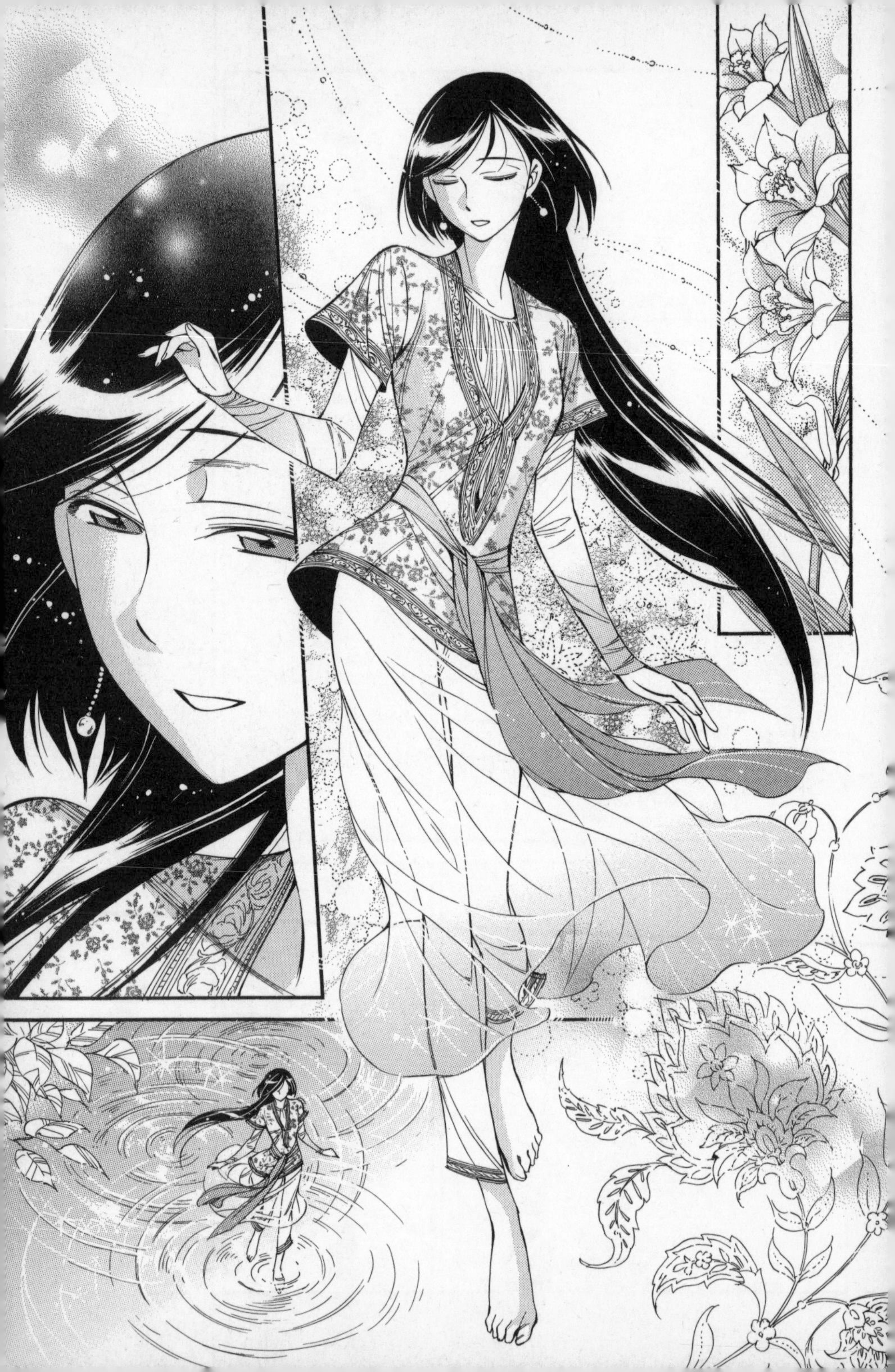

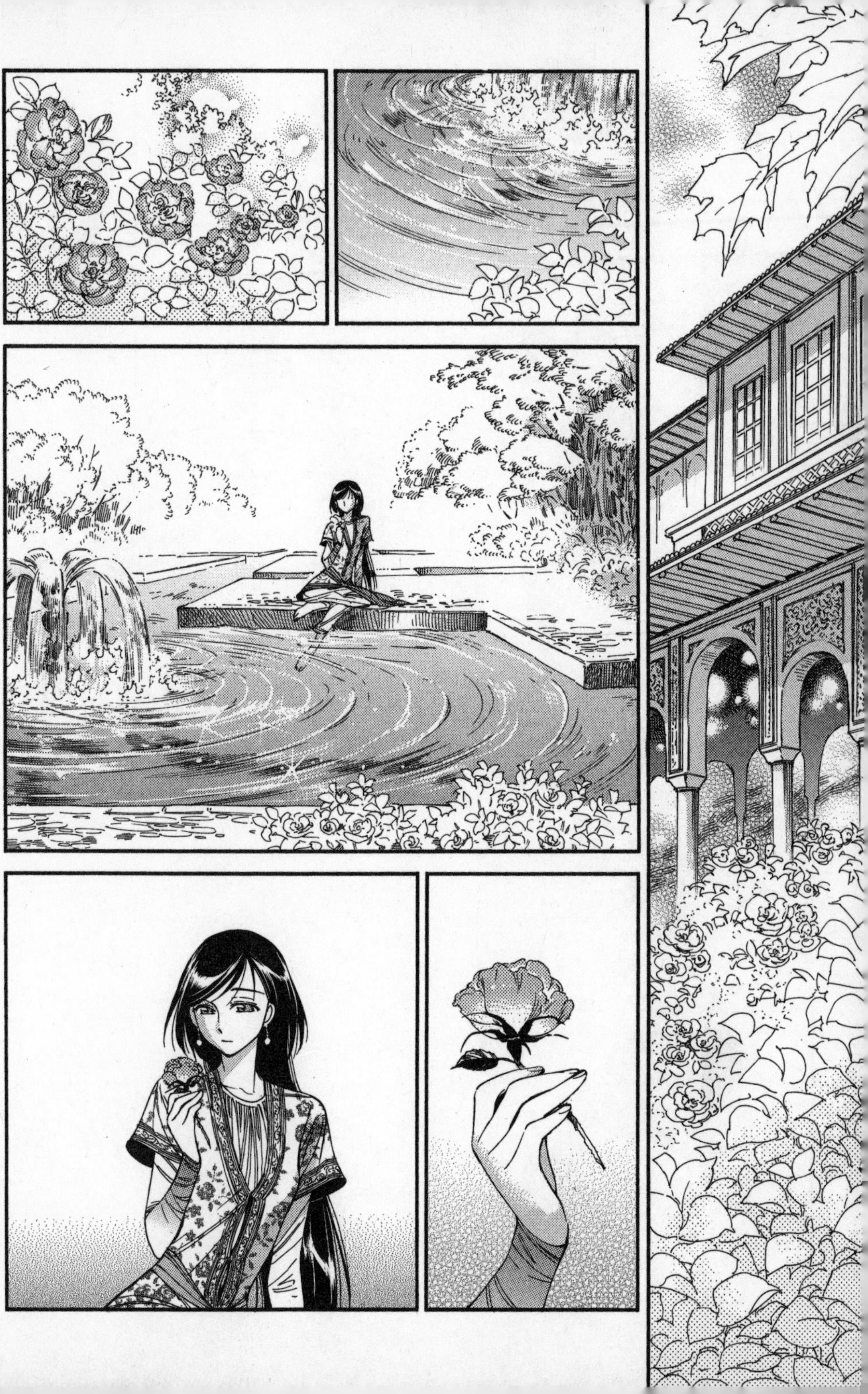

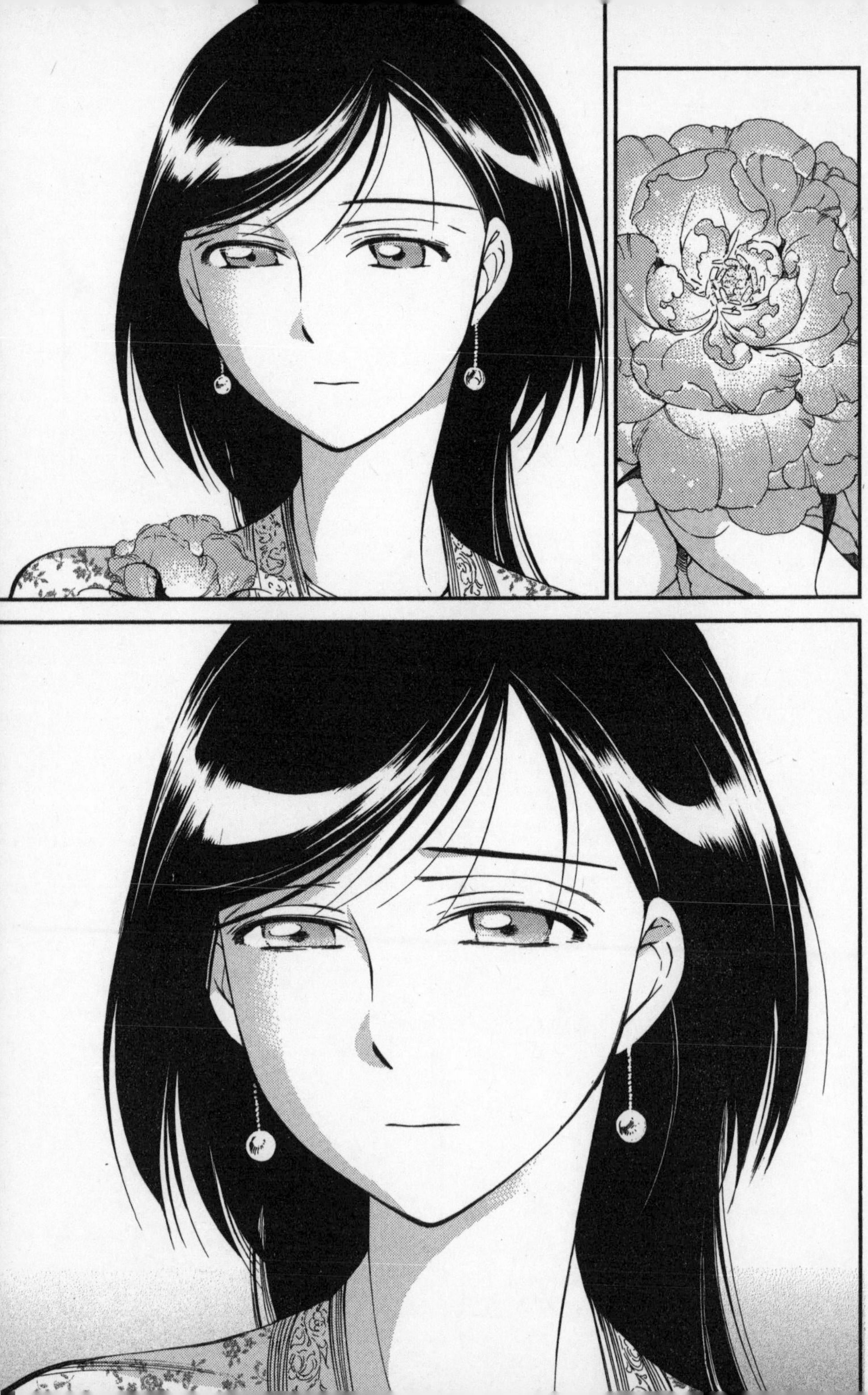

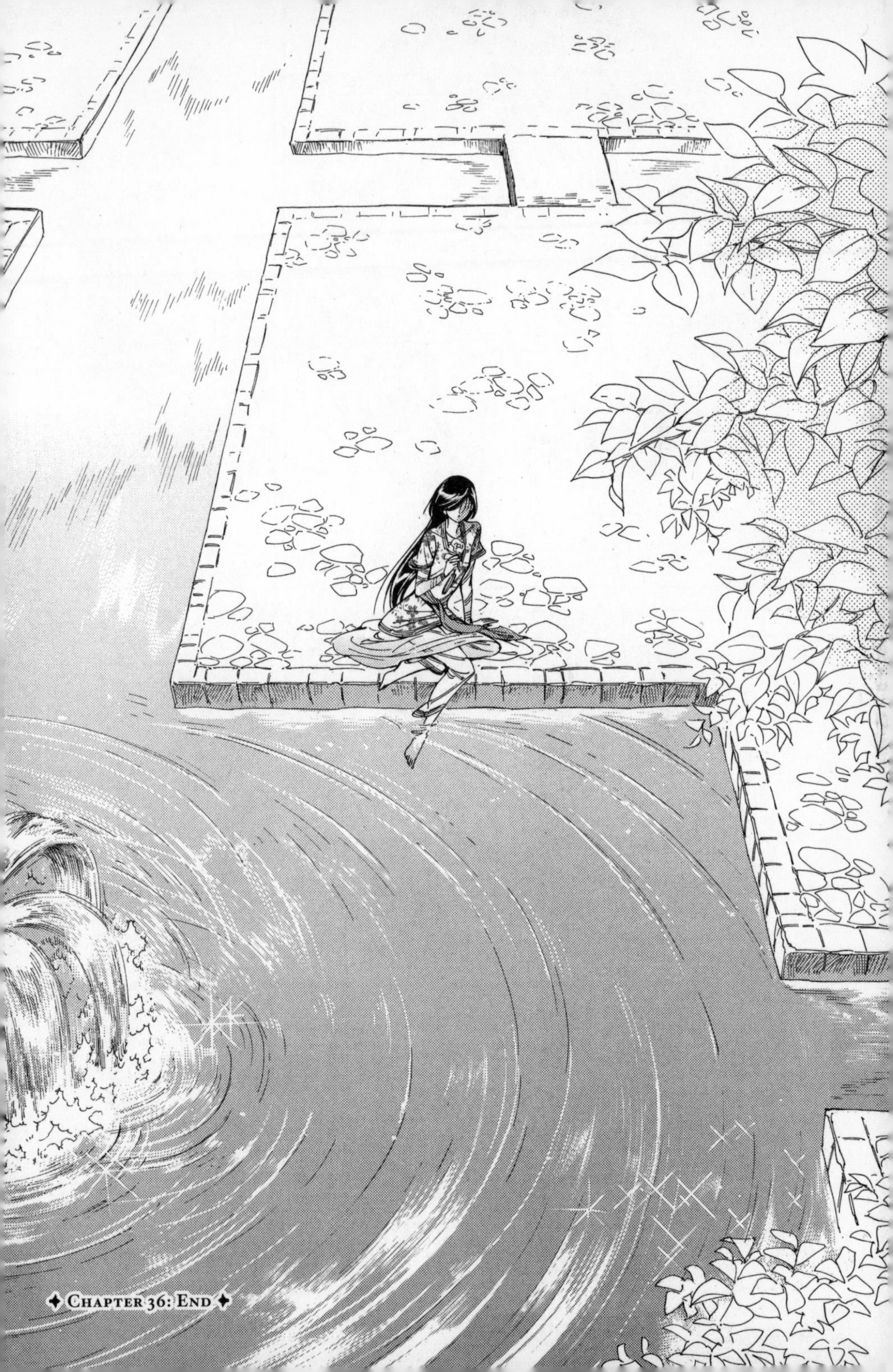

✦ Chapter 36: End ✦

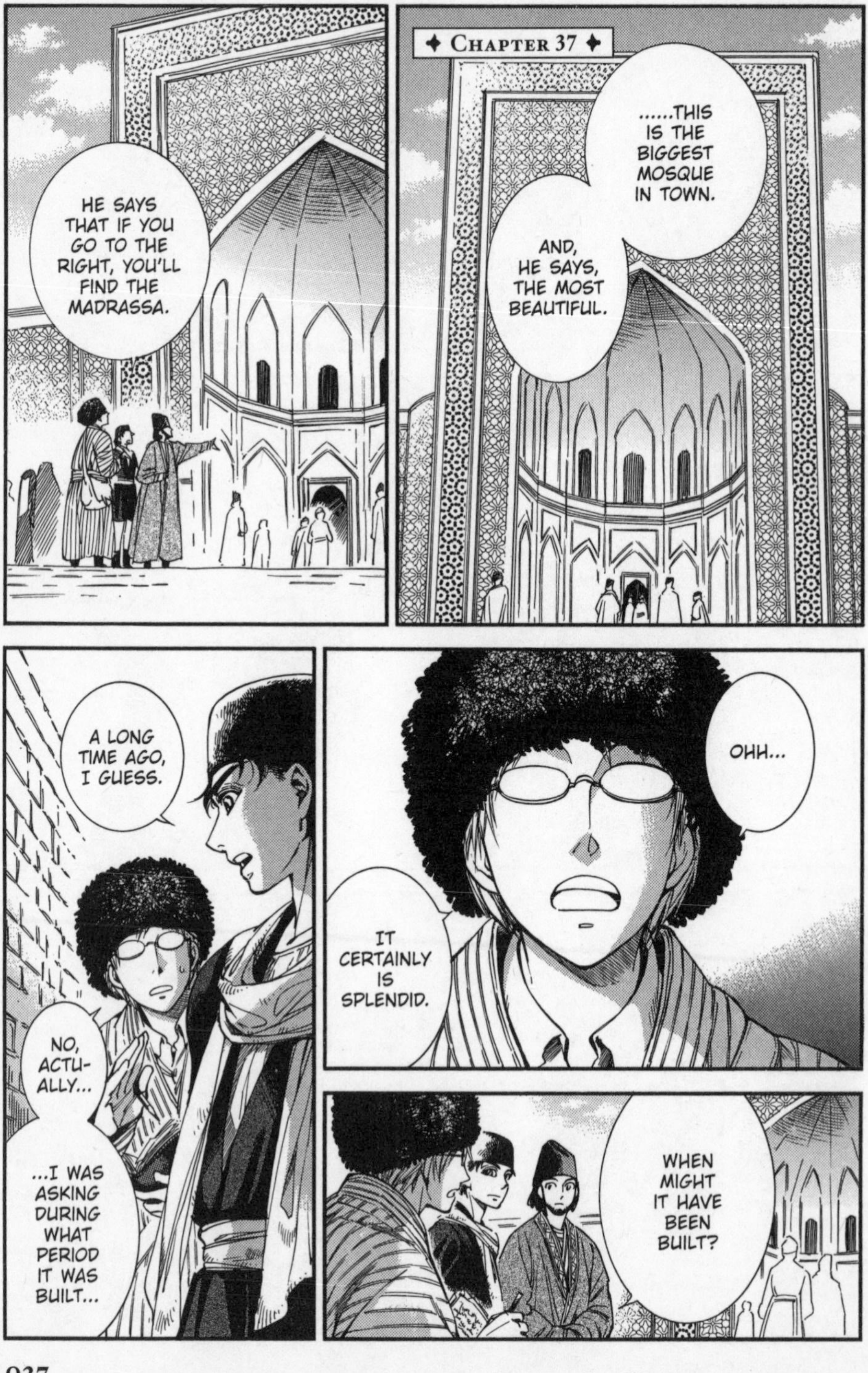
CHAPTER 37
......THIS IS THE BIGGEST MOSQUE IN TOWN.
AND, HE SAYS, THE MOST BEAUTIFUL.
HE SAYS THAT IF YOU GO TO THE RIGHT, YOU'LL FIND THE MADRASSA.
OHH...
IT CERTAINLY IS SPLENDID.
WHEN MIGHT IT HAVE BEEN BUILT?
A LONG TIME AGO, I GUESS.
NO, ACTUALLY...
...I WAS ASKING DURING WHAT PERIOD IT WAS BUILT...

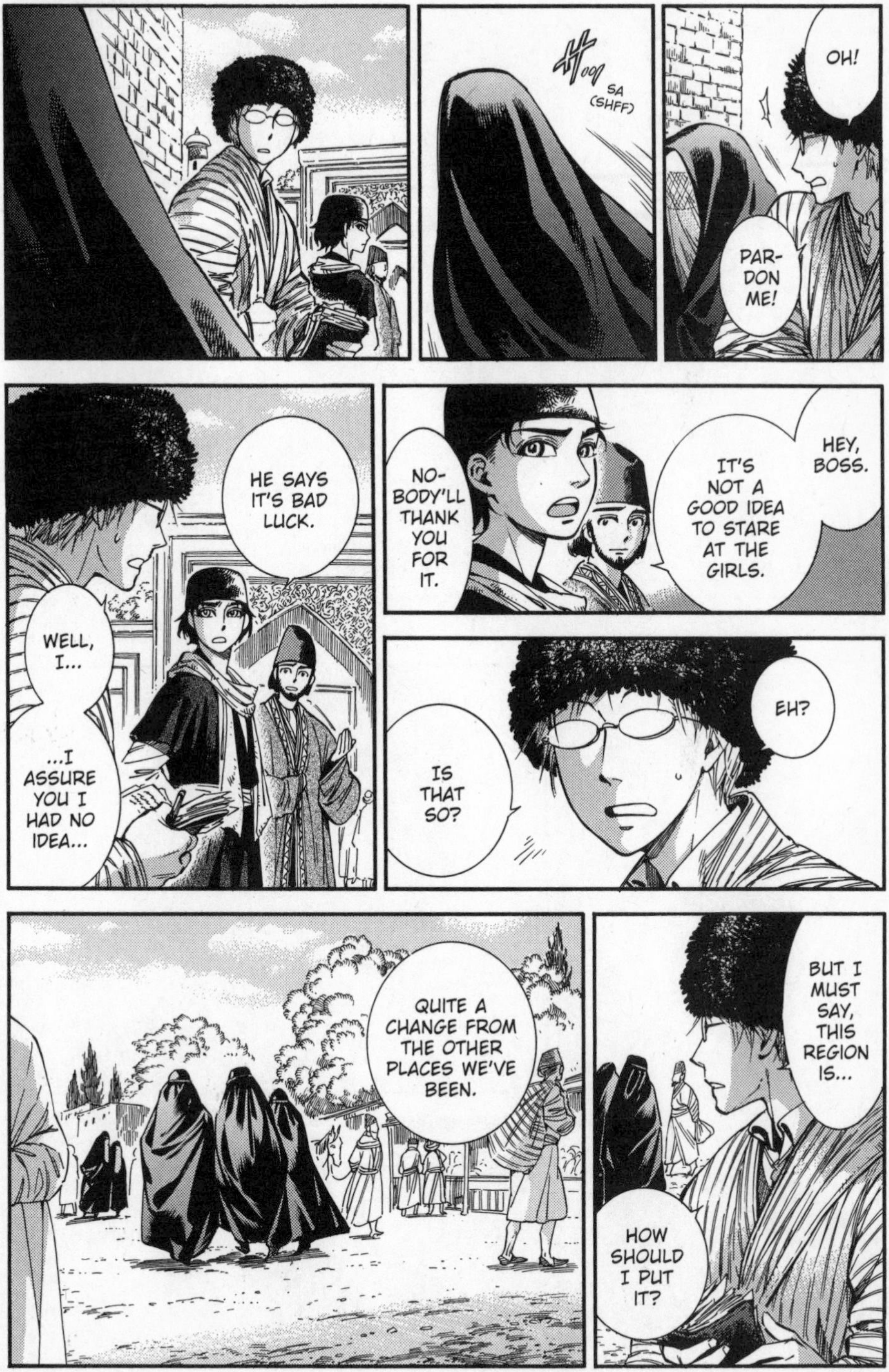
OH!
PAR-DON ME!
SA (SHFF)
HEY, BOSS.
IT'S NOT A GOOD IDEA TO STARE AT THE GIRLS.
NO-BODY'LL THANK YOU FOR IT.
EH?
IS THAT SO?
HE SAYS IT'S BAD LUCK.
WELL, I...
...I ASSURE YOU I HAD NO IDEA...
BUT I MUST SAY, THIS REGION IS...
HOW SHOULD I PUT IT?
QUITE A CHANGE FROM THE OTHER PLACES WE'VE BEEN.

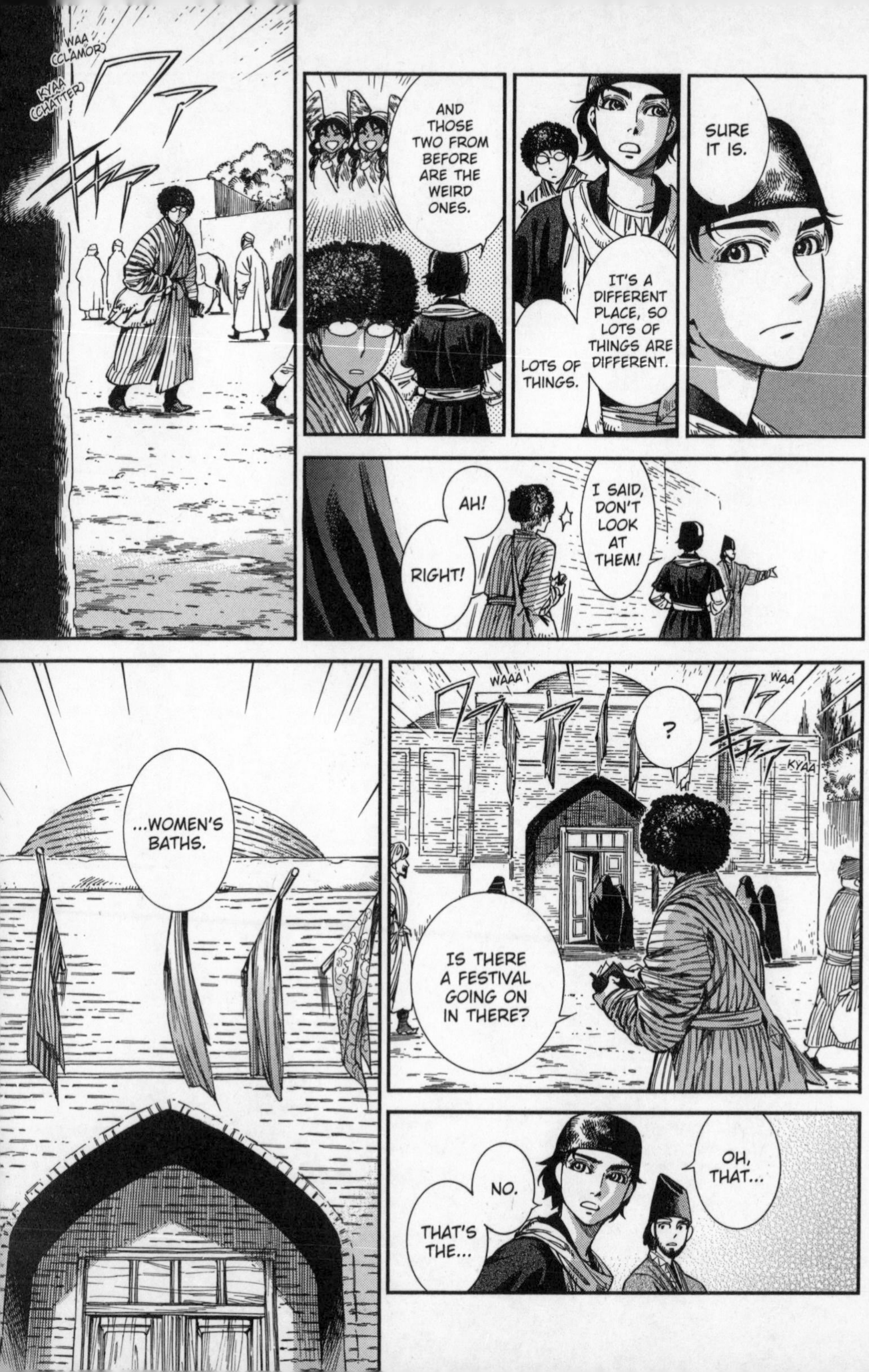
SURE IT IS.
IT'S A DIFFERENT PLACE, SO LOTS OF THINGS ARE DIFFERENT.
LOTS OF THINGS.
AND THOSE TWO FROM BEFORE ARE THE WEIRD ONES.
I SAID, DON'T LOOK AT THEM!
AH!
RIGHT!
WAA (CLAMOR)
KYAA (CHATTER)
WAA
?
KYAA
WAAA
IS THERE A FESTIVAL GOING ON IN THERE?
OH, THAT...
NO.
THAT'S THE...
...WOMEN'S BATHS.

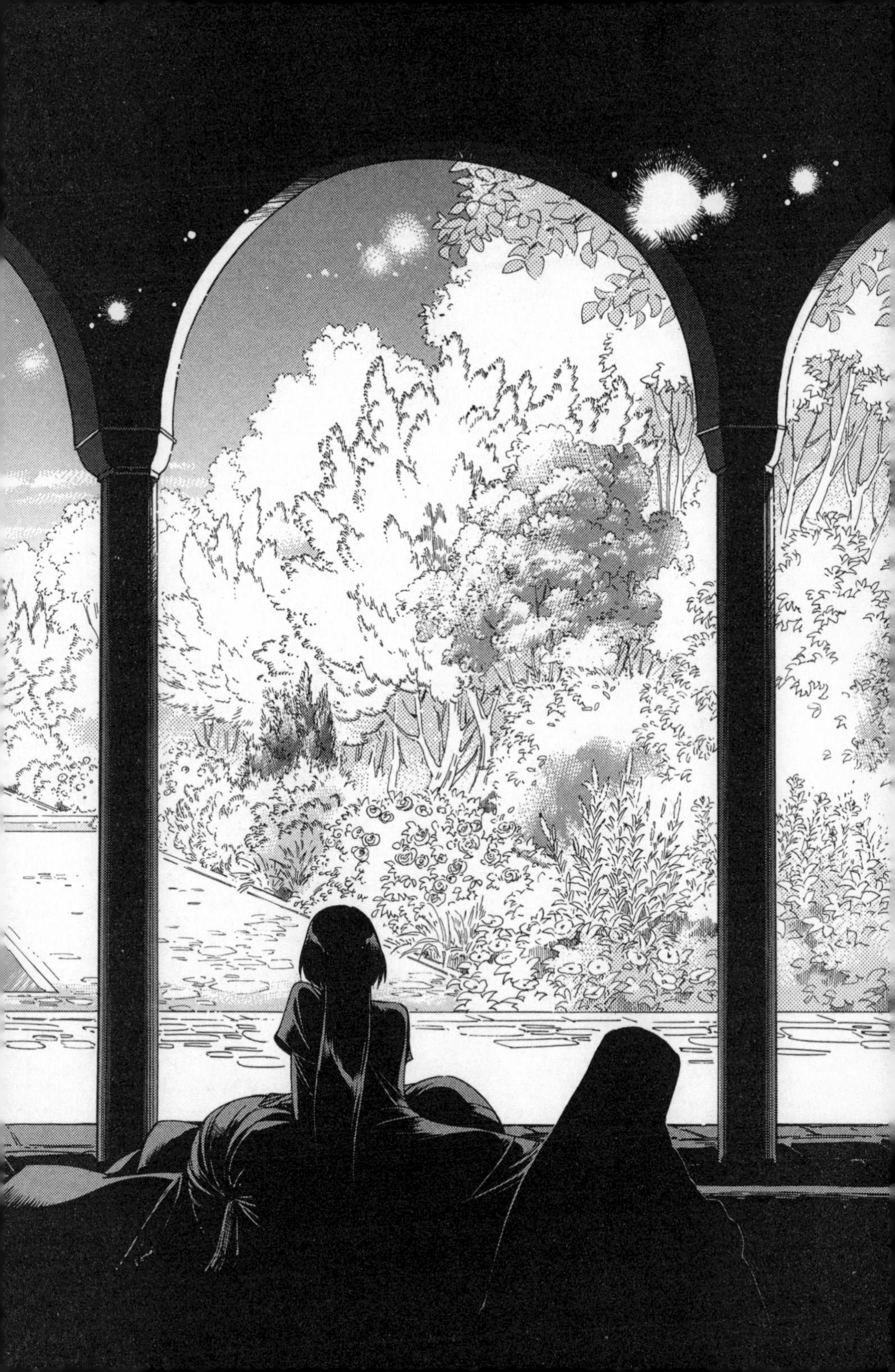

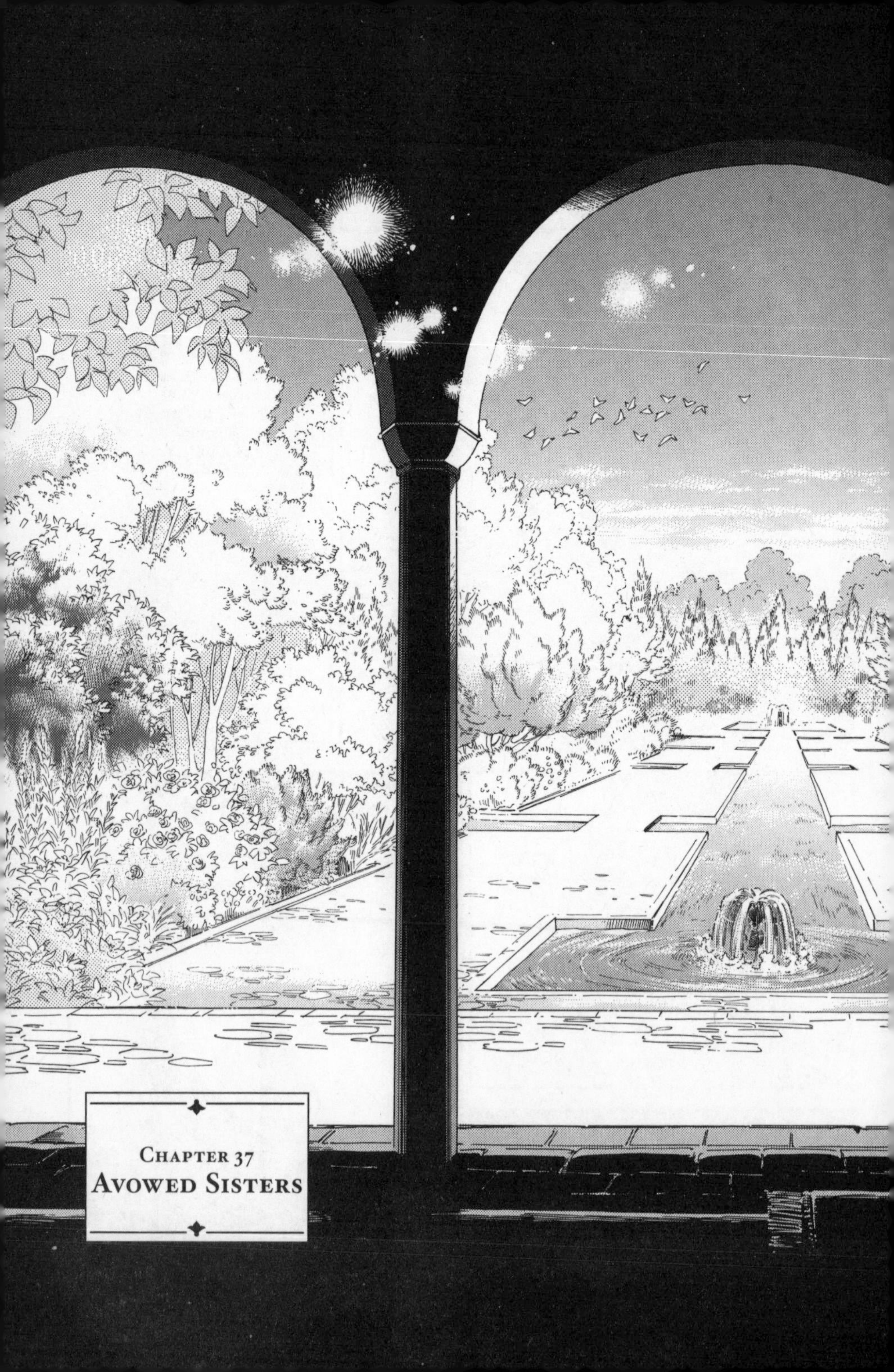
CHAPTER 37
AVOWED SISTERS

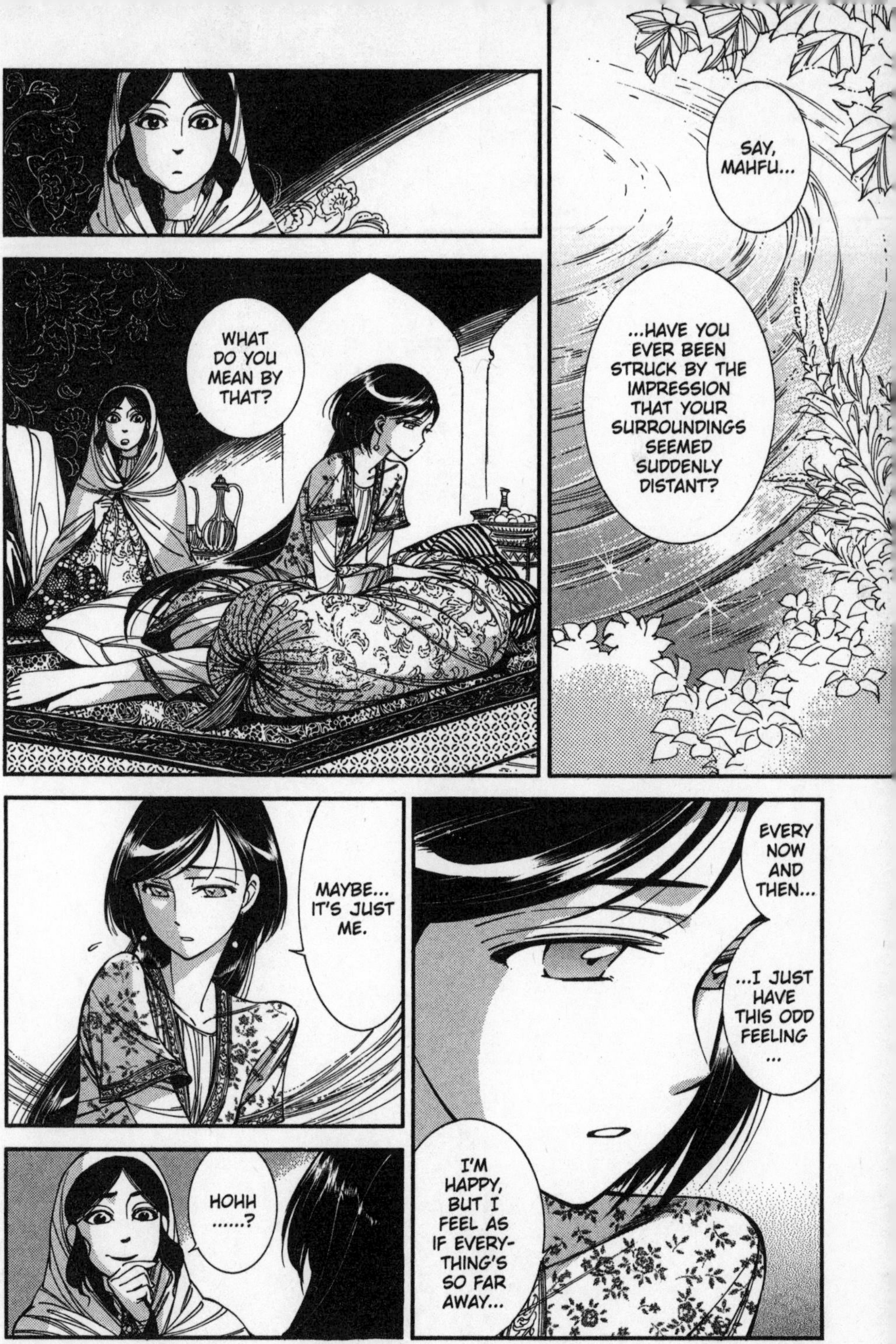
SAY, MAHFU...
...HAVE YOU EVER BEEN STRUCK BY THE IMPRESSION THAT YOUR SURROUNDINGS SEEMED SUDDENLY DISTANT?
WHAT DO YOU MEAN BY THAT?
EVERY NOW AND THEN...
...I JUST HAVE THIS ODD FEELING...
I'M HAPPY, BUT I FEEL AS IF EVERY-THING'S SO FAR AWAY...
MAYBE... IT'S JUST ME.
HOHH ......?

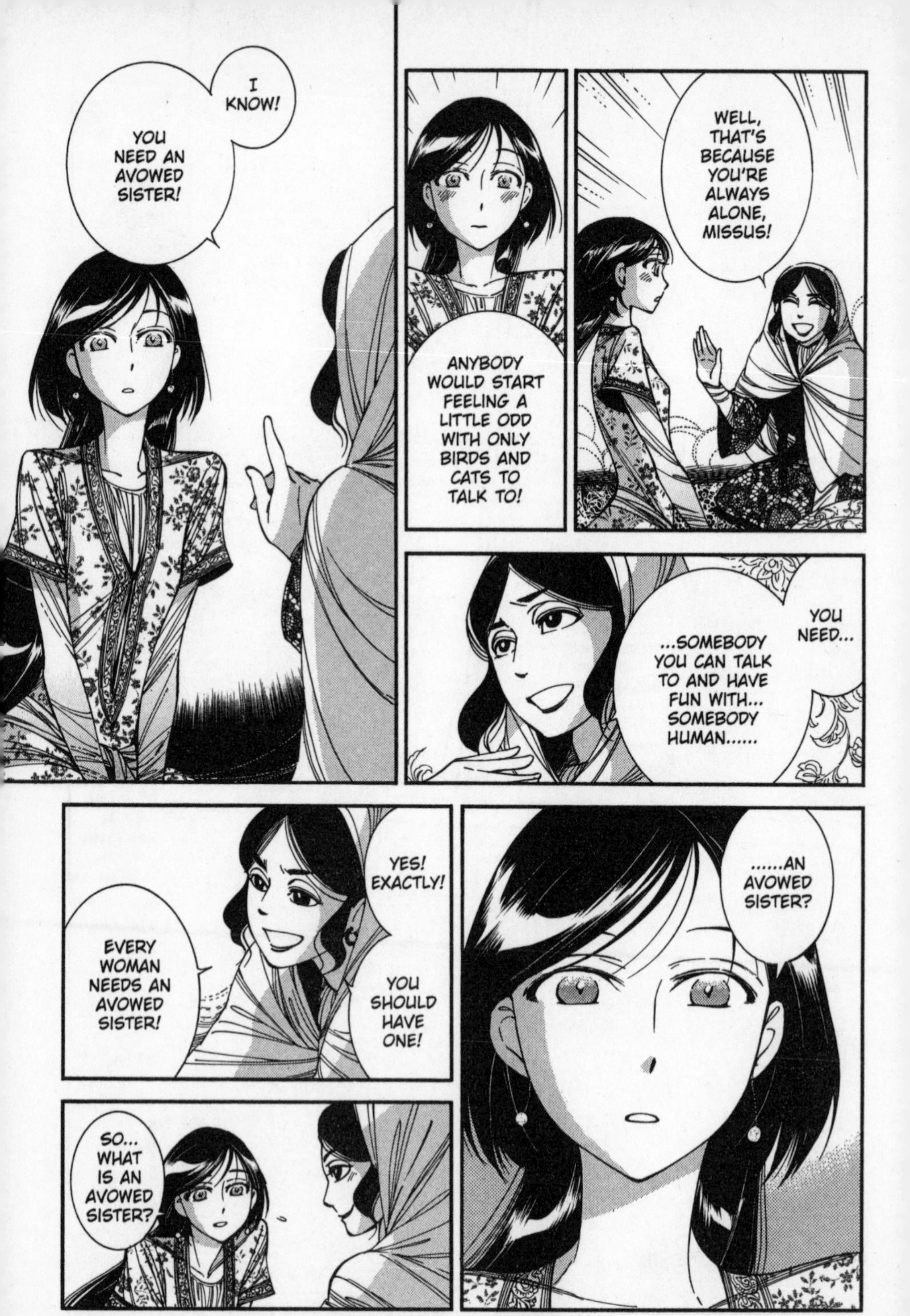
WELL, THAT'S BECAUSE YOU'RE ALWAYS ALONE, MISSUS!
ANYBODY WOULD START FEELING A LITTLE ODD WITH ONLY BIRDS AND CATS TO TALK TO!
YOU NEED...
...SOMEBODY YOU CAN TALK TO AND HAVE FUN WITH... SOMEBODY HUMAN......
I KNOW!
YOU NEED AN AVOWED SISTER!
......AN AVOWED SISTER?
YES! EXACTLY!
YOU SHOULD HAVE ONE!
EVERY WOMAN NEEDS AN AVOWED SISTER!
SO... WHAT IS AN AVOWED SISTER?

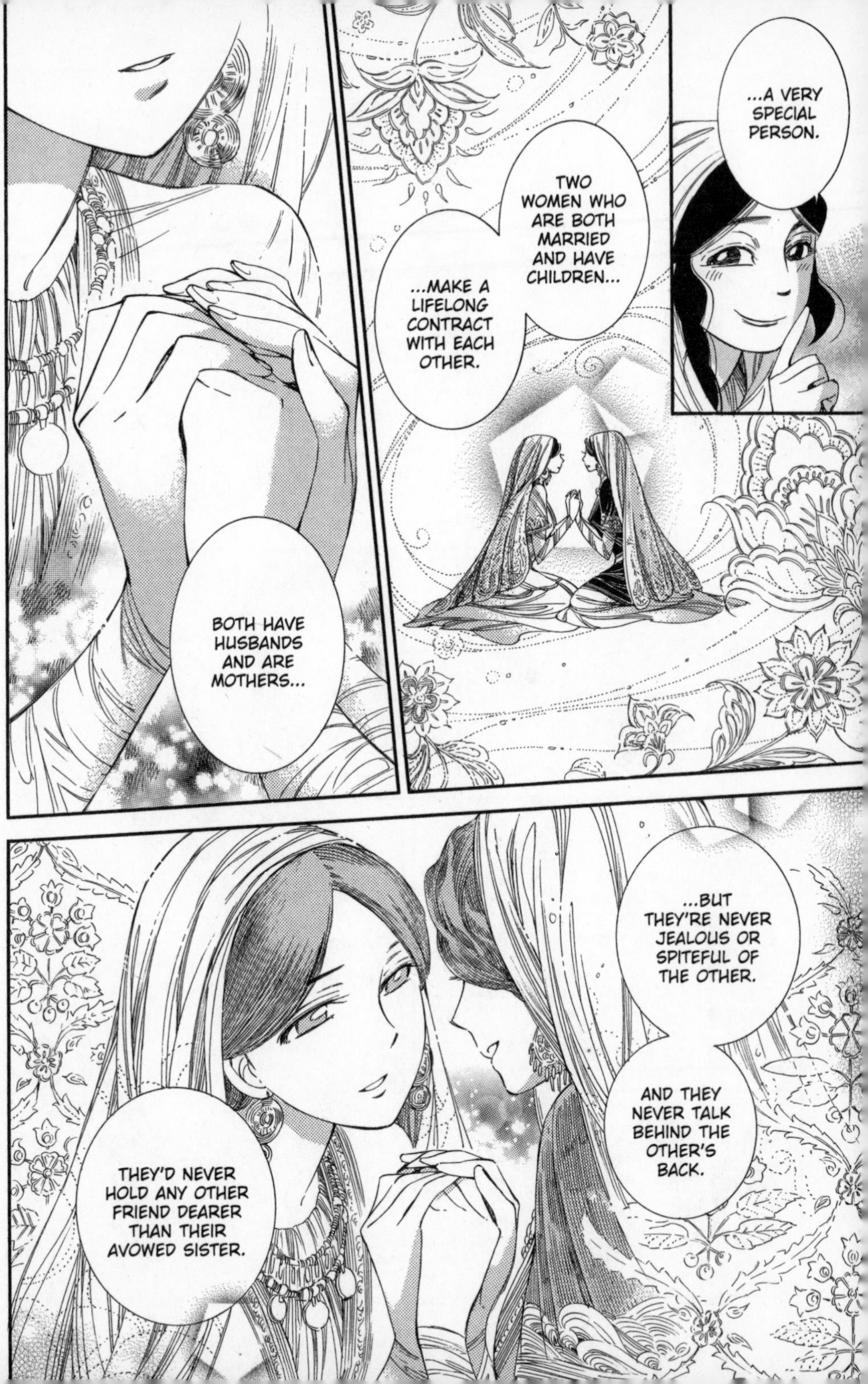
...A VERY SPECIAL PERSON.
TWO WOMEN WHO ARE BOTH MARRIED AND HAVE CHILDREN...
...MAKE A LIFELONG CONTRACT WITH EACH OTHER.
BOTH HAVE HUSBANDS AND ARE MOTHERS...
...BUT THEY'RE NEVER JEALOUS OR SPITEFUL OF THE OTHER.
AND THEY NEVER TALK BEHIND THE OTHER'S BACK.
THEY'D NEVER HOLD ANY OTHER FRIEND DEARER THAN THEIR AVOWED SISTER.

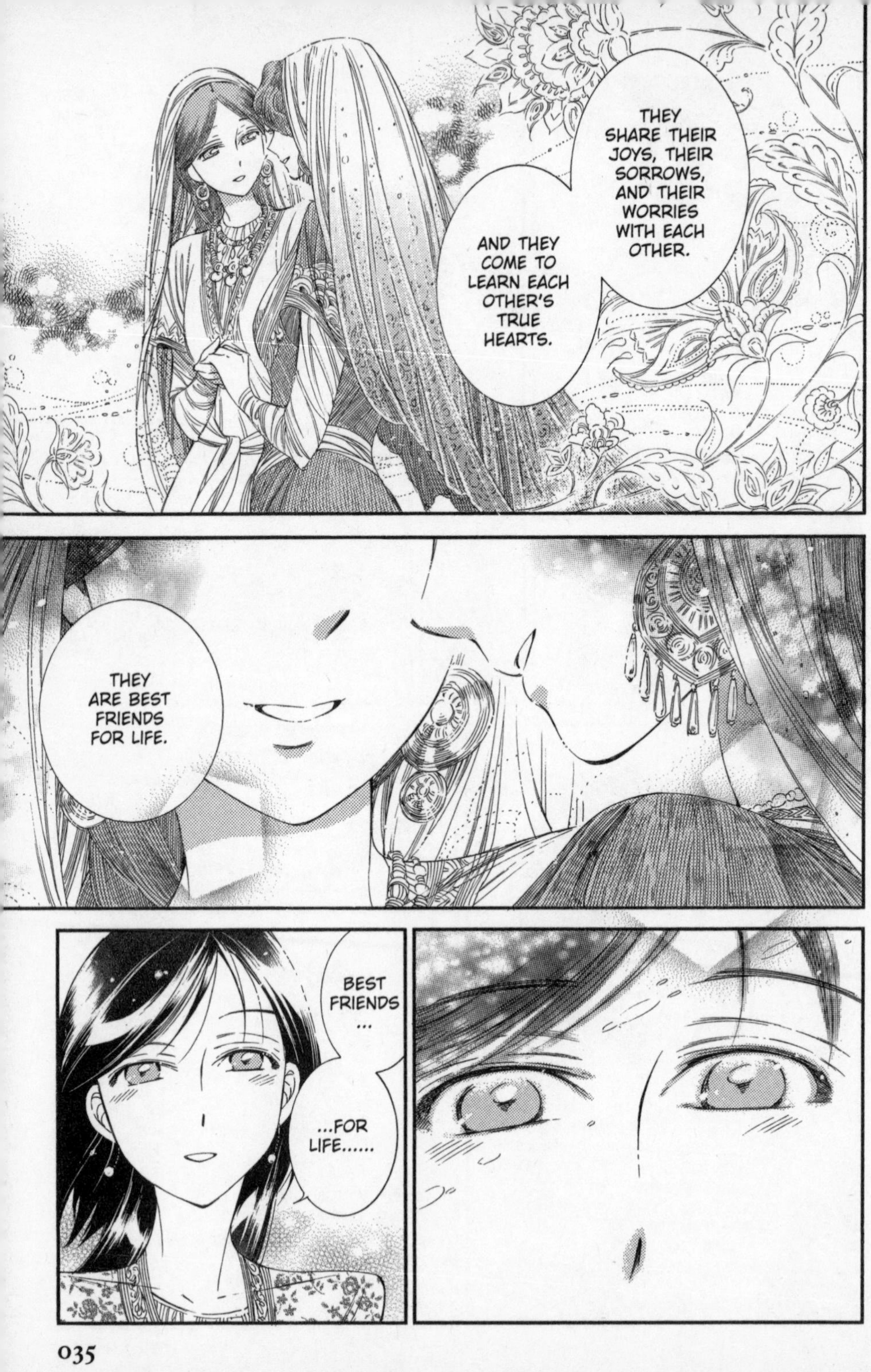
THEY SHARE THEIR JOYS, THEIR SORROWS, AND THEIR WORRIES WITH EACH OTHER.
AND THEY COME TO LEARN EACH OTHER'S TRUE HEARTS.
THEY ARE BEST FRIENDS FOR LIFE.
BEST FRIENDS ...
...FOR LIFE......

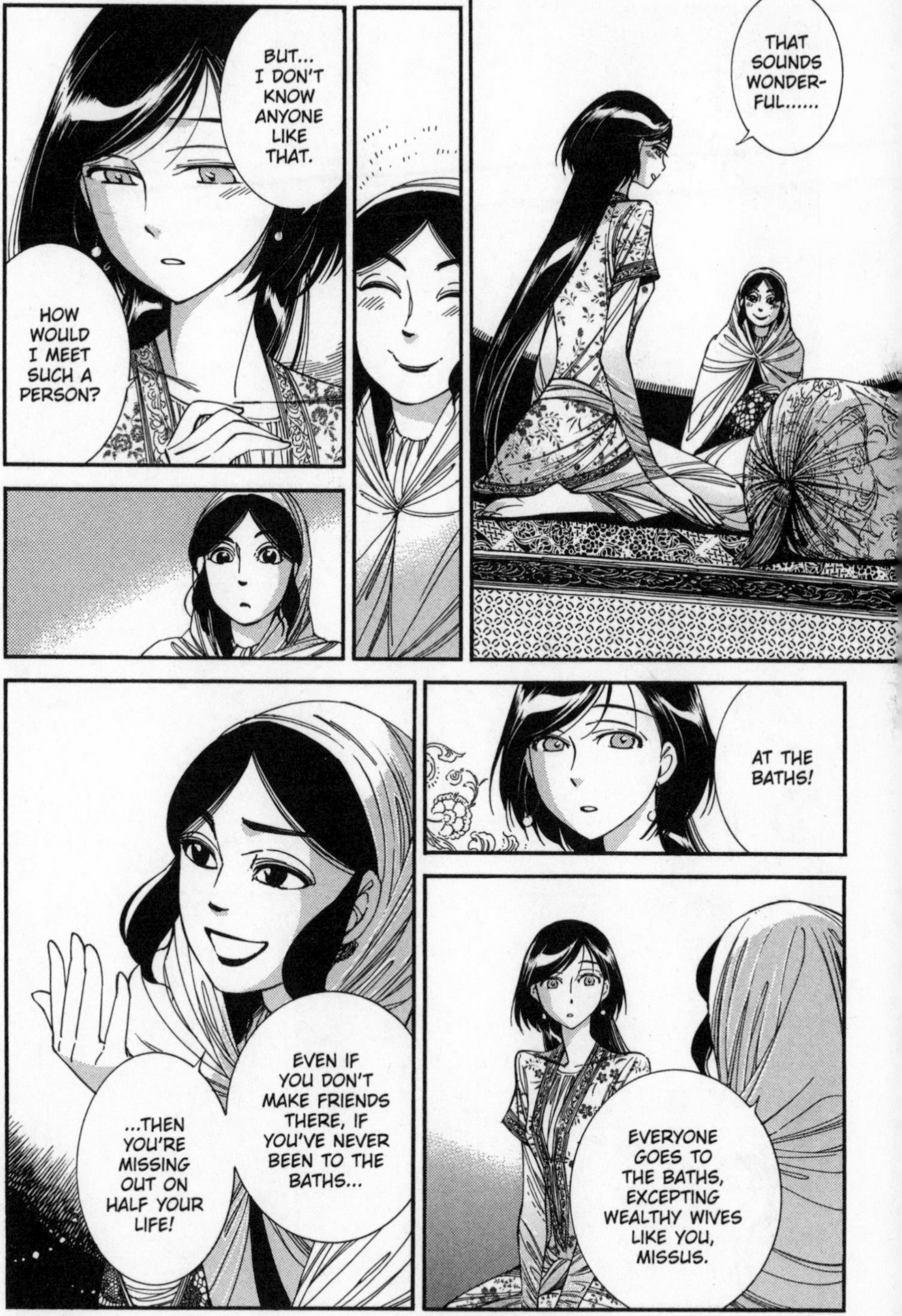
THAT SOUNDS WONDERFUL......
BUT... I DON'T KNOW ANYONE LIKE THAT.
HOW WOULD I MEET SUCH A PERSON?
AT THE BATHS!
EVERYONE GOES TO THE BATHS, EXCEPTING WEALTHY WIVES LIKE YOU, MISSUS.
EVEN IF YOU DON'T MAKE FRIENDS THERE, IF YOU'VE NEVER BEEN TO THE BATHS...
...THEN YOU'RE MISSING OUT ON HALF YOUR LIFE!

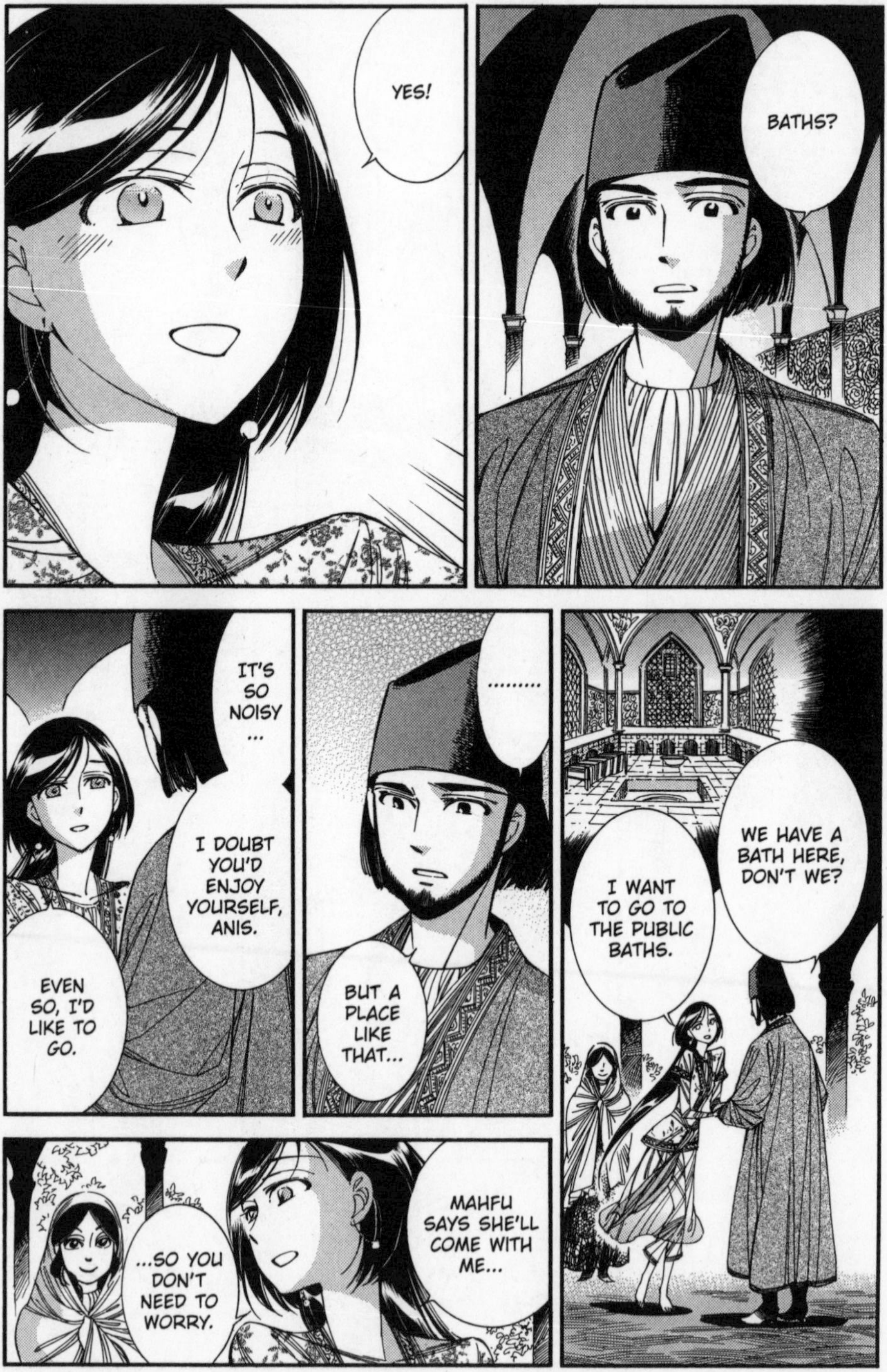
BATHS?
YES!
WE HAVE A BATH HERE, DON'T WE?
I WANT TO GO TO THE PUBLIC BATHS.
....
BUT A PLACE LIKE THAT...
IT'S SO NOISY ...
I DOUBT YOU'D ENJOY YOURSELF, ANIS.
EVEN SO, I'D LIKE TO GO.
MAHFU SAYS SHE'LL COME WITH ME...
...SO YOU DON'T NEED TO WORRY.

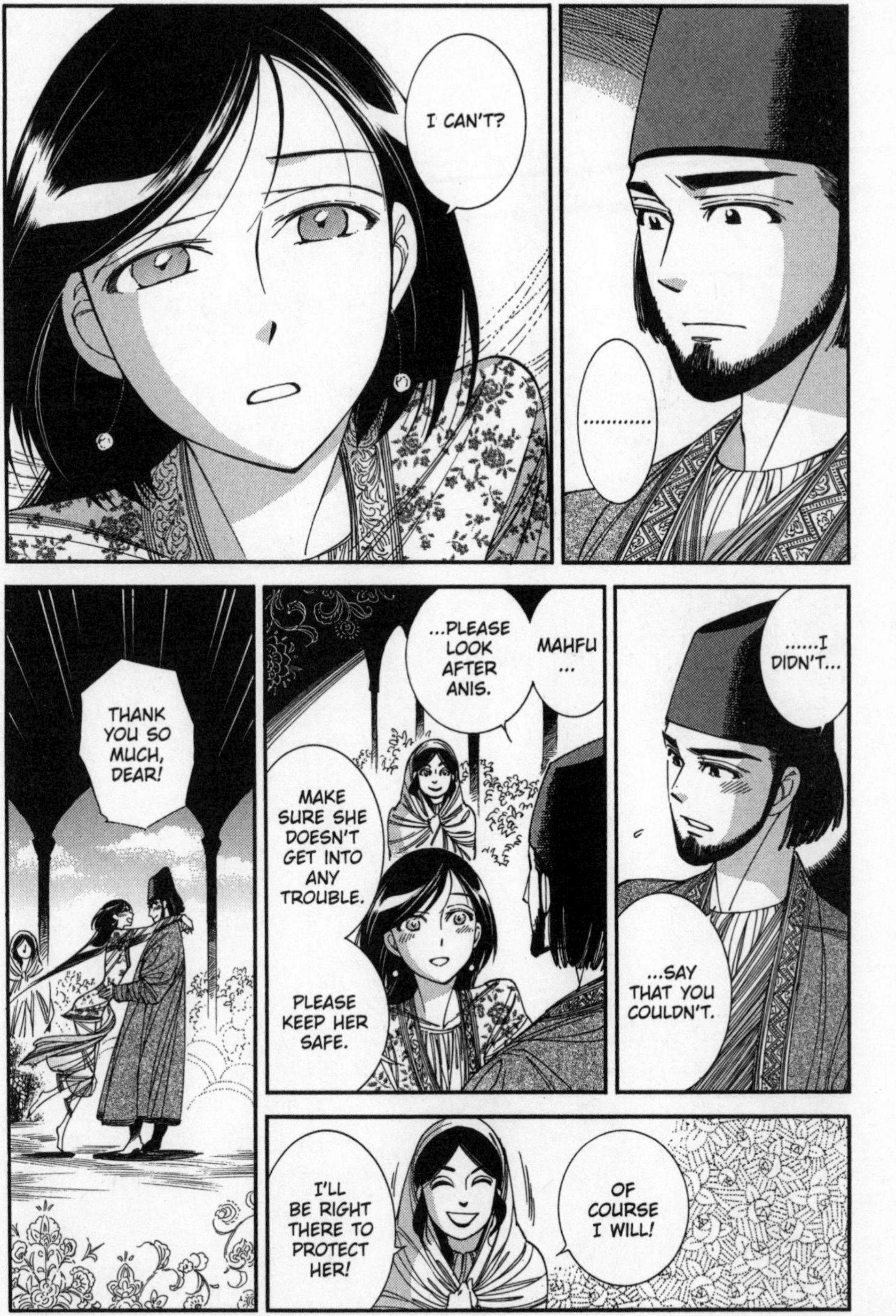
....
I CAN'T?
......I DIDN'T...
...SAY THAT YOU COULDN'T.
MAHFU...
...PLEASE LOOK AFTER ANIS.
MAKE SURE SHE DOESN'T GET INTO ANY TROUBLE.
PLEASE KEEP HER SAFE.
OF COURSE I WILL!
I'LL BE RIGHT THERE TO PROTECT HER!
THANK YOU SO MUCH, DEAR!

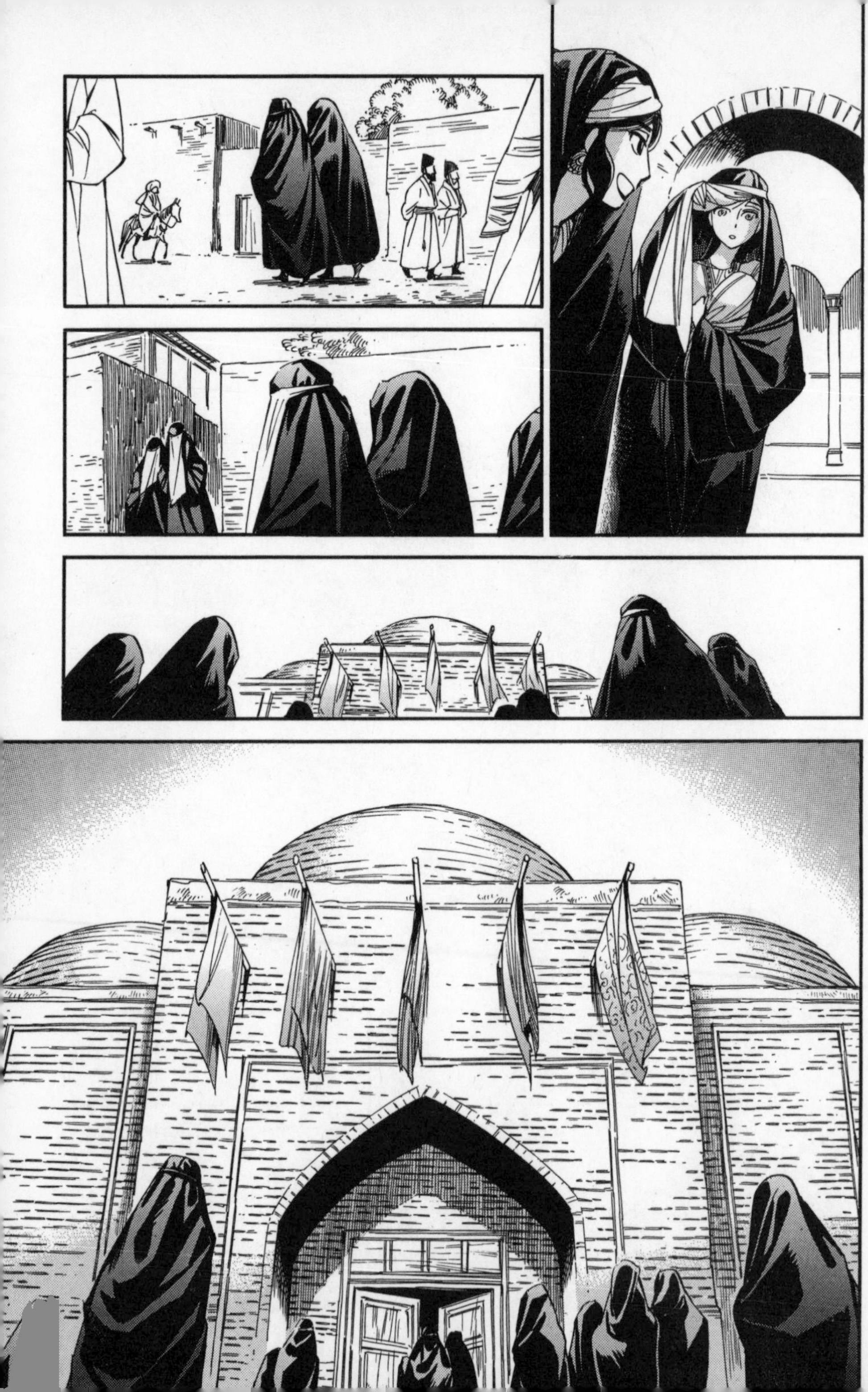

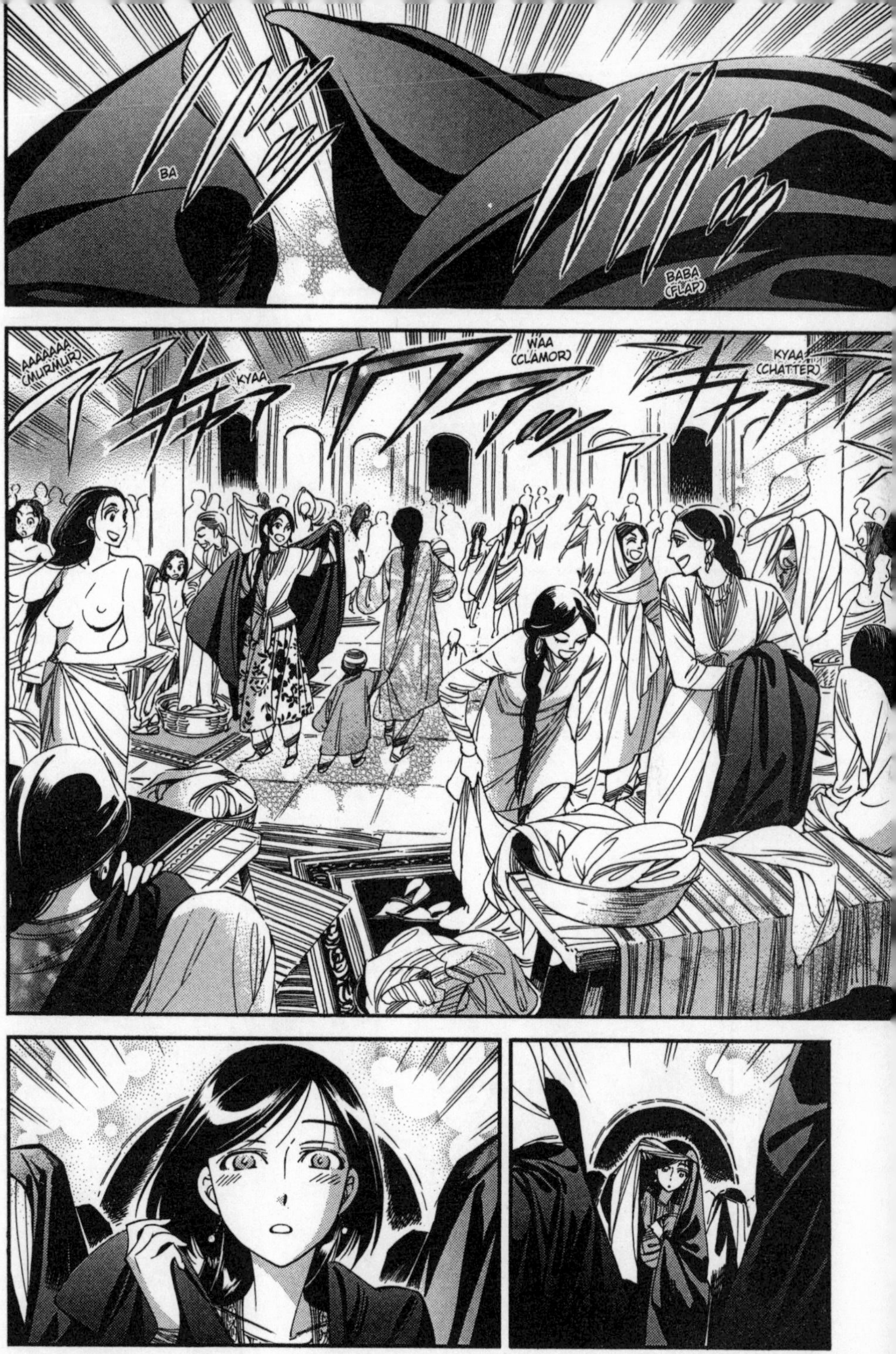
BA
BABA (FLAP)
KYAA (CHATTER)
WAA (CLAMOR)
KYAA
AAAAAAA (MURMUR)

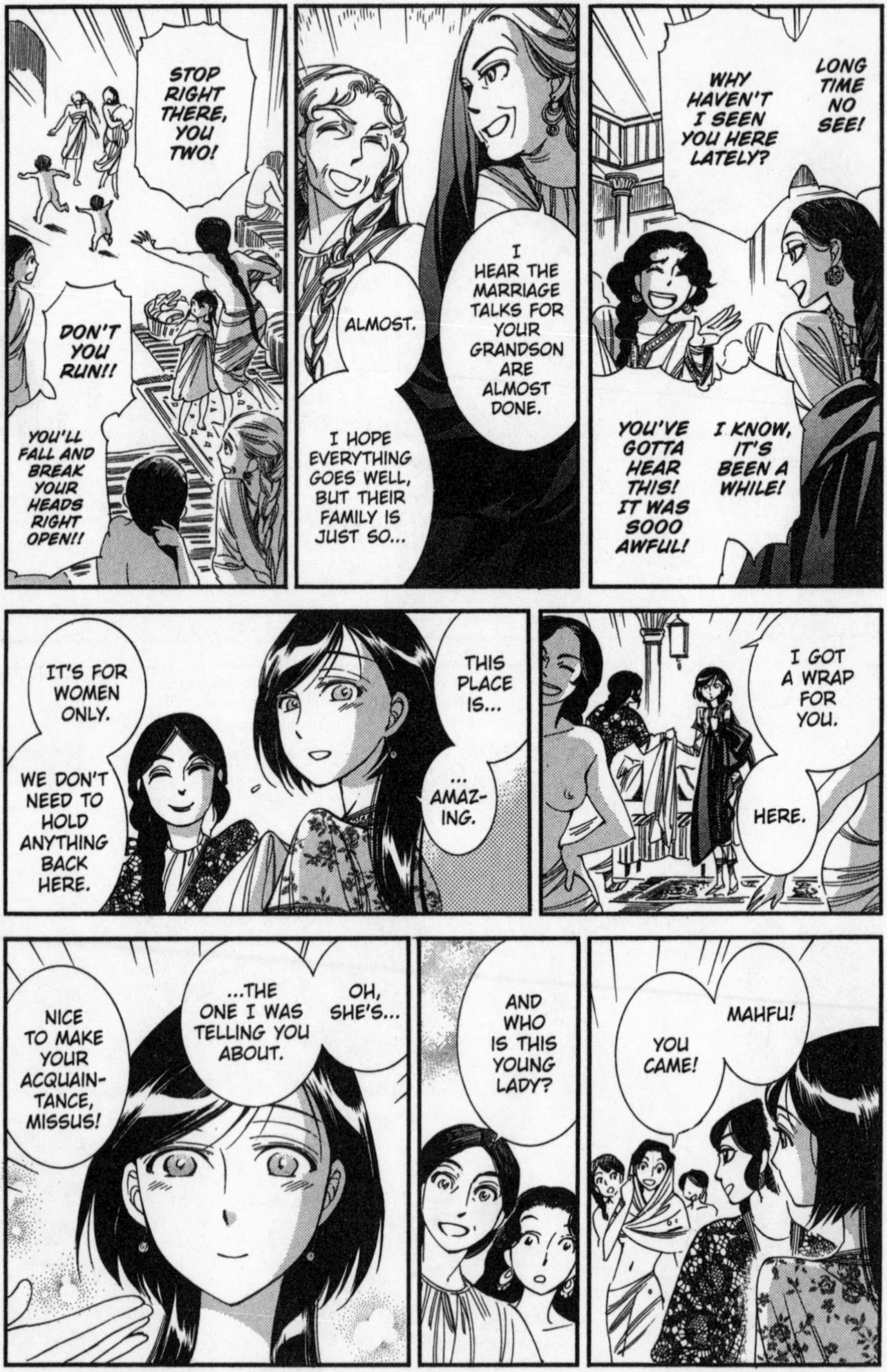
LONG TIME NO SEE!
WHY HAVEN'T I SEEN YOU HERE LATELY?
I KNOW, IT'S BEEN A WHILE!
YOU'VE GOTTA HEAR THIS! IT WAS SOOO AWFUL!
I HEAR THE MARRIAGE TALKS FOR YOUR GRANDSON ARE ALMOST DONE.
ALMOST.
I HOPE EVERYTHING GOES WELL, BUT THEIR FAMILY IS JUST SO...
STOP RIGHT THERE, YOU TWO!
DON'T YOU RUN!!
YOU'LL FALL AND BREAK YOUR HEADS RIGHT OPEN!!
I GOT A WRAP FOR YOU.
HERE.
THIS PLACE IS...
...AMAZ-ING.
IT'S FOR WOMEN ONLY.
WE DON'T NEED TO HOLD ANYTHING BACK HERE.
MAHFU!
YOU CAME!
AND WHO IS THIS YOUNG LADY?
OH, SHE'S...
...THE ONE I WAS TELLING YOU ABOUT.
NICE TO MAKE YOUR ACQUAINTANCE, MISSUS!

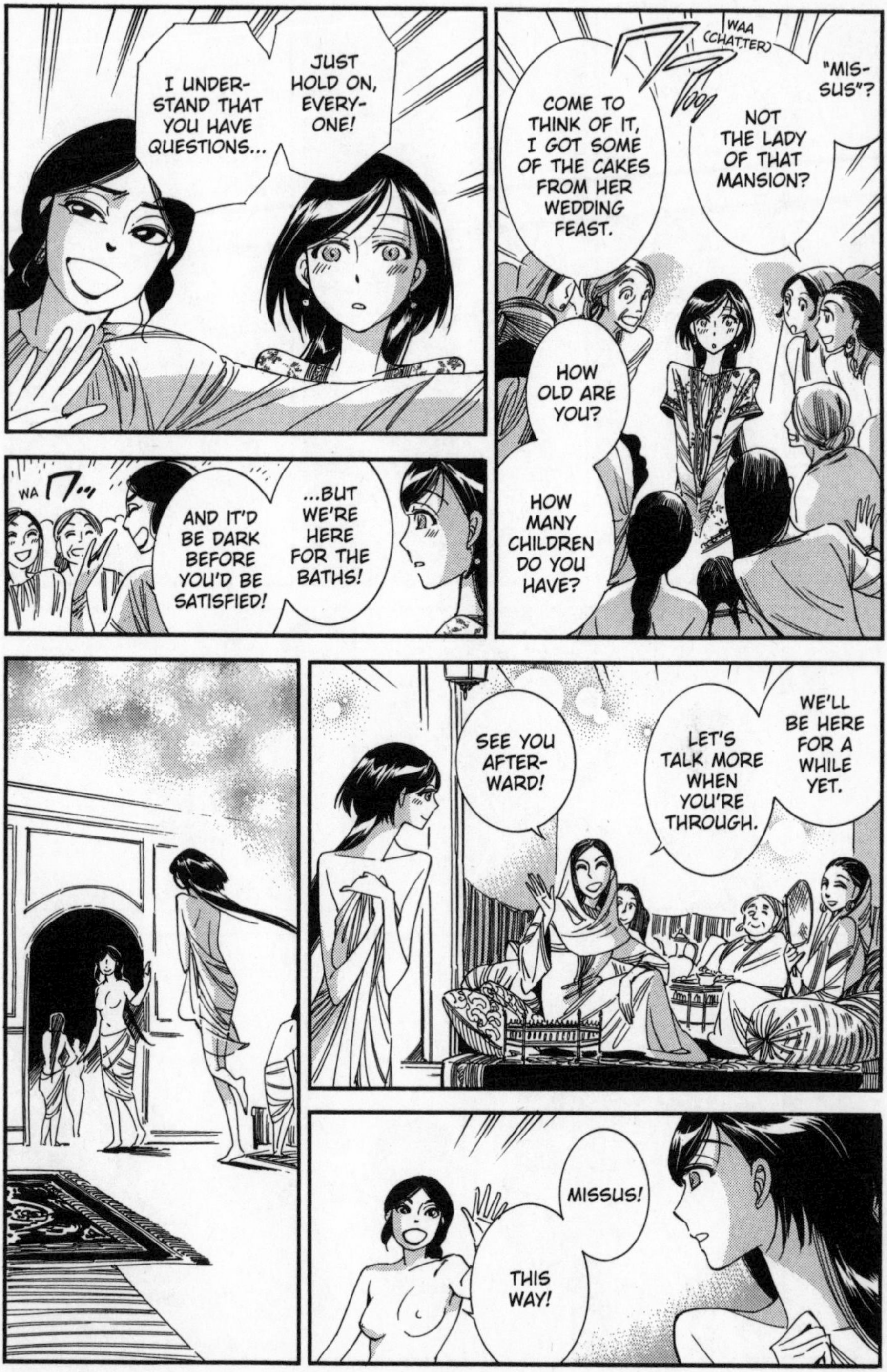
WAA (CHATTER)
"MIS-SUS"?
NOT THE LADY OF THAT MANSION?
COME TO THINK OF IT, I GOT SOME OF THE CAKES FROM HER WEDDING FEAST.
HOW OLD ARE YOU?
HOW MANY CHILDREN DO YOU HAVE?
JUST HOLD ON, EVERY-ONE!
I UNDER-STAND THAT YOU HAVE QUESTIONS...
...BUT WE'RE HERE FOR THE BATHS!
AND IT'D BE DARK BEFORE YOU'D BE SATISFIED!
WA
WE'LL BE HERE FOR A WHILE YET.
LET'S TALK MORE WHEN YOU'RE THROUGH.
SEE YOU AFTER-WARD!
MISSUS!
THIS WAY!

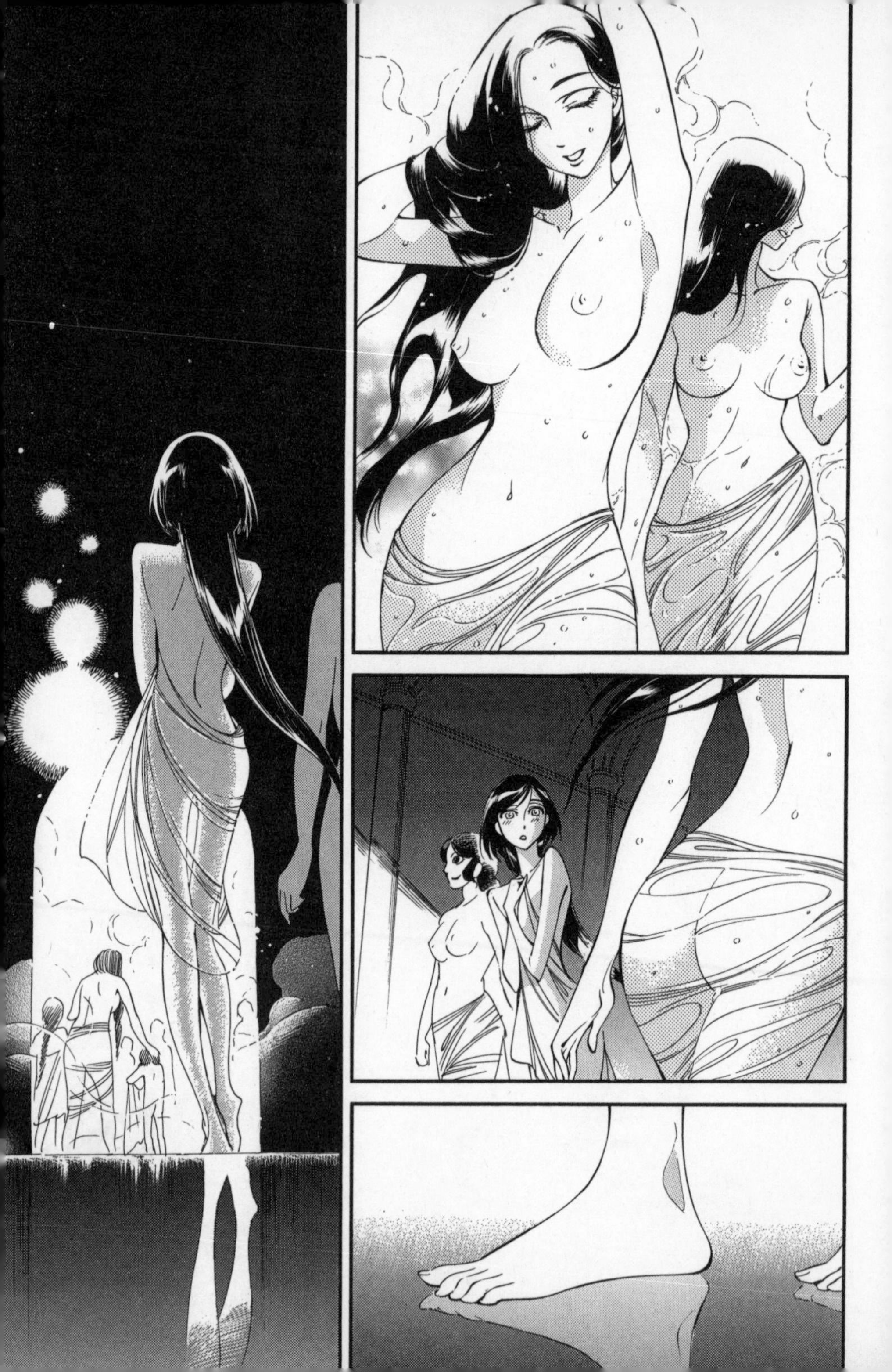

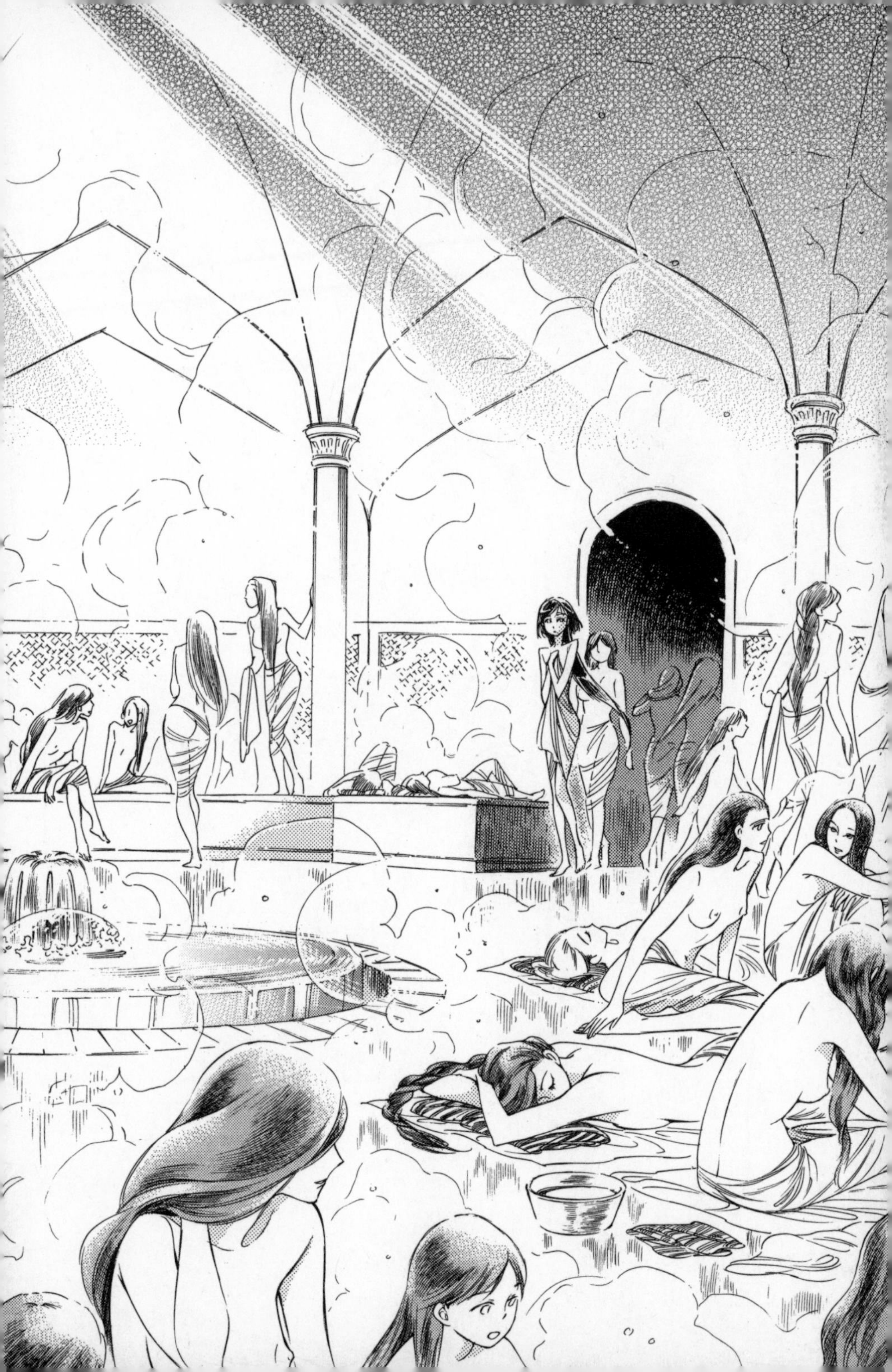

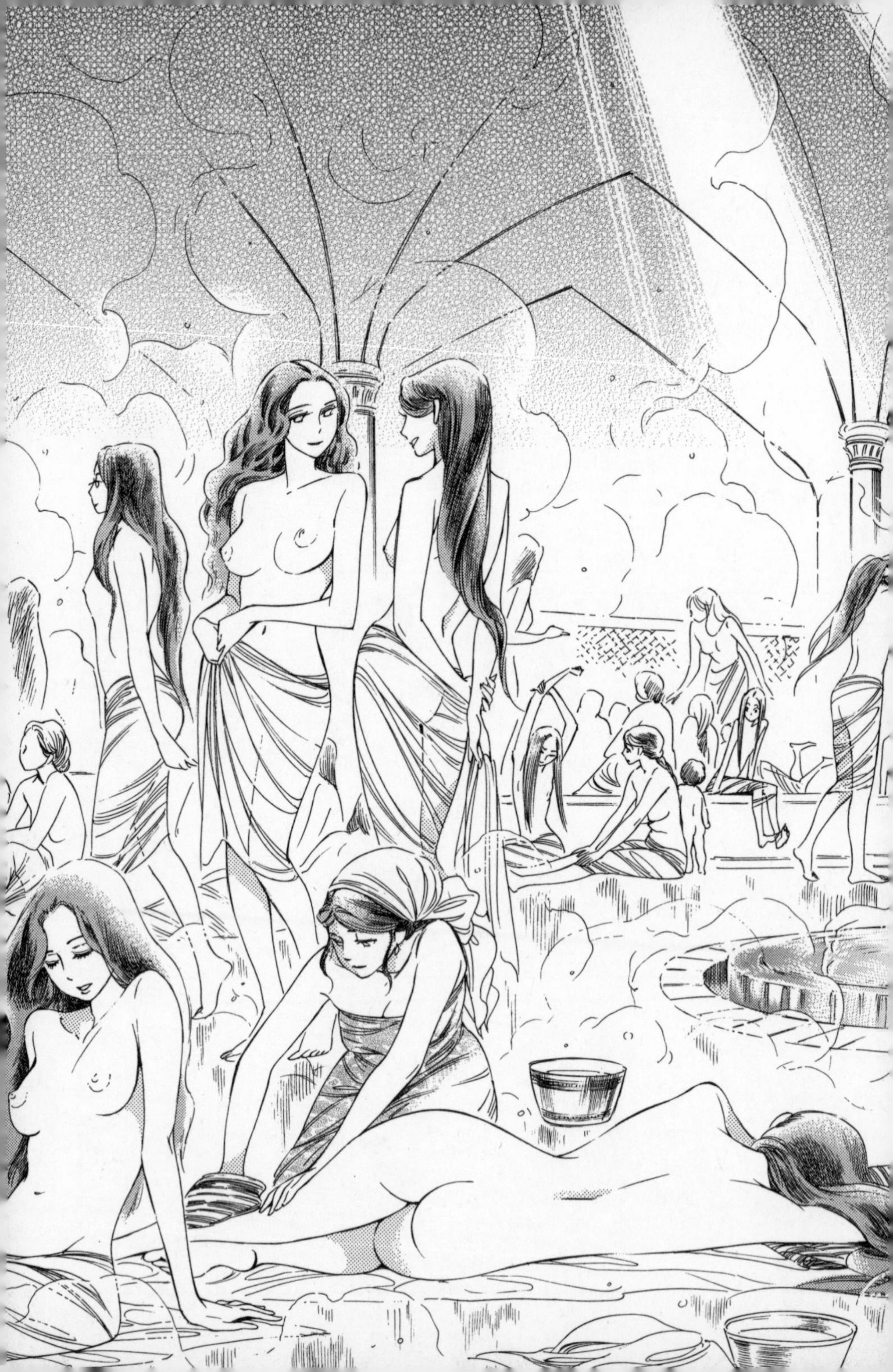

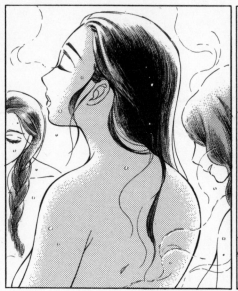
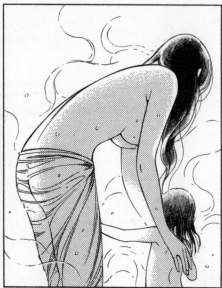
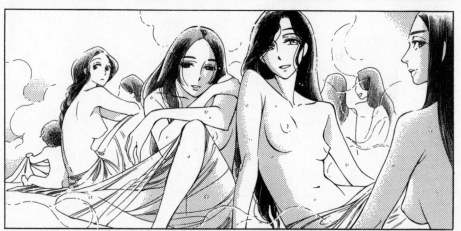
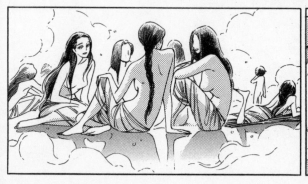
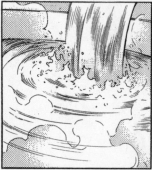

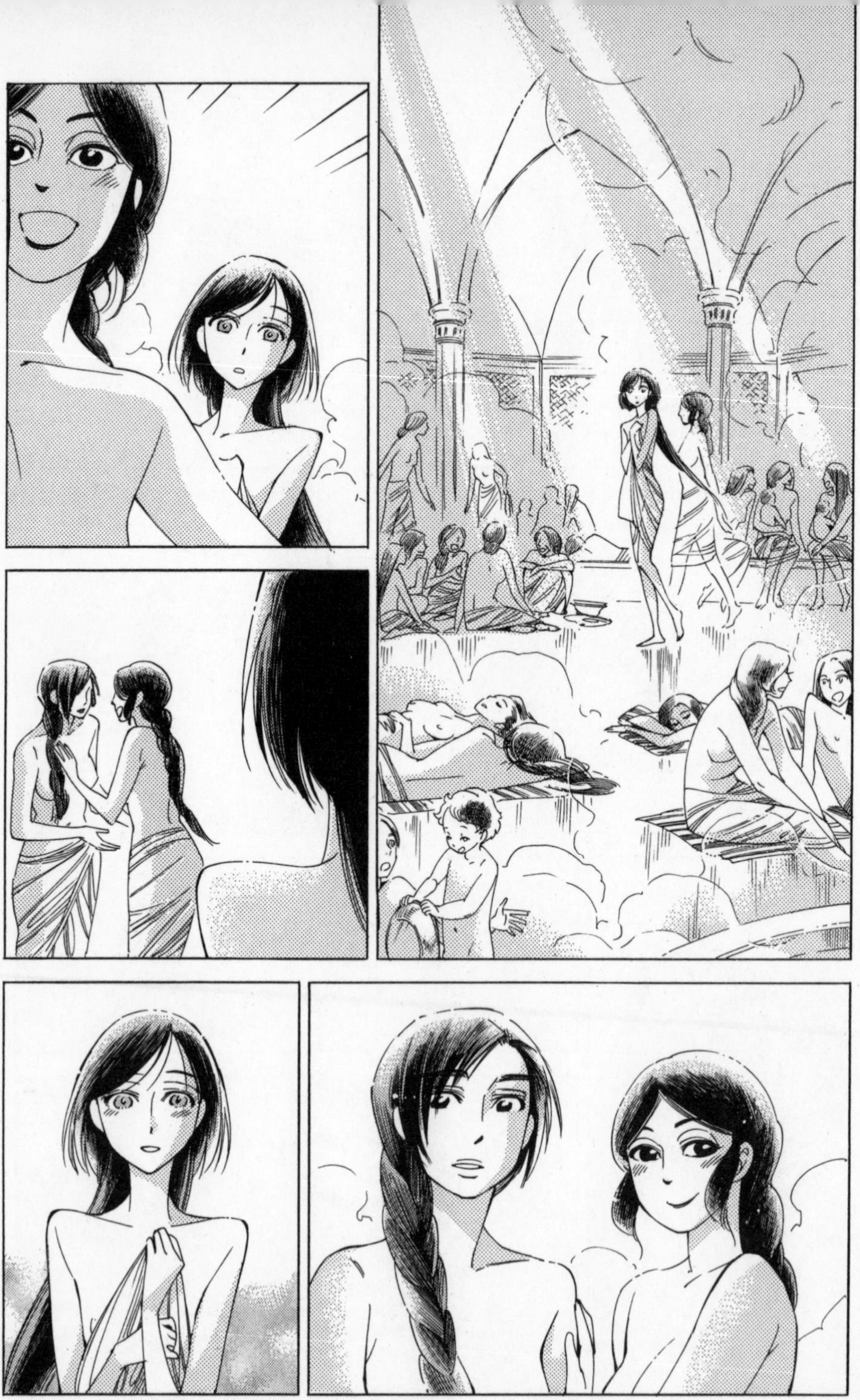

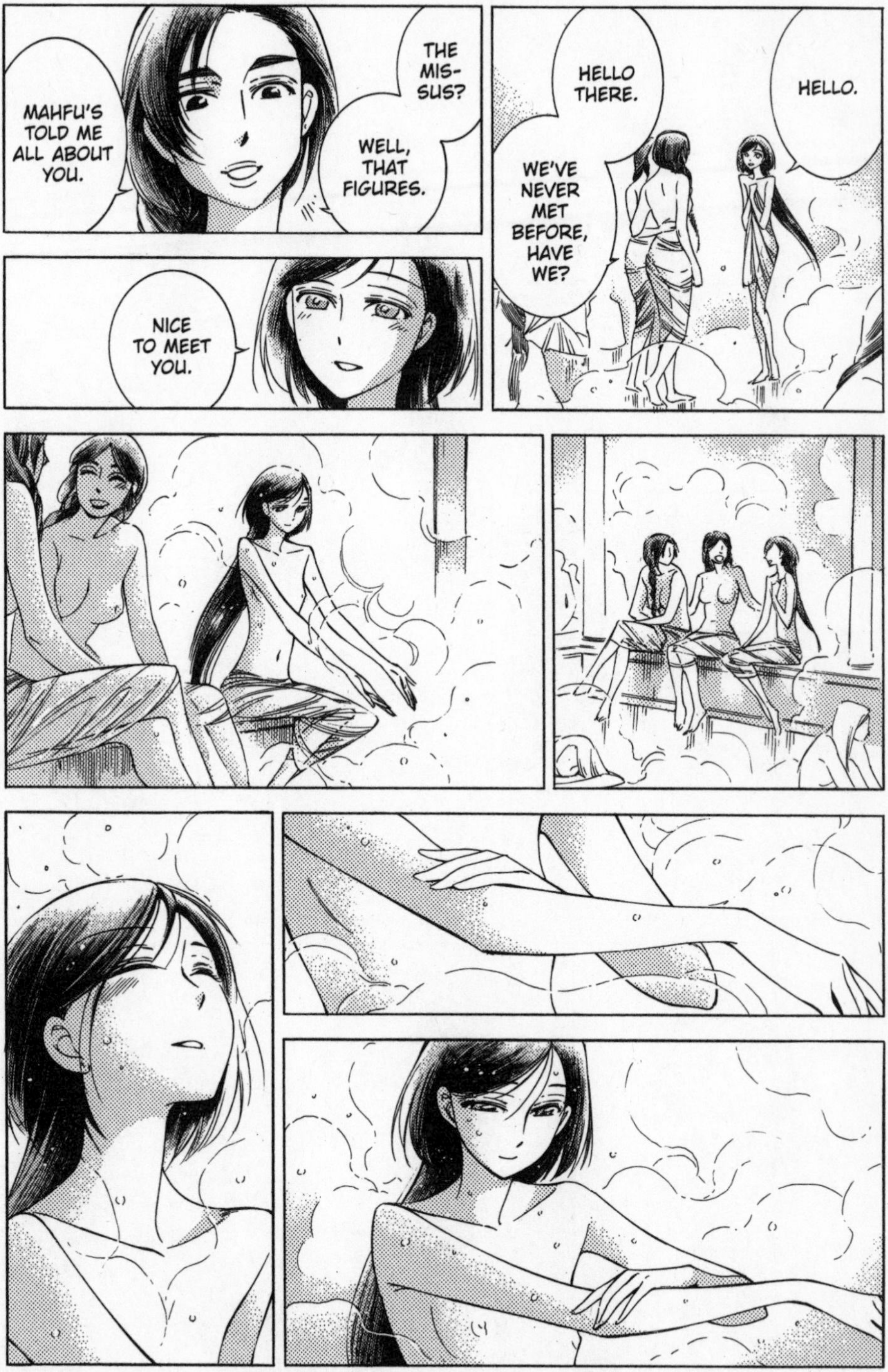
HELLO.
HELLO THERE.
WE'VE NEVER MET BEFORE, HAVE WE?
THE MIS-SUS?
MAHFU'S TOLD ME ALL ABOUT YOU.
WELL, THAT FIGURES.
NICE TO MEET YOU.

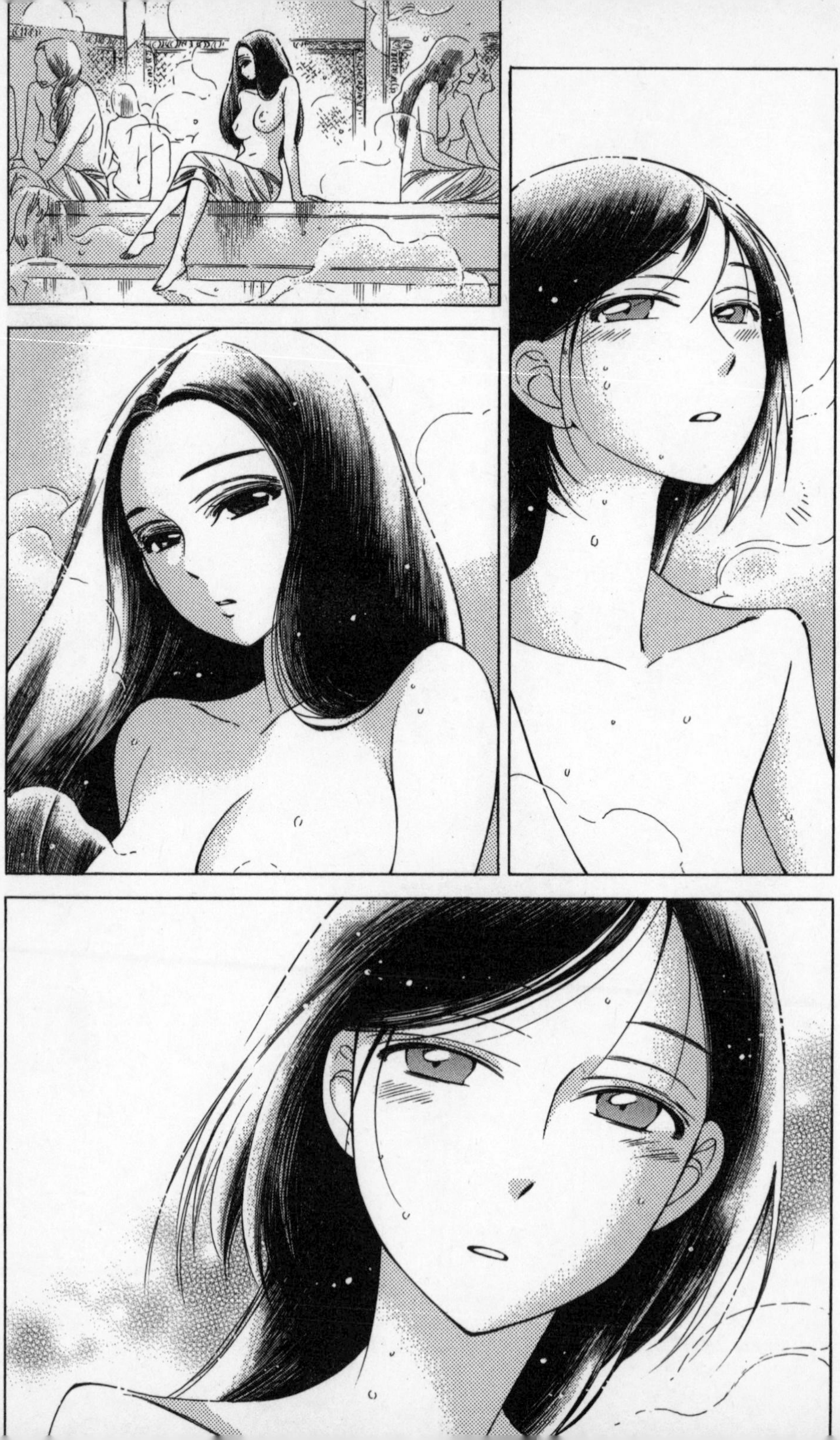

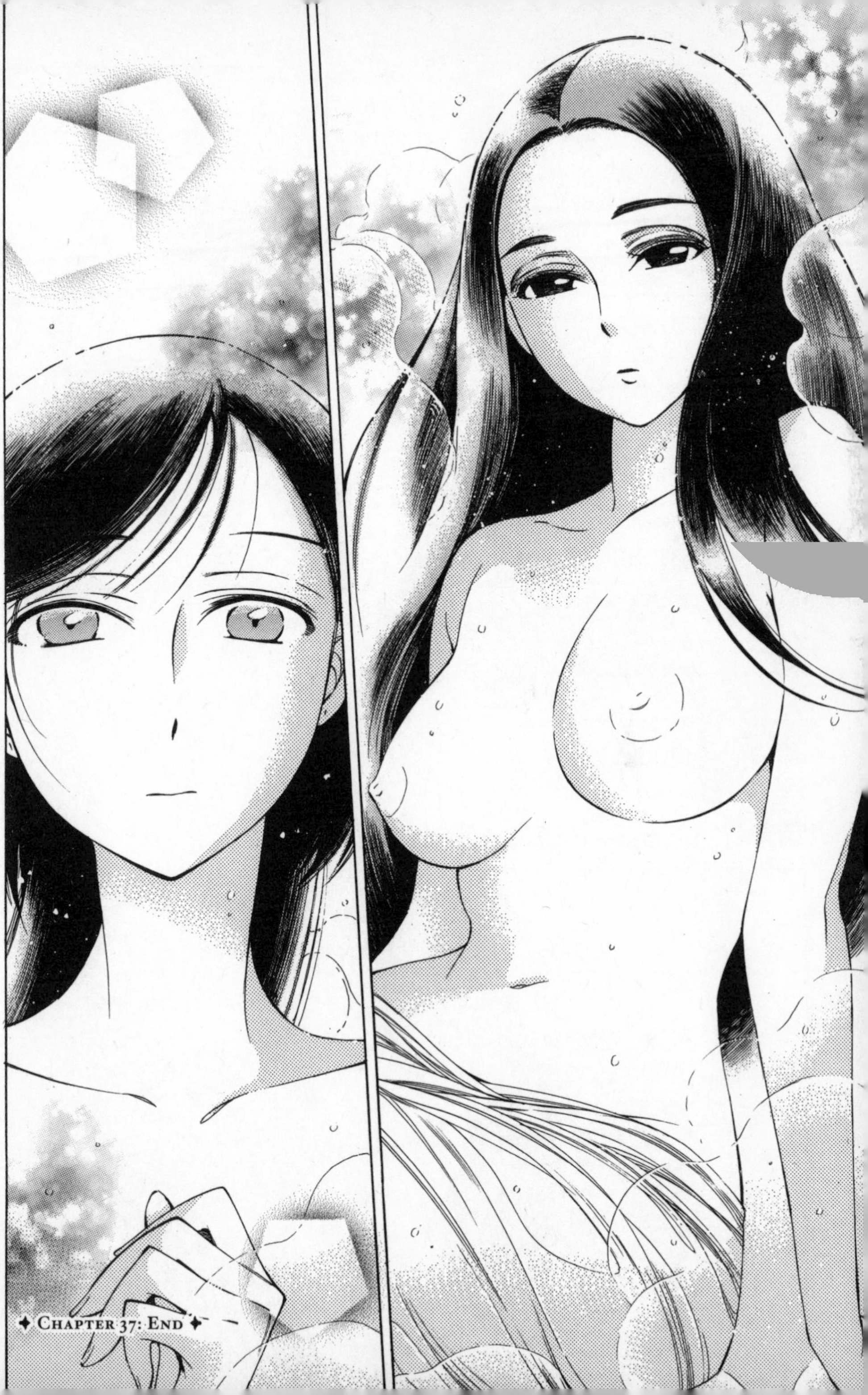
Chapter 37: End

Chapter 38
Men's Baths

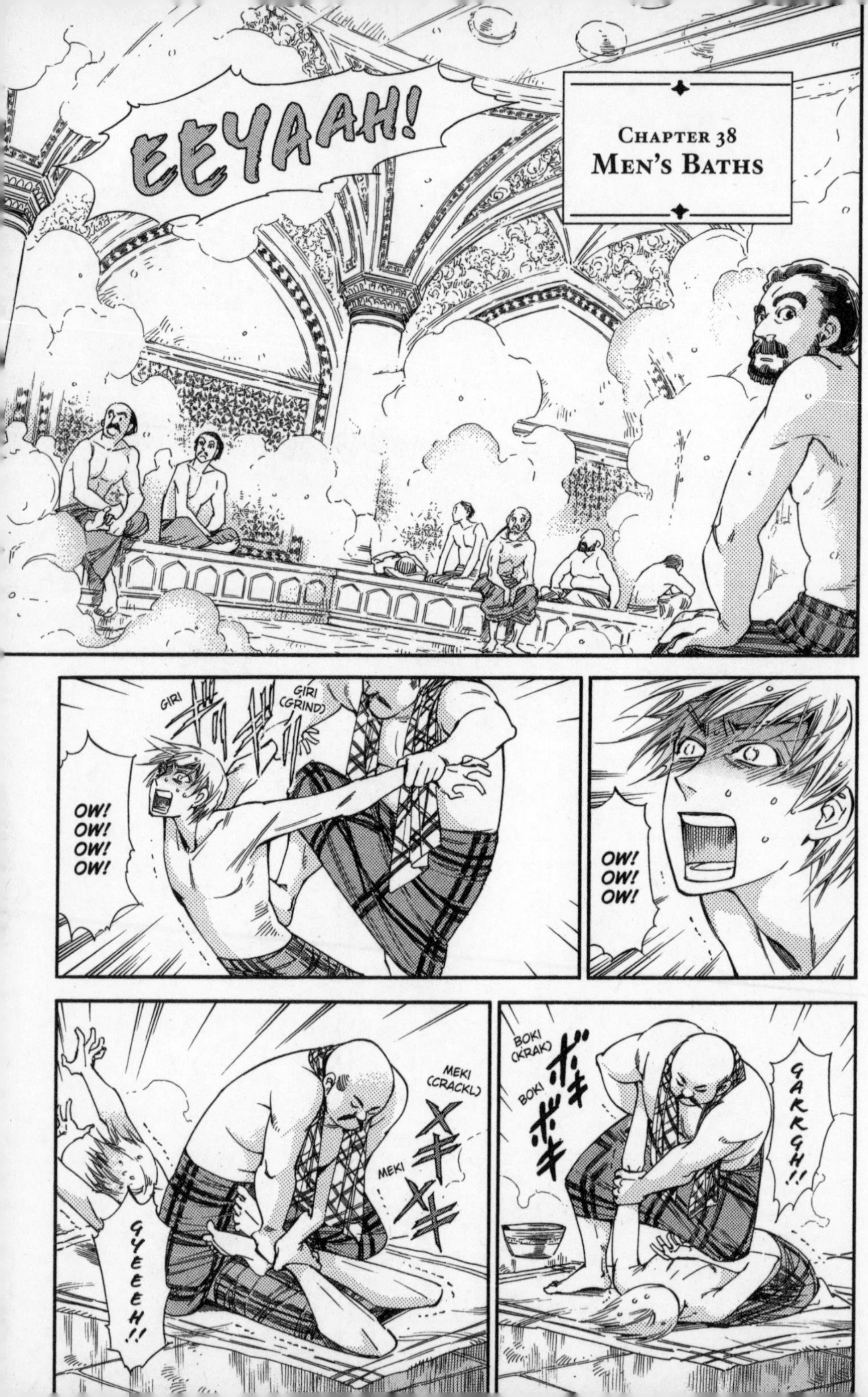
EEYAAH!
OW! OW! OW!
GIRI
GIRI (GRIND)
OW! OW! OW! OW!
BOKI (KRAK)
BOKI
GARRGH!!
MEKI (CRACKL)
MEKI
GYEEEEH!!

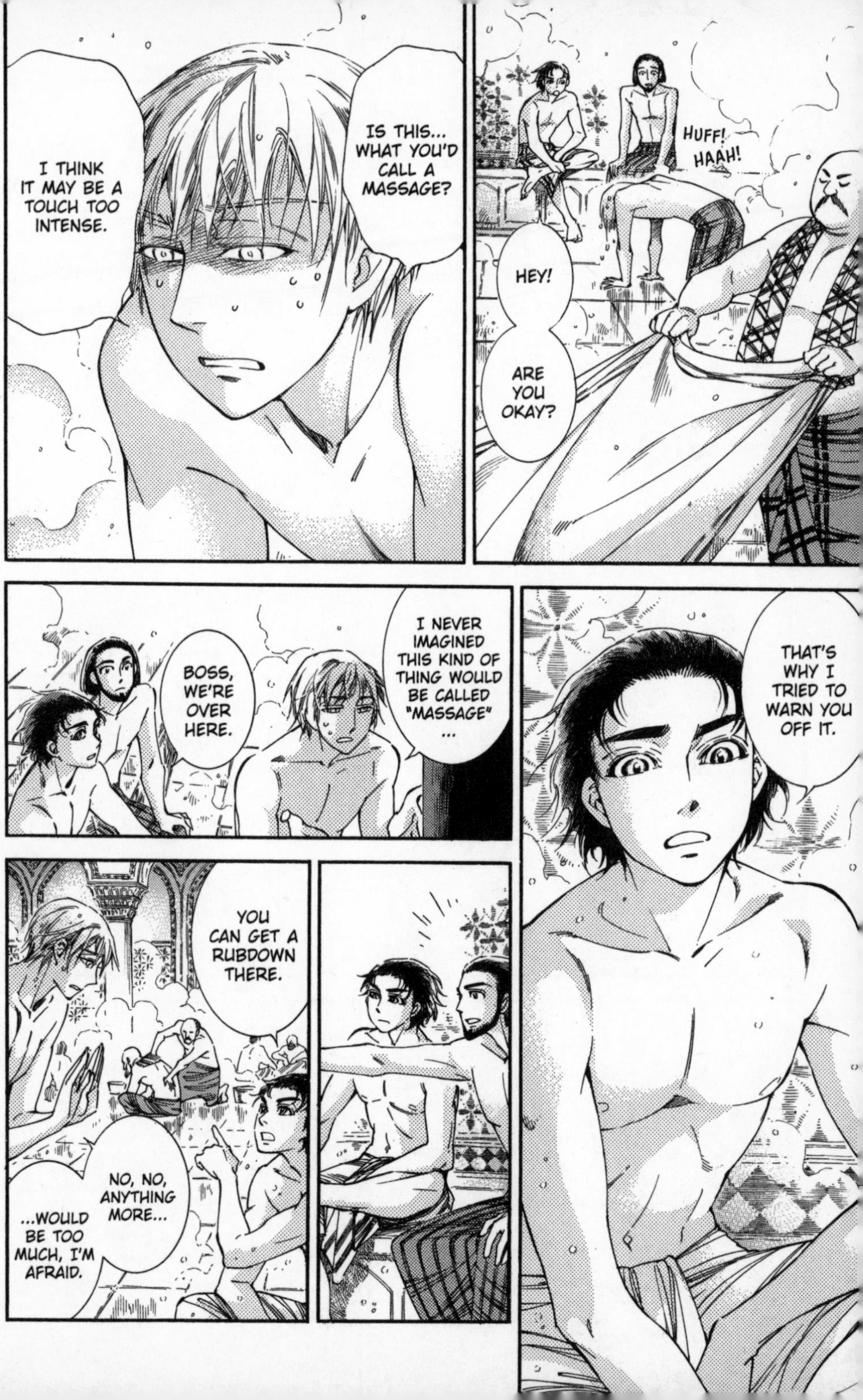
HUFF! HAAH!
HEY!
ARE YOU OKAY?
IS THIS... WHAT YOU'D CALL A MASSAGE?
I THINK IT MAY BE A TOUCH TOO INTENSE.
THAT'S WHY I TRIED TO WARN YOU OFF IT.
I NEVER IMAGINED THIS KIND OF THING WOULD BE CALLED "MASSAGE"...
BOSS, WE'RE OVER HERE.
YOU CAN GET A RUBDOWN THERE.
NO, NO, ANYTHING MORE...
...WOULD BE TOO MUCH, I'M AFRAID.

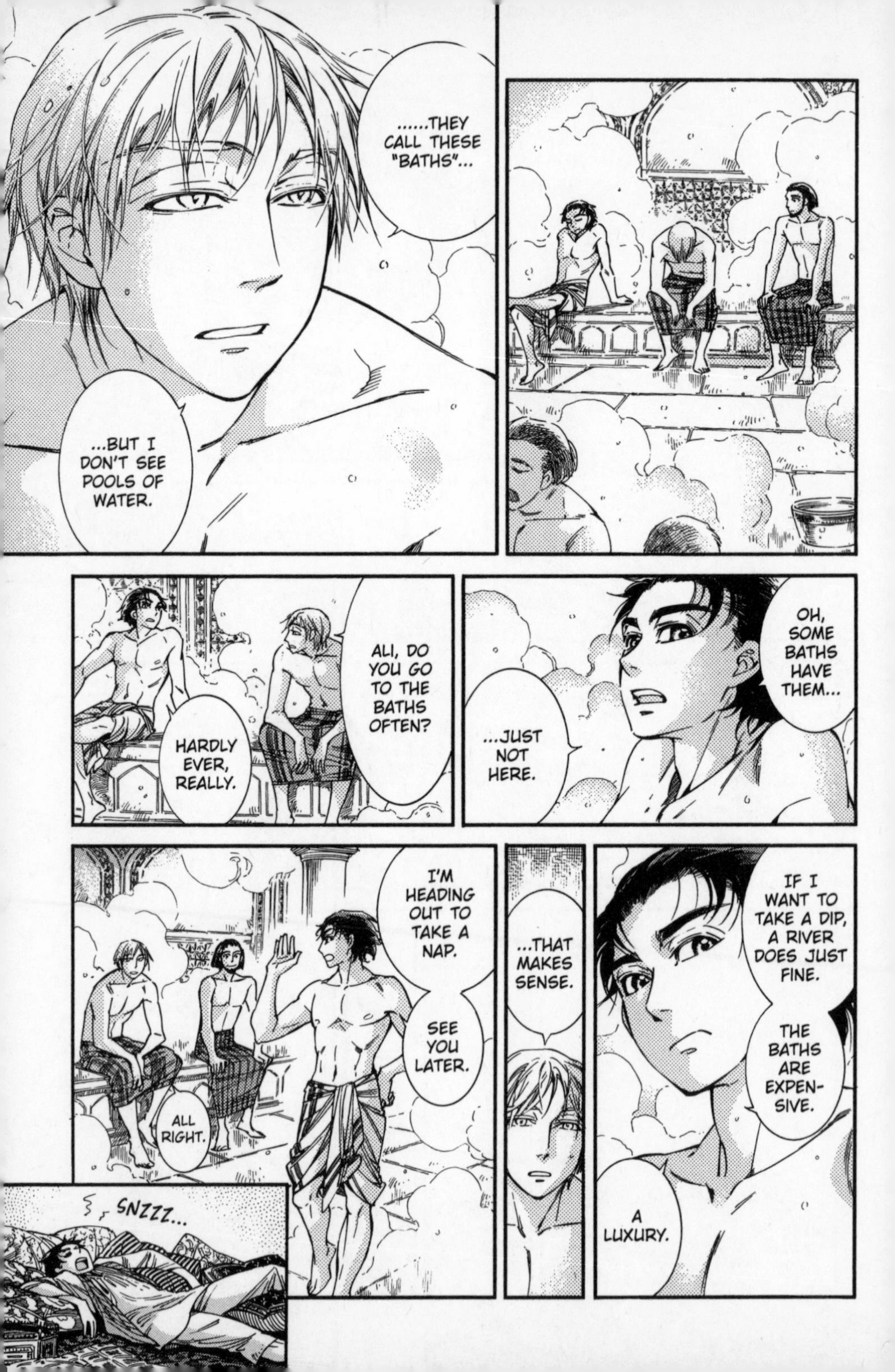
......THEY CALL THESE "BATHS"...
...BUT I DON'T SEE POOLS OF WATER.
OH, SOME BATHS HAVE THEM...
...JUST NOT HERE.
ALI, DO YOU GO TO THE BATHS OFTEN?
HARDLY EVER, REALLY.
IF I WANT TO TAKE A DIP, A RIVER DOES JUST FINE.
THE BATHS ARE EXPEN-SIVE.
A LUXURY.
...THAT MAKES SENSE.
I'M HEADING OUT TO TAKE A NAP.
SEE YOU LATER.
ALL RIGHT.
SNZZZ...

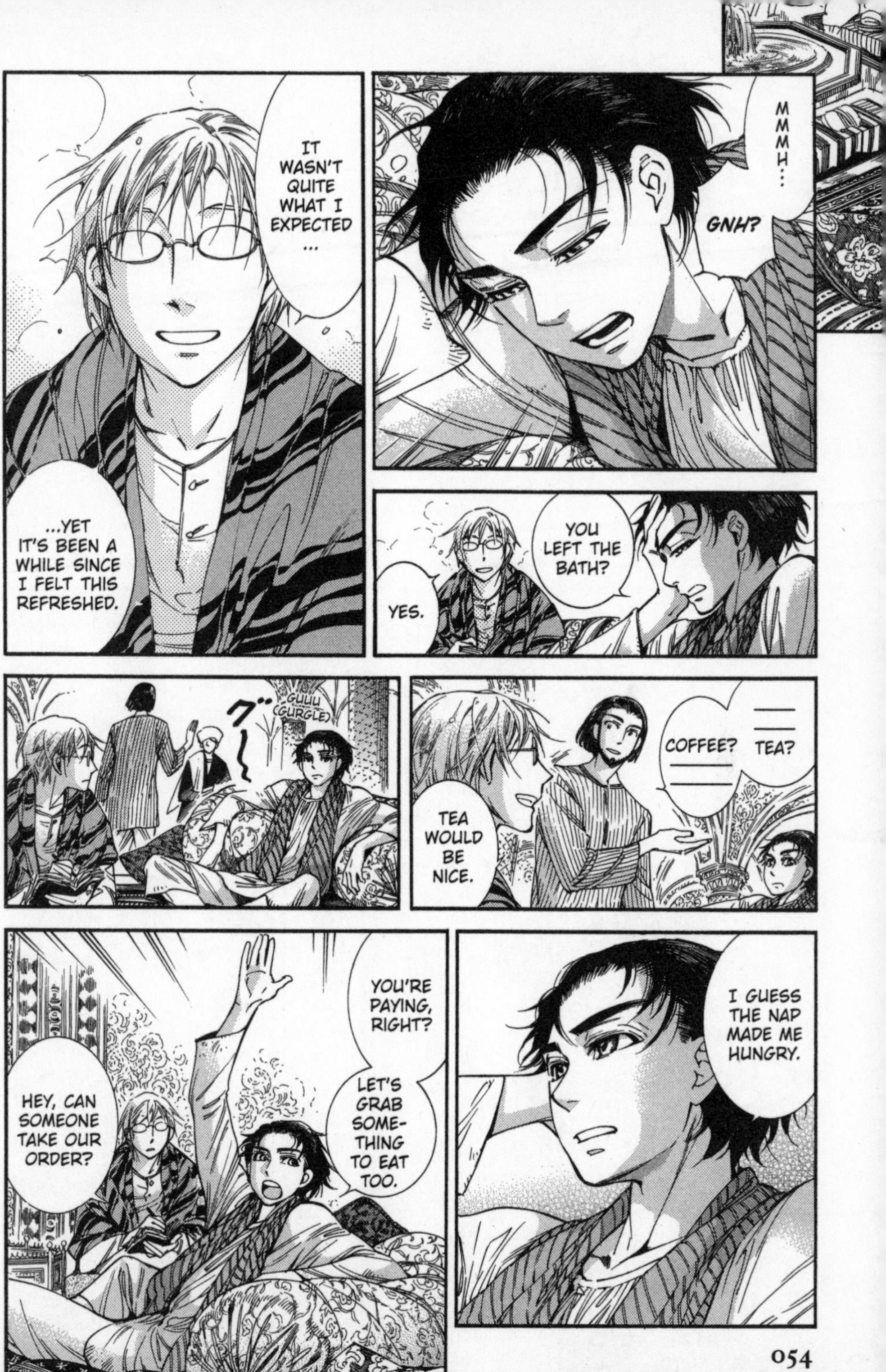

MMMH...
GNH?
YOU LEFT THE BATH?
YES.
IT WASN'T QUITE WHAT I EXPECTED ...
...YET IT'S BEEN A WHILE SINCE I FELT THIS REFRESHED.
—— —— TEA?
COFFEE? —— ——
TEA WOULD BE NICE.
GUUU (GURGLE)
I GUESS THE NAP MADE ME HUNGRY.
YOU'RE PAYING, RIGHT?
LET'S GRAB SOME-THING TO EAT TOO.
HEY, CAN SOMEONE TAKE OUR ORDER?

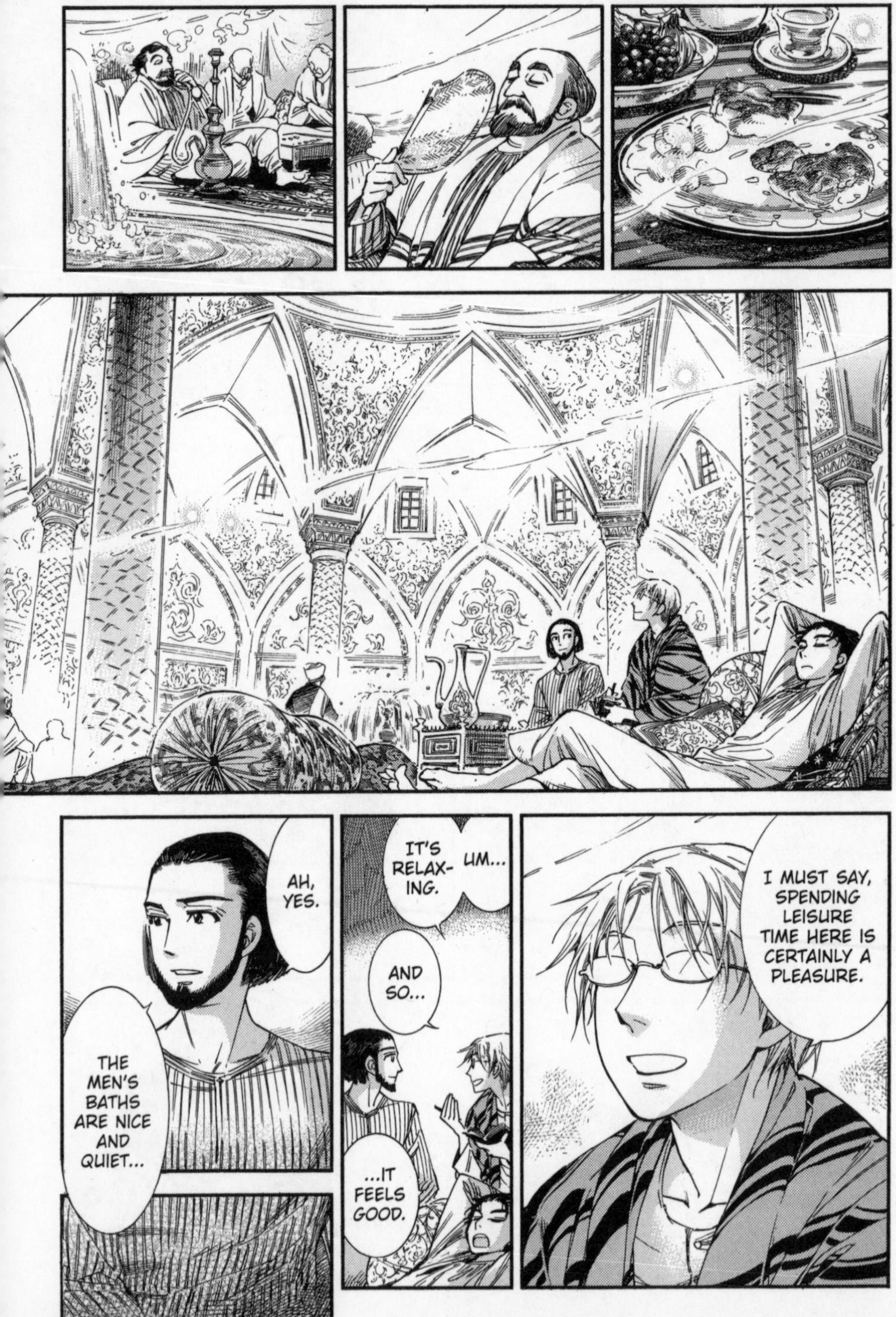
I MUST SAY, SPENDING LEISURE TIME HERE IS CERTAINLY A PLEASURE.
UM...
IT'S RELAX-ING.
AND SO...
...IT FEELS GOOD.
AH, YES.
THE MEN'S BATHS ARE NICE AND QUIET...

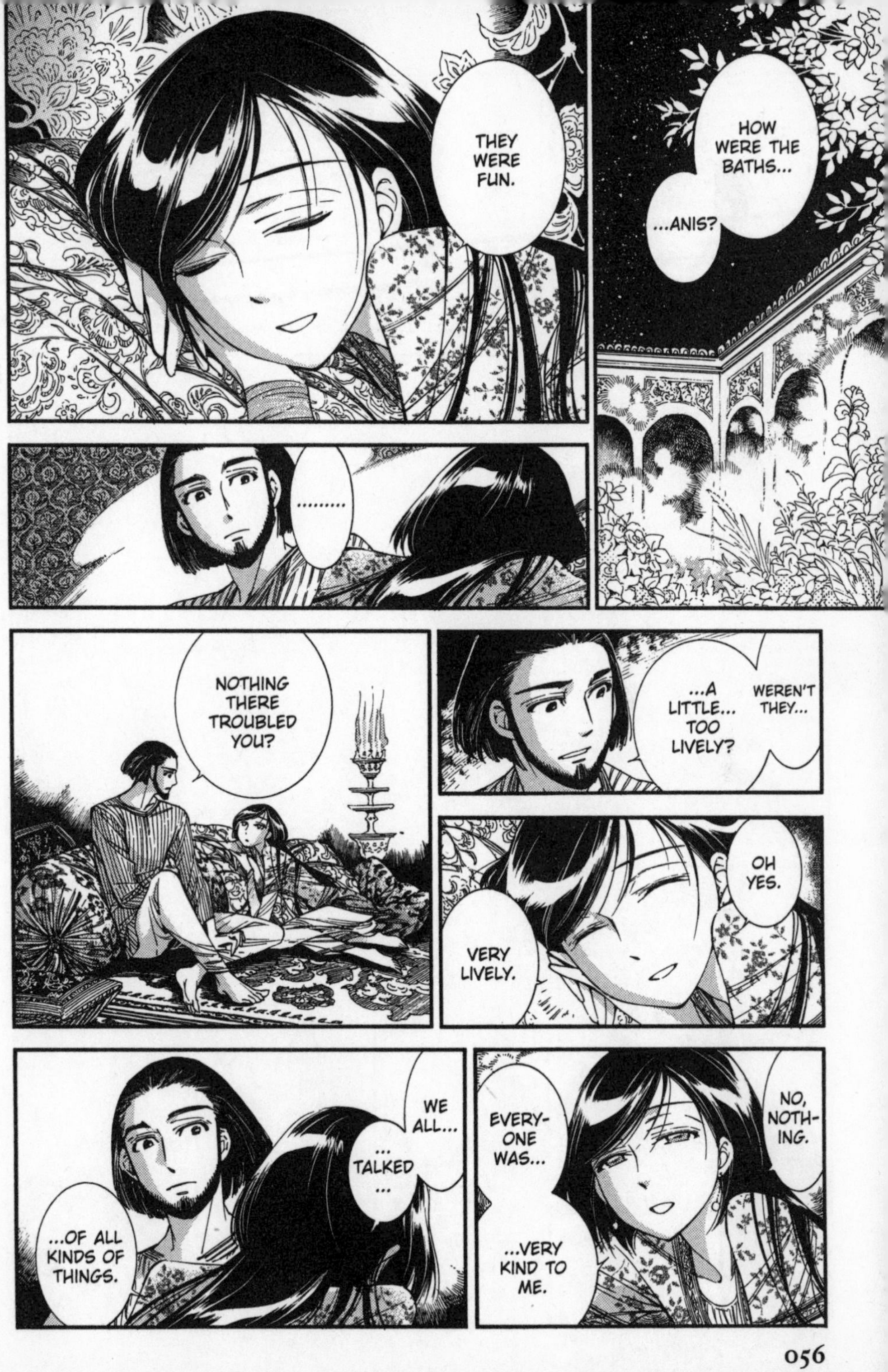
HOW WERE THE BATHS...
...ANIS?
THEY WERE FUN.
....
WEREN'T THEY...
...A LITTLE... TOO LIVELY?
OH YES.
VERY LIVELY.
NOTHING THERE TROUBLED YOU?
NO, NOTH-ING.
EVERY-ONE WAS...
...VERY KIND TO ME.
WE ALL...
...TALKED...
...OF ALL KINDS OF THINGS.

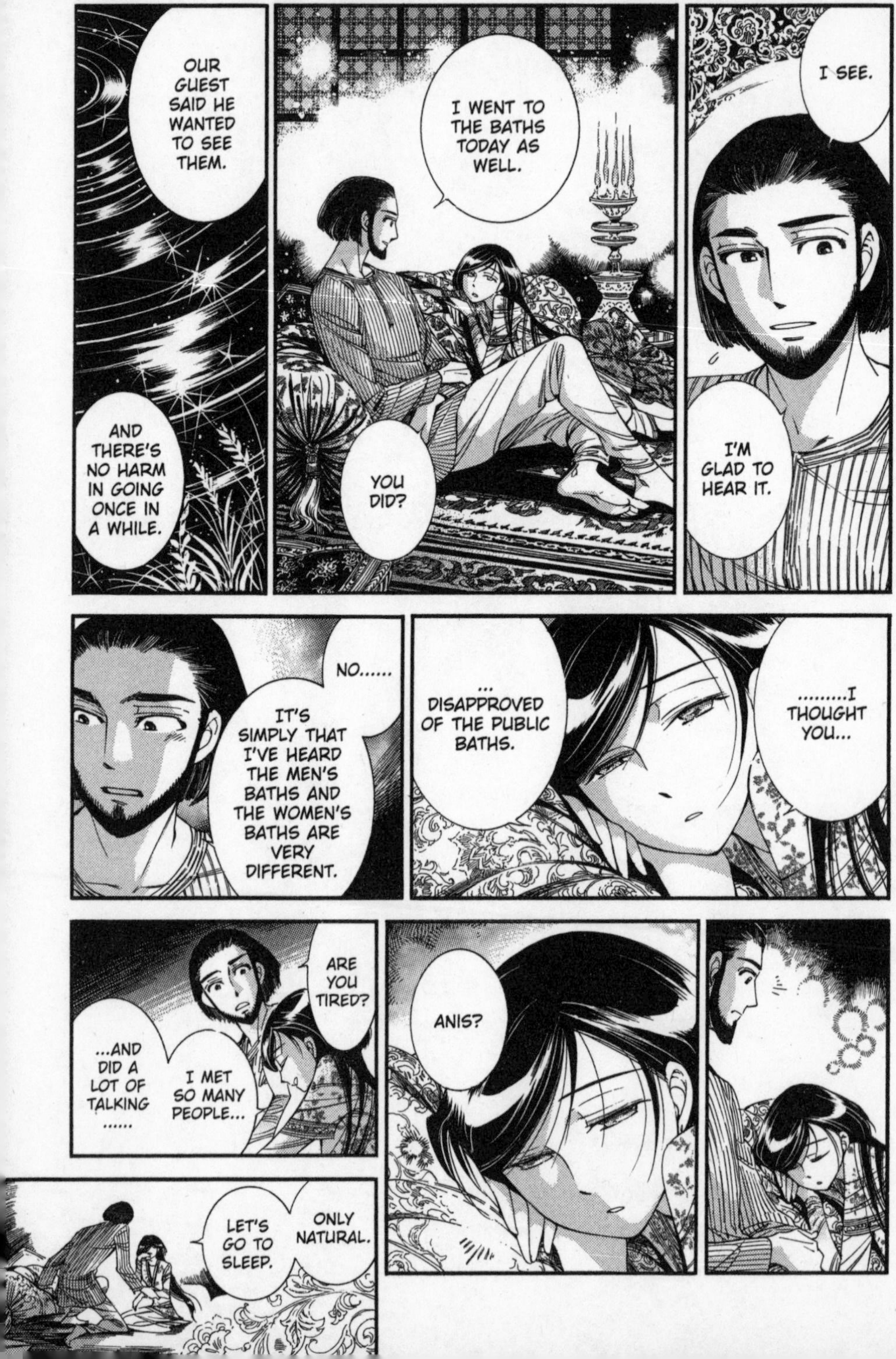
I SEE.
I'M GLAD TO HEAR IT.
I WENT TO THE BATHS TODAY AS WELL.
YOU DID?
OUR GUEST SAID HE WANTED TO SEE THEM.
AND THERE'S NO HARM IN GOING ONCE IN A WHILE.
.........I THOUGHT YOU...
...DISAPPROVED OF THE PUBLIC BATHS.
NO......
IT'S SIMPLY THAT I'VE HEARD THE MEN'S BATHS AND THE WOMEN'S BATHS ARE VERY DIFFERENT.
ANIS?
ARE YOU TIRED?
I MET SO MANY PEOPLE...
...AND DID A LOT OF TALKING......
ONLY NATURAL.
LET'S GO TO SLEEP.

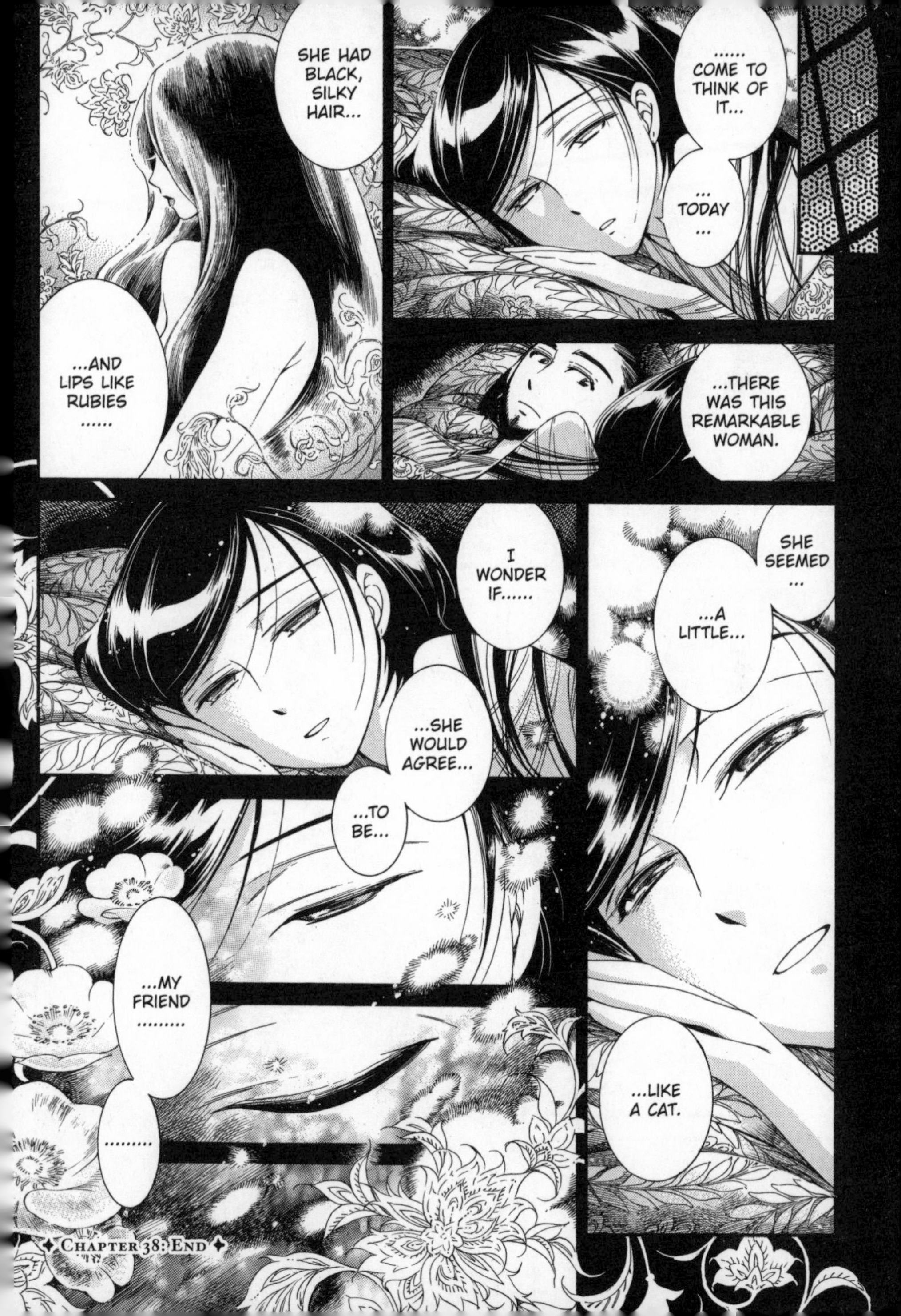
......COME TO THINK OF IT...
...TODAY...
...THERE WAS THIS REMARKABLE WOMAN.
SHE HAD BLACK, SILKY HAIR...
...AND LIPS LIKE RUBIES ......
SHE SEEMED ...
...A LITTLE...
...LIKE A CAT.
I WONDER IF......
...SHE WOULD AGREE...
...TO BE...
...MY FRIEND ....
....
Chapter 38: End

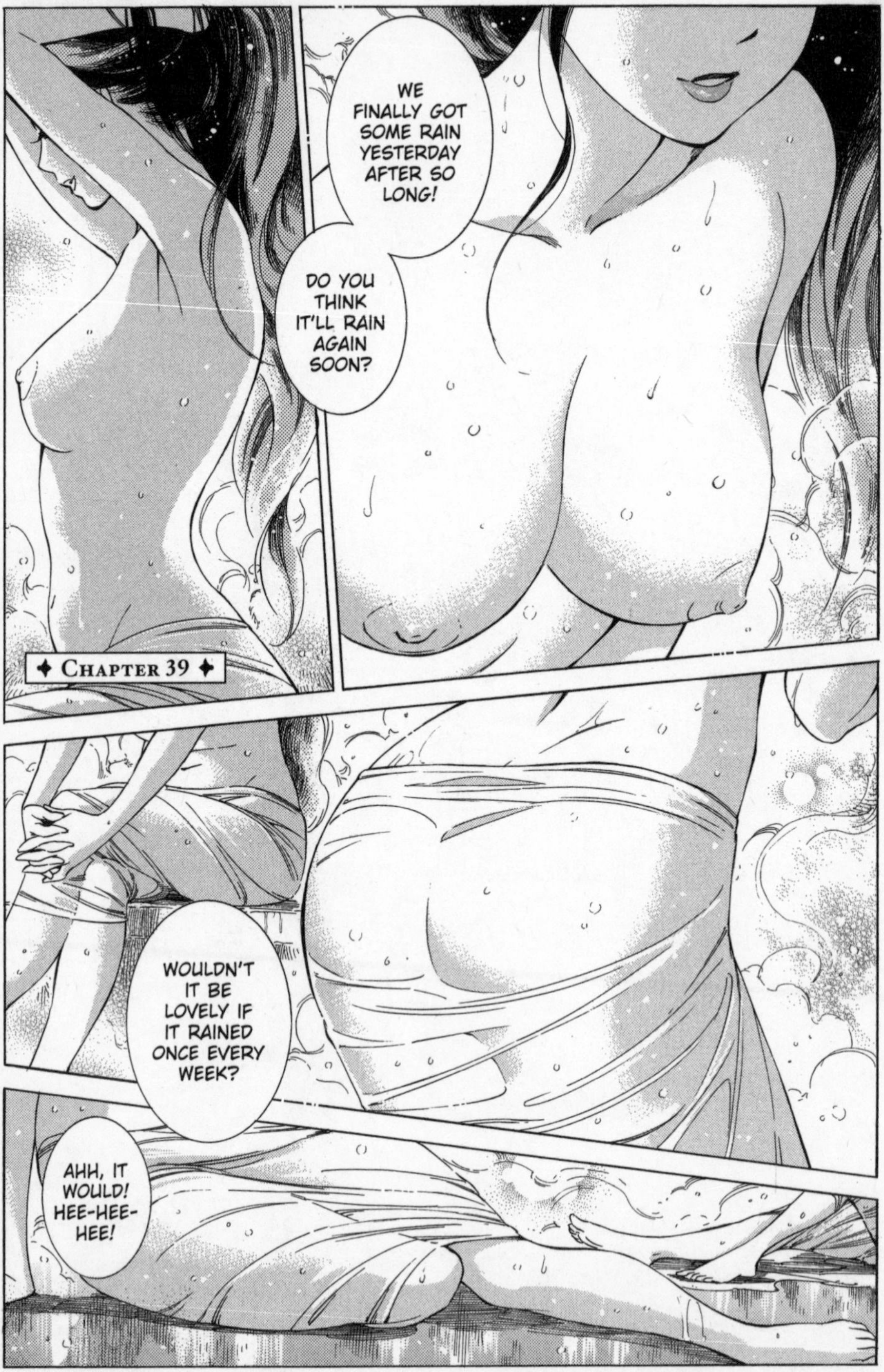
WE FINALLY GOT SOME RAIN YESTERDAY AFTER SO LONG!
DO YOU THINK IT'LL RAIN AGAIN SOON?
✦ CHAPTER 39 ✦
WOULDN'T IT BE LOVELY IF IT RAINED ONCE EVERY WEEK?
AHH, IT WOULD! HEE-HEE-HEE!

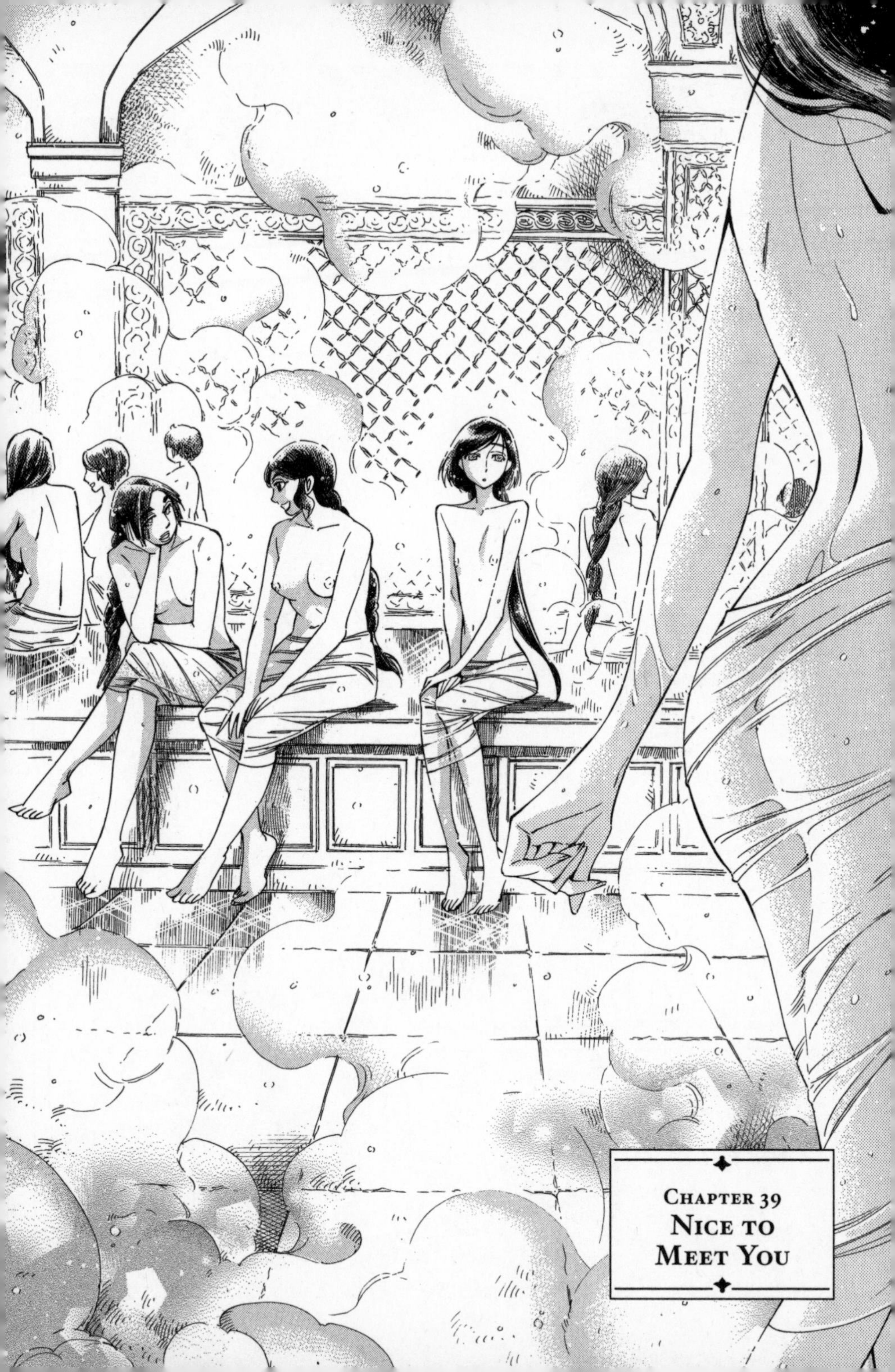
Chapter 39
Nice to Meet You

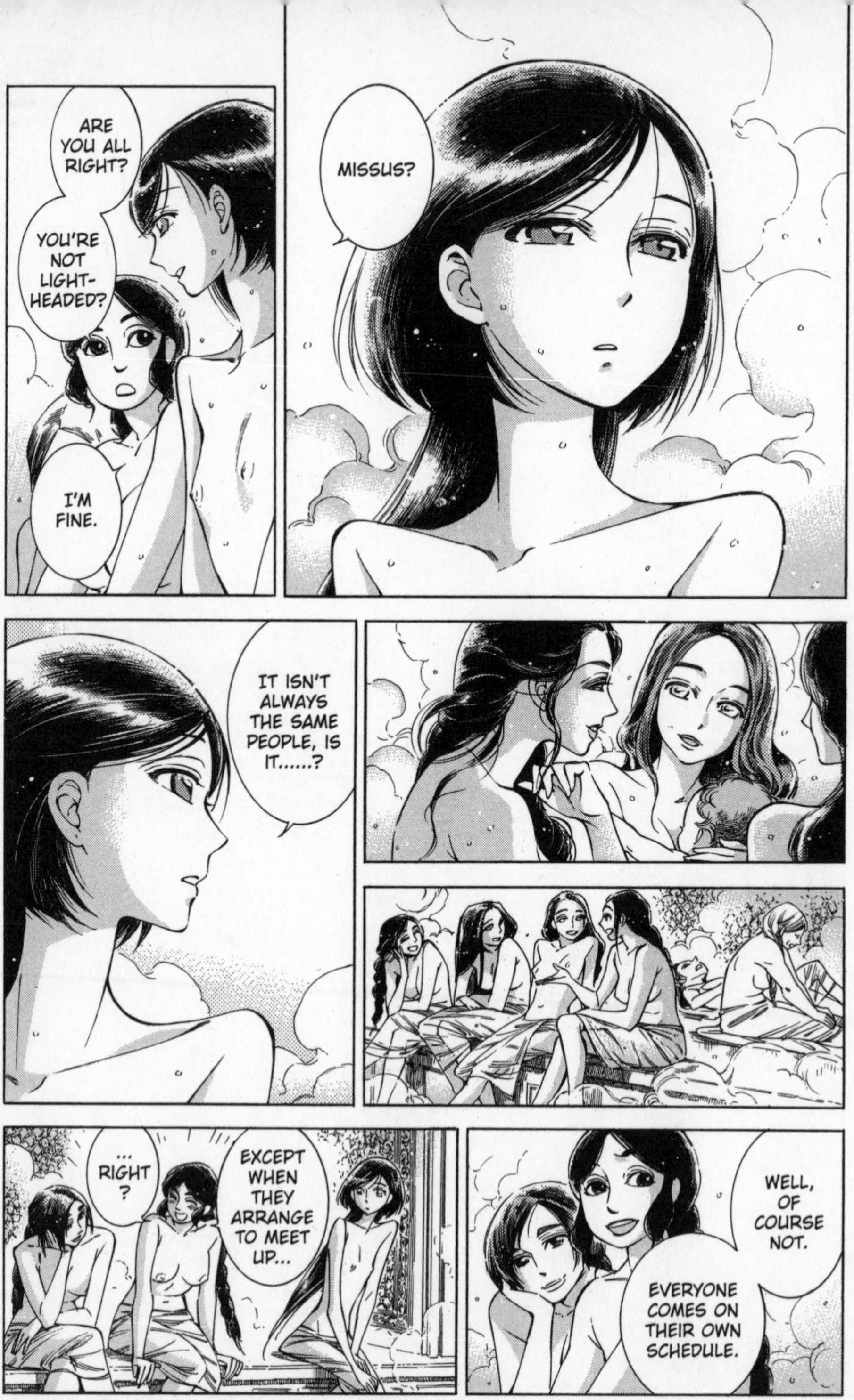
MISSUS?
ARE YOU ALL RIGHT?
YOU'RE NOT LIGHT-HEADED?
I'M FINE.
IT ISN'T ALWAYS THE SAME PEOPLE, IS IT......?
WELL, OF COURSE NOT.
EVERYONE COMES ON THEIR OWN SCHEDULE.
EXCEPT WHEN THEY ARRANGE TO MEET UP...
... RIGHT?

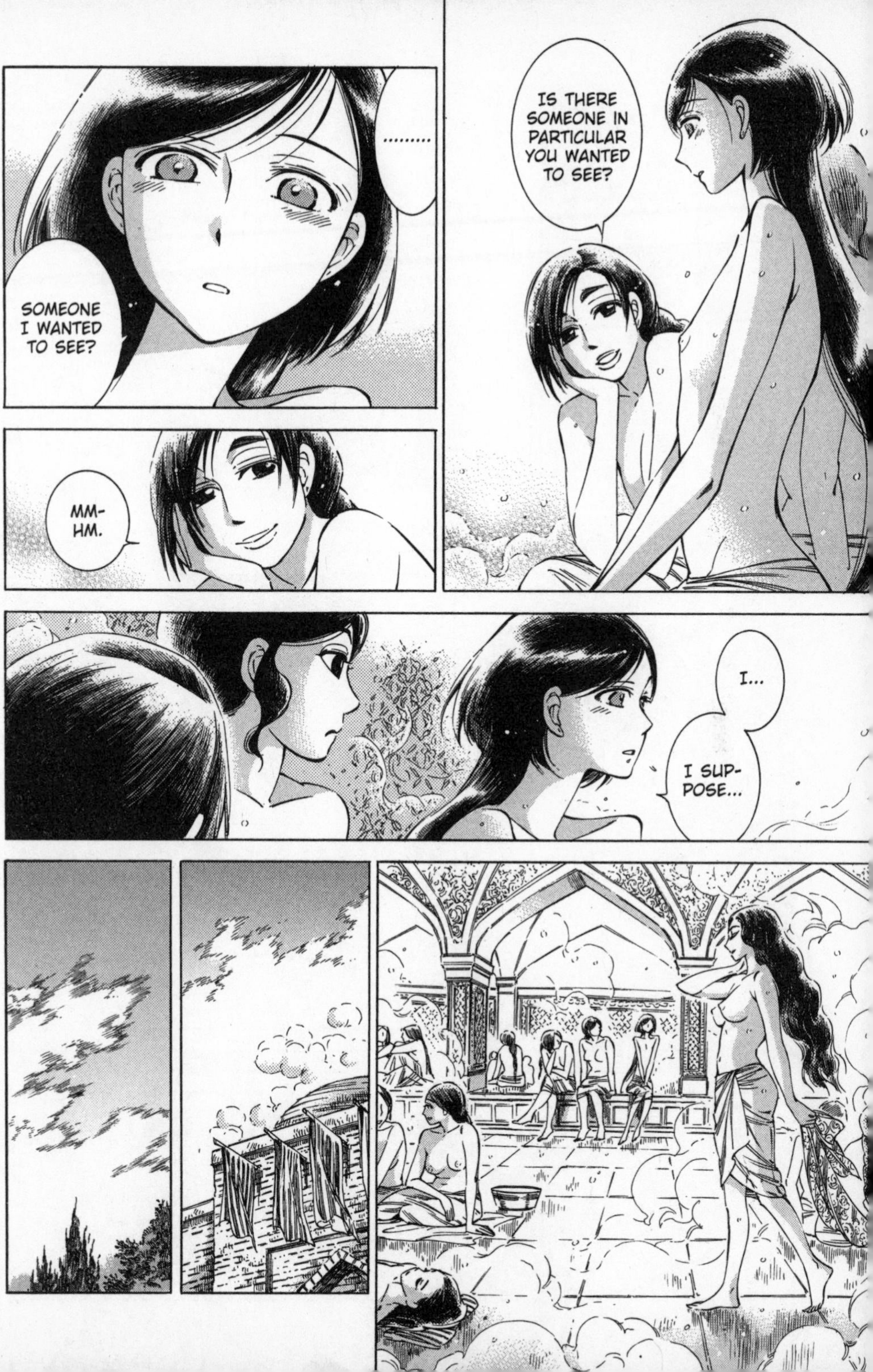
IS THERE SOMEONE IN PARTICULAR YOU WANTED TO SEE?
....
SOMEONE I WANTED TO SEE?
MM-HM.
I...
I SUP-POSE...

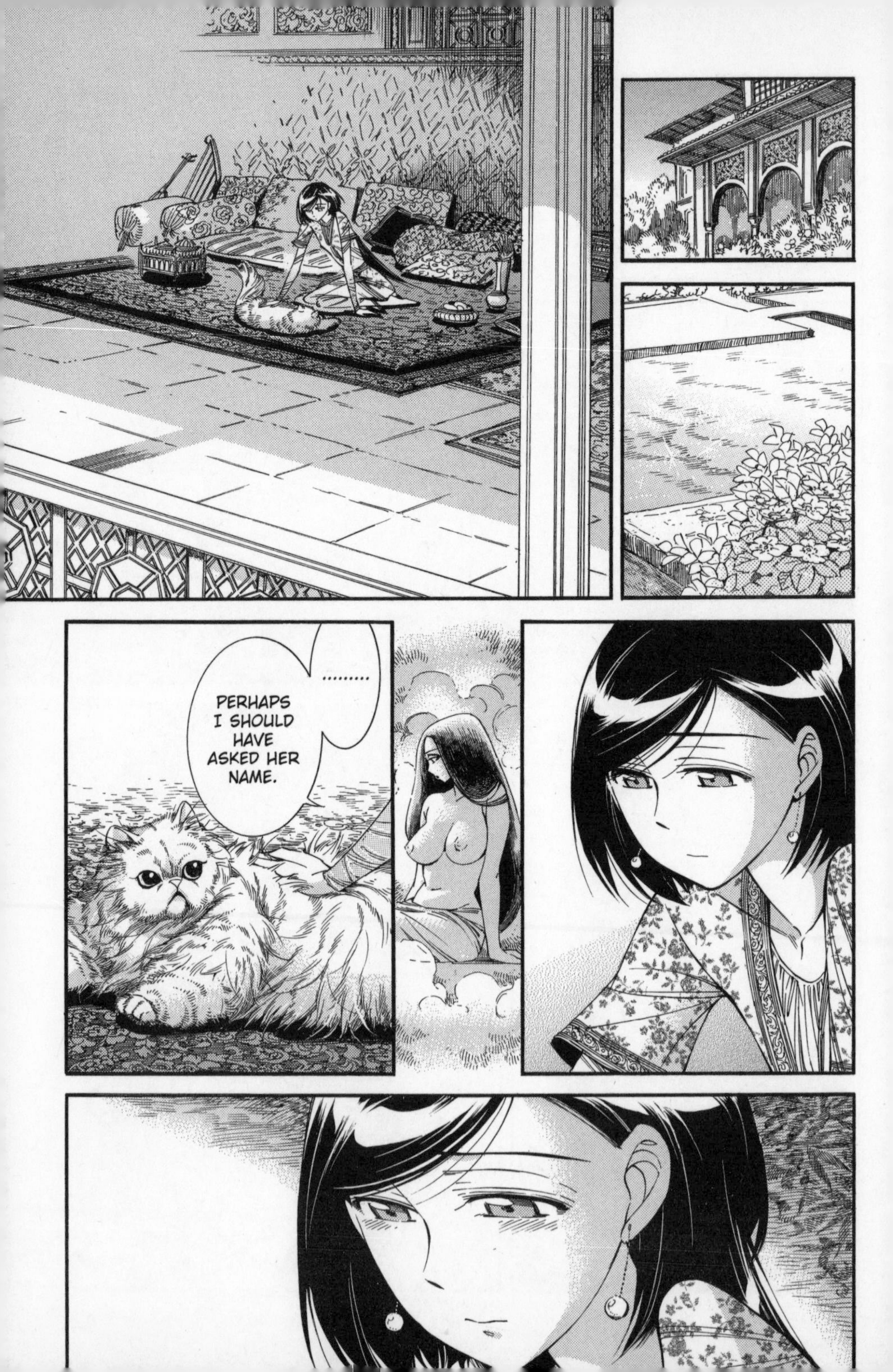

....
PERHAPS I SHOULD HAVE ASKED HER NAME.

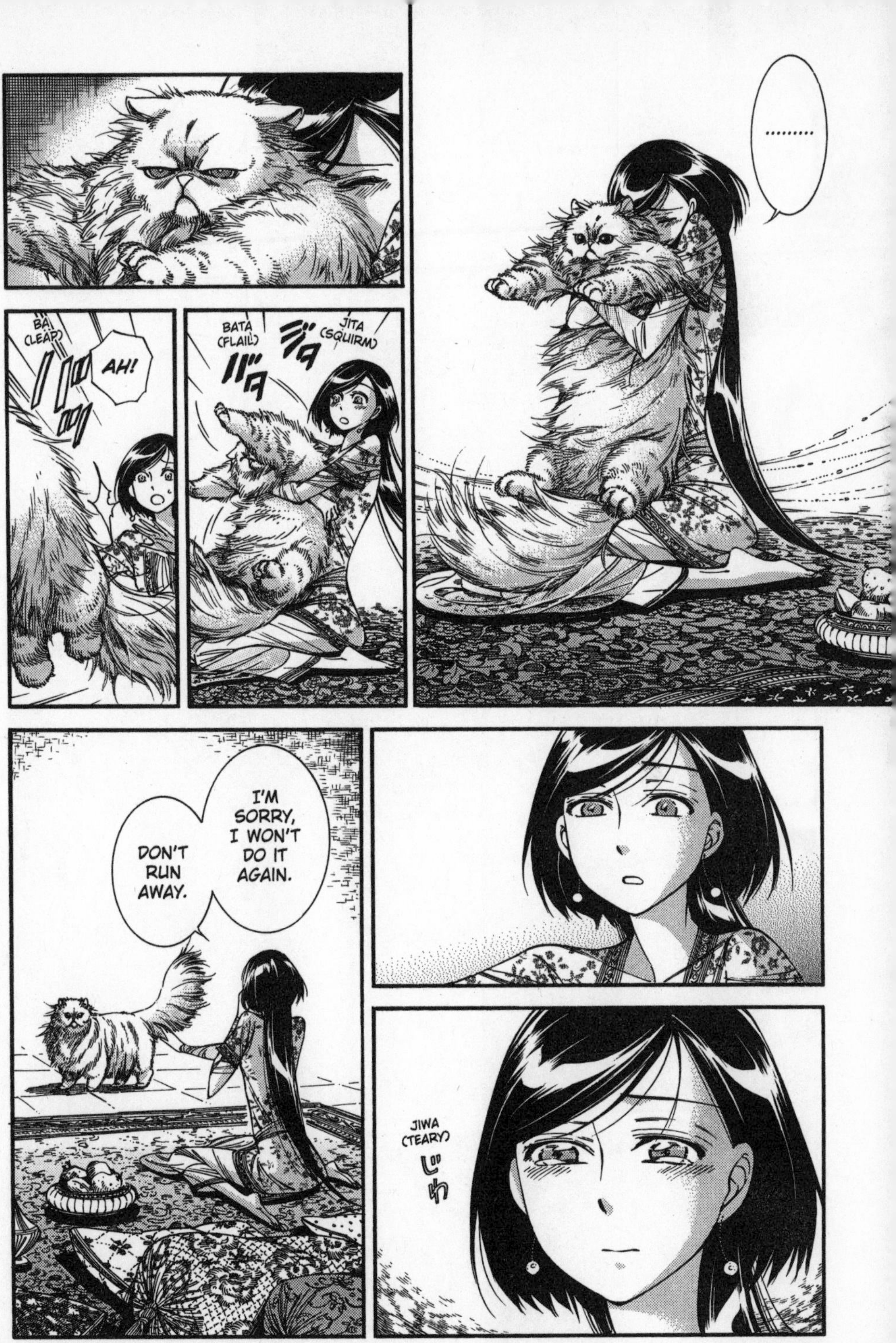
....
BATA (FLAIL)
JITA (SQUIRM)
BA (LEAP)
AH!
JIWA (TEARY)
I'M SORRY, I WON'T DO IT AGAIN.
DON'T RUN AWAY.

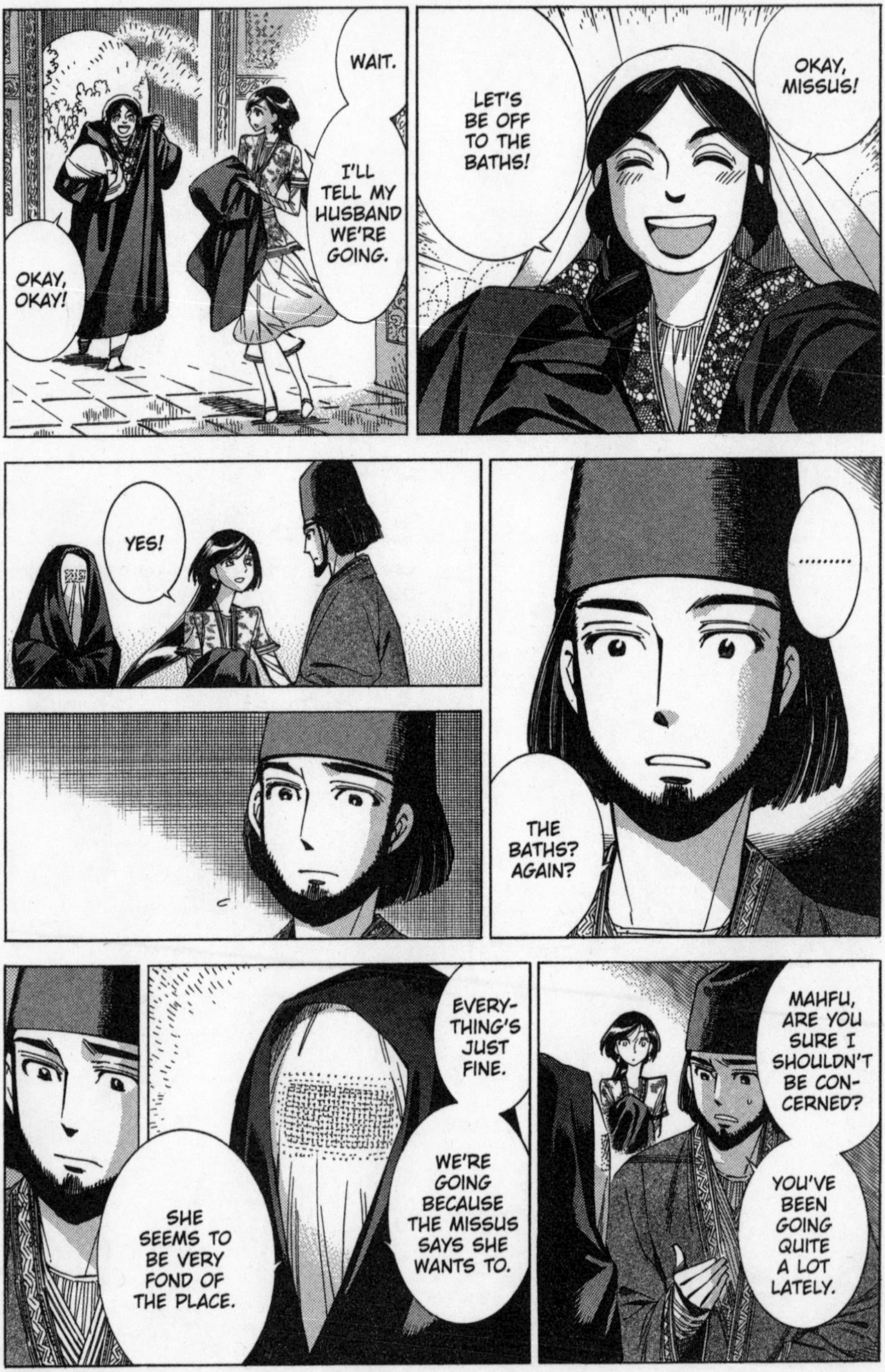
OKAY, MISSUS!
LET'S BE OFF TO THE BATHS!
WAIT.
I'LL TELL MY HUSBAND WE'RE GOING.
OKAY, OKAY!
....
THE BATHS? AGAIN?
YES!
MAHFU, ARE YOU SURE I SHOULDN'T BE CON-CERNED?
YOU'VE BEEN GOING QUITE A LOT LATELY.
EVERY-THING'S JUST FINE.
WE'RE GOING BECAUSE THE MISSUS SAYS SHE WANTS TO.
SHE SEEMS TO BE VERY FOND OF THE PLACE.

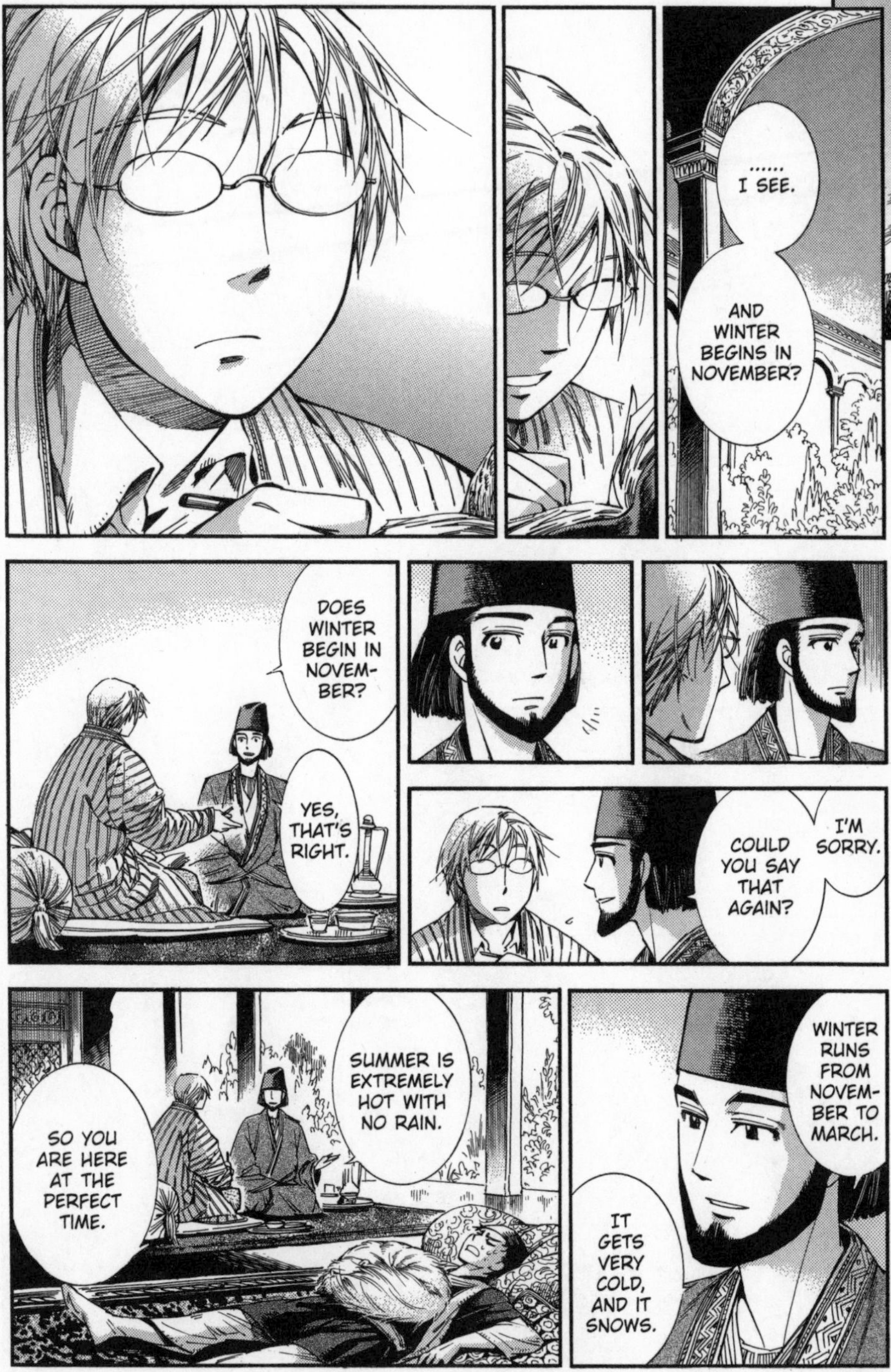
......
I SEE.
AND WINTER BEGINS IN NOVEMBER?
I'M SORRY.
COULD YOU SAY THAT AGAIN?
DOES WINTER BEGIN IN NOVEM-BER?
YES, THAT'S RIGHT.
WINTER RUNS FROM NOVEM-BER TO MARCH.
IT GETS VERY COLD, AND IT SNOWS.
SUMMER IS EXTREMELY HOT WITH NO RAIN.
SO YOU ARE HERE AT THE PERFECT TIME.

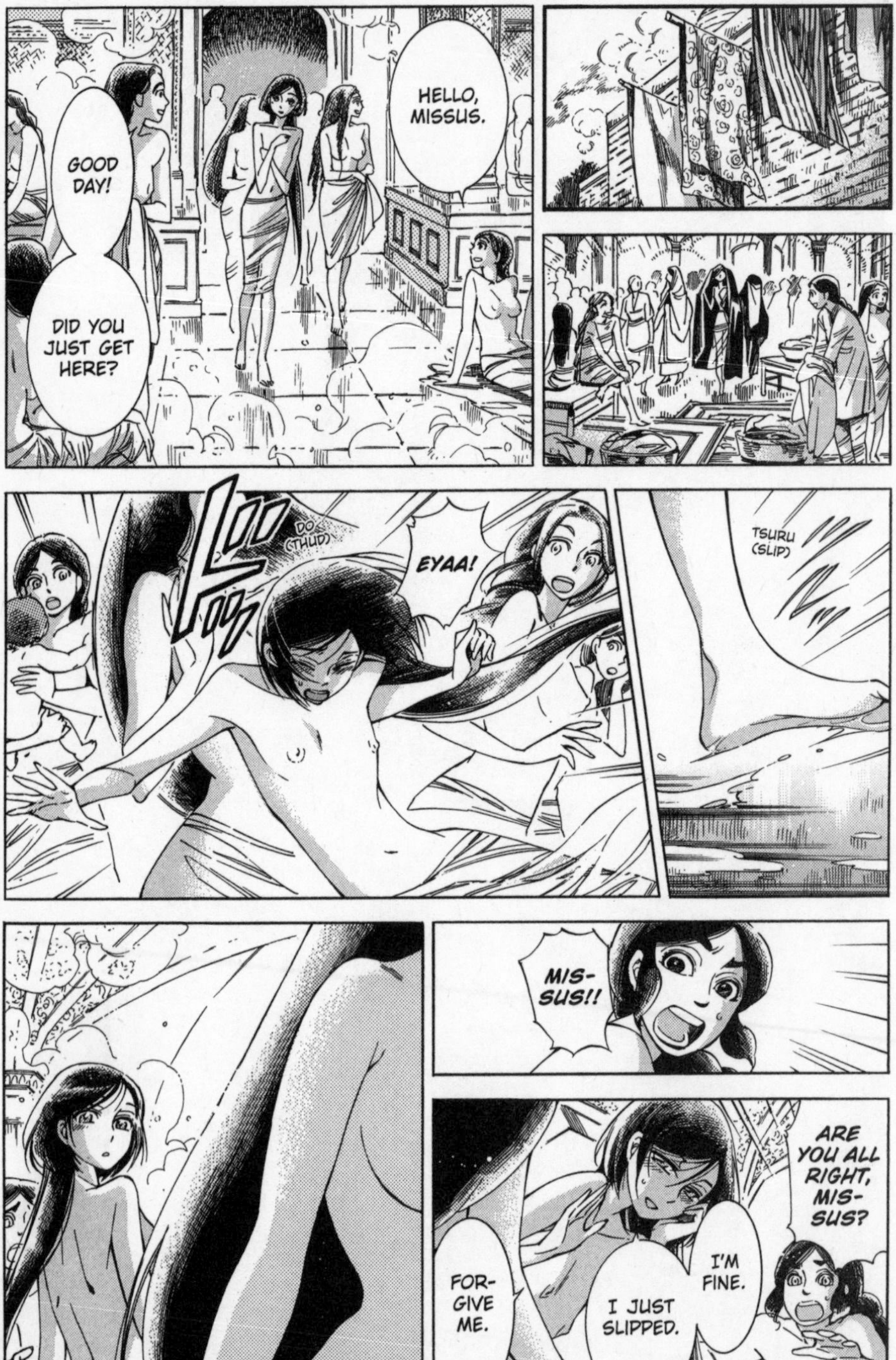
HELLO, MISSUS.
GOOD DAY!
DID YOU JUST GET HERE?
TSURU (SLIP)
DO (THUD)
EYAA!
MIS-SUS!!
ARE YOU ALL RIGHT, MIS-SUS?
I'M FINE.
I JUST SLIPPED.
FOR-GIVE ME.

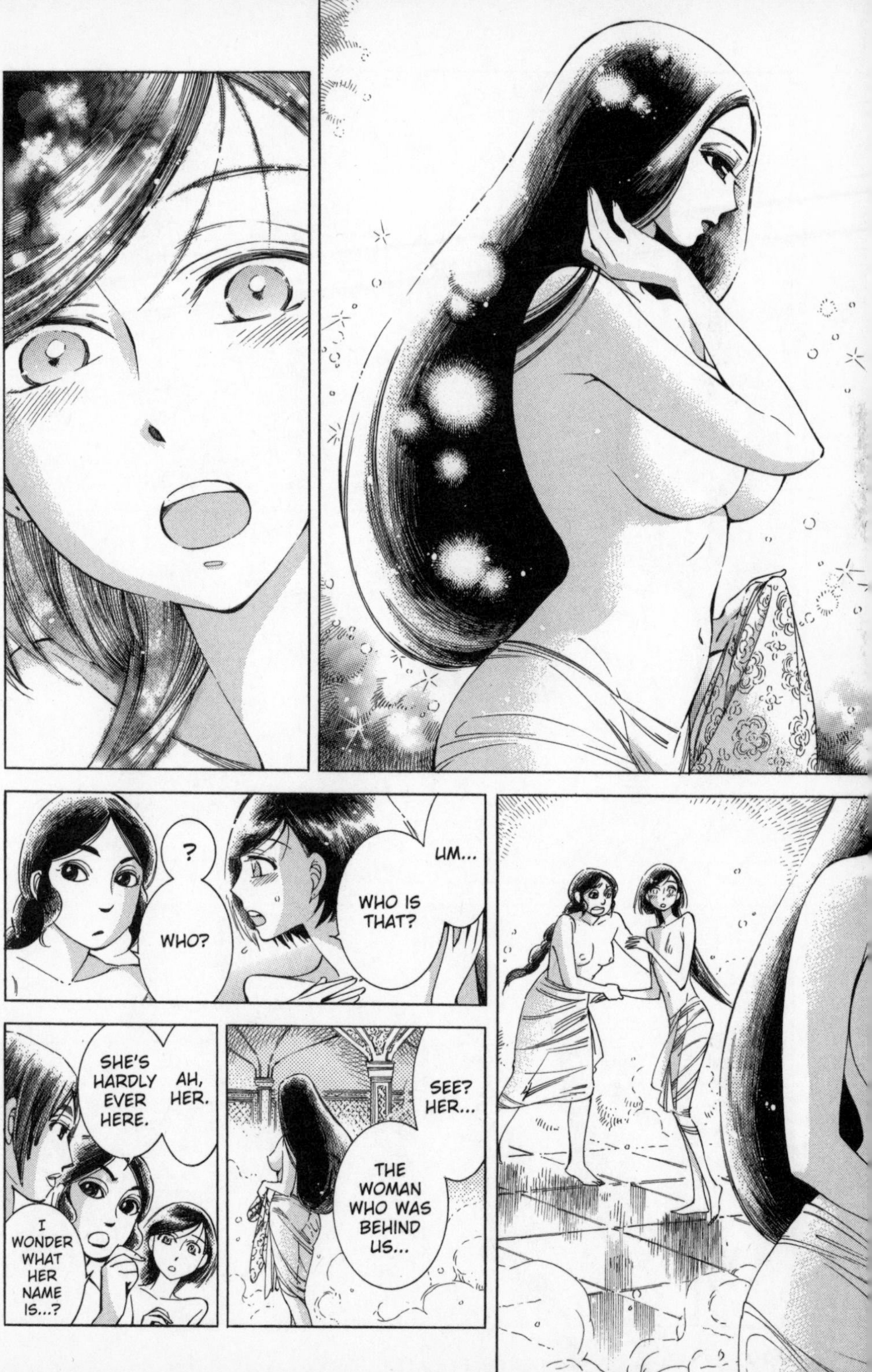
UM... WHO IS THAT?
?
WHO?
SEE? HER...
THE WOMAN WHO WAS BEHIND US...
AH, HER.
SHE'S HARDLY EVER HERE.
I WONDER WHAT HER NAME IS...?

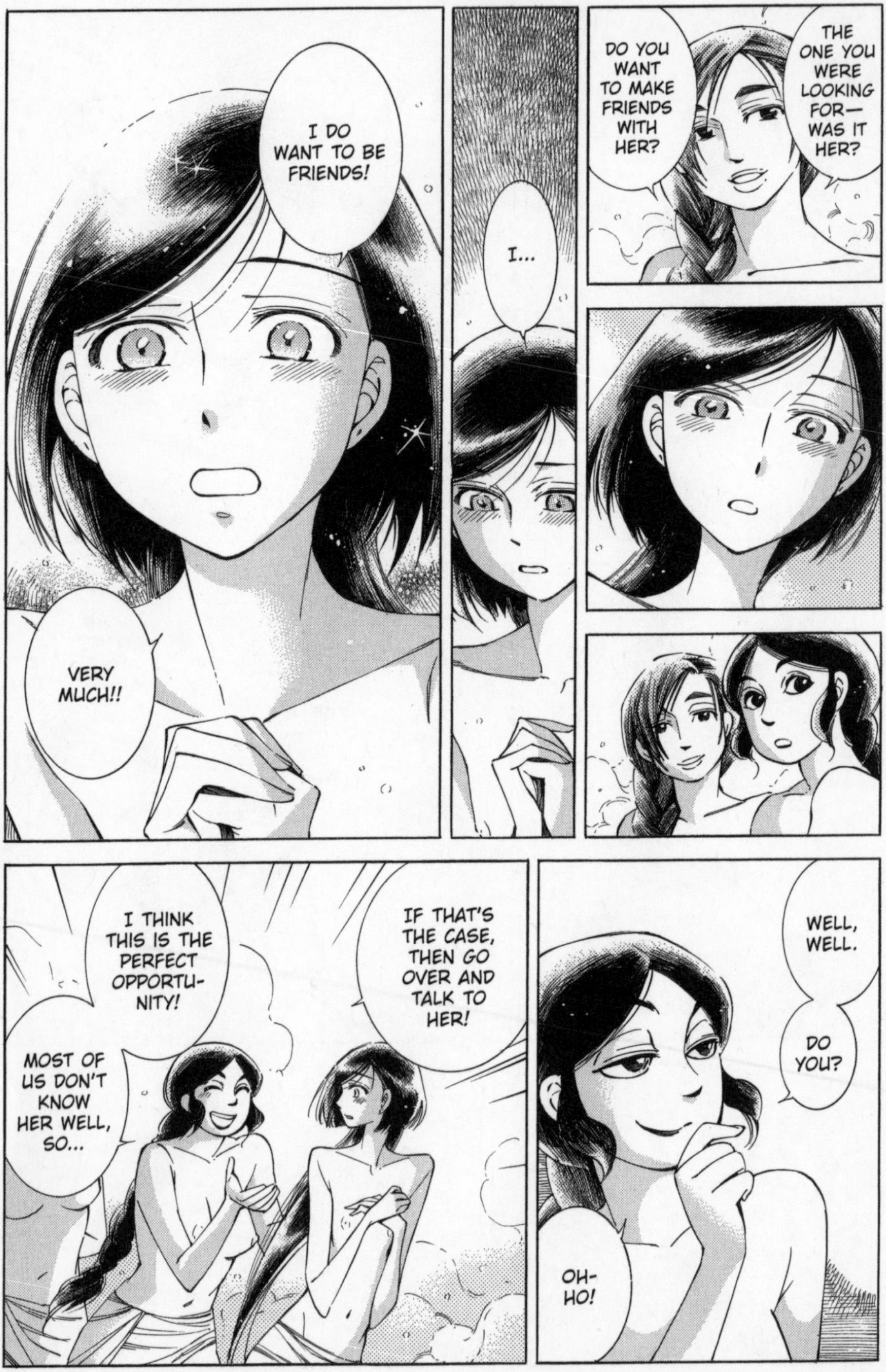
THE ONE YOU WERE LOOKING FOR—WAS IT HER?
DO YOU WANT TO MAKE FRIENDS WITH HER?
I...
I DO WANT TO BE FRIENDS!
VERY MUCH!!
WELL, WELL.
DO YOU?
OH-HO!
IF THAT'S THE CASE, THEN GO OVER AND TALK TO HER!
I THINK THIS IS THE PERFECT OPPORTU-NITY!
MOST OF US DON'T KNOW HER WELL, SO...

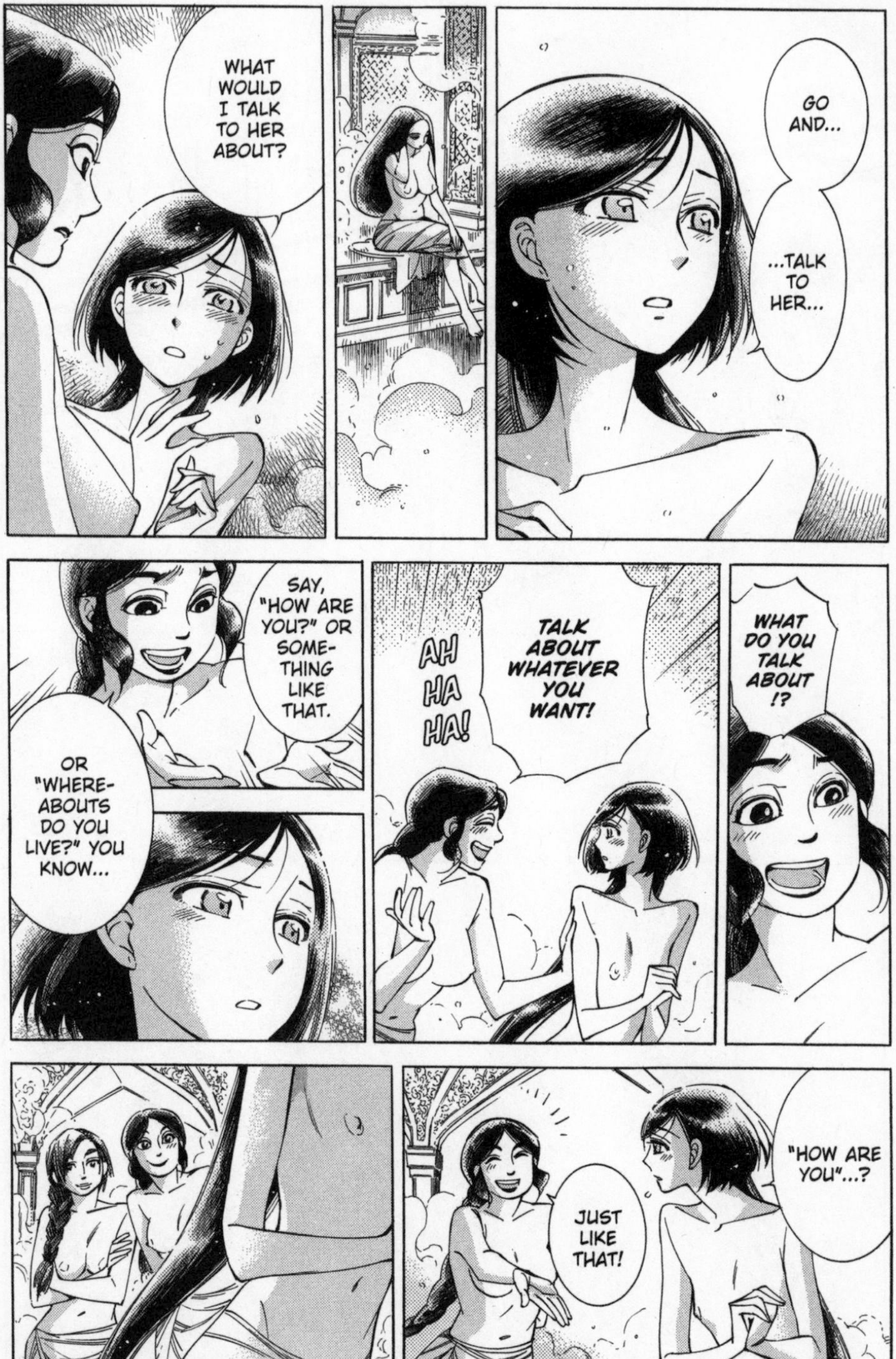
GO AND...
...TALK TO HER...
WHAT WOULD I TALK TO HER ABOUT?
WHAT DO YOU TALK ABOUT !?
TALK ABOUT WHATEVER YOU WANT!
AH HA HA!
SAY, "HOW ARE YOU?" OR SOME-THING LIKE THAT.
OR "WHERE-ABOUTS DO YOU LIVE?" YOU KNOW...
"HOW ARE YOU"...?
JUST LIKE THAT!

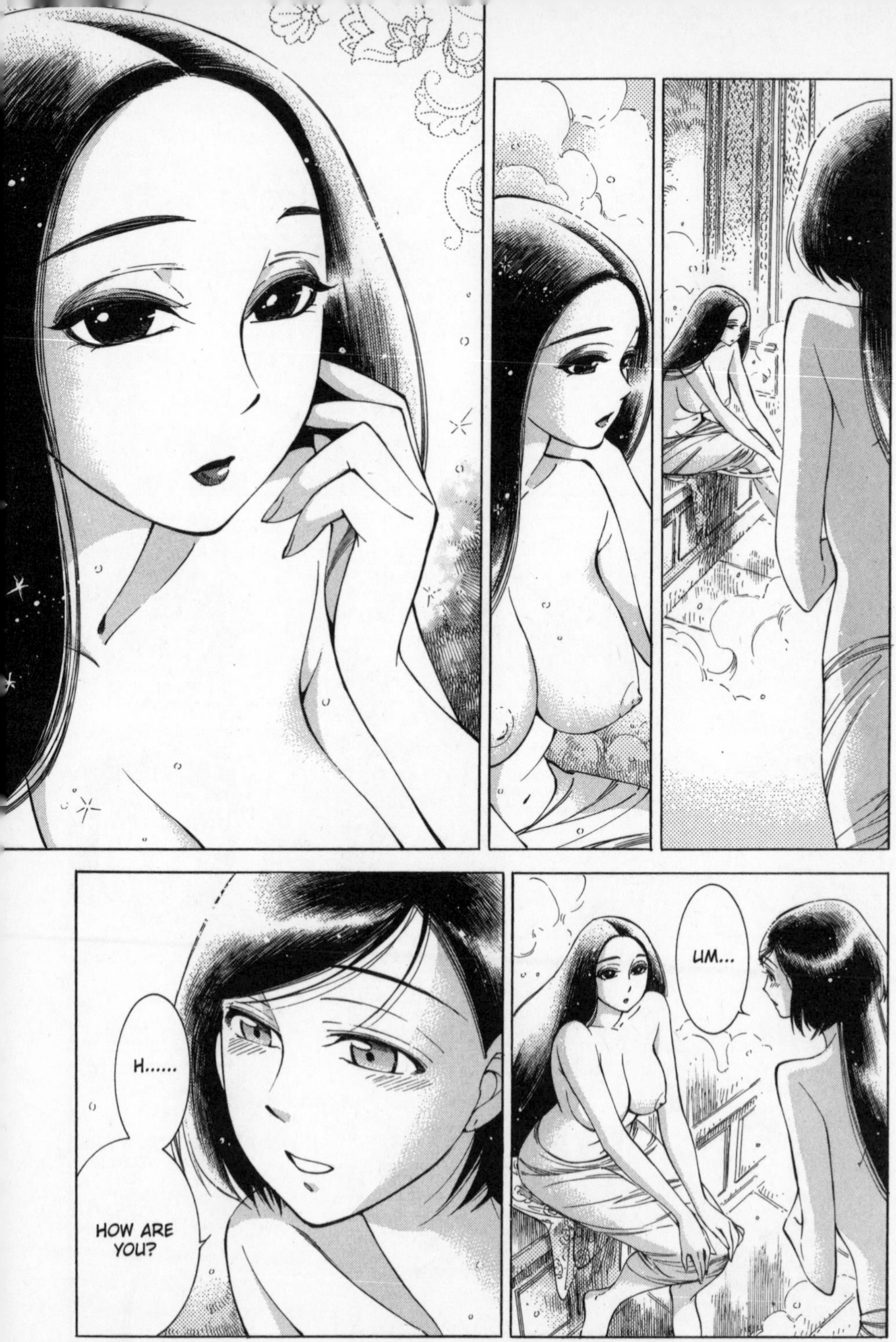
UM...
H......
HOW ARE YOU?

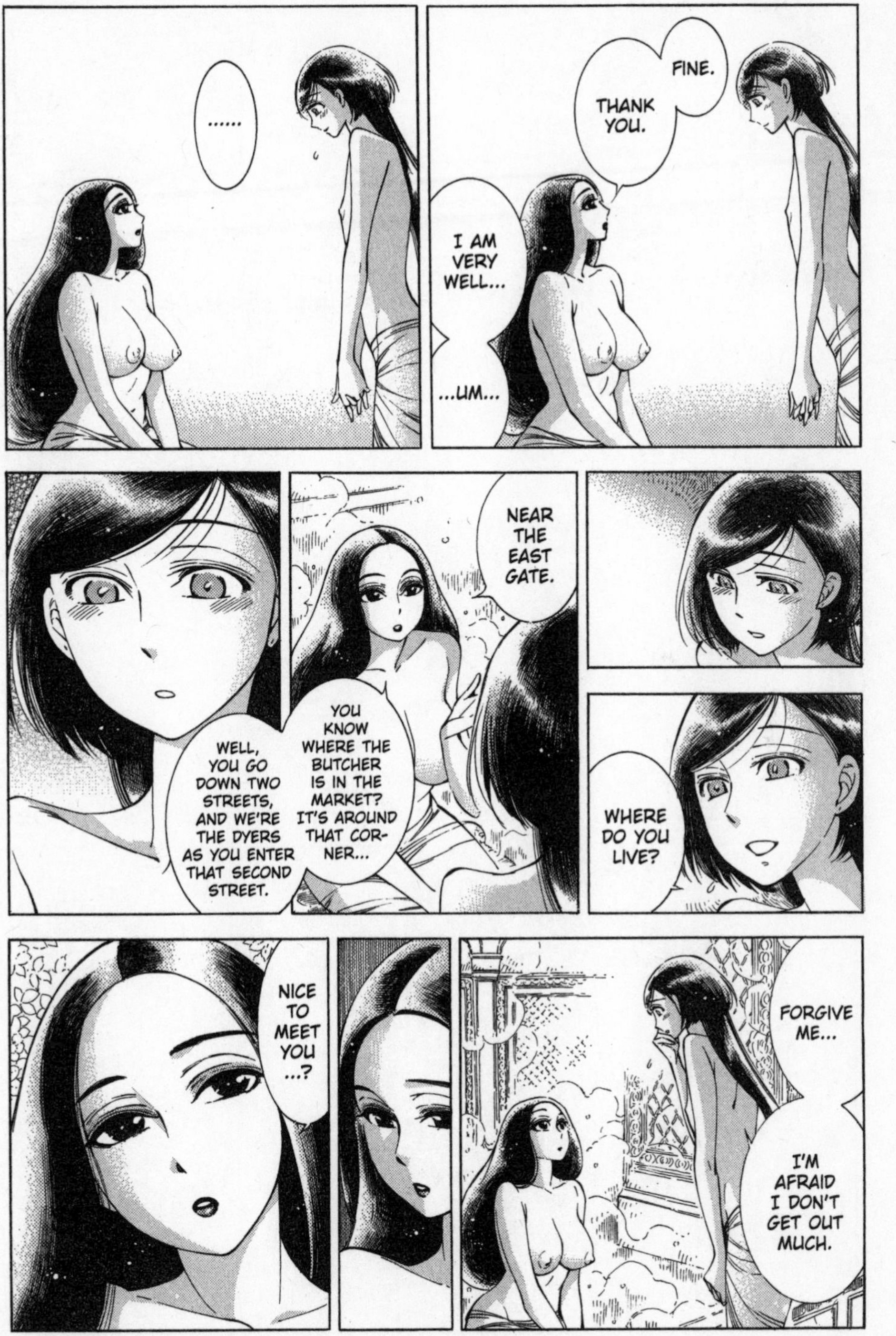
FINE.
THANK YOU.
I AM VERY WELL...
...UM...
......
WHERE DO YOU LIVE?
NEAR THE EAST GATE.
YOU KNOW WHERE THE BUTCHER IS IN THE MARKET? IT'S AROUND THAT CORNER...
WELL, YOU GO DOWN TWO STREETS, AND WE'RE THE DYERS AS YOU ENTER THAT SECOND STREET.
FORGIVE ME...
I'M AFRAID I DON'T GET OUT MUCH.
NICE TO MEET YOU ...?

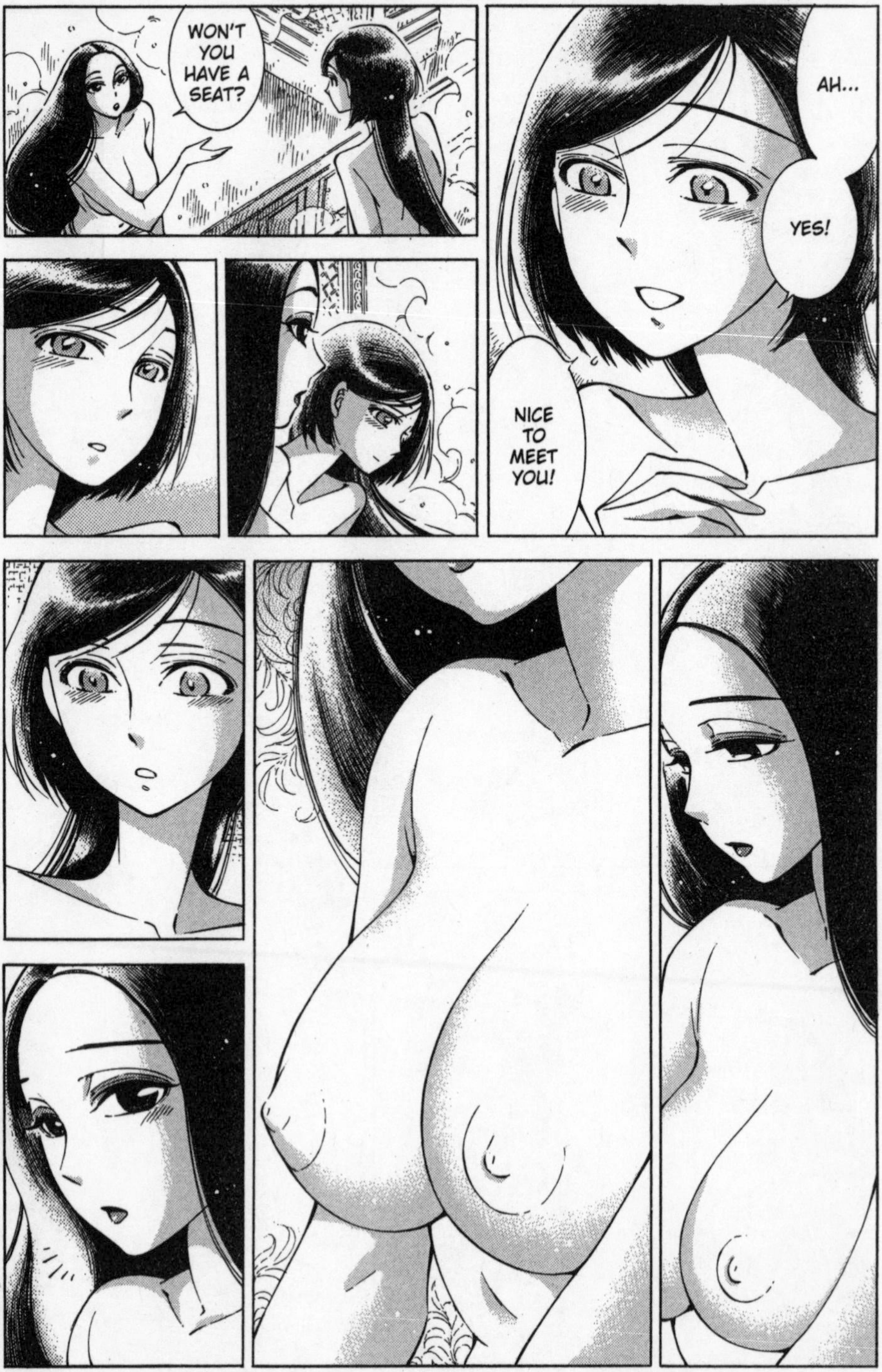
AH...
YES!
NICE TO MEET YOU!
WON'T YOU HAVE A SEAT?

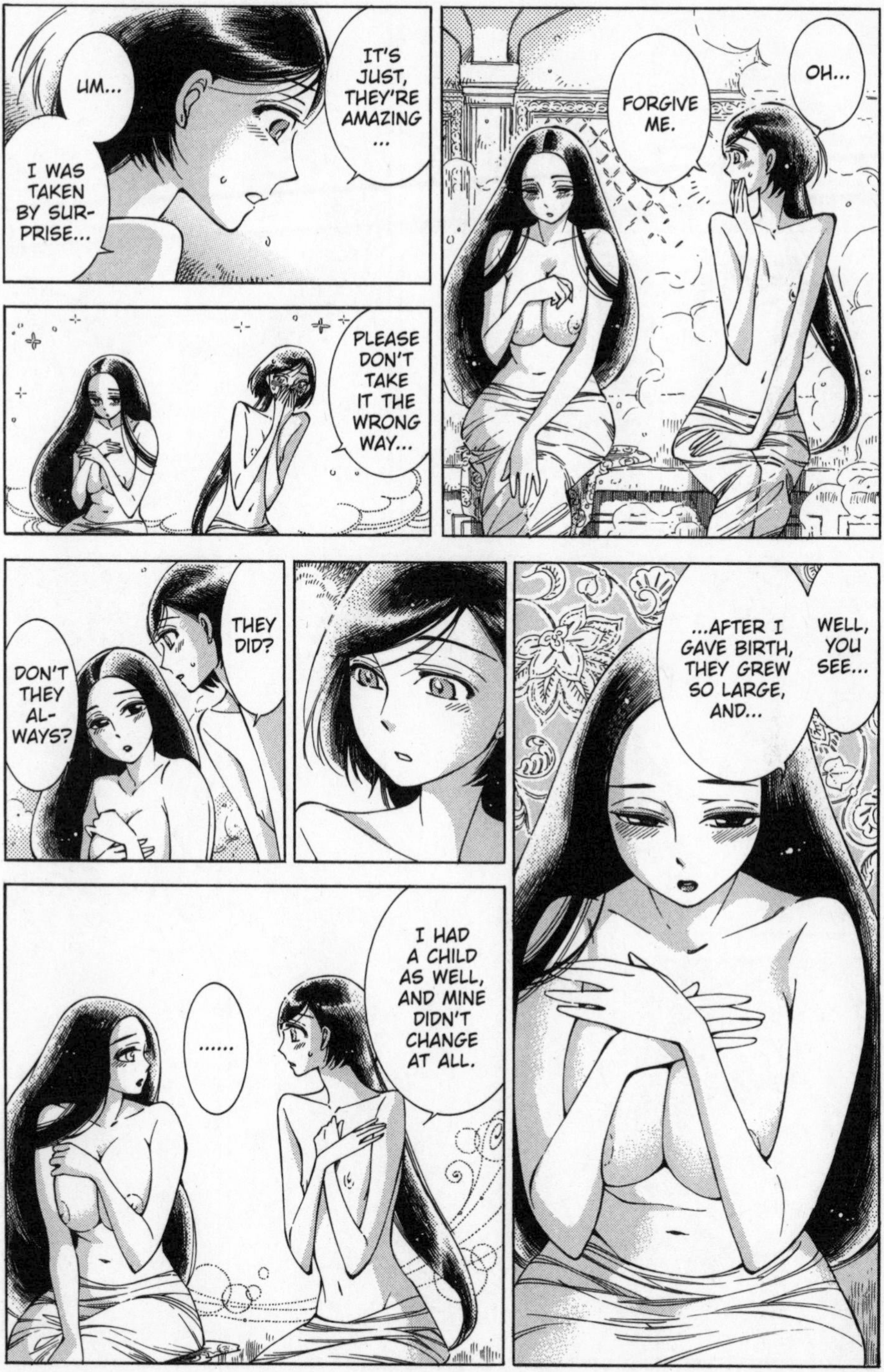
OH...
FORGIVE ME.
IT'S JUST, THEY'RE AMAZING...
UM...
I WAS TAKEN BY SURPRISE...
PLEASE DON'T TAKE IT THE WRONG WAY...
WELL, YOU SEE...
...AFTER I GAVE BIRTH, THEY GREW SO LARGE, AND...
THEY DID?
DON'T THEY ALWAYS?
I HAD A CHILD AS WELL, AND MINE DIDN'T CHANGE AT ALL.
......

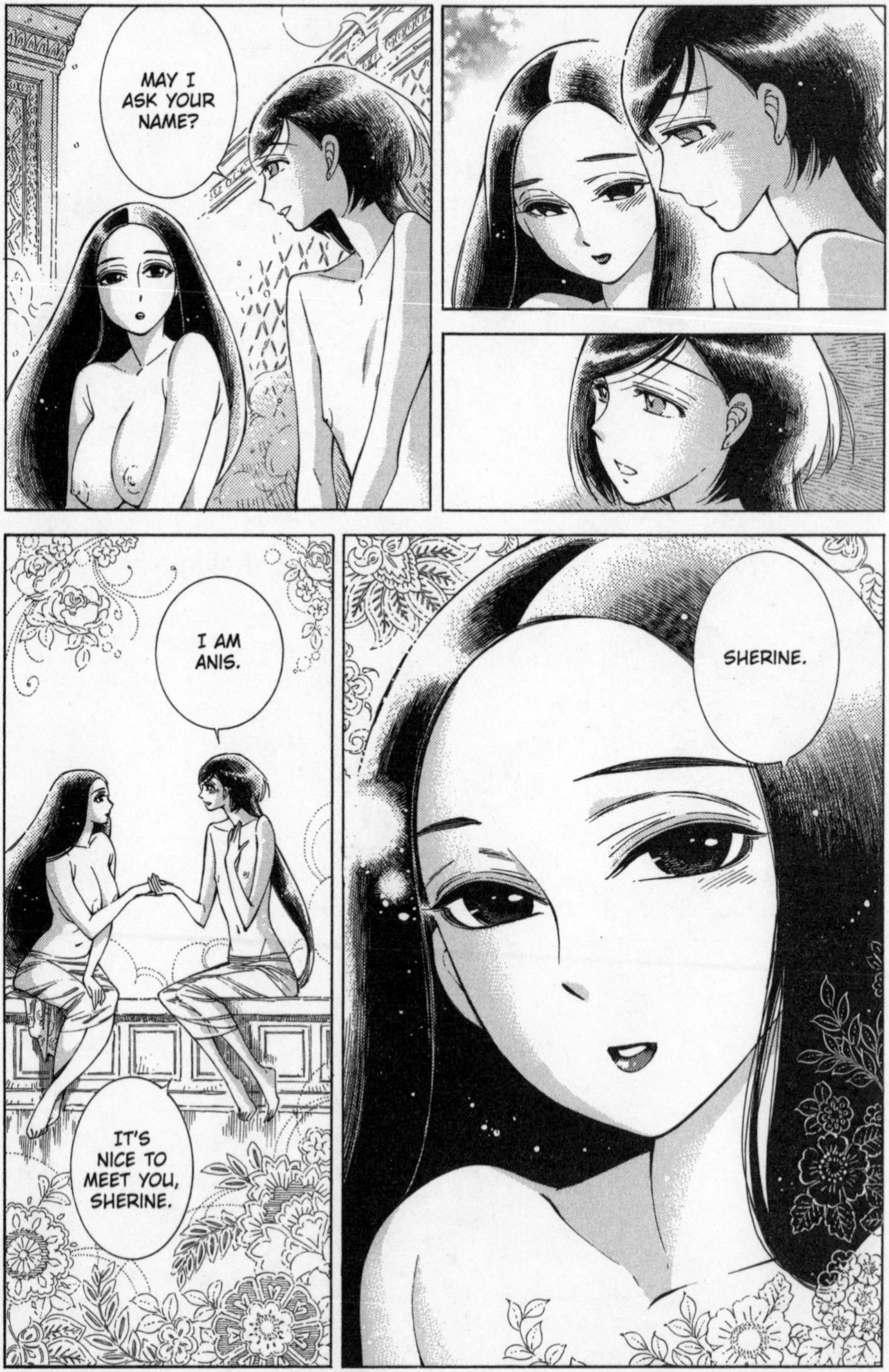
MAY I ASK YOUR NAME?
SHERINE.
I AM ANIS.
IT'S NICE TO MEET YOU, SHERINE.

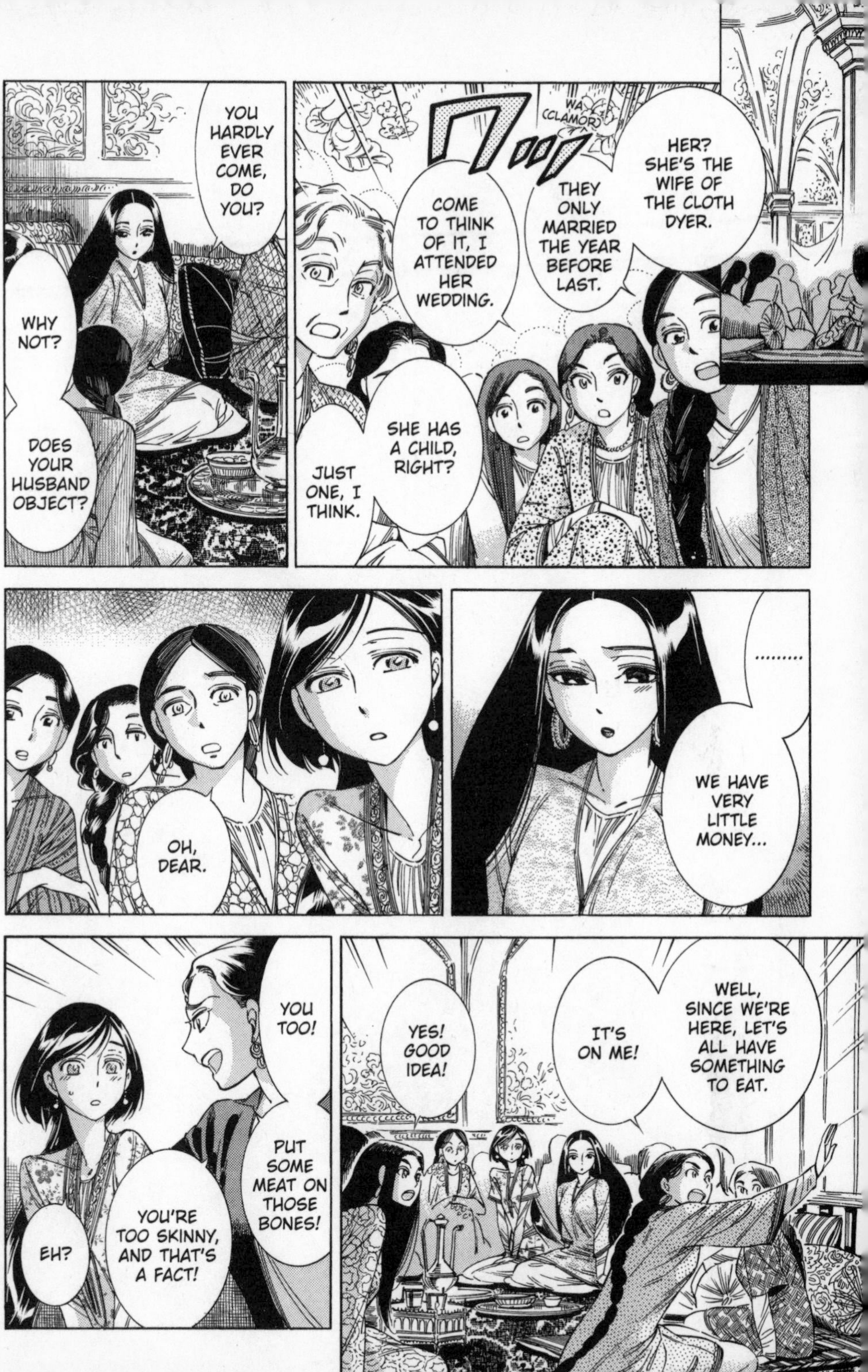
WA (CLAMOR)
HER? SHE'S THE WIFE OF THE CLOTH DYER.
THEY ONLY MARRIED THE YEAR BEFORE LAST.
COME TO THINK OF IT, I ATTENDED HER WEDDING.
SHE HAS A CHILD, RIGHT?
JUST ONE, I THINK.
YOU HARDLY EVER COME, DO YOU?
WHY NOT?
DOES YOUR HUSBAND OBJECT?
....
WE HAVE VERY LITTLE MONEY...
OH, DEAR.
WELL, SINCE WE'RE HERE, LET'S ALL HAVE SOMETHING TO EAT.
IT'S ON ME!
YES! GOOD IDEA!
YOU TOO!
PUT SOME MEAT ON THOSE BONES!
YOU'RE TOO SKINNY, AND THAT'S A FACT!
EH?

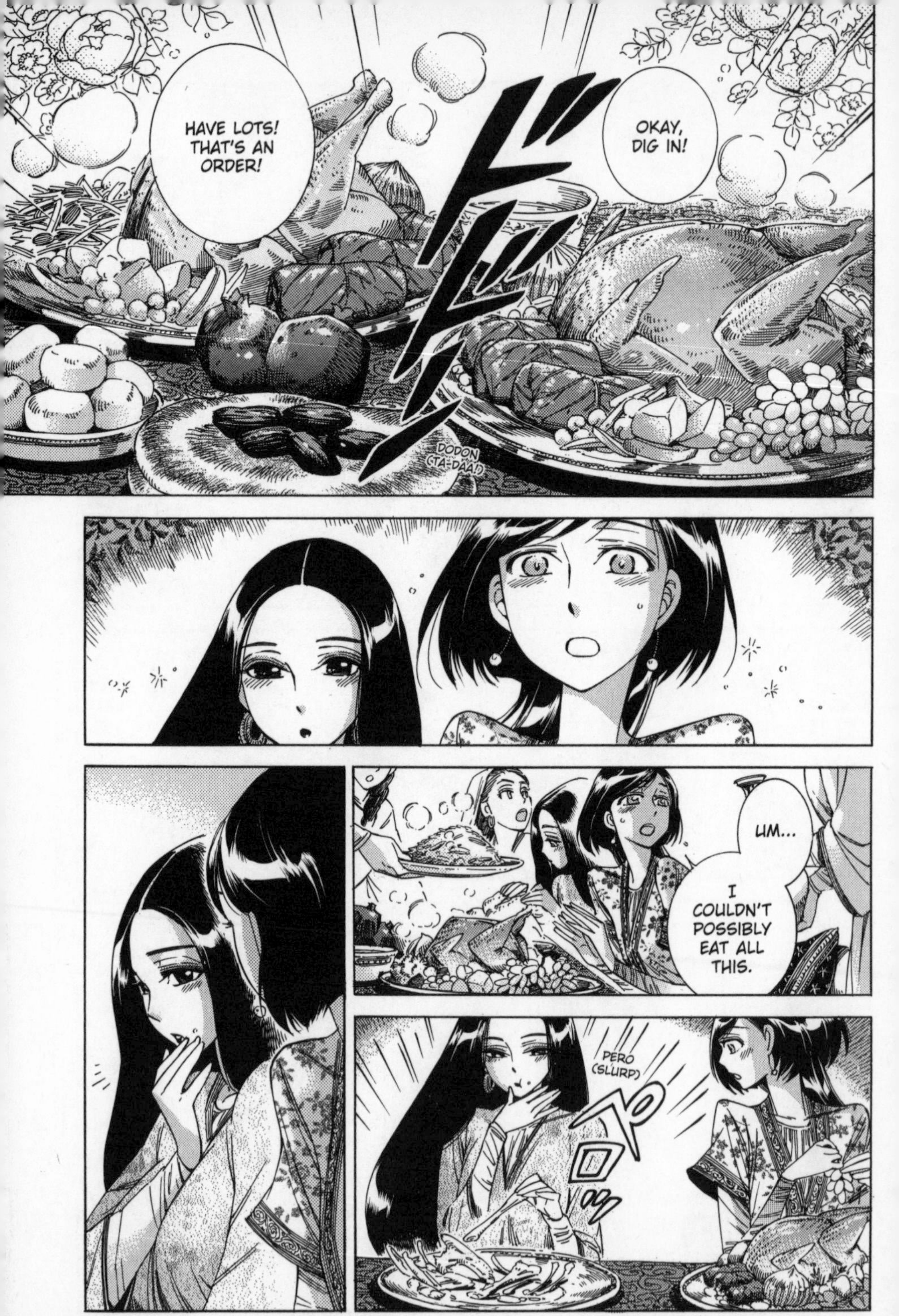
OKAY, DIG IN!
HAVE LOTS! THAT'S AN ORDER!
DODON (TA-DAA!)
UM...
I COULDN'T POSSIBLY EAT ALL THIS.
PERO (SLURP)

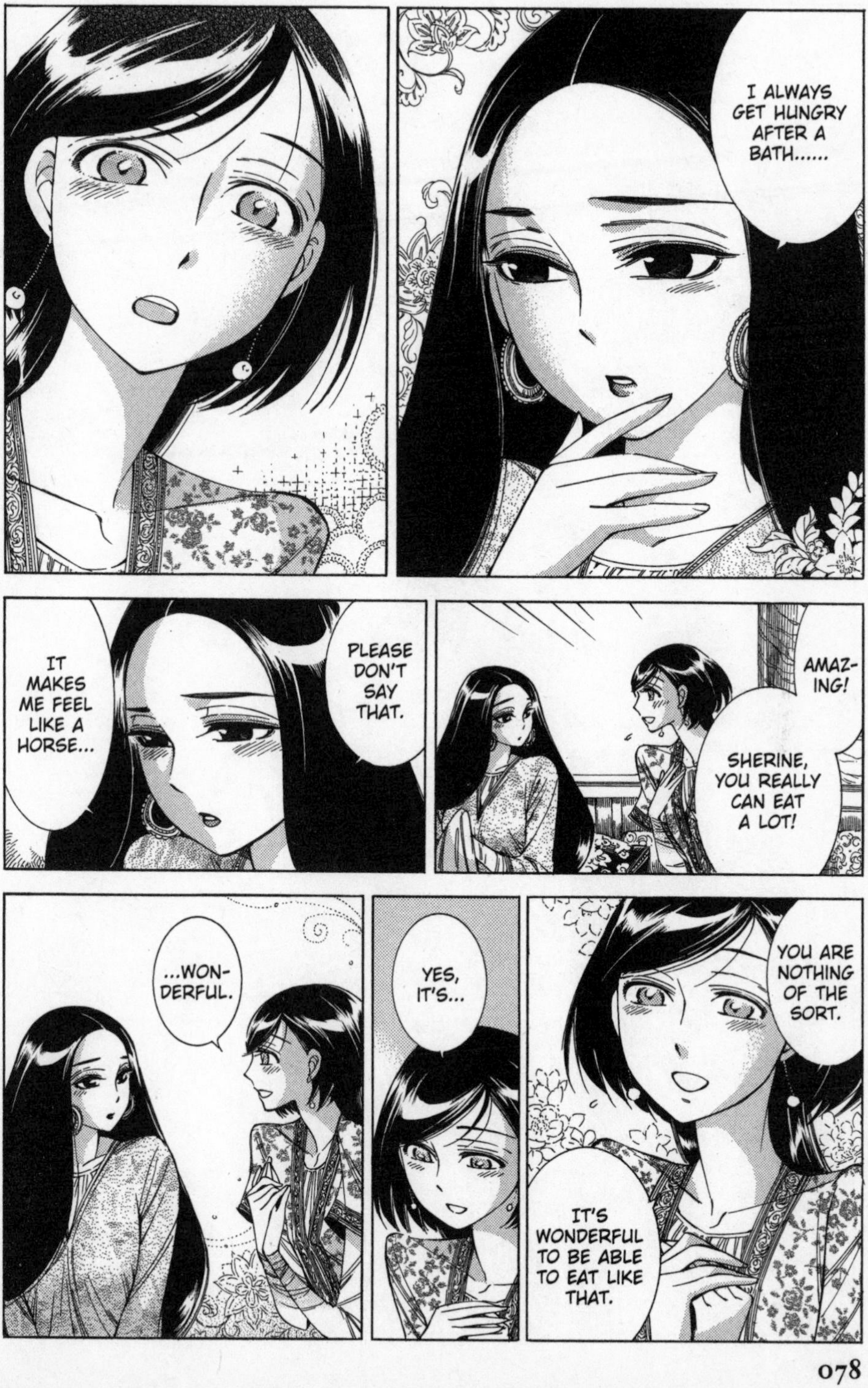
I ALWAYS GET HUNGRY AFTER A BATH......
AMAZ-ING!
SHERINE, YOU REALLY CAN EAT A LOT!
PLEASE DON'T SAY THAT.
IT MAKES ME FEEL LIKE A HORSE...
YOU ARE NOTHING OF THE SORT.
IT'S WONDERFUL TO BE ABLE TO EAT LIKE THAT.
YES, IT'S...
...WON-DERFUL.

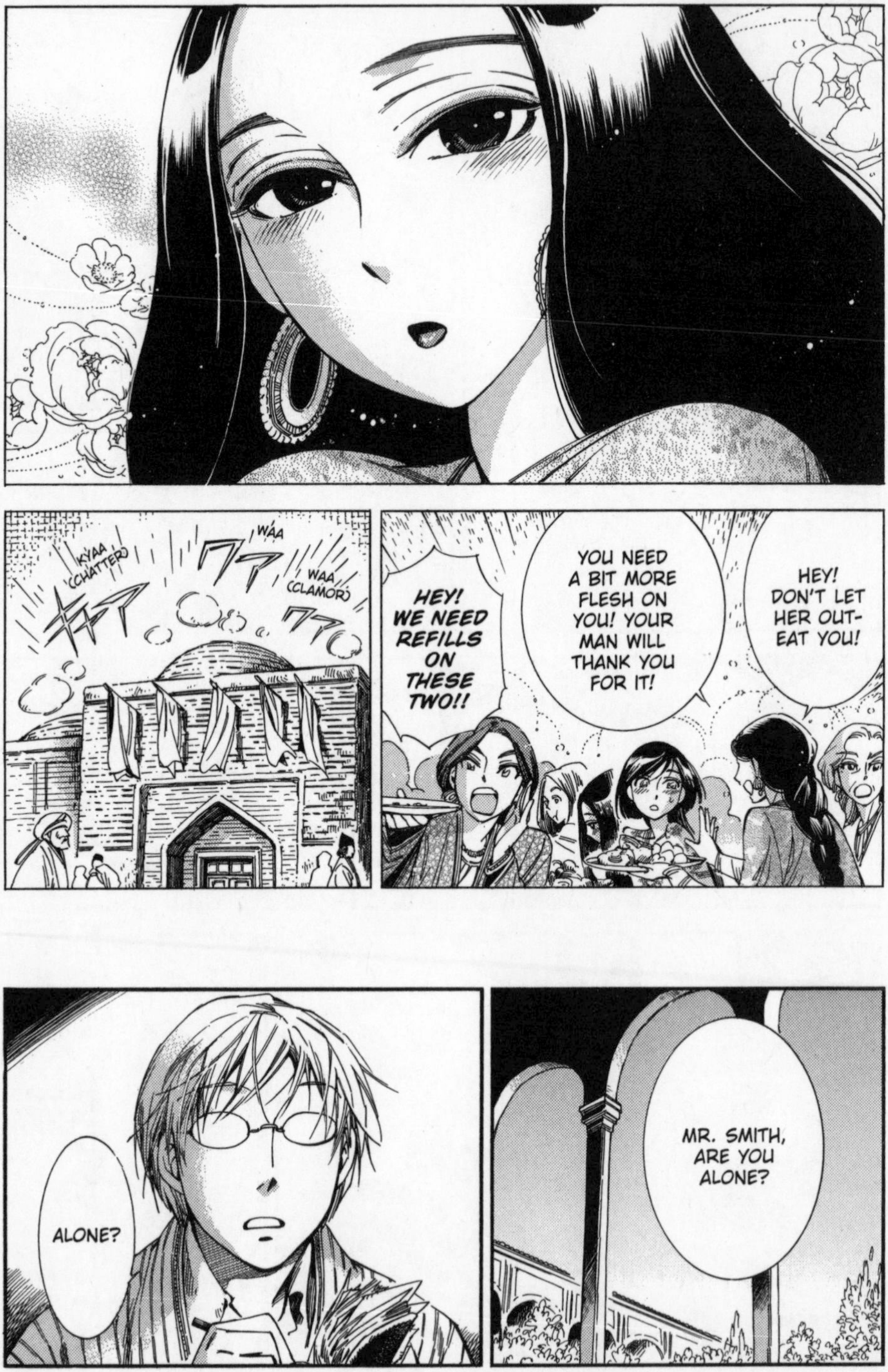
HEY! DON'T LET HER OUT-EAT YOU!
YOU NEED A BIT MORE FLESH ON YOU! YOUR MAN WILL THANK YOU FOR IT!
HEY! WE NEED REFILLS ON THESE TWO!!
WAA (CLAMOR)
ワア
WAA
ワア
KYAA (CHATTER)
キャア
MR. SMITH, ARE YOU ALONE?
ALONE?

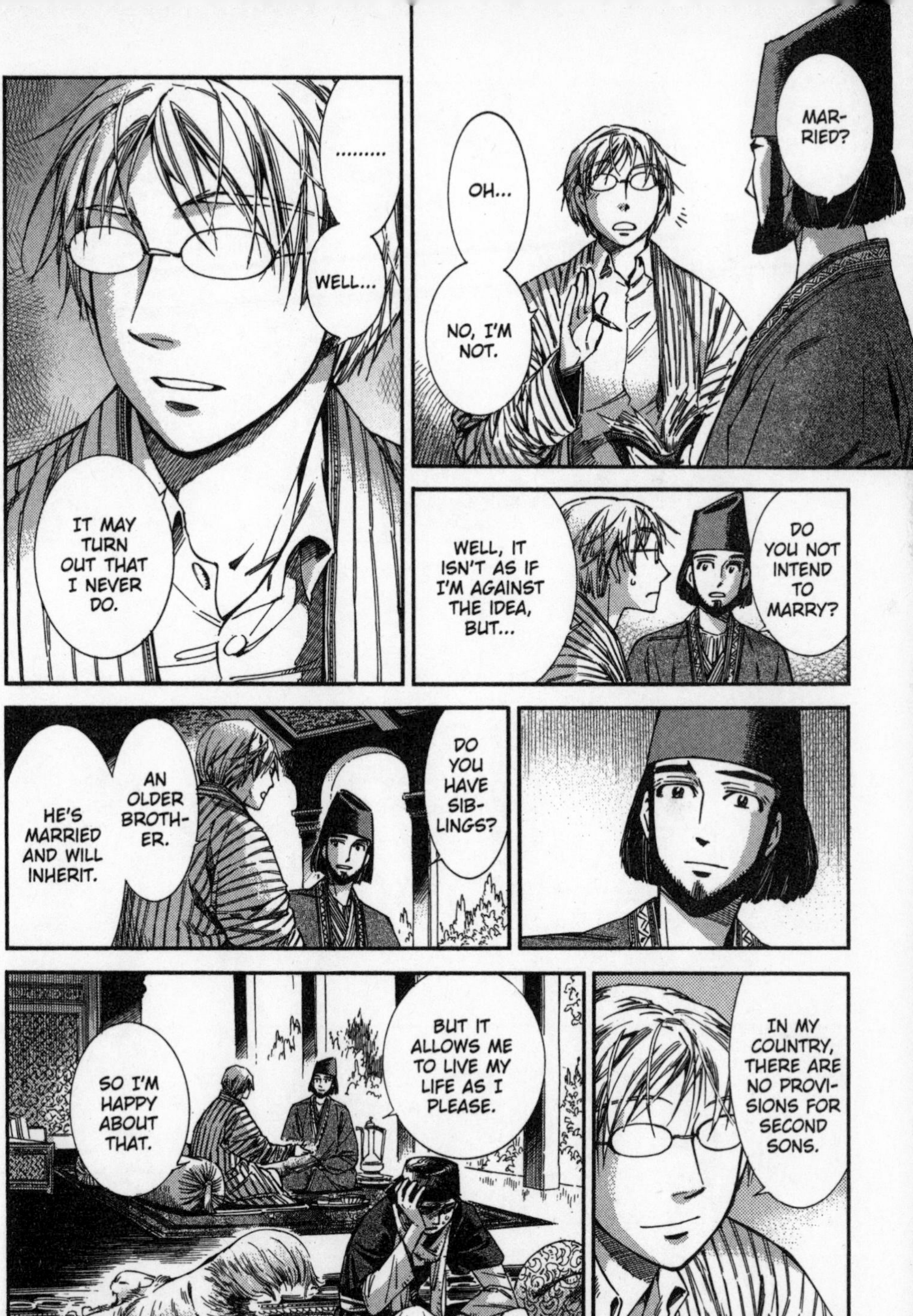
MARRIED?
OH...
NO, I'M NOT.
DO YOU NOT INTEND TO MARRY?
WELL, IT ISN'T AS IF I'M AGAINST THE IDEA, BUT...
....
WELL...
IT MAY TURN OUT THAT I NEVER DO.
DO YOU HAVE SIBLINGS?
AN OLDER BROTHER.
HE'S MARRIED AND WILL INHERIT.
IN MY COUNTRY, THERE ARE NO PROVISIONS FOR SECOND SONS.
BUT IT ALLOWS ME TO LIVE MY LIFE AS I PLEASE.
SO I'M HAPPY ABOUT THAT.

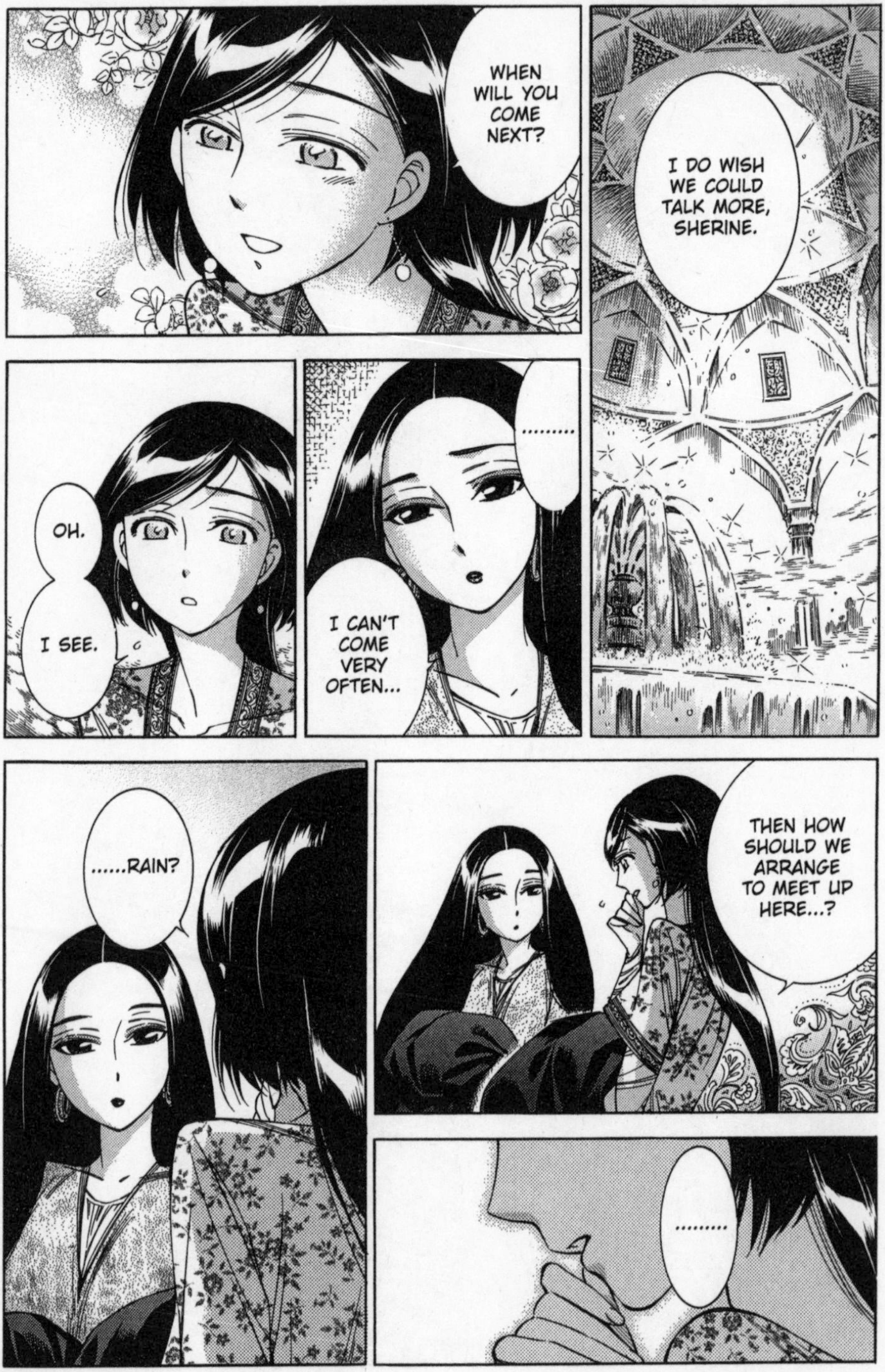
I DO WISH WE COULD TALK MORE, SHERINE.
WHEN WILL YOU COME NEXT?
....
I CAN'T COME VERY OFTEN...
OH.
I SEE.
THEN HOW SHOULD WE ARRANGE TO MEET UP HERE...?
....
......RAIN?

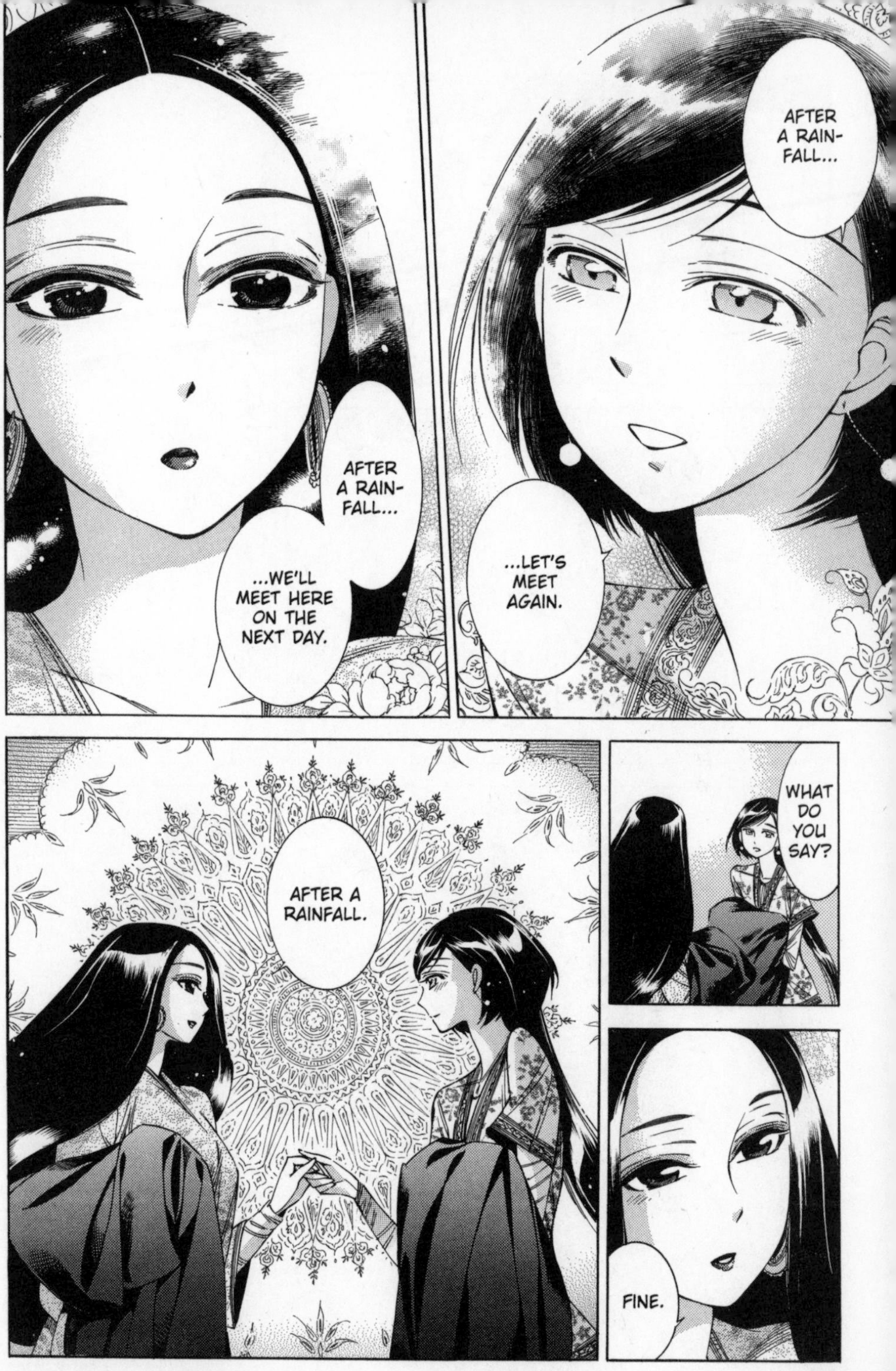
AFTER A RAIN-FALL...
...LET'S MEET AGAIN.
AFTER A RAIN-FALL...
...WE'LL MEET HERE ON THE NEXT DAY.
WHAT DO YOU SAY?
FINE.
AFTER A RAINFALL.

✦ Chapter 39: End ✦

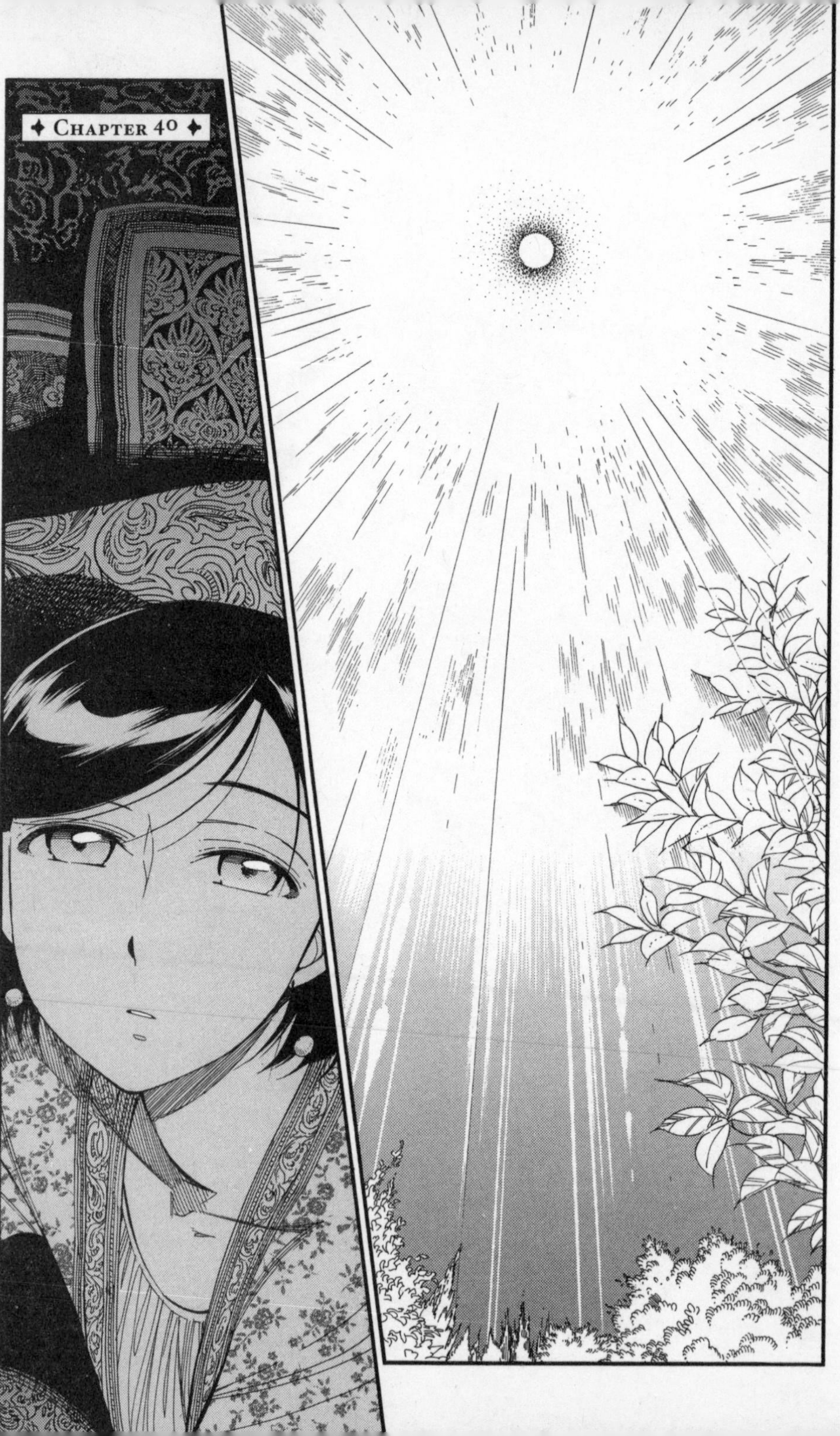
CHAPTER 40

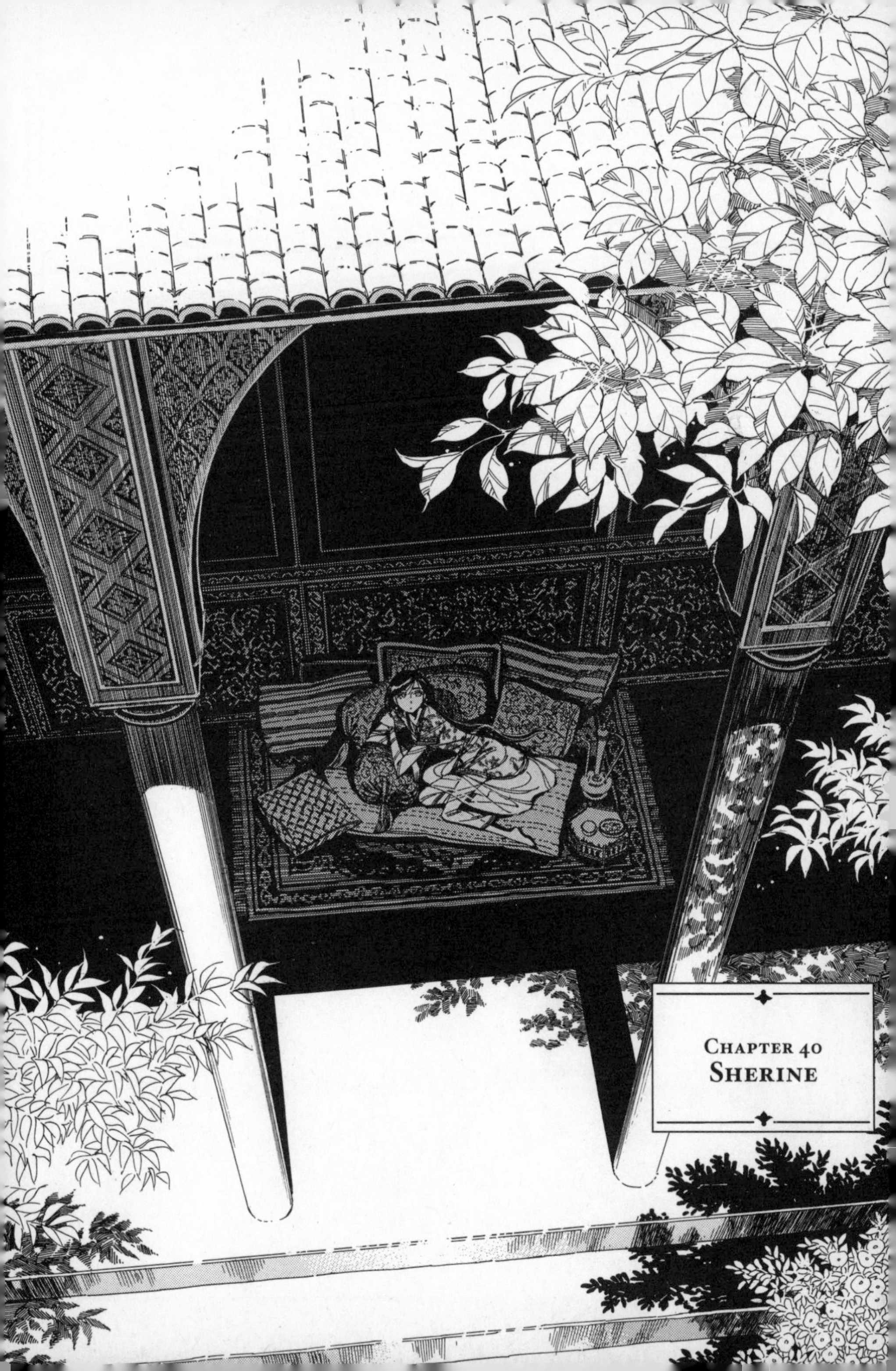
Chapter 40
Sherine

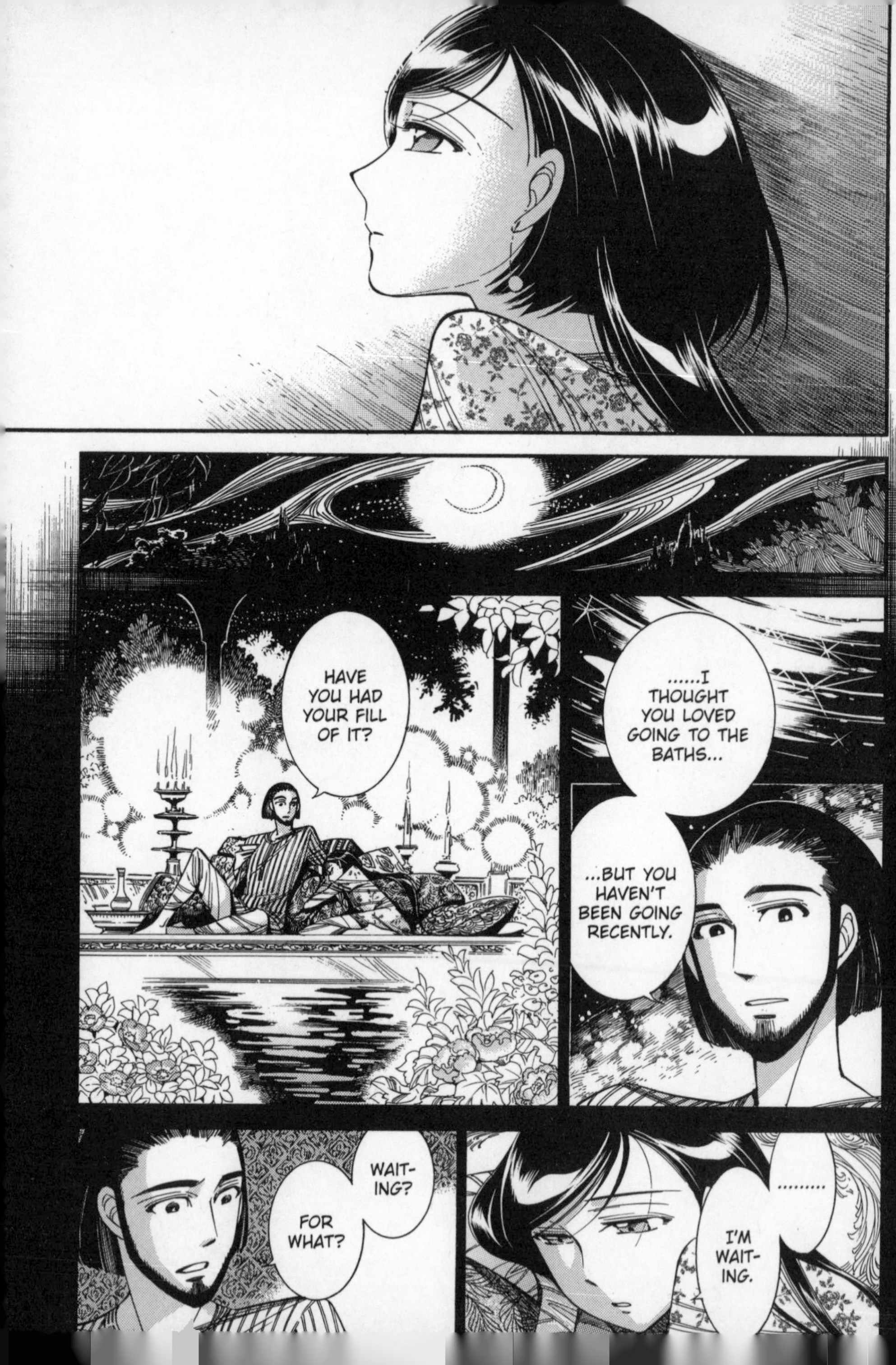
......I THOUGHT YOU LOVED GOING TO THE BATHS...
...BUT YOU HAVEN'T BEEN GOING RECENTLY.
HAVE YOU HAD YOUR FILL OF IT?
....
I'M WAIT-ING.
WAIT-ING?
FOR WHAT?

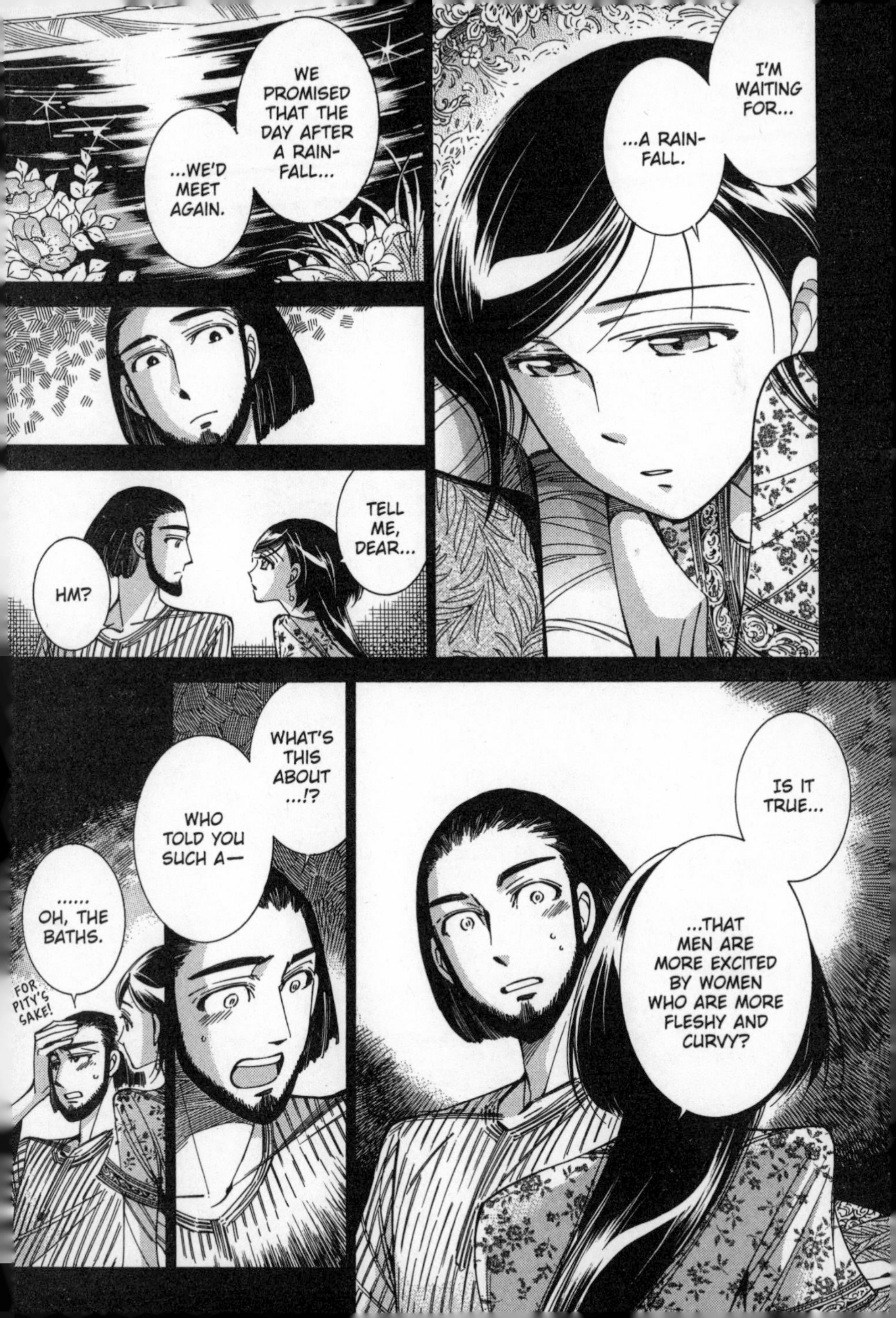
I'M WAITING FOR...
...A RAIN-FALL.
WE PROMISED THAT THE DAY AFTER A RAIN-FALL...
...WE'D MEET AGAIN.
TELL ME, DEAR...
HM?
IS IT TRUE...
...THAT MEN ARE MORE EXCITED BY WOMEN WHO ARE MORE FLESHY AND CURVY?
WHAT'S THIS ABOUT ...!?
WHO TOLD YOU SUCH A—
...... OH, THE BATHS.
FOR PITY'S SAKE!

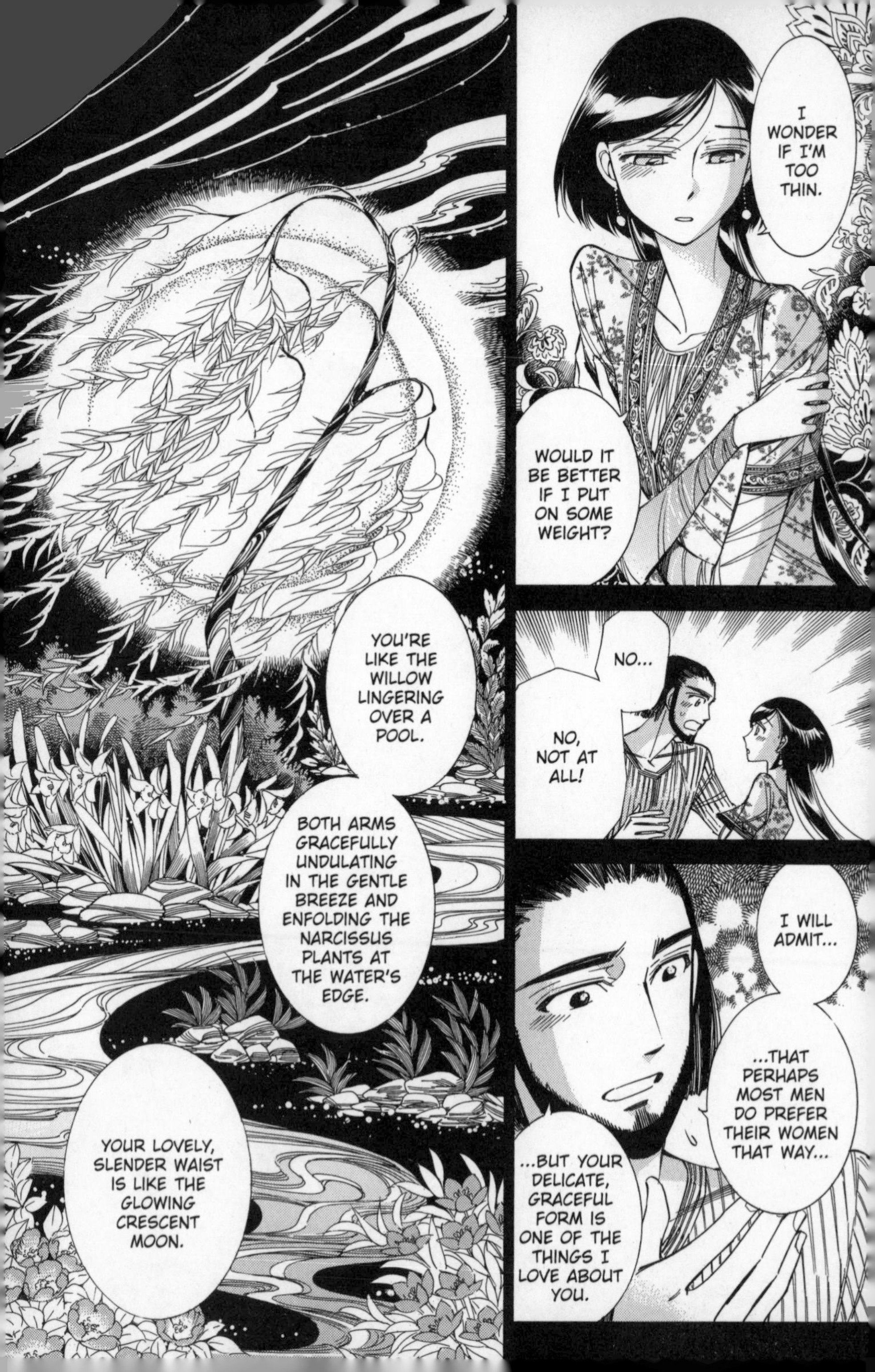
I WONDER IF I'M TOO THIN.
WOULD IT BE BETTER IF I PUT ON SOME WEIGHT?
NO...
NO, NOT AT ALL!
I WILL ADMIT...
...THAT PERHAPS MOST MEN DO PREFER THEIR WOMEN THAT WAY...
...BUT YOUR DELICATE, GRACEFUL FORM IS ONE OF THE THINGS I LOVE ABOUT YOU.
YOU'RE LIKE THE WILLOW LINGERING OVER A POOL.
BOTH ARMS GRACEFULLY UNDULATING IN THE GENTLE BREEZE AND ENFOLDING THE NARCISSUS PLANTS AT THE WATER'S EDGE.
YOUR LOVELY, SLENDER WAIST IS LIKE THE GLOWING CRESCENT MOON.

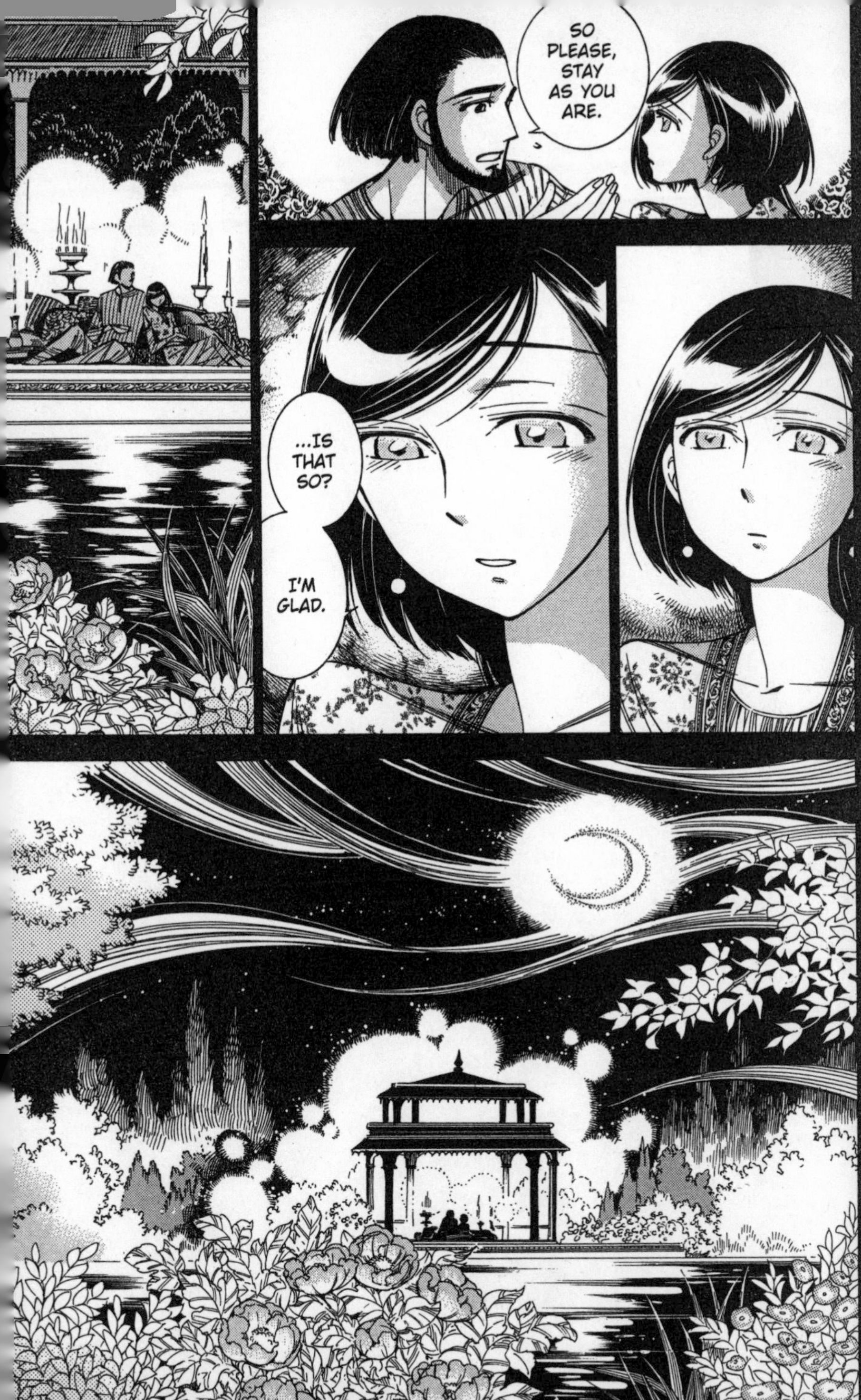
SO PLEASE, STAY AS YOU ARE.
...IS THAT SO?
I'M GLAD.

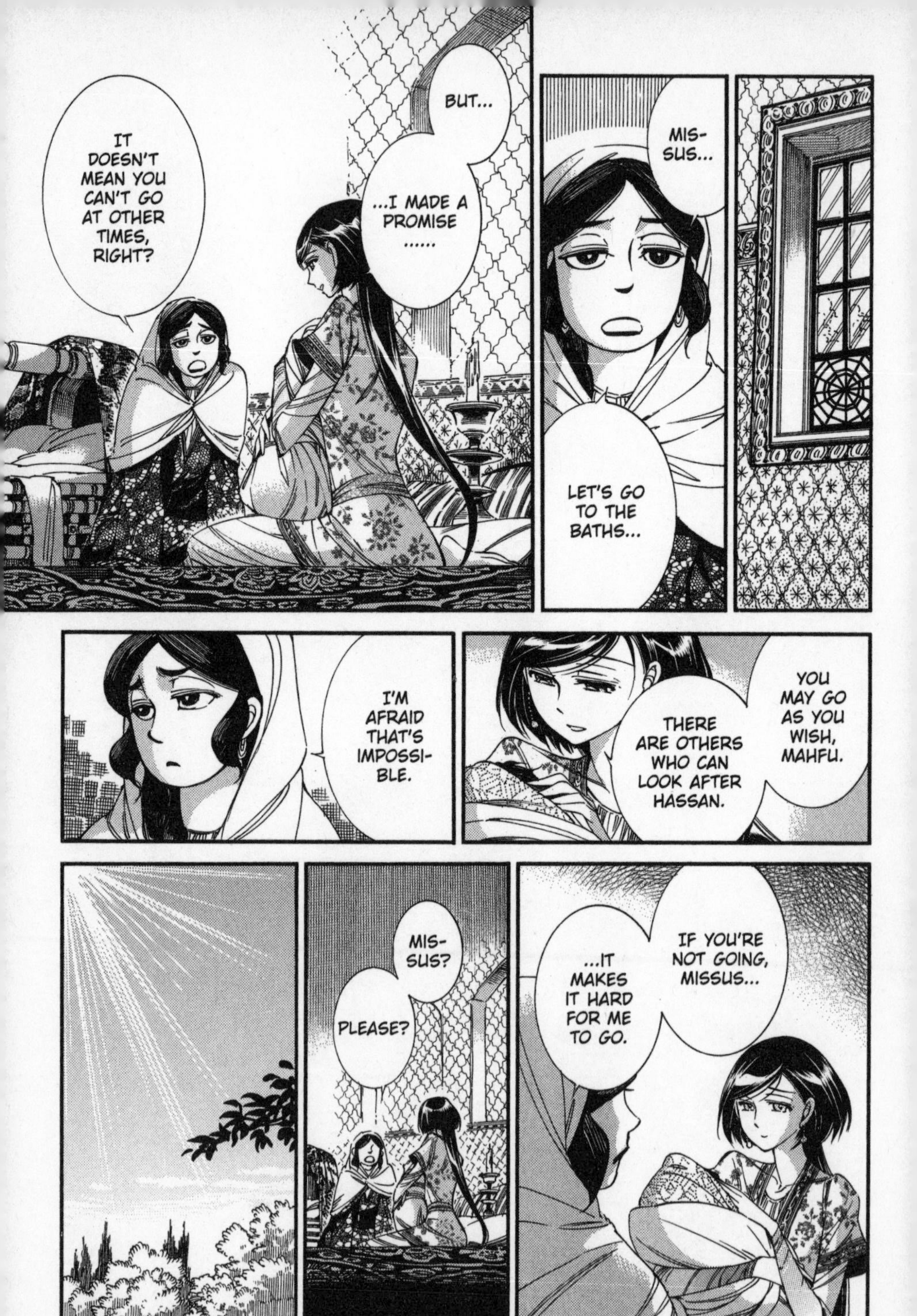
MIS-SUS...
LET'S GO TO THE BATHS...
BUT...
...I MADE A PROMISE ......
IT DOESN'T MEAN YOU CAN'T GO AT OTHER TIMES, RIGHT?
YOU MAY GO AS YOU WISH, MAHFU.
THERE ARE OTHERS WHO CAN LOOK AFTER HASSAN.
I'M AFRAID THAT'S IMPOSSIBLE.
IF YOU'RE NOT GOING, MISSUS...
...IT MAKES IT HARD FOR ME TO GO.
MIS-SUS?
PLEASE?

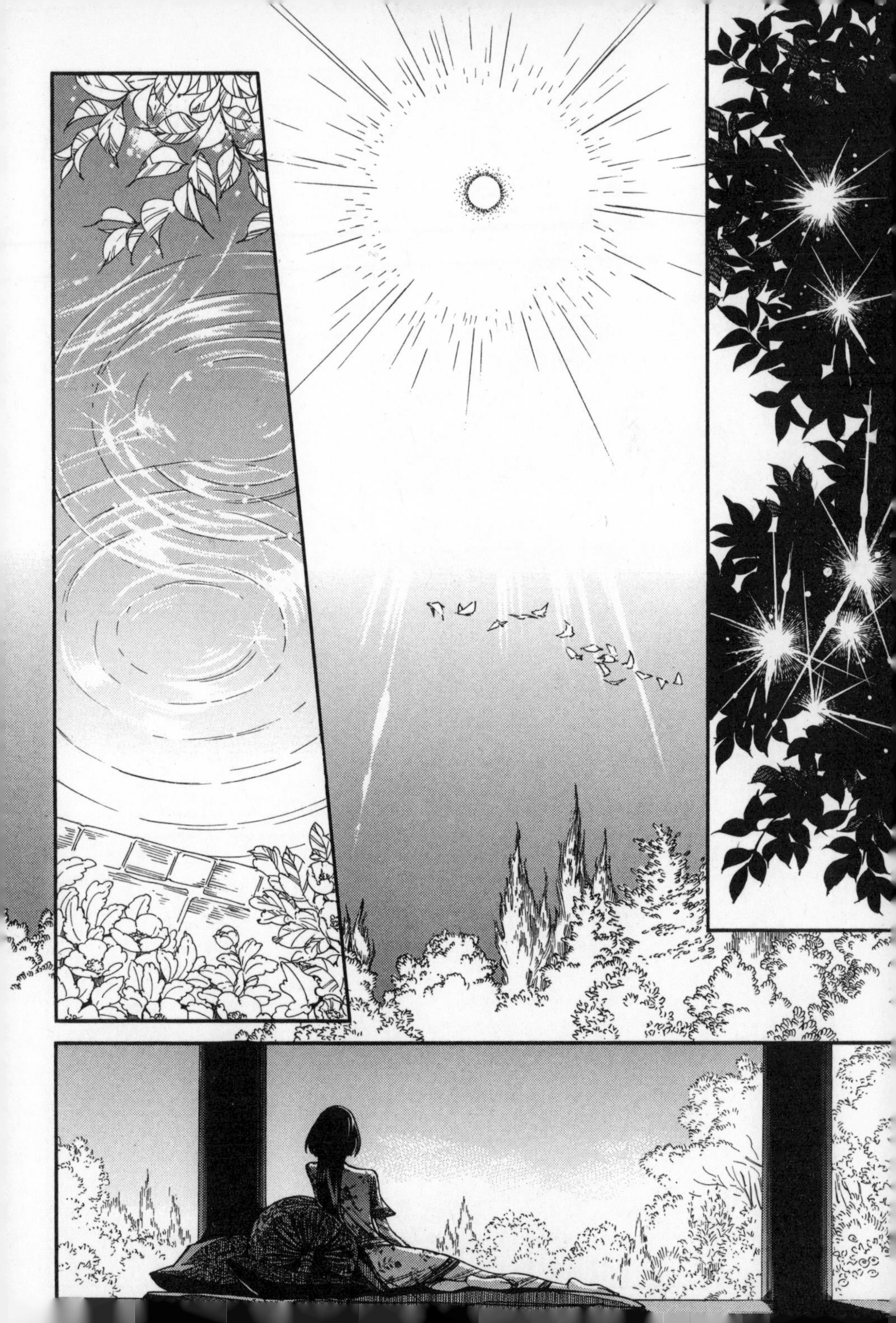

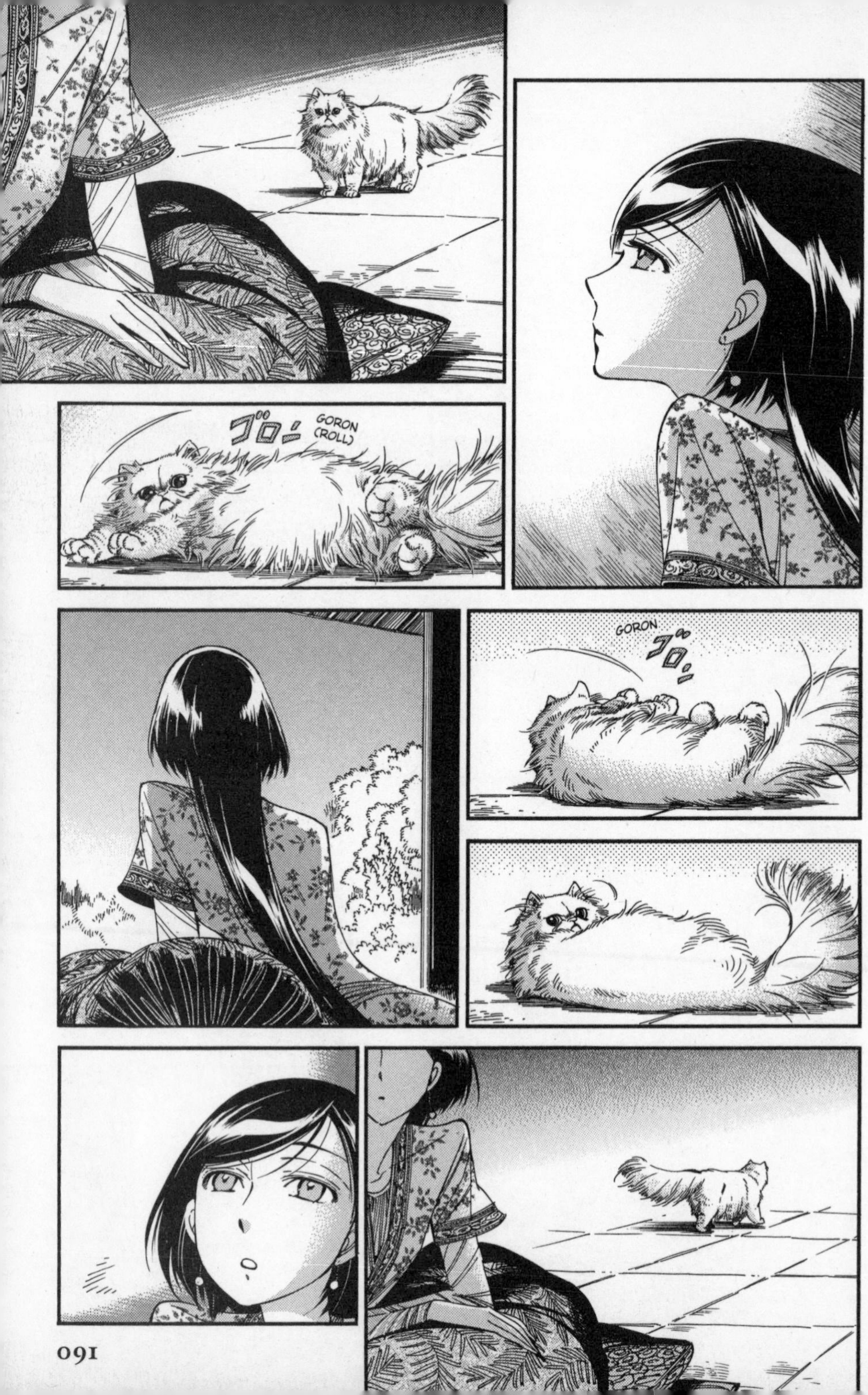
ゴロン
GORON
(ROLL)
GORON
ゴロン

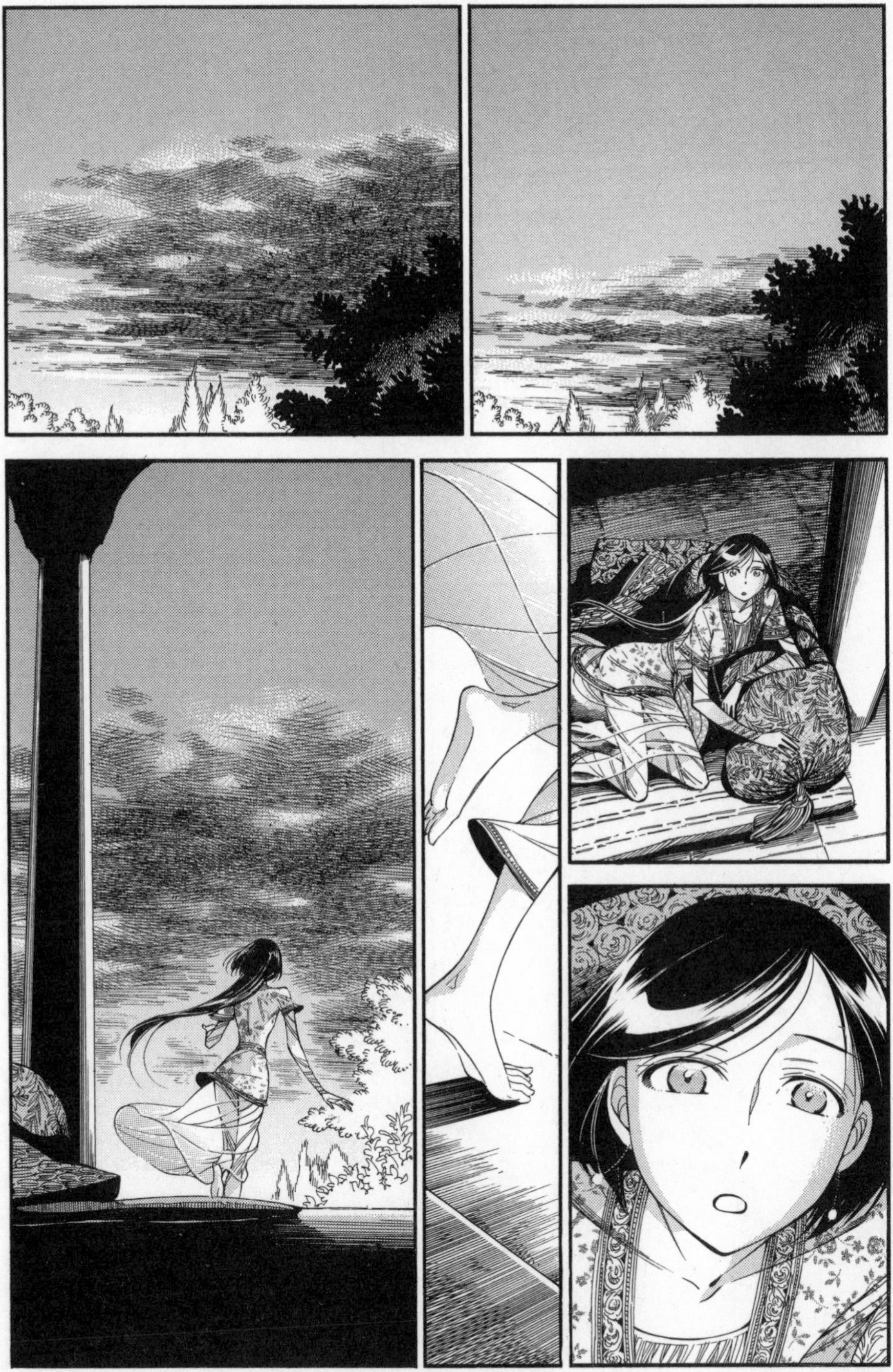

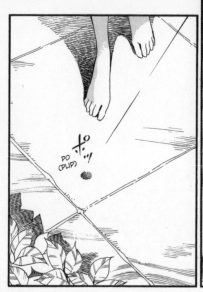

PO
(PLIP)

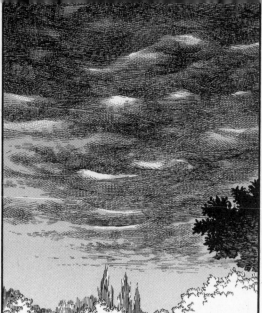

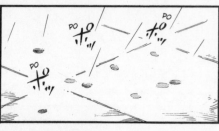

PO

PO

PO

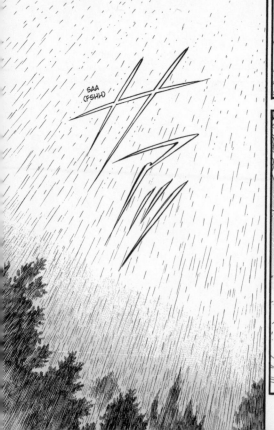

SAA
(FSHH)

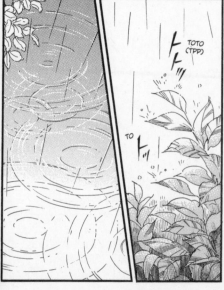

TOTO
(TPP)

TO

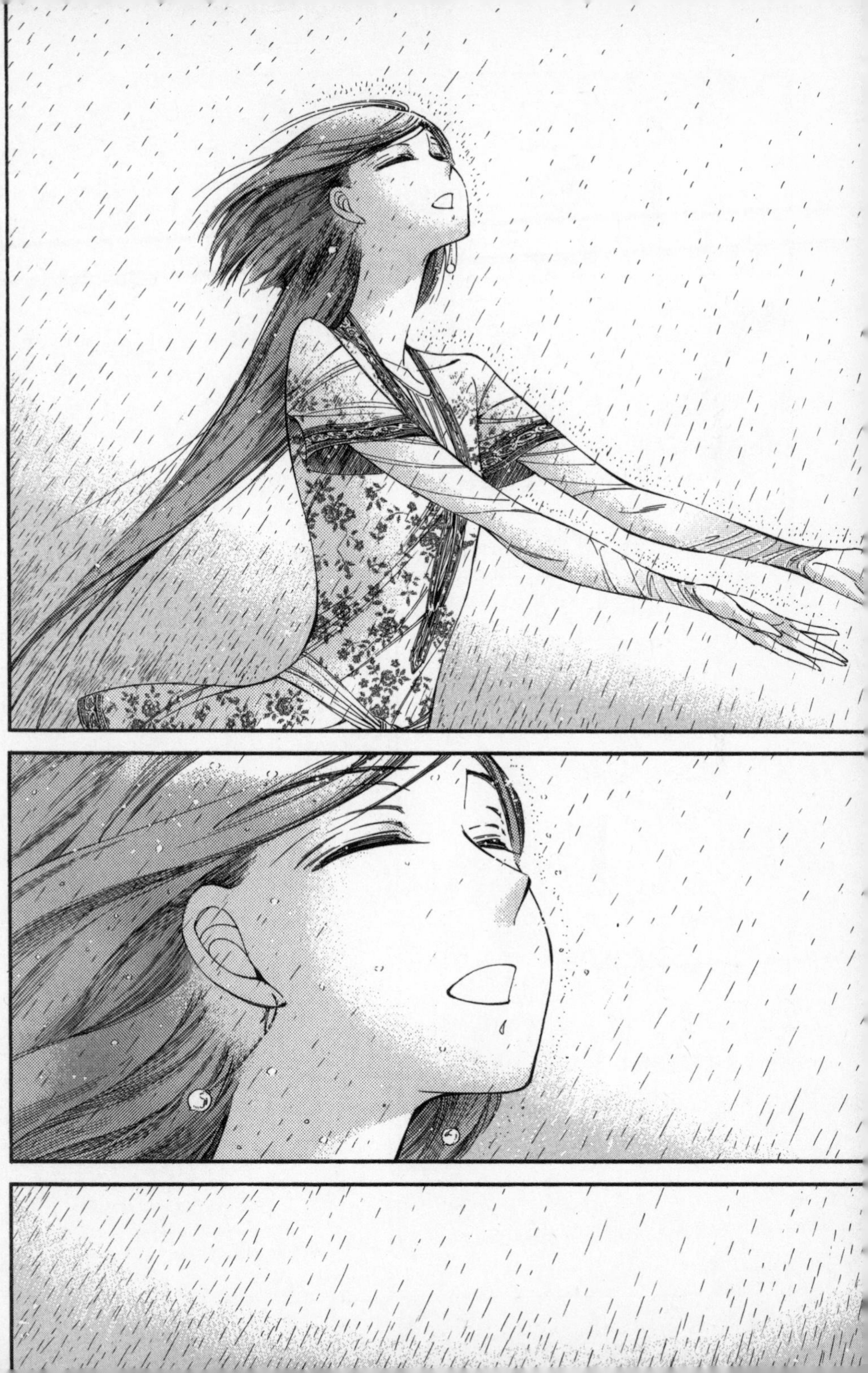

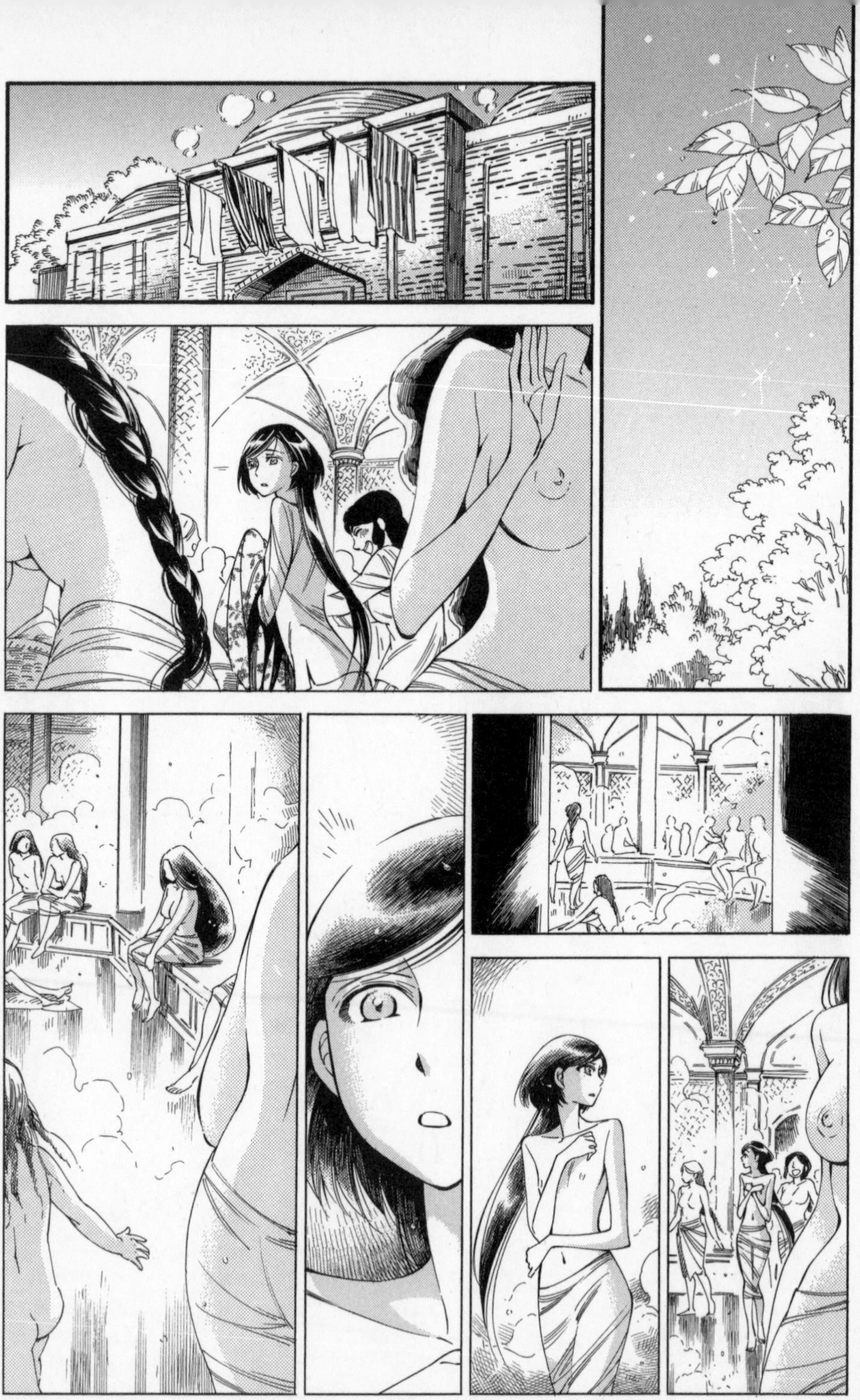

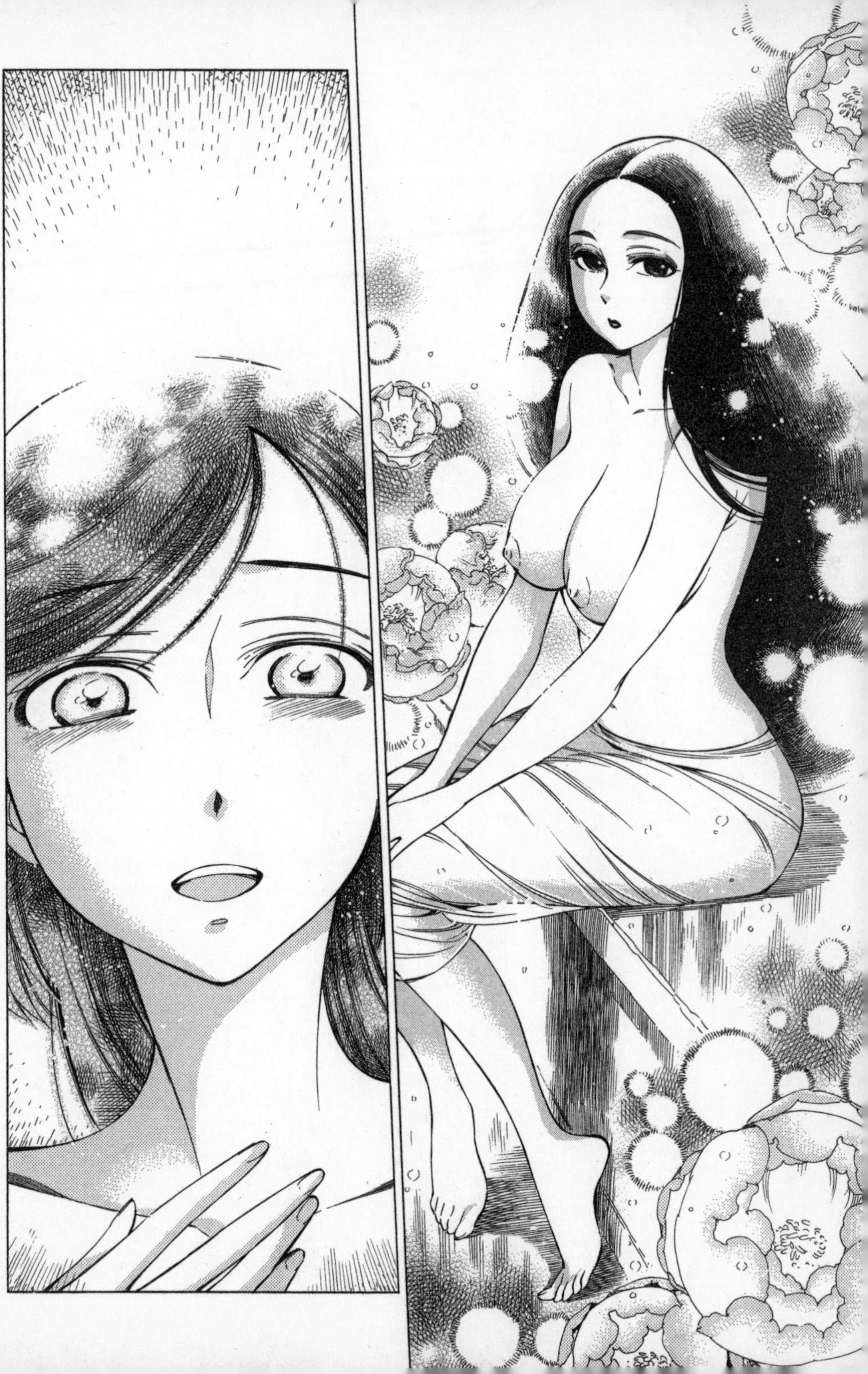

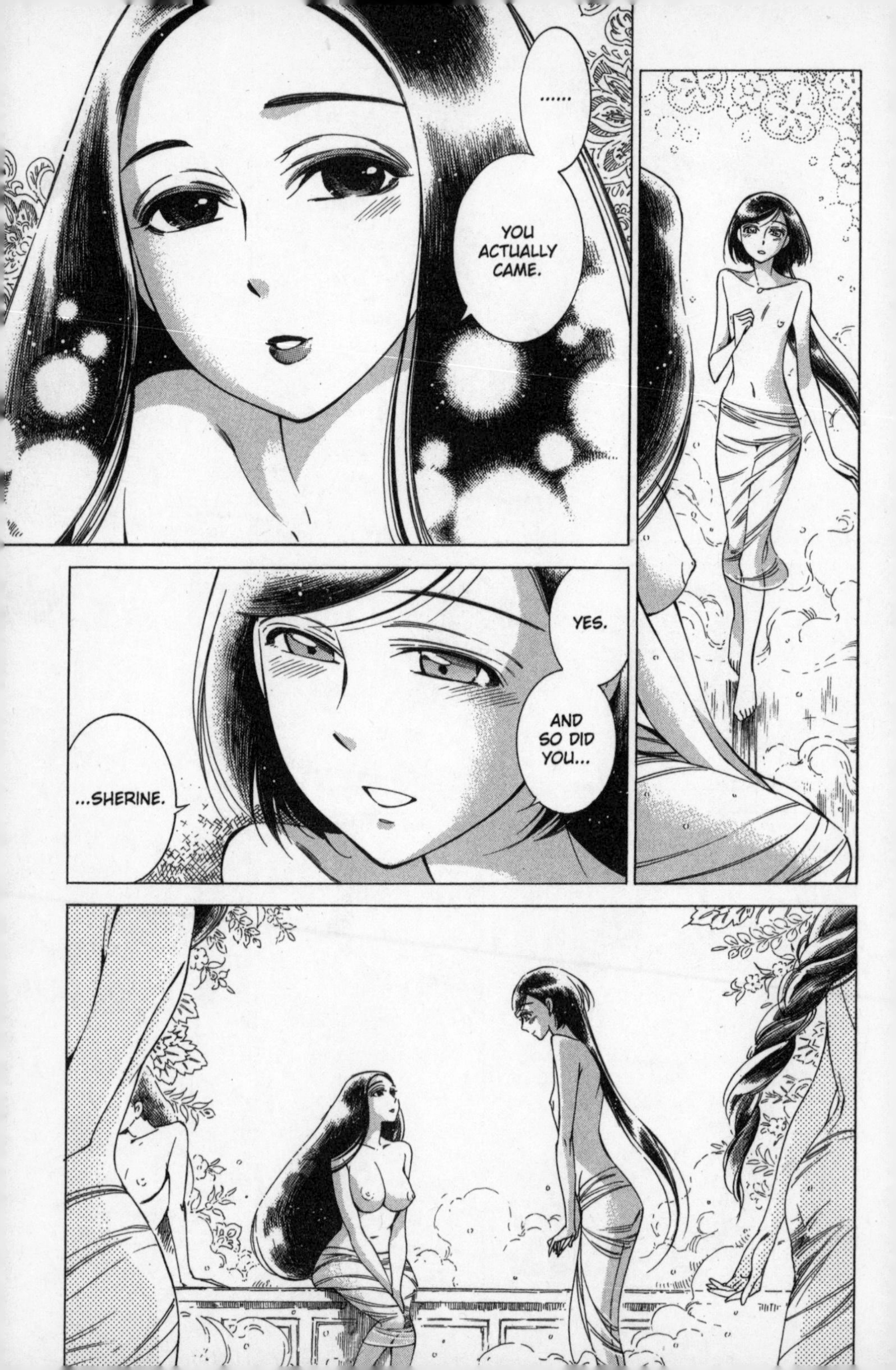
......
YOU ACTUALLY CAME.
YES.
AND SO DID YOU...
...SHERINE.

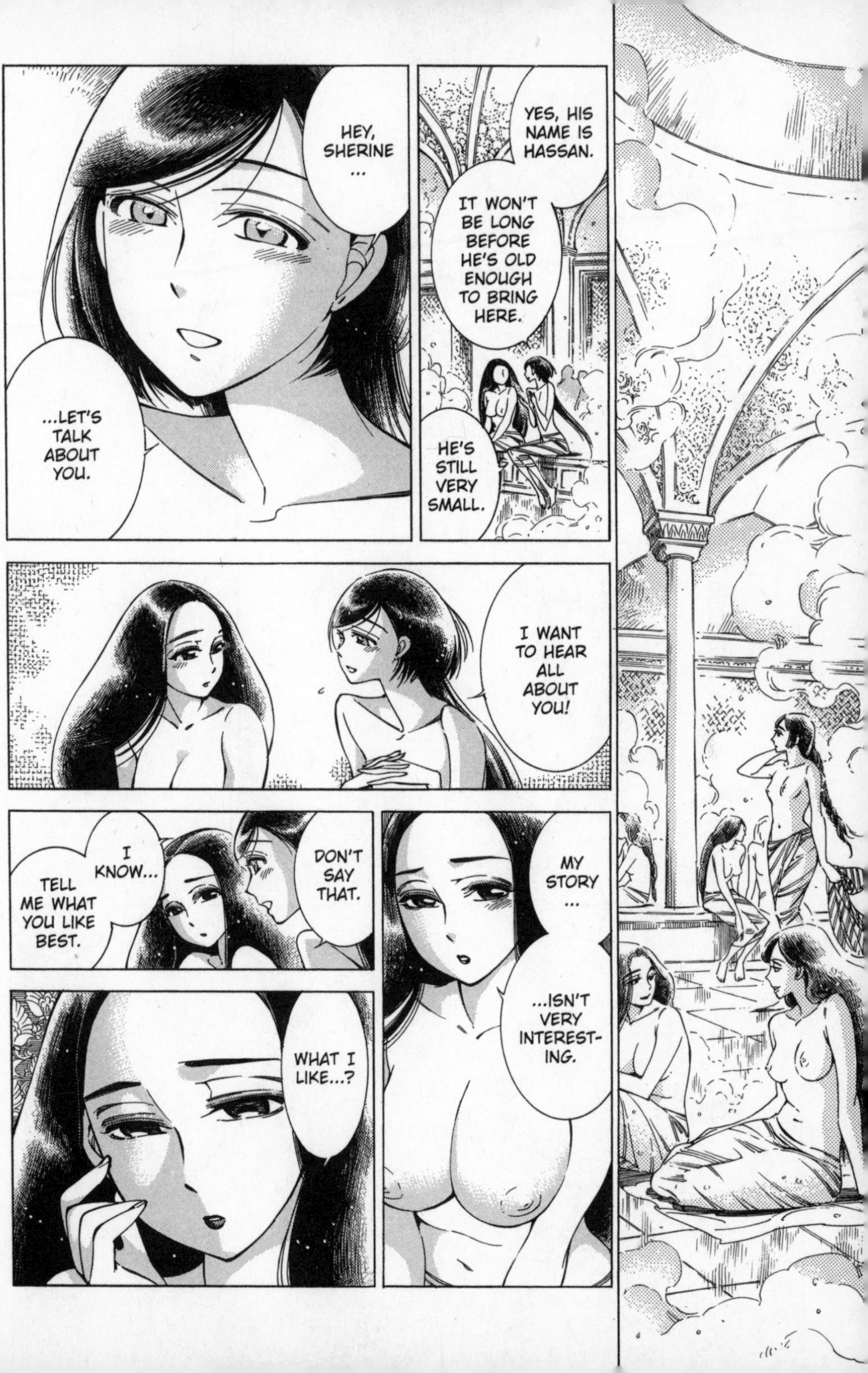
YES, HIS NAME IS HASSAN.
IT WON'T BE LONG BEFORE HE'S OLD ENOUGH TO BRING HERE.
HE'S STILL VERY SMALL.
HEY, SHERINE ...
...LET'S TALK ABOUT YOU.
I WANT TO HEAR ALL ABOUT YOU!
MY STORY ...
...ISN'T VERY INTEREST-ING.
DON'T SAY THAT.
I KNOW...
TELL ME WHAT YOU LIKE BEST.
WHAT I LIKE...?

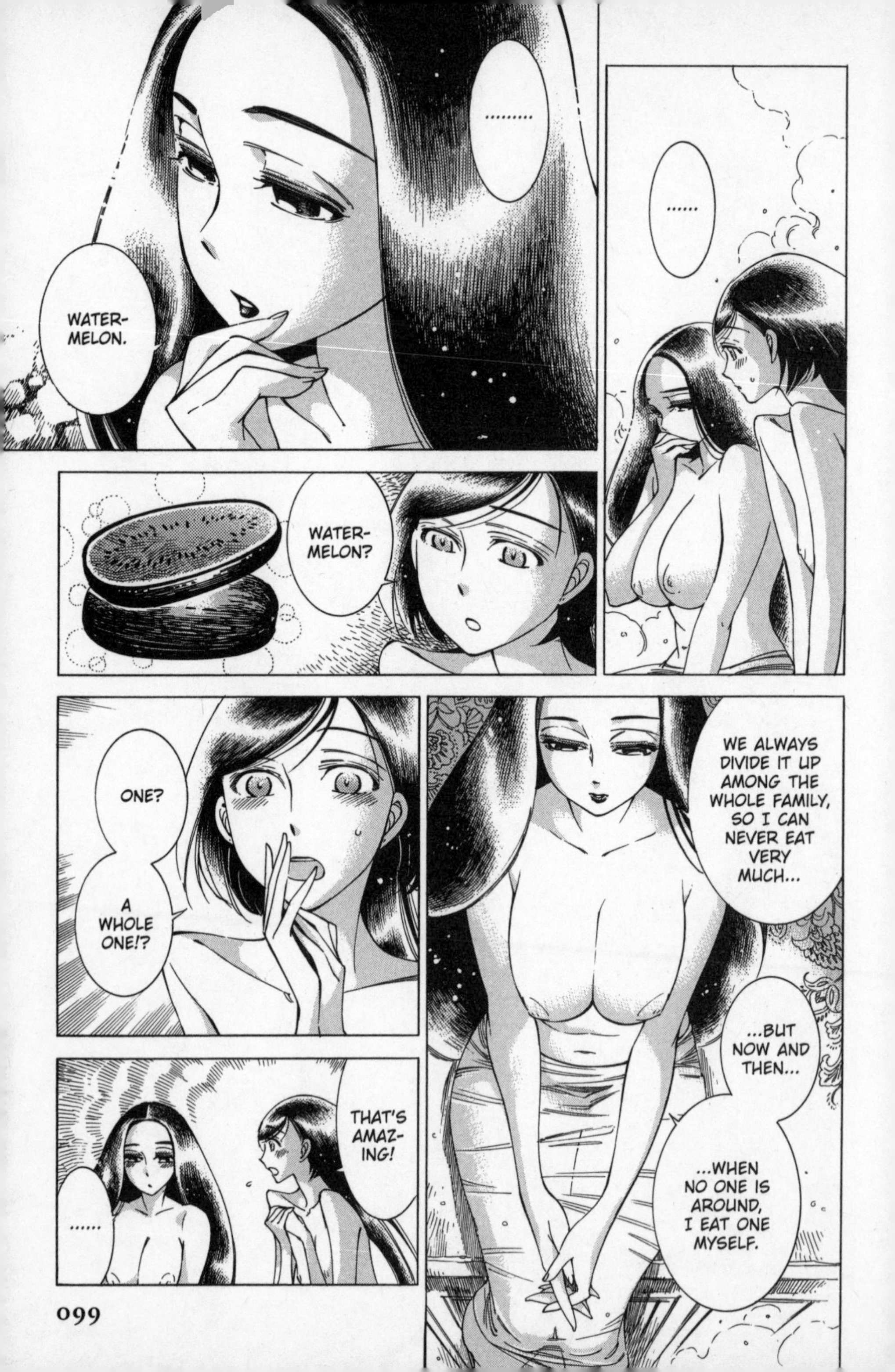

......
....
WATER-MELON.
WATER-MELON?
WE ALWAYS DIVIDE IT UP AMONG THE WHOLE FAMILY, SO I CAN NEVER EAT VERY MUCH...
...BUT NOW AND THEN...
...WHEN NO ONE IS AROUND, I EAT ONE MYSELF.
ONE?
A WHOLE ONE!?
THAT'S AMAZ-ING!
......

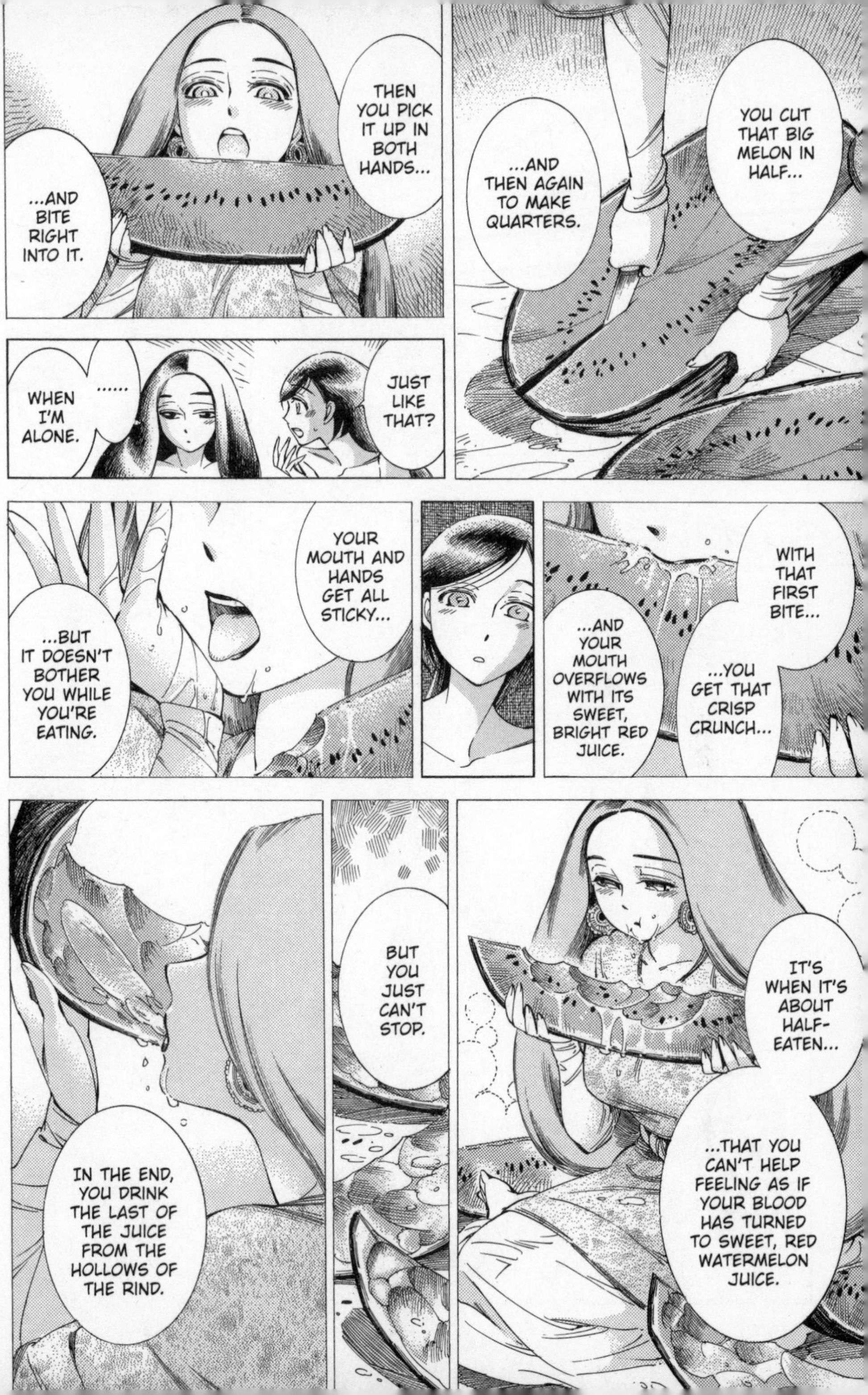
YOU CUT THAT BIG MELON IN HALF...
...AND THEN AGAIN TO MAKE QUARTERS.
THEN YOU PICK IT UP IN BOTH HANDS...
...AND BITE RIGHT INTO IT.
JUST LIKE THAT?
......
WHEN I'M ALONE.
WITH THAT FIRST BITE...
...YOU GET THAT CRISP CRUNCH...
...AND YOUR MOUTH OVERFLOWS WITH ITS SWEET, BRIGHT RED JUICE.
YOUR MOUTH AND HANDS GET ALL STICKY...
...BUT IT DOESN'T BOTHER YOU WHILE YOU'RE EATING.
IT'S WHEN IT'S ABOUT HALF-EATEN...
...THAT YOU CAN'T HELP FEELING AS IF YOUR BLOOD HAS TURNED TO SWEET, RED WATERMELON JUICE.
BUT YOU JUST CAN'T STOP.
IN THE END, YOU DRINK THE LAST OF THE JUICE FROM THE HOLLOWS OF THE RIND.

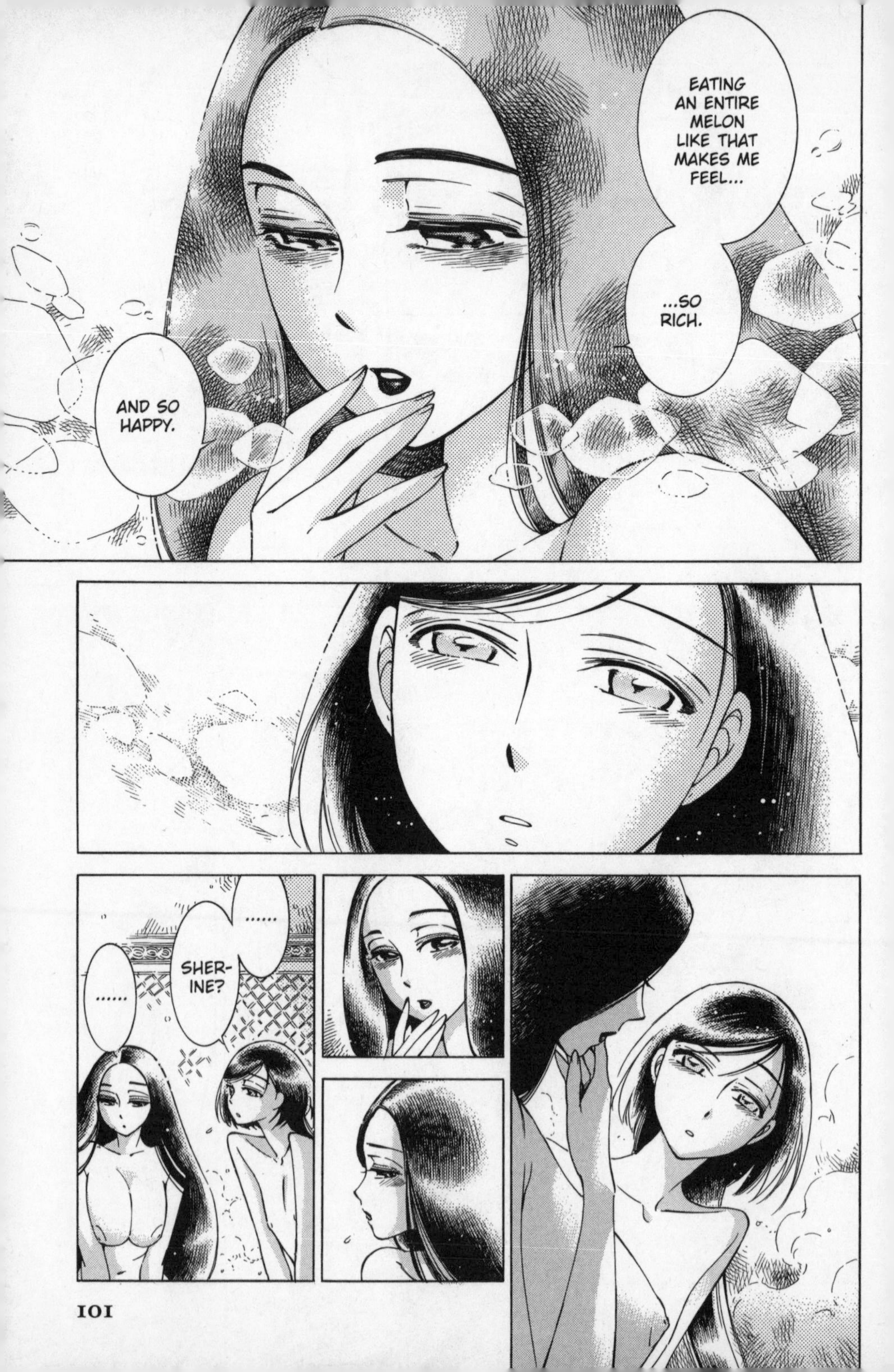
EATING AN ENTIRE MELON LIKE THAT MAKES ME FEEL...
...SO RICH.
AND SO HAPPY.
......
SHER-INE?
......

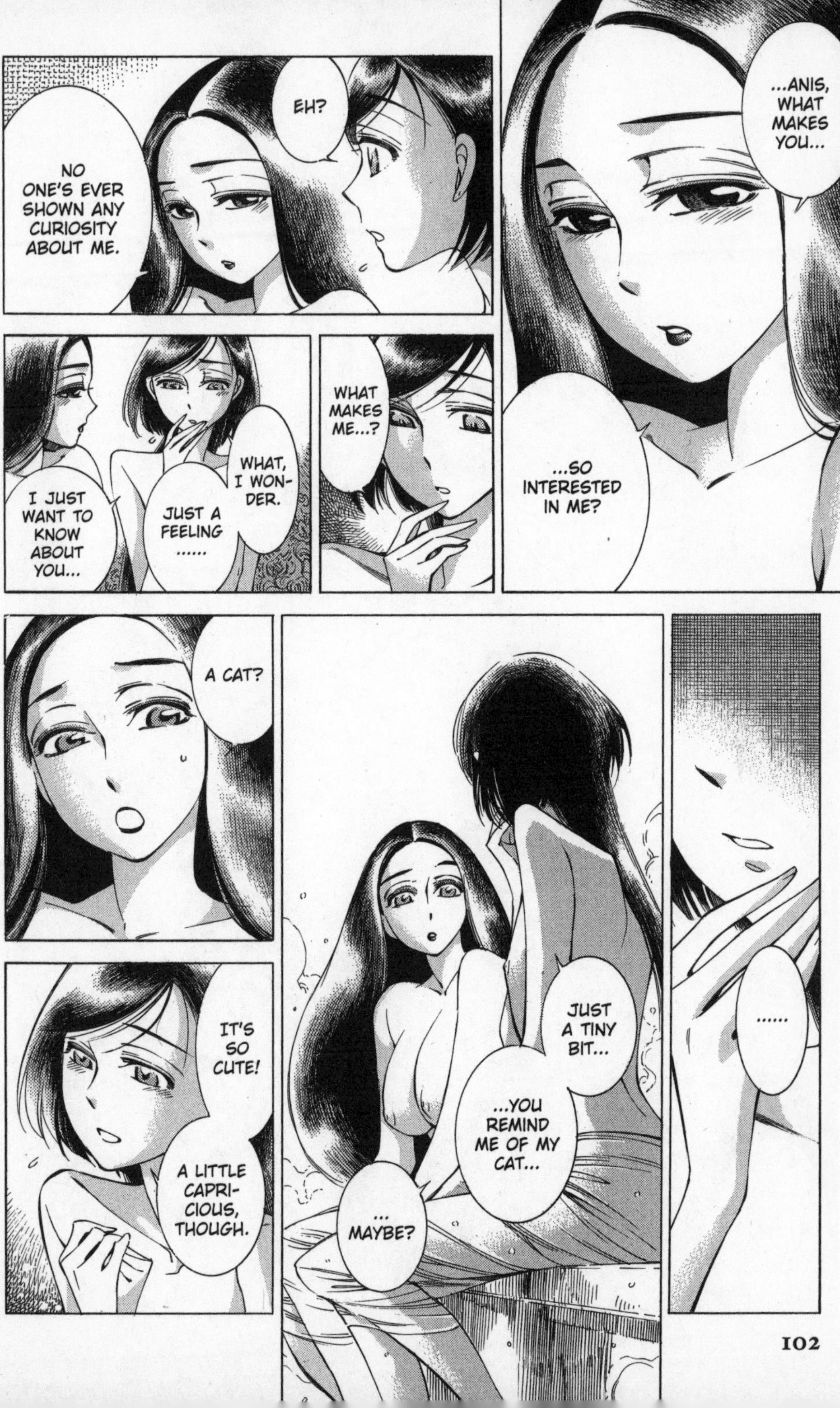
...ANIS, WHAT MAKES YOU...
...SO INTERESTED IN ME?
EH?
NO ONE'S EVER SHOWN ANY CURIOSITY ABOUT ME.
WHAT MAKES ME...?
WHAT, I WONDER.
JUST A FEELING ......
I JUST WANT TO KNOW ABOUT YOU...
......
JUST A TINY BIT...
...YOU REMIND ME OF MY CAT...
... MAYBE?
A CAT?
IT'S SO CUTE!
A LITTLE CAPRICIOUS, THOUGH.

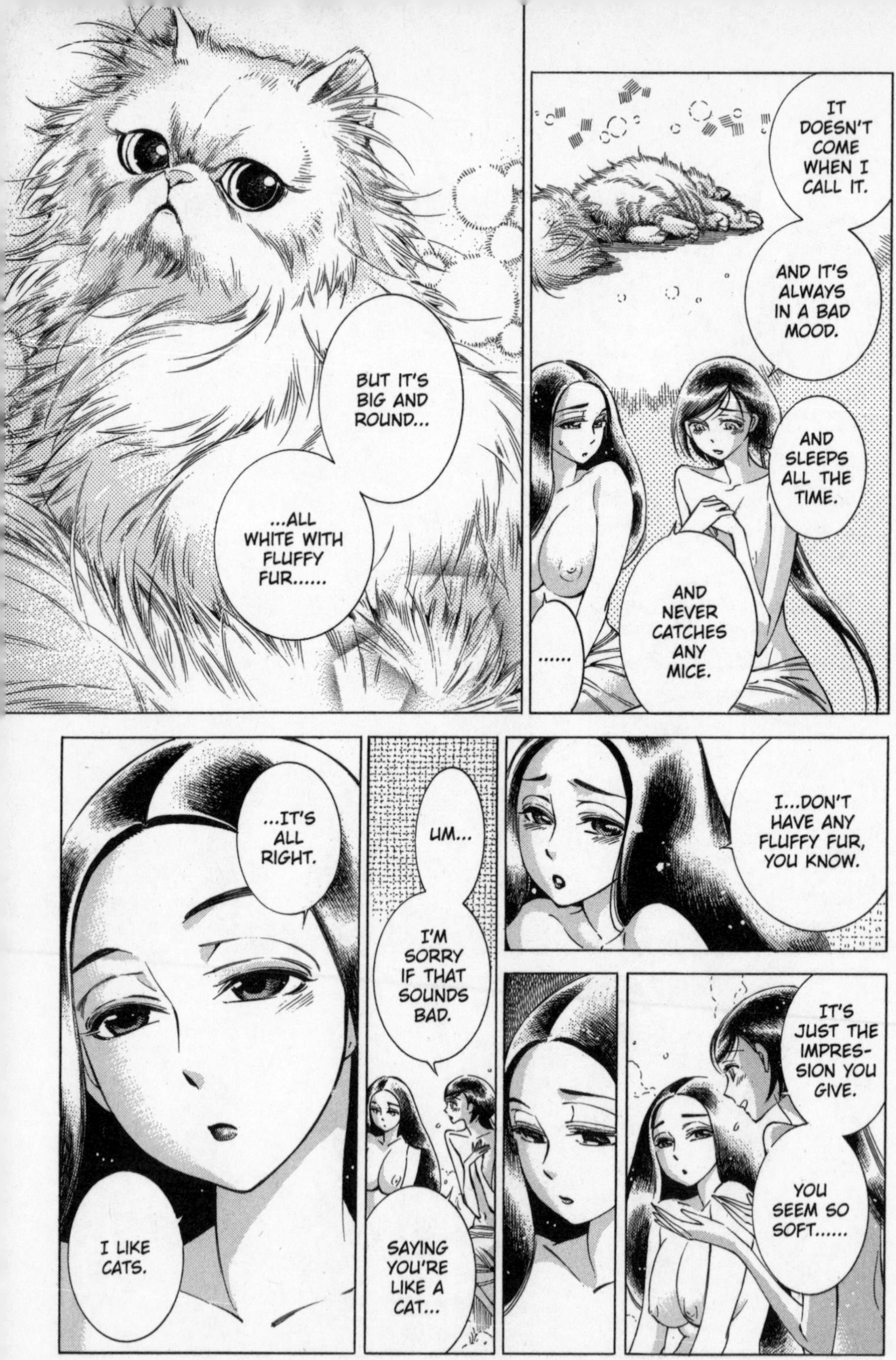
IT DOESN'T COME WHEN I CALL IT.
AND IT'S ALWAYS IN A BAD MOOD.
AND SLEEPS ALL THE TIME.
AND NEVER CATCHES ANY MICE.
......
BUT IT'S BIG AND ROUND...
...ALL WHITE WITH FLUFFY FUR......
I...DON'T HAVE ANY FLUFFY FUR, YOU KNOW.
IT'S JUST THE IMPRES-SION YOU GIVE.
YOU SEEM SO SOFT......
UM...
I'M SORRY IF THAT SOUNDS BAD.
SAYING YOU'RE LIKE A CAT...
...IT'S ALL RIGHT.
I LIKE CATS.

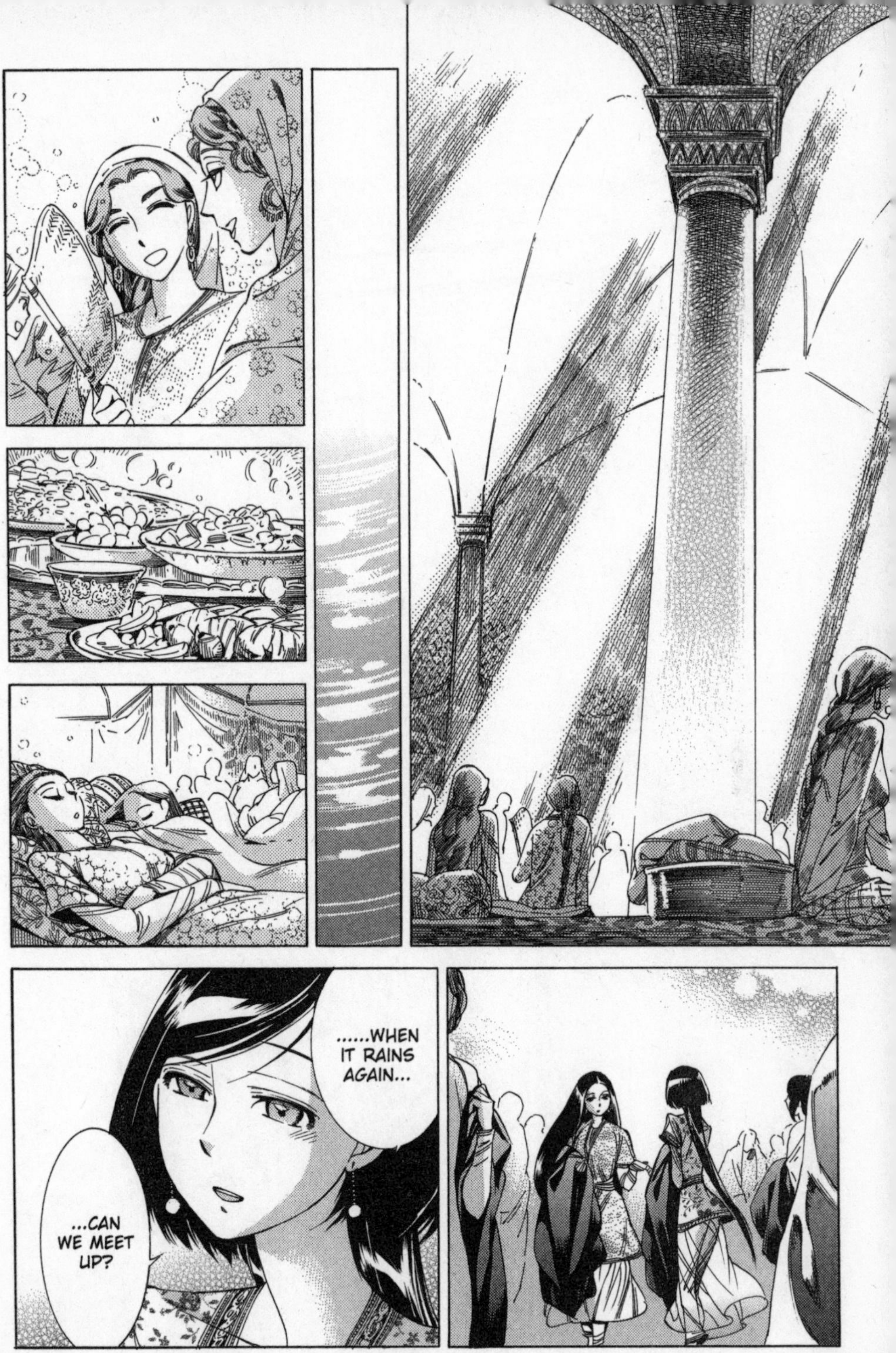
......WHEN IT RAINS AGAIN...
...CAN WE MEET UP?

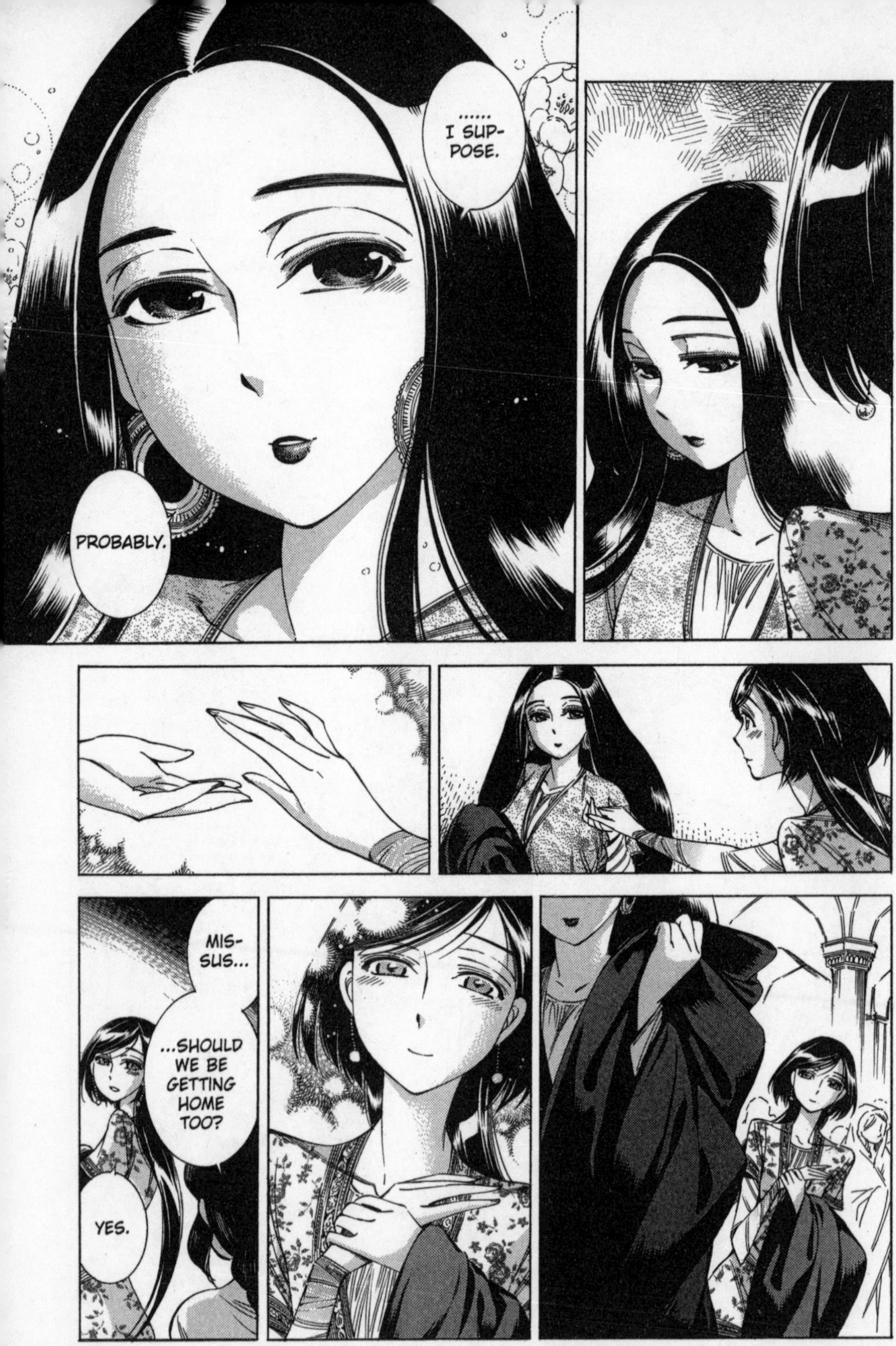
......
I SUP-POSE.
PROBABLY.
MIS-SUS...
...SHOULD WE BE GETTING HOME TOO?
YES.

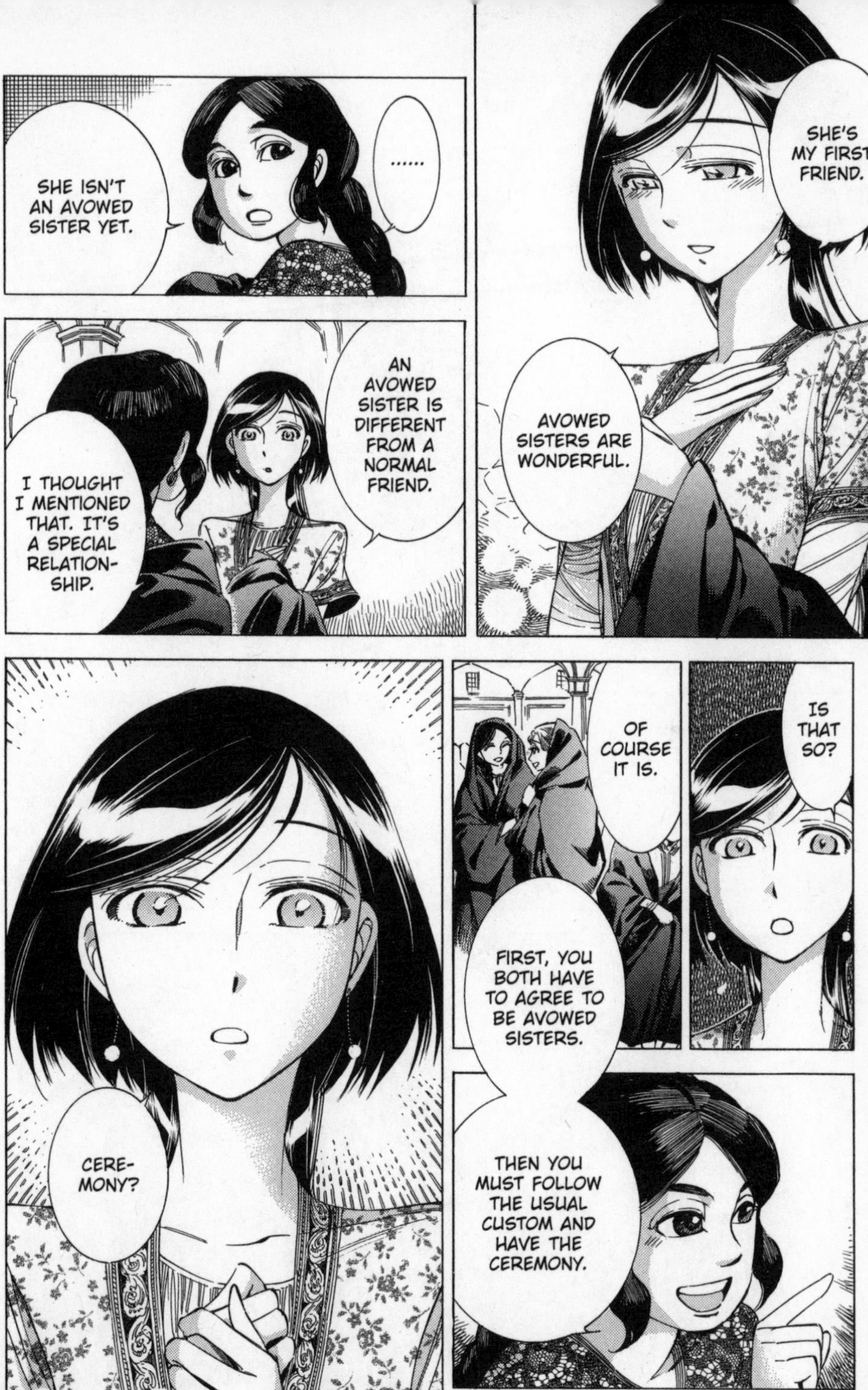
SHE'S MY FIRST FRIEND.
AVOWED SISTERS ARE WONDERFUL.
......
SHE ISN'T AN AVOWED SISTER YET.
AN AVOWED SISTER IS DIFFERENT FROM A NORMAL FRIEND.
I THOUGHT I MENTIONED THAT. IT'S A SPECIAL RELATION-SHIP.
IS THAT SO?
OF COURSE IT IS.
FIRST, YOU BOTH HAVE TO AGREE TO BE AVOWED SISTERS.
THEN YOU MUST FOLLOW THE USUAL CUSTOM AND HAVE THE CEREMONY.
CERE-MONY?

✦ Chapter 40: End ✦

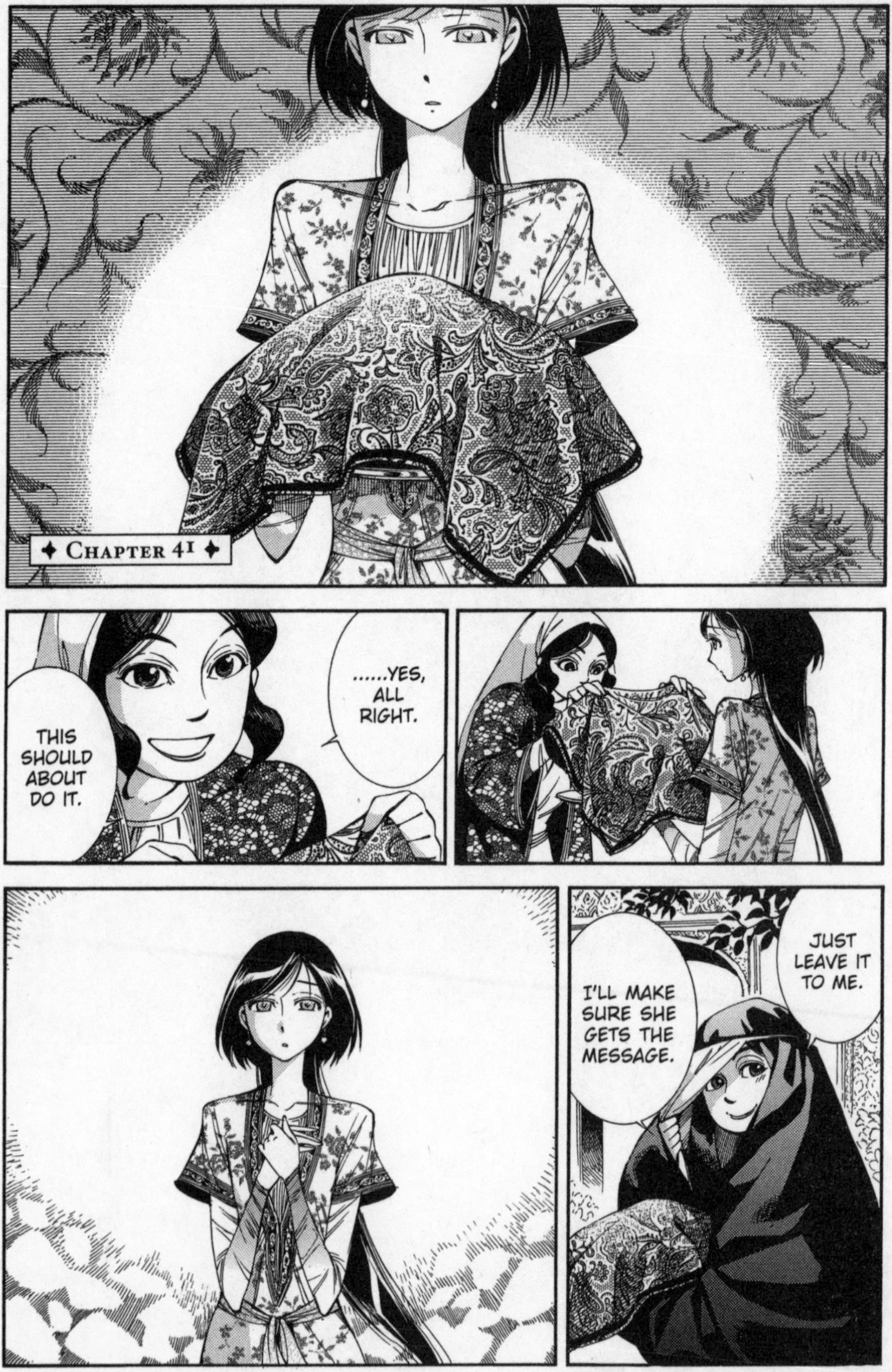
✦ Chapter 41 ✦
......YES, ALL RIGHT.
THIS SHOULD ABOUT DO IT.
JUST LEAVE IT TO ME.
I'LL MAKE SURE SHE GETS THE MESSAGE.

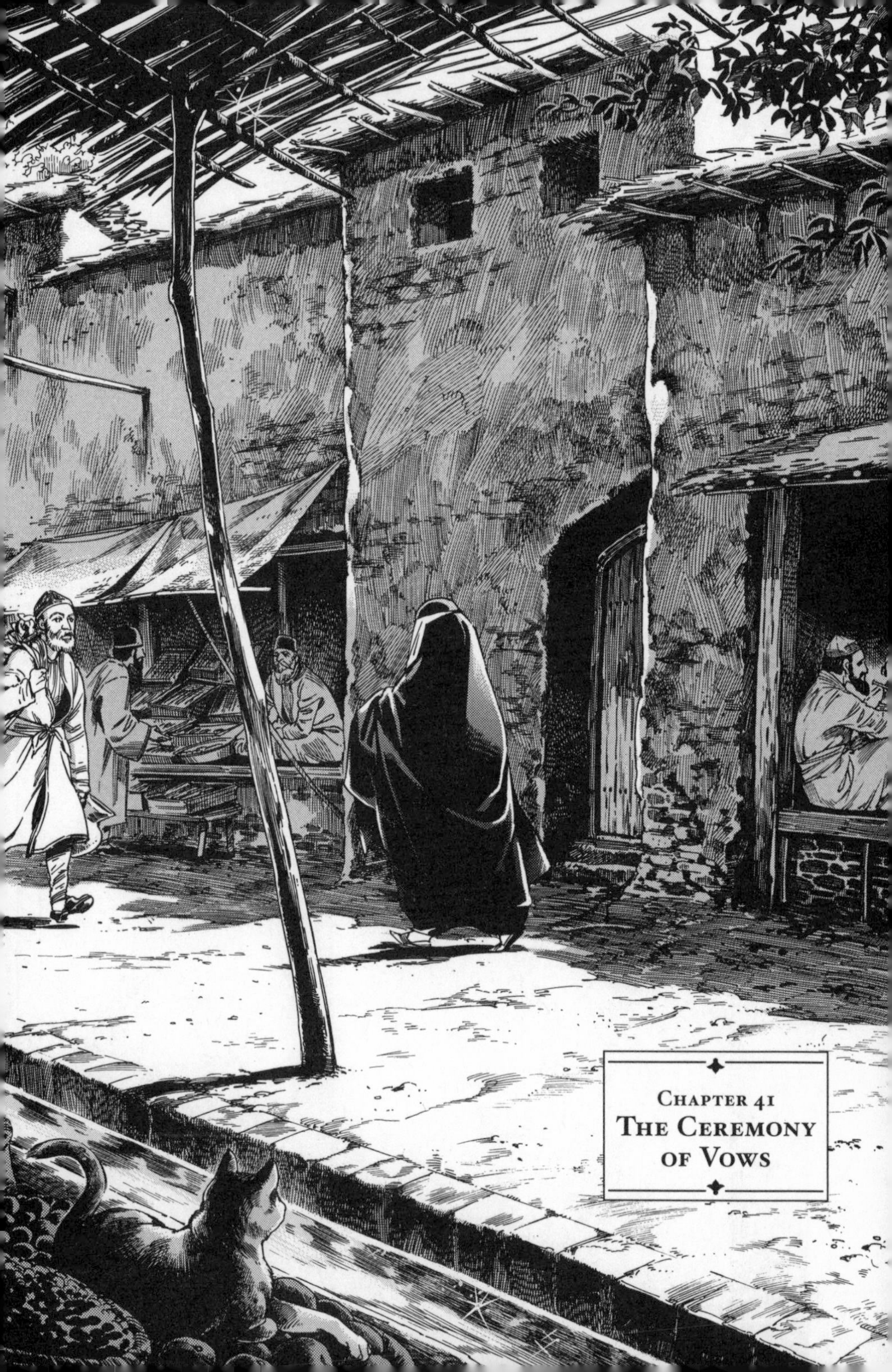
CHAPTER 41
THE CEREMONY OF VOWS

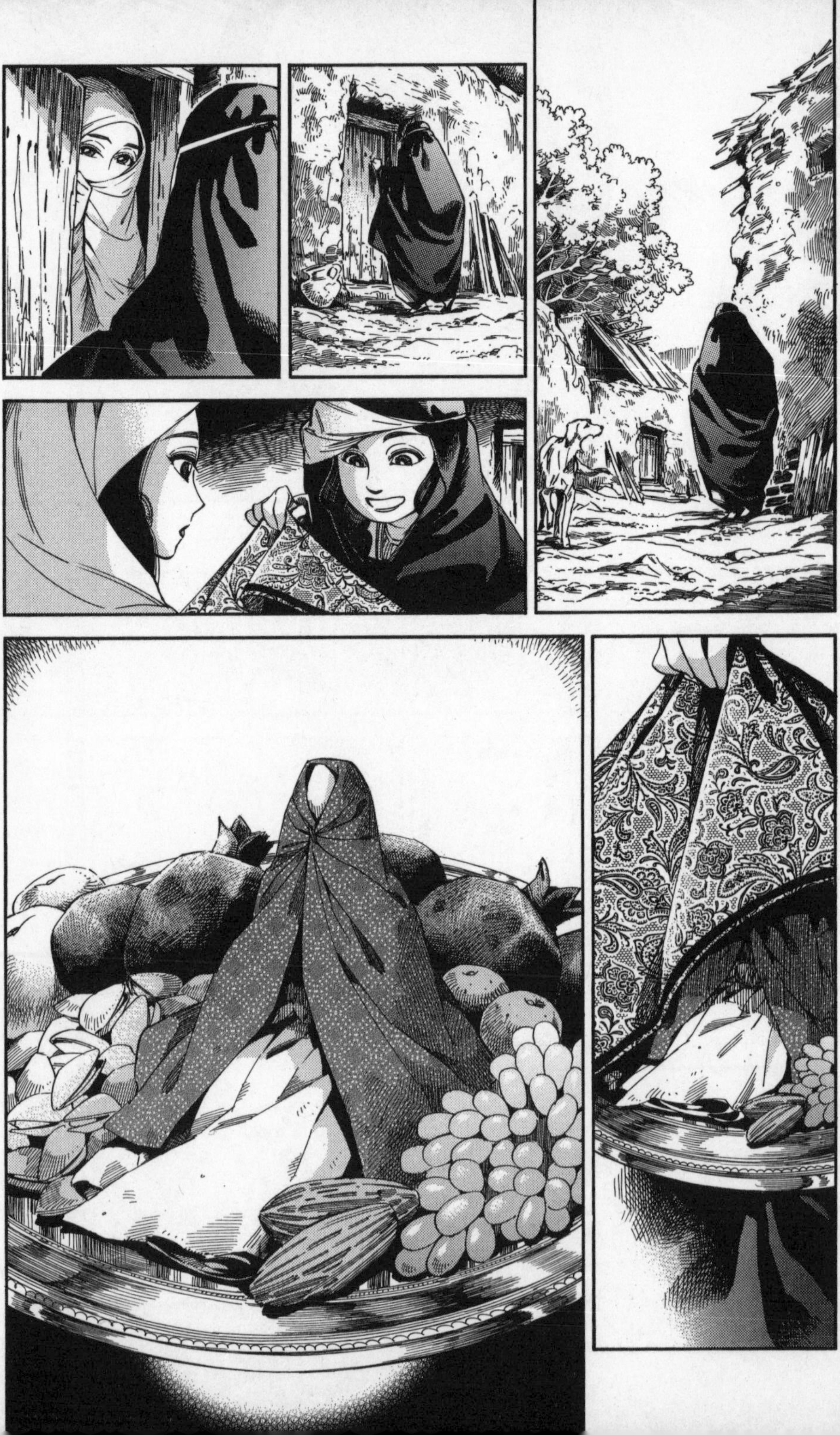

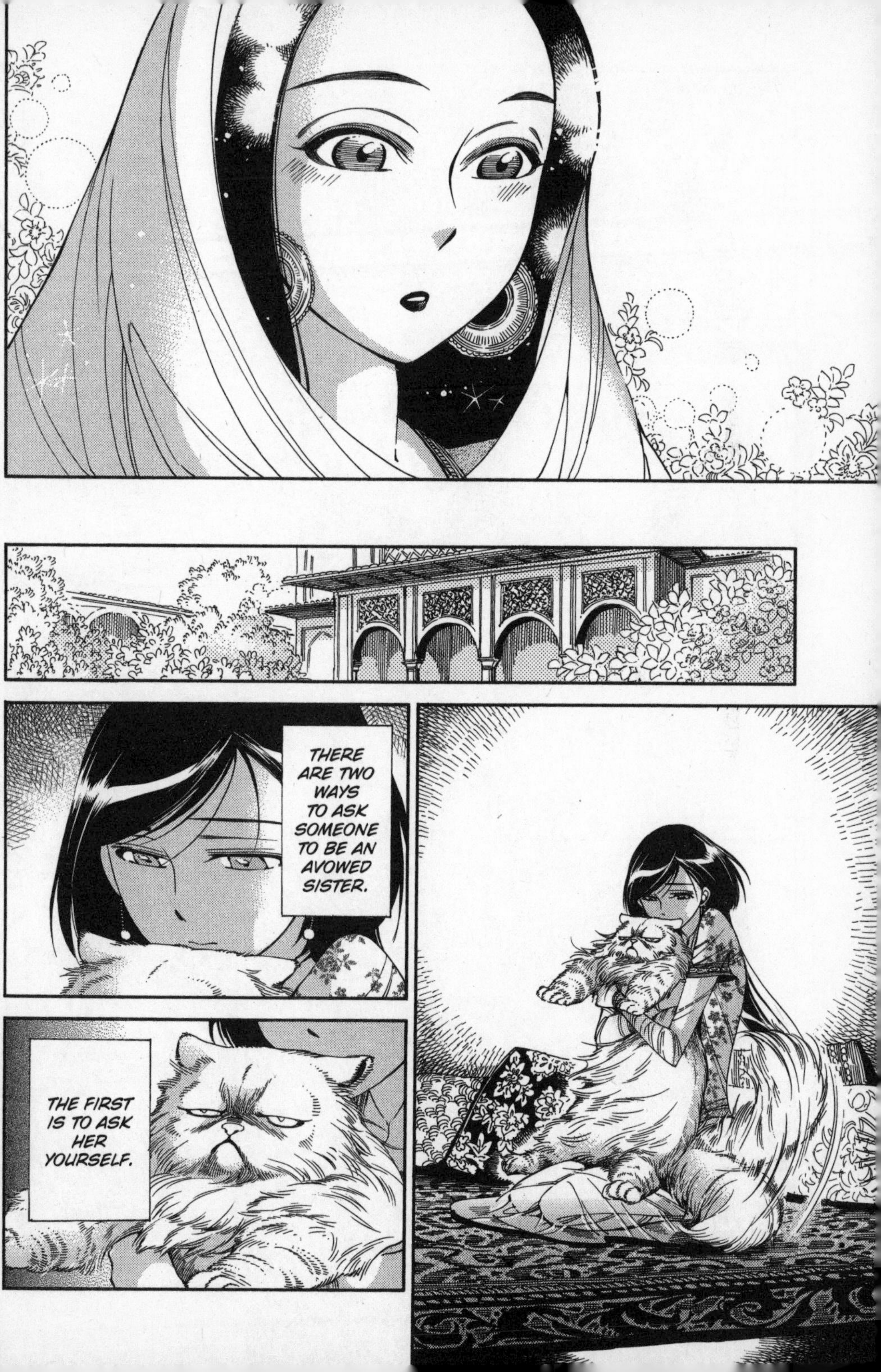
THERE ARE TWO WAYS TO ASK SOMEONE TO BE AN AVOWED SISTER.
THE FIRST IS TO ASK HER YOURSELF.

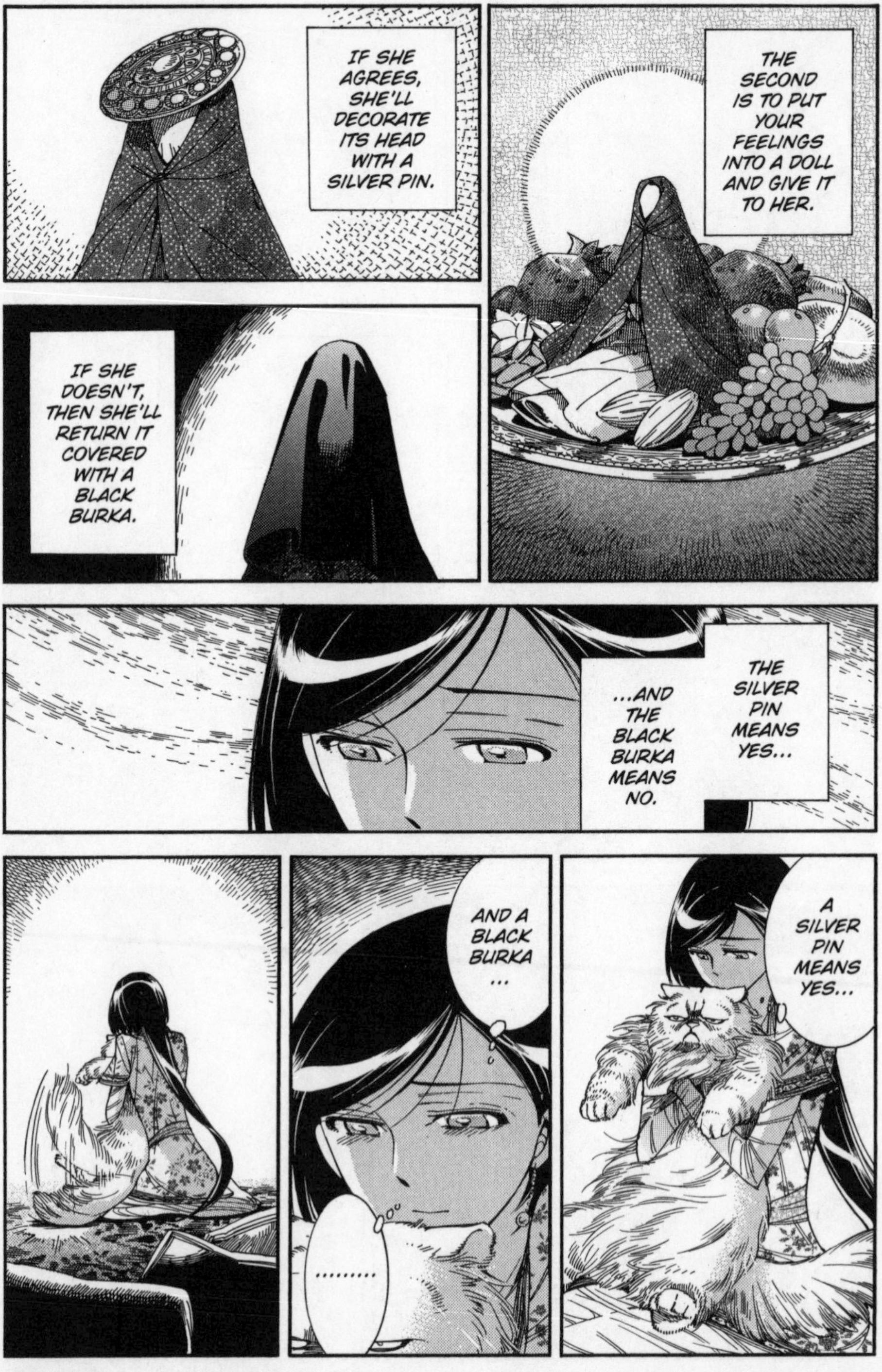
THE SECOND IS TO PUT YOUR FEELINGS INTO A DOLL AND GIVE IT TO HER.
IF SHE AGREES, SHE'LL DECORATE ITS HEAD WITH A SILVER PIN.
IF SHE DOESN'T, THEN SHE'LL RETURN IT COVERED WITH A BLACK BURKA.
THE SILVER PIN MEANS YES...
...AND THE BLACK BURKA MEANS NO.
A SILVER PIN MEANS YES...
AND A BLACK BURKA ...
....

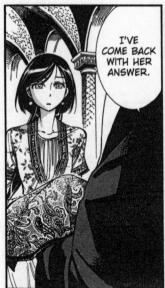

I'VE COME BACK WITH HER ANSWER.

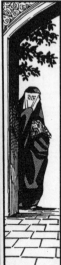

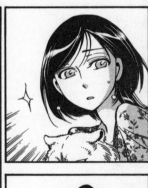

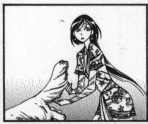

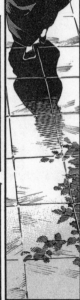

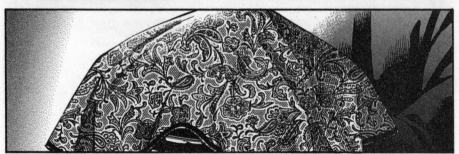

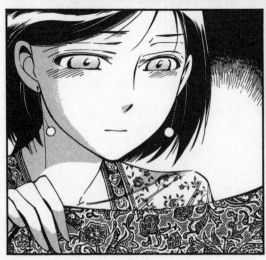

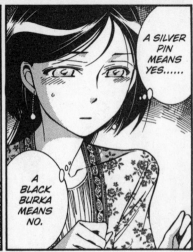

A SILVER PIN MEANS YES......

A BLACK BURKA MEANS NO.

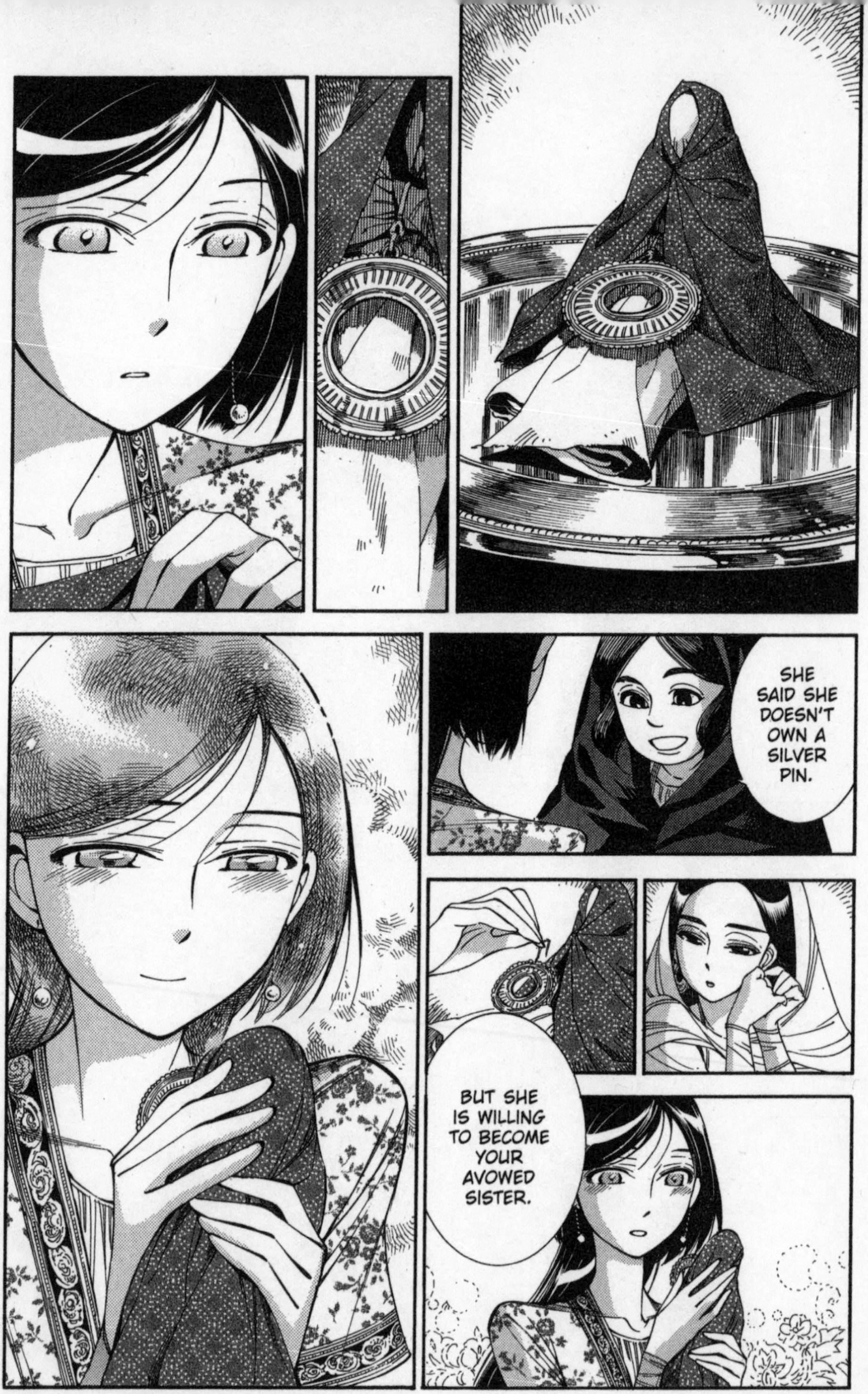
SHE SAID SHE DOESN'T OWN A SILVER PIN.
BUT SHE IS WILLING TO BECOME YOUR AVOWED SISTER.

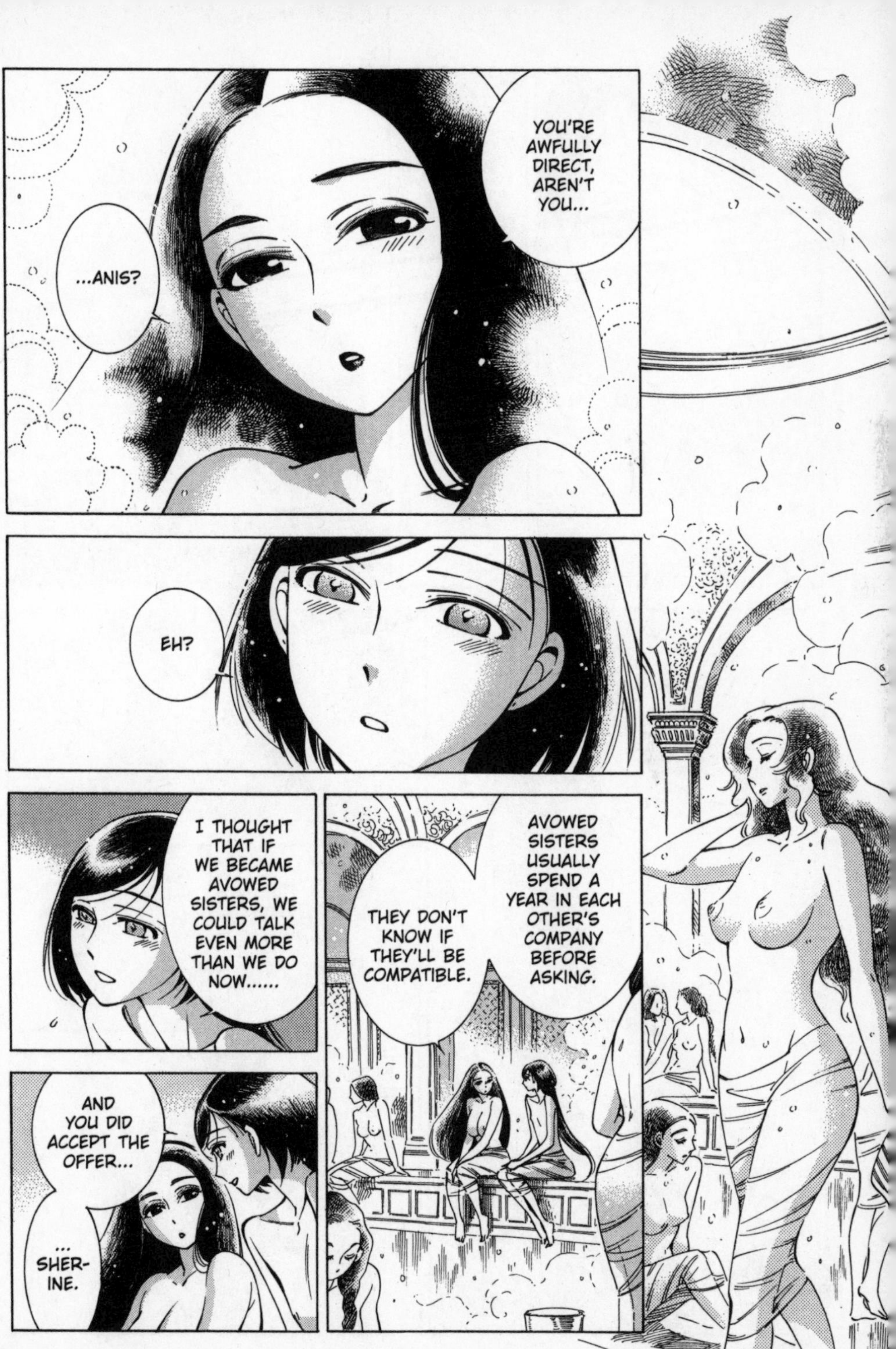
YOU'RE AWFULLY DIRECT, AREN'T YOU...
...ANIS?
EH?
AVOWED SISTERS USUALLY SPEND A YEAR IN EACH OTHER'S COMPANY BEFORE ASKING.
THEY DON'T KNOW IF THEY'LL BE COMPATIBLE.
I THOUGHT THAT IF WE BECAME AVOWED SISTERS, WE COULD TALK EVEN MORE THAN WE DO NOW......
AND YOU DID ACCEPT THE OFFER...
...SHER-INE.

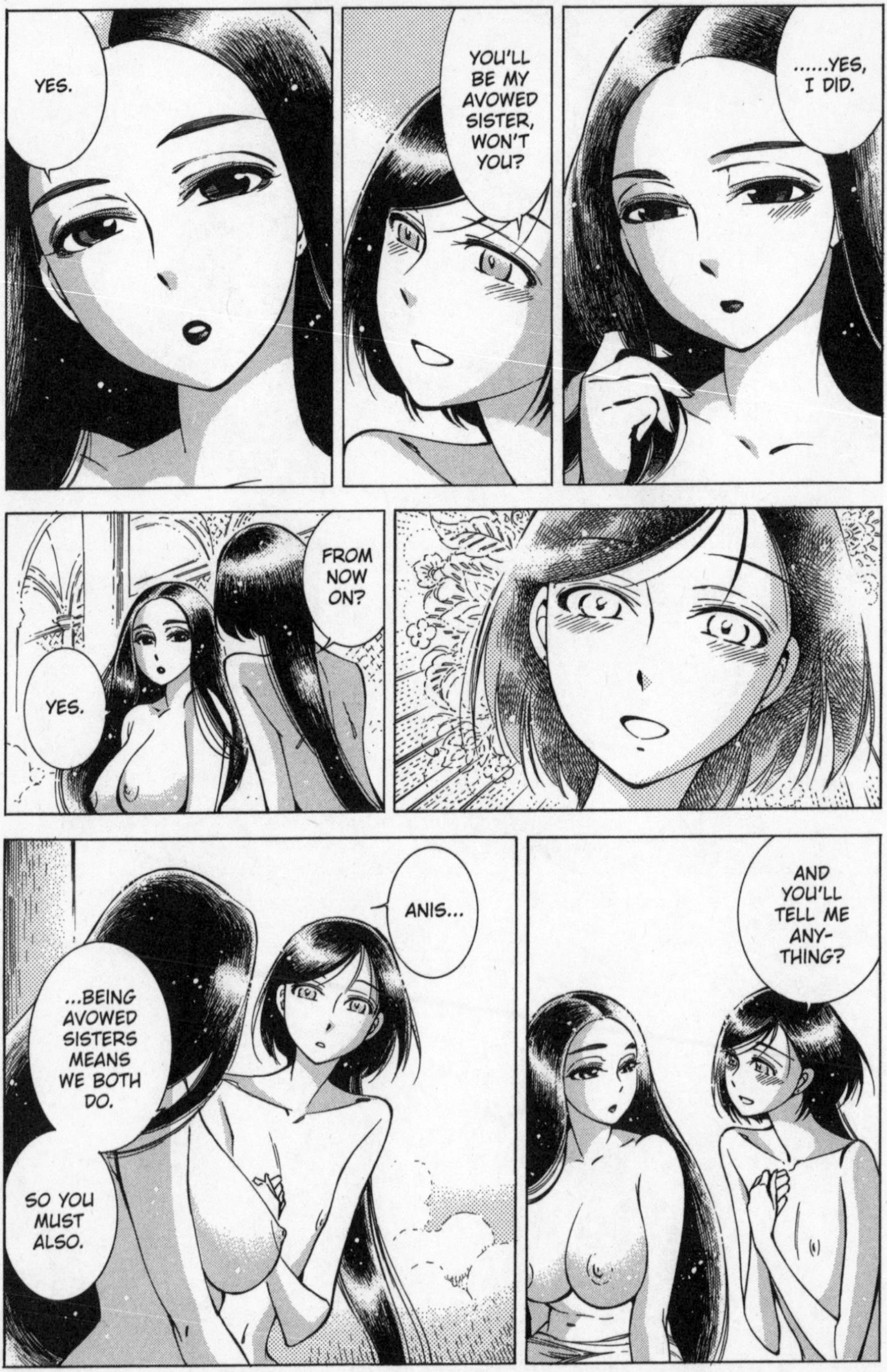
......YES, I DID.
YOU'LL BE MY AVOWED SISTER, WON'T YOU?
YES.
FROM NOW ON?
YES.
AND YOU'LL TELL ME ANY-THING?
ANIS...
...BEING AVOWED SISTERS MEANS WE BOTH DO.
SO YOU MUST ALSO.

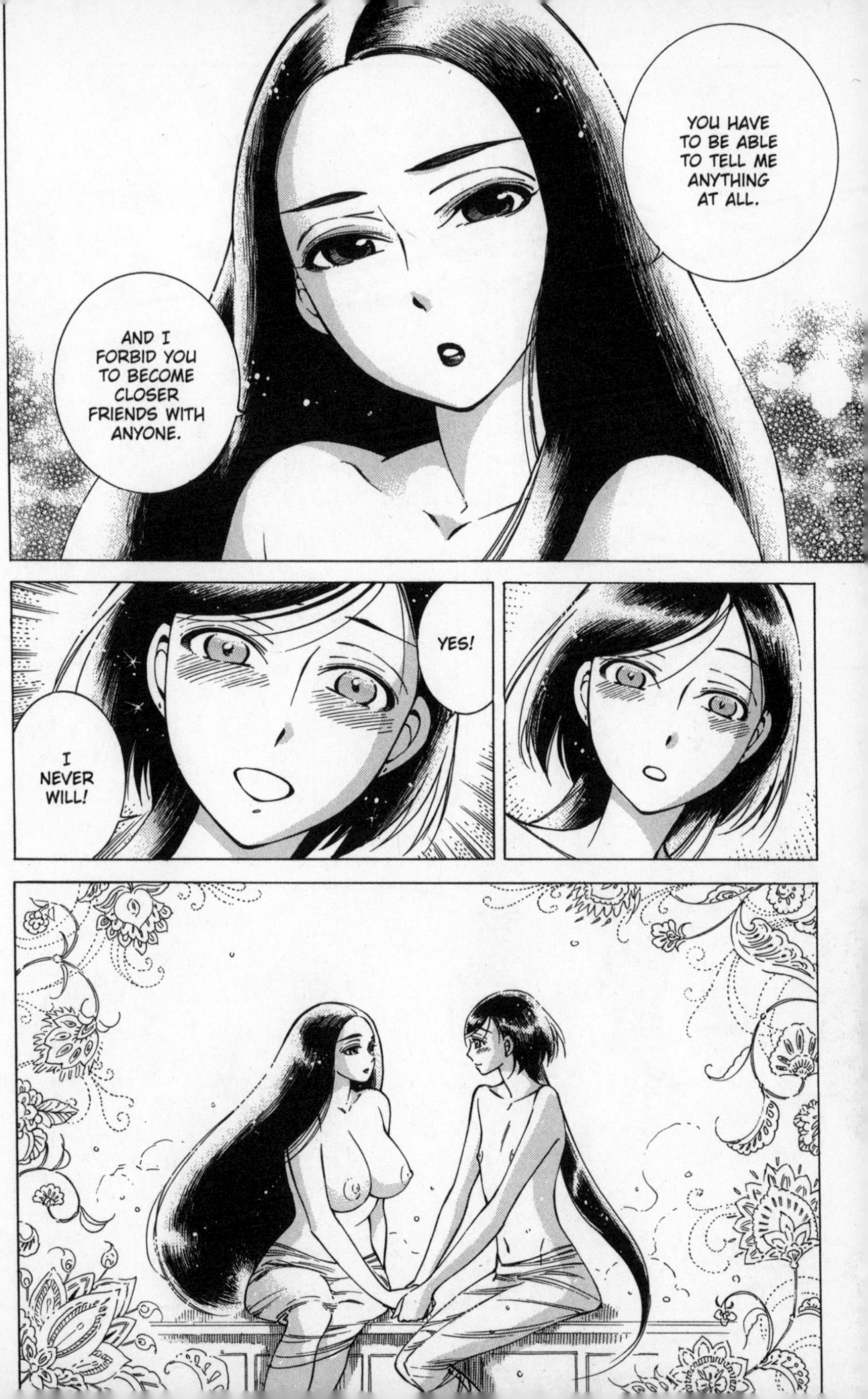
YOU HAVE TO BE ABLE TO TELL ME ANYTHING AT ALL.
AND I FORBID YOU TO BECOME CLOSER FRIENDS WITH ANYONE.
YES!
I NEVER WILL!

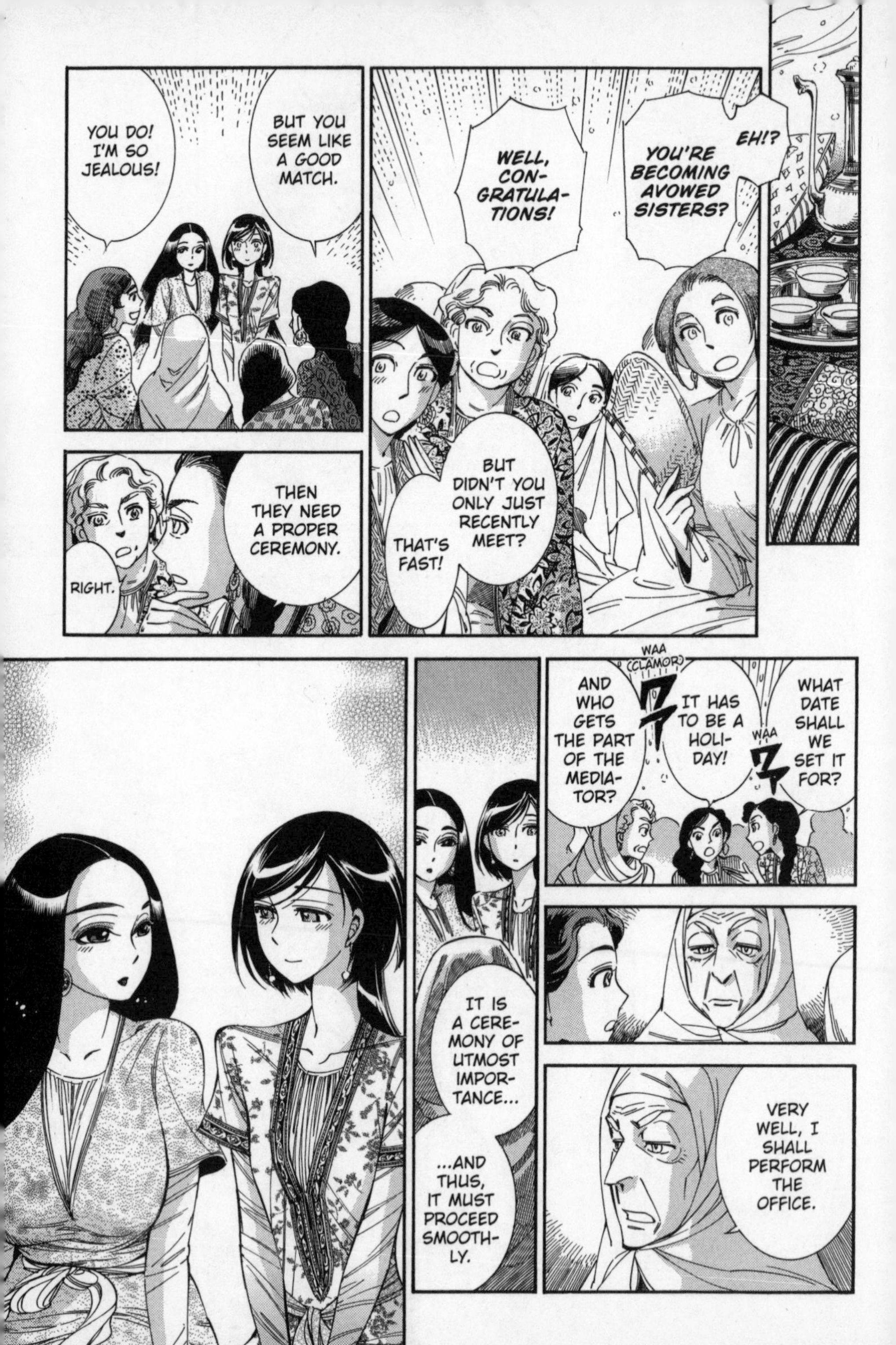
EH!?
YOU'RE BECOMING AVOWED SISTERS?
WELL, CONGRATULATIONS!
BUT DIDN'T YOU ONLY JUST RECENTLY MEET?
THAT'S FAST!
BUT YOU SEEM LIKE A GOOD MATCH.
YOU DO! I'M SO JEALOUS!
THEN THEY NEED A PROPER CEREMONY.
RIGHT.
WHAT DATE SHALL WE SET IT FOR?
WAA
IT HAS TO BE A HOLIDAY!
WAA (CLAMOR)
AND WHO GETS THE PART OF THE MEDIATOR?
VERY WELL, I SHALL PERFORM THE OFFICE.
IT IS A CEREMONY OF UTMOST IMPORTANCE...
...AND THUS, IT MUST PROCEED SMOOTHLY.

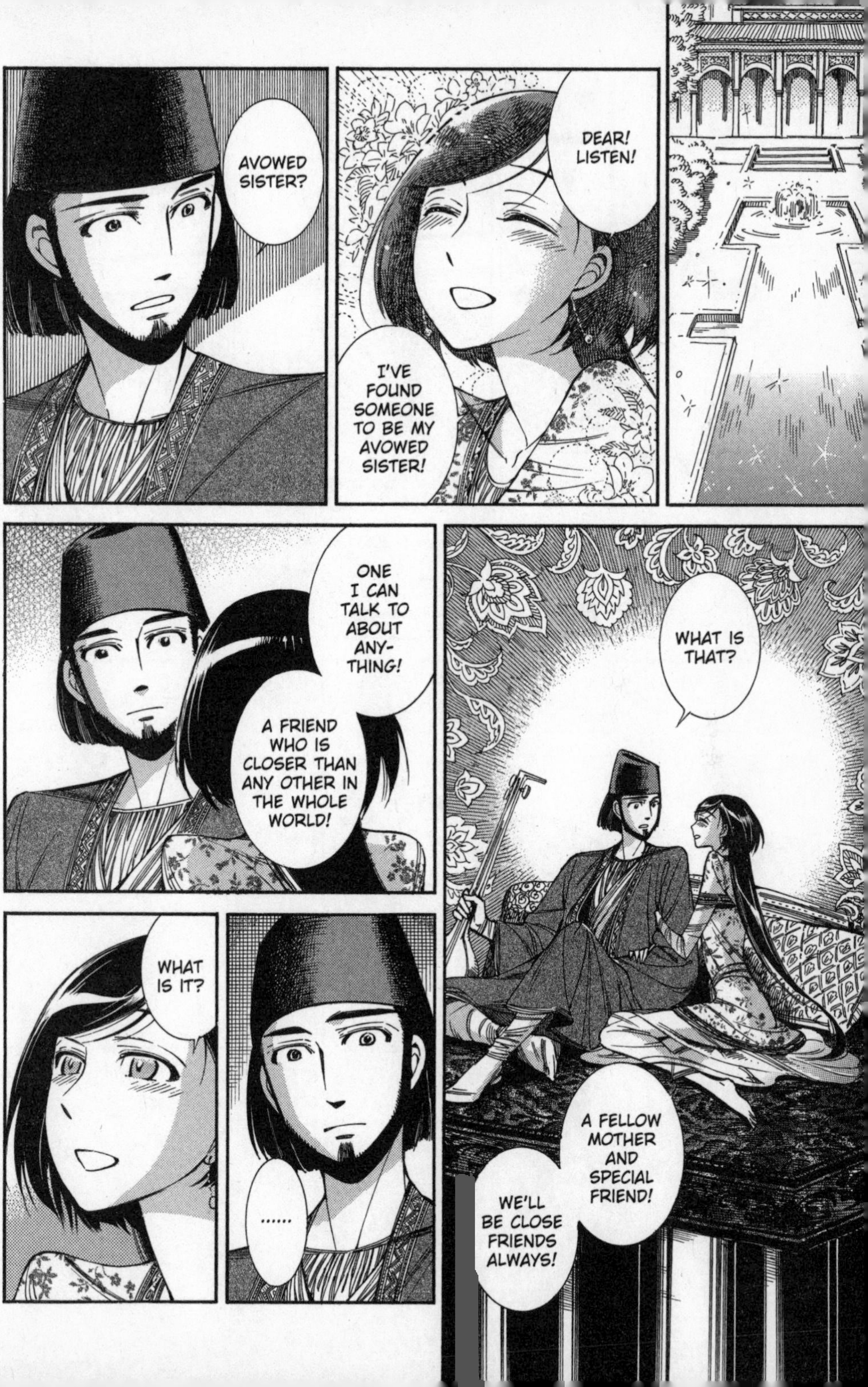
DEAR! LISTEN!
I'VE FOUND SOMEONE TO BE MY AVOWED SISTER!
AVOWED SISTER?
WHAT IS THAT?
A FELLOW MOTHER AND SPECIAL FRIEND!
WE'LL BE CLOSE FRIENDS ALWAYS!
ONE I CAN TALK TO ABOUT ANY-THING!
A FRIEND WHO IS CLOSER THAN ANY OTHER IN THE WHOLE WORLD!
......
WHAT IS IT?

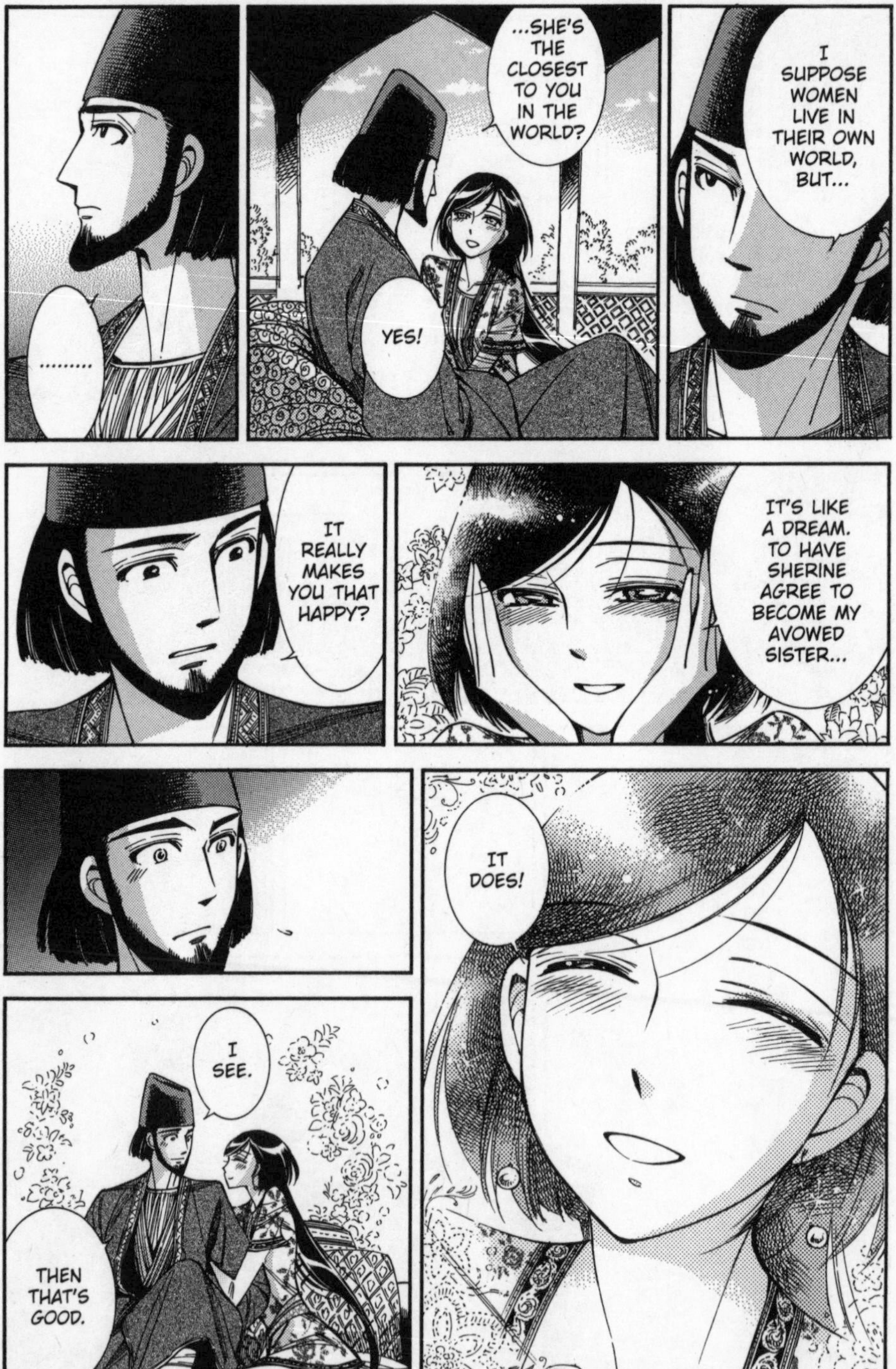
I SUPPOSE WOMEN LIVE IN THEIR OWN WORLD, BUT...
...SHE'S THE CLOSEST TO YOU IN THE WORLD?
YES!
....
IT'S LIKE A DREAM. TO HAVE SHERINE AGREE TO BECOME MY AVOWED SISTER...
IT REALLY MAKES YOU THAT HAPPY?
IT DOES!
I SEE.
THEN THAT'S GOOD.

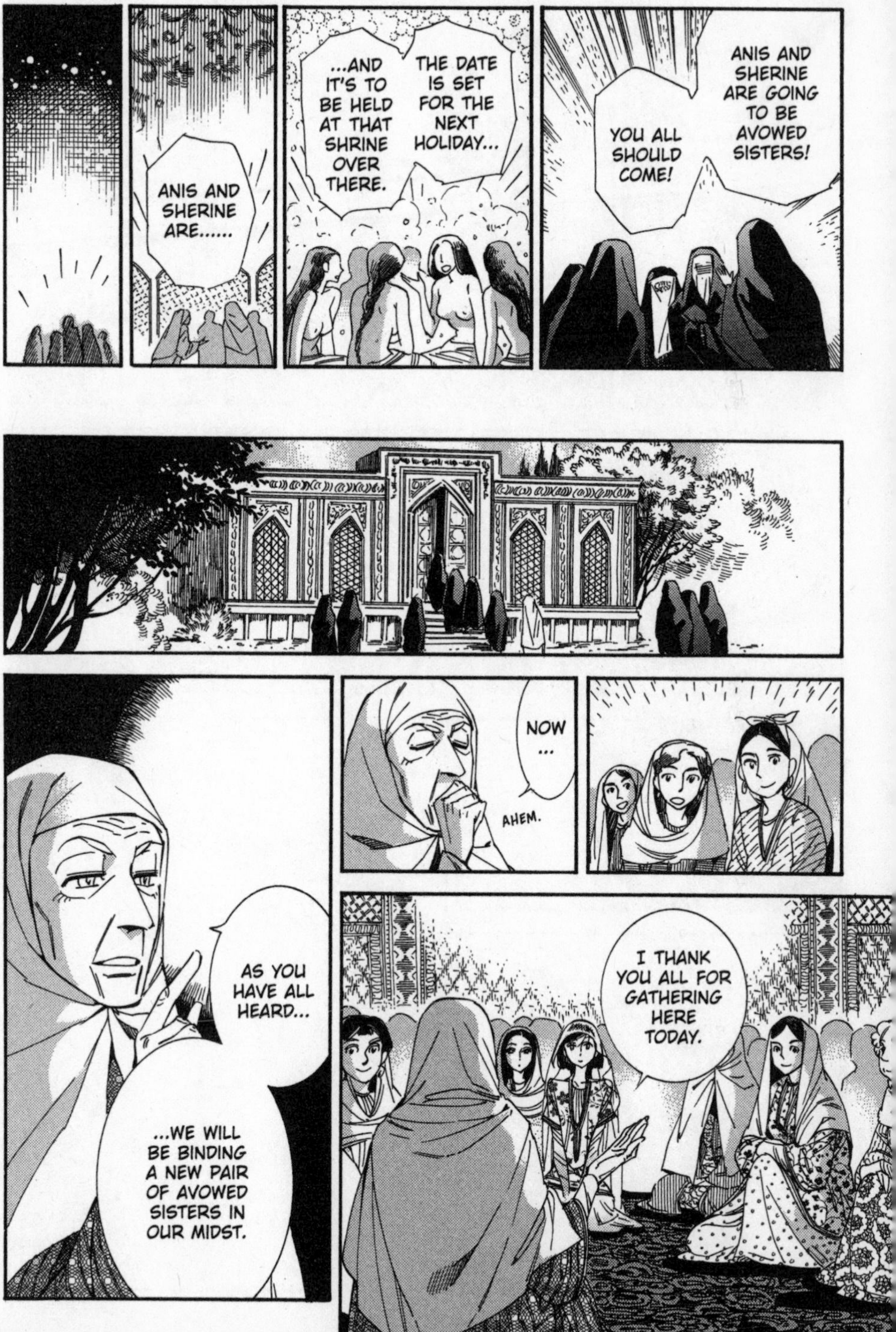
ANIS AND SHERINE ARE GOING TO BE AVOWED SISTERS!
YOU ALL SHOULD COME!
THE DATE IS SET FOR THE NEXT HOLIDAY...
...AND IT'S TO BE HELD AT THAT SHRINE OVER THERE.
ANIS AND SHERINE ARE......
NOW ...
AHEM.
I THANK YOU ALL FOR GATHERING HERE TODAY.
AS YOU HAVE ALL HEARD...
...WE WILL BE BINDING A NEW PAIR OF AVOWED SISTERS IN OUR MIDST.

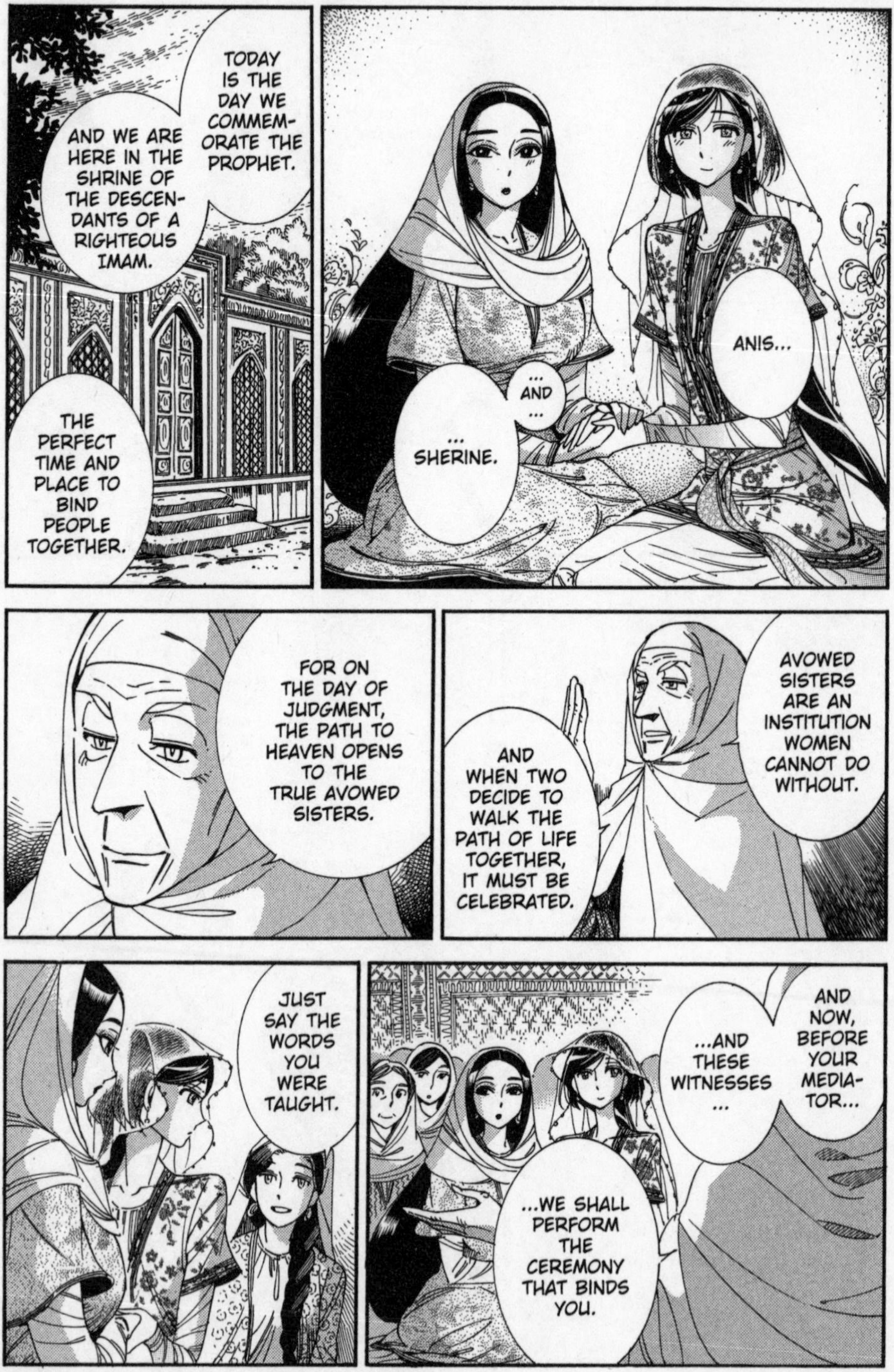
ANIS...
...AND...
...SHERINE.
TODAY IS THE DAY WE COMMEMORATE THE PROPHET.
AND WE ARE HERE IN THE SHRINE OF THE DESCENDANTS OF A RIGHTEOUS IMAM.
THE PERFECT TIME AND PLACE TO BIND PEOPLE TOGETHER.
AVOWED SISTERS ARE AN INSTITUTION WOMEN CANNOT DO WITHOUT.
AND WHEN TWO DECIDE TO WALK THE PATH OF LIFE TOGETHER, IT MUST BE CELEBRATED.
FOR ON THE DAY OF JUDGMENT, THE PATH TO HEAVEN OPENS TO THE TRUE AVOWED SISTERS.
AND NOW, BEFORE YOUR MEDIATOR...
...AND THESE WITNESSES...
...WE SHALL PERFORM THE CEREMONY THAT BINDS YOU.
JUST SAY THE WORDS YOU WERE TAUGHT.

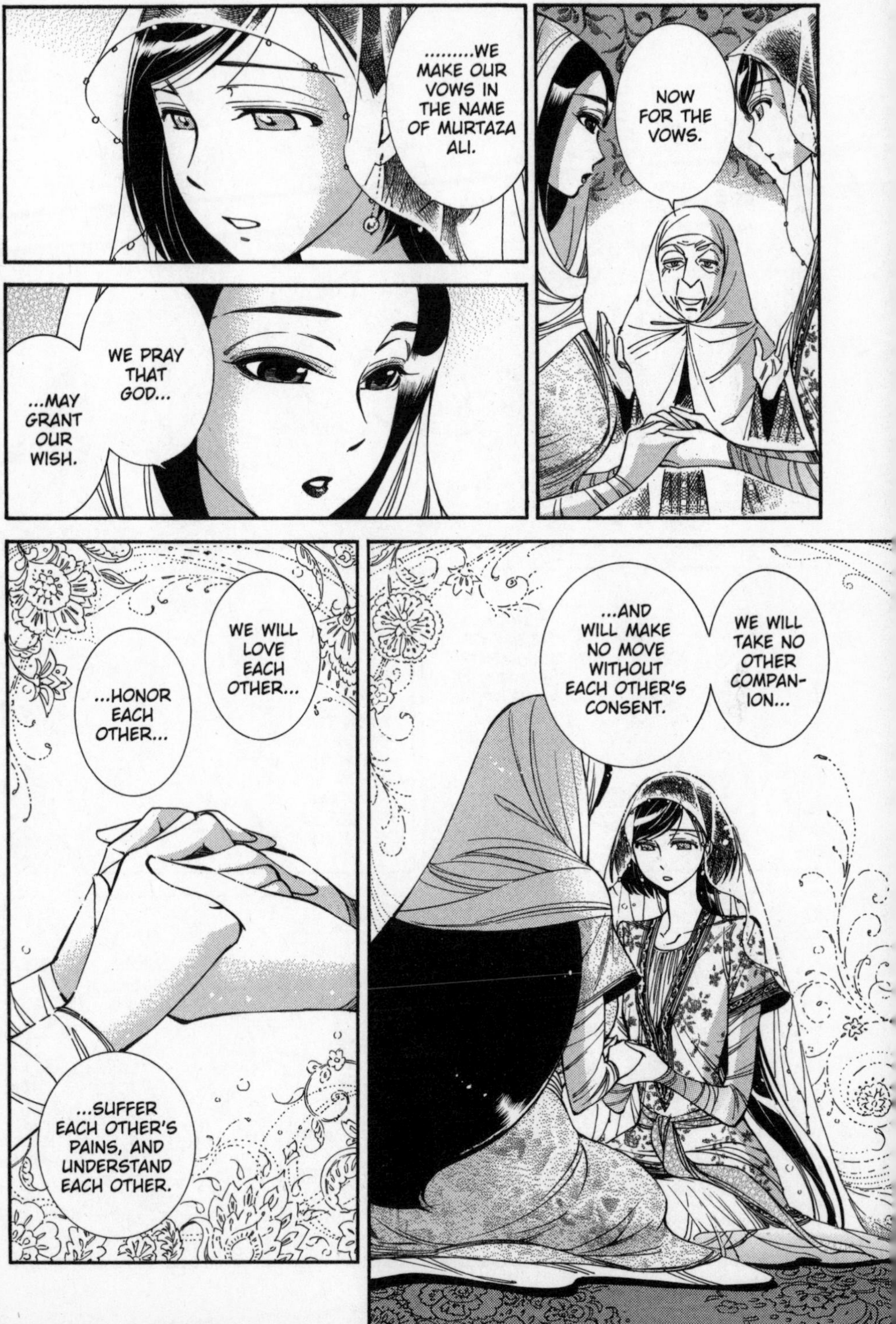
NOW FOR THE VOWS.
.........WE MAKE OUR VOWS IN THE NAME OF MURTAZA ALI.
WE PRAY THAT GOD...
...MAY GRANT OUR WISH.
WE WILL TAKE NO OTHER COMPANION...
...AND WILL MAKE NO MOVE WITHOUT EACH OTHER'S CONSENT.
WE WILL LOVE EACH OTHER...
...HONOR EACH OTHER...
...SUFFER EACH OTHER'S PAINS, AND UNDERSTAND EACH OTHER.

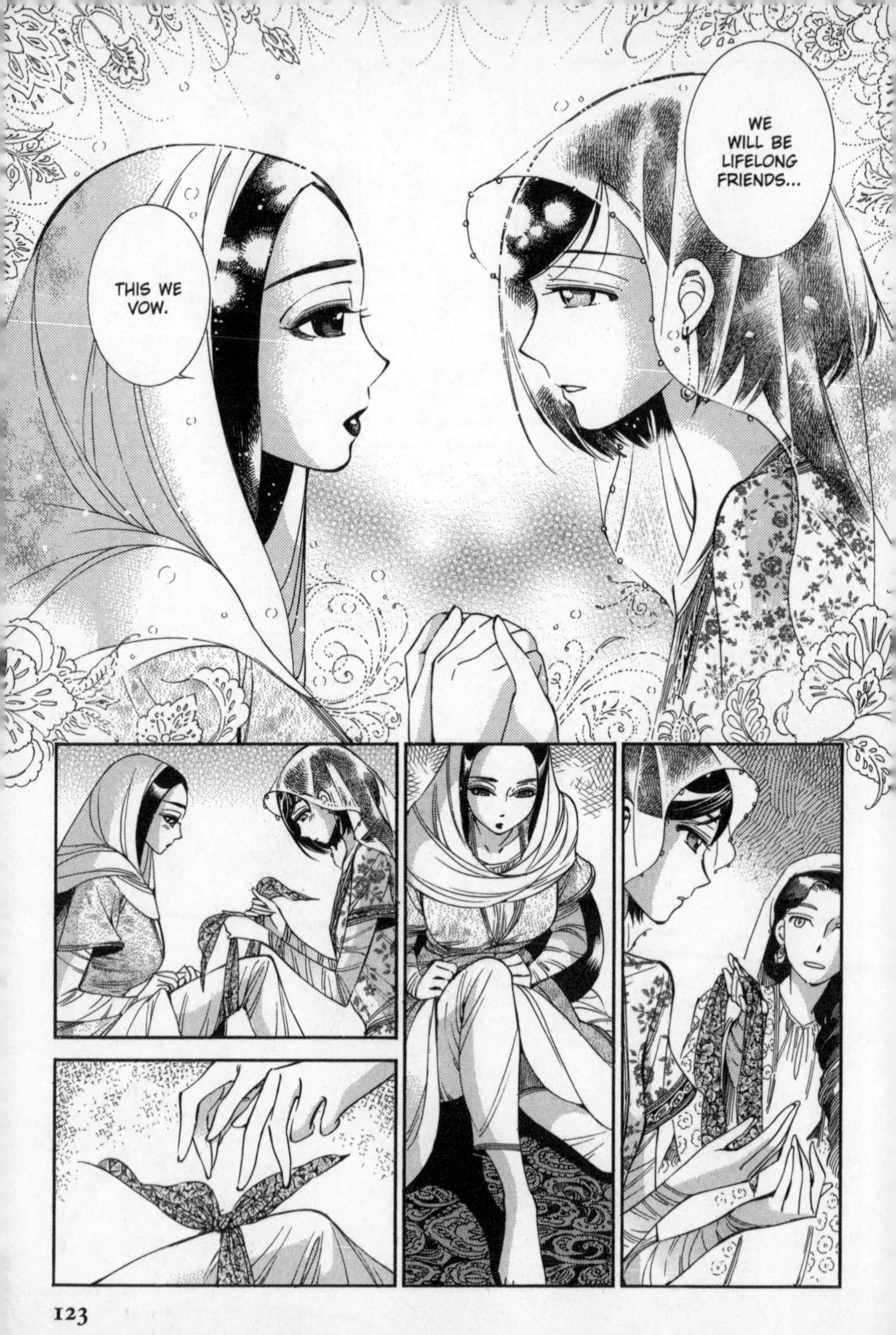
WE WILL BE LIFELONG FRIENDS...
THIS WE VOW.

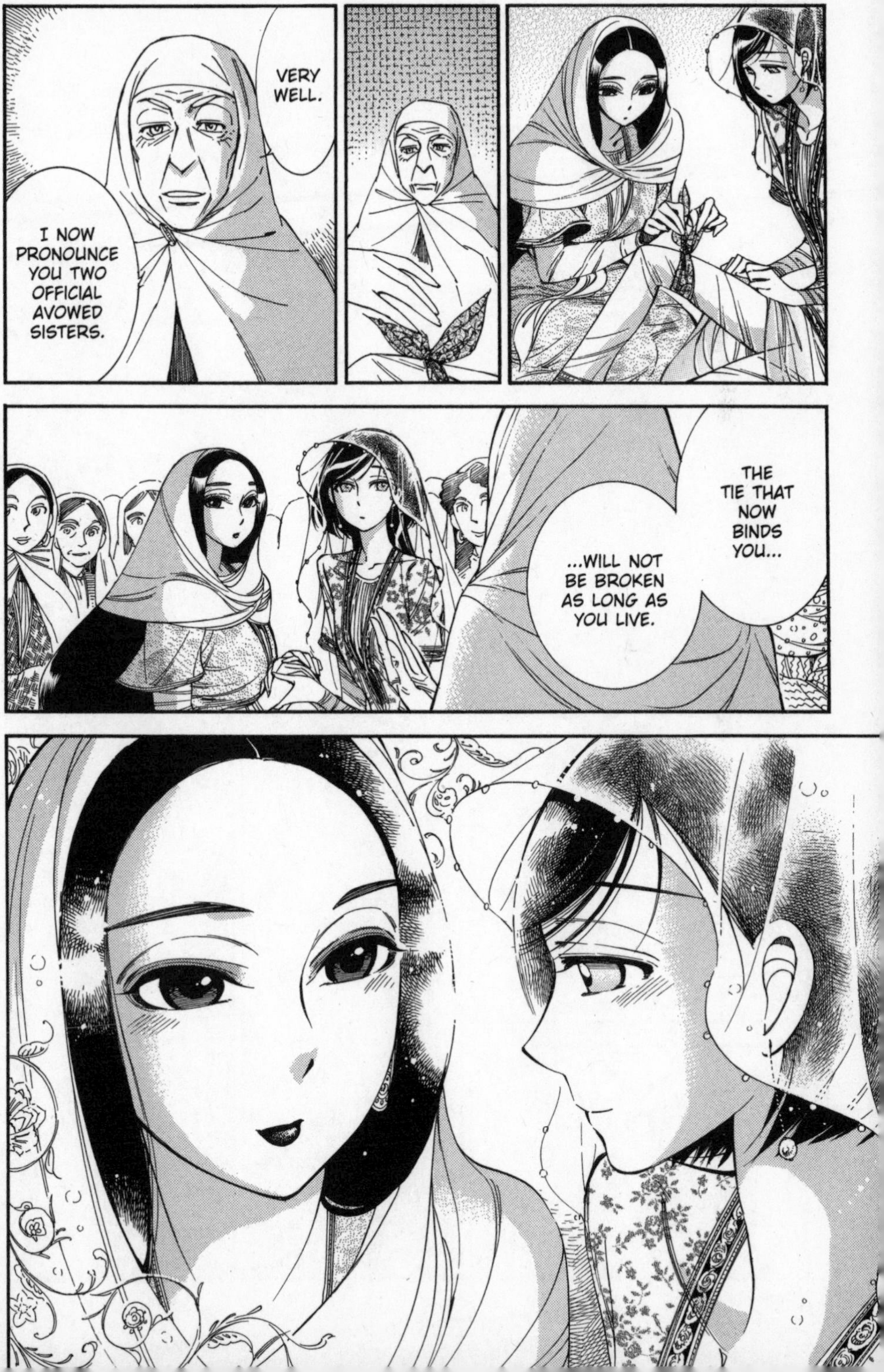
VERY WELL.
I NOW PRONOUNCE YOU TWO OFFICIAL AVOWED SISTERS.
THE TIE THAT NOW BINDS YOU...
...WILL NOT BE BROKEN AS LONG AS YOU LIVE.

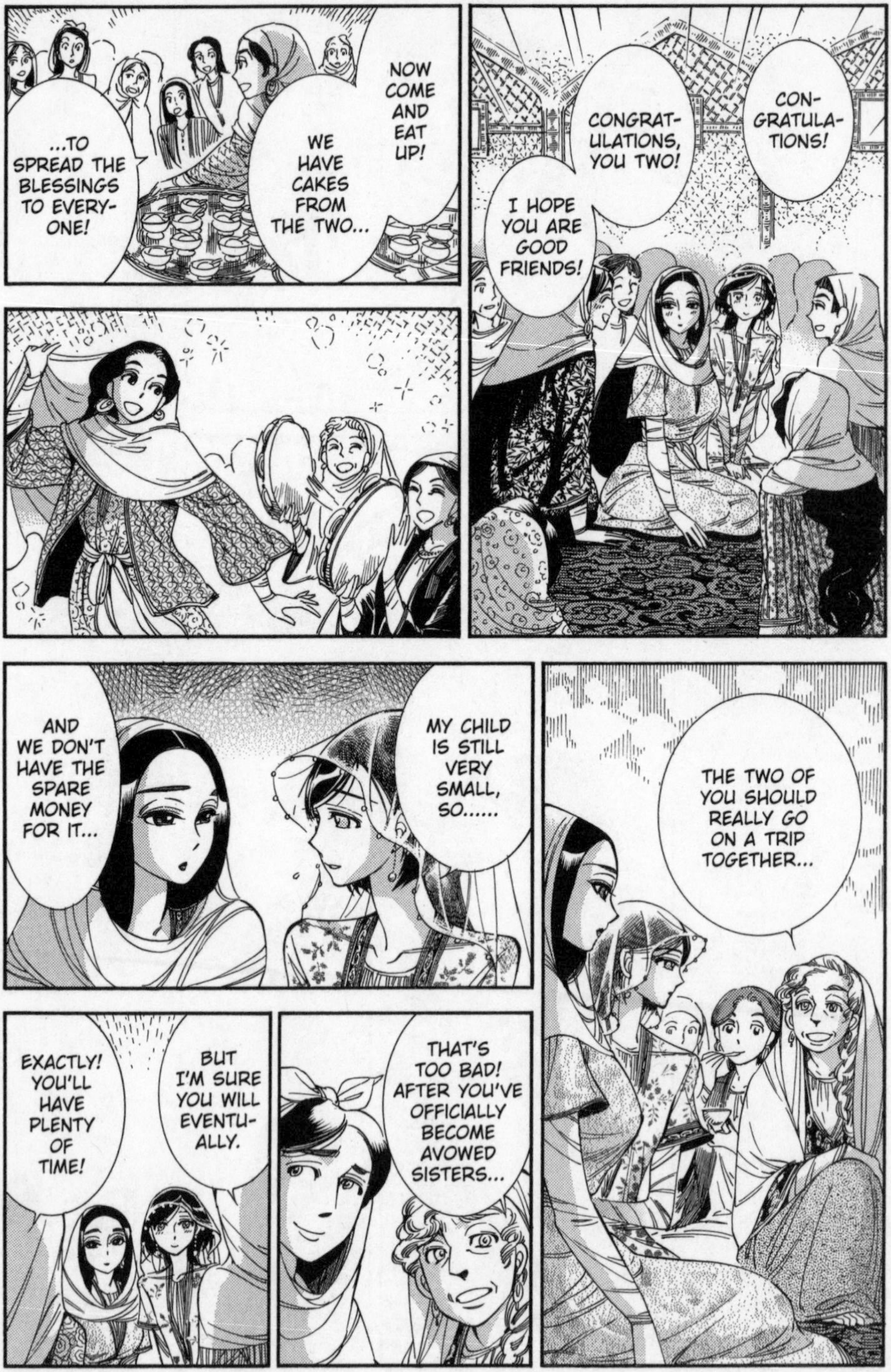
CON-GRATULA-TIONS!
CONGRAT-ULATIONS, YOU TWO!
I HOPE YOU ARE GOOD FRIENDS!
NOW COME AND EAT UP!
WE HAVE CAKES FROM THE TWO...
...TO SPREAD THE BLESSINGS TO EVERY-ONE!
THE TWO OF YOU SHOULD REALLY GO ON A TRIP TOGETHER...
MY CHILD IS STILL VERY SMALL, SO......
AND WE DON'T HAVE THE SPARE MONEY FOR IT...
THAT'S TOO BAD! AFTER YOU'VE OFFICIALLY BECOME AVOWED SISTERS...
BUT I'M SURE YOU WILL EVENTU-ALLY.
EXACTLY! YOU'LL HAVE PLENTY OF TIME!

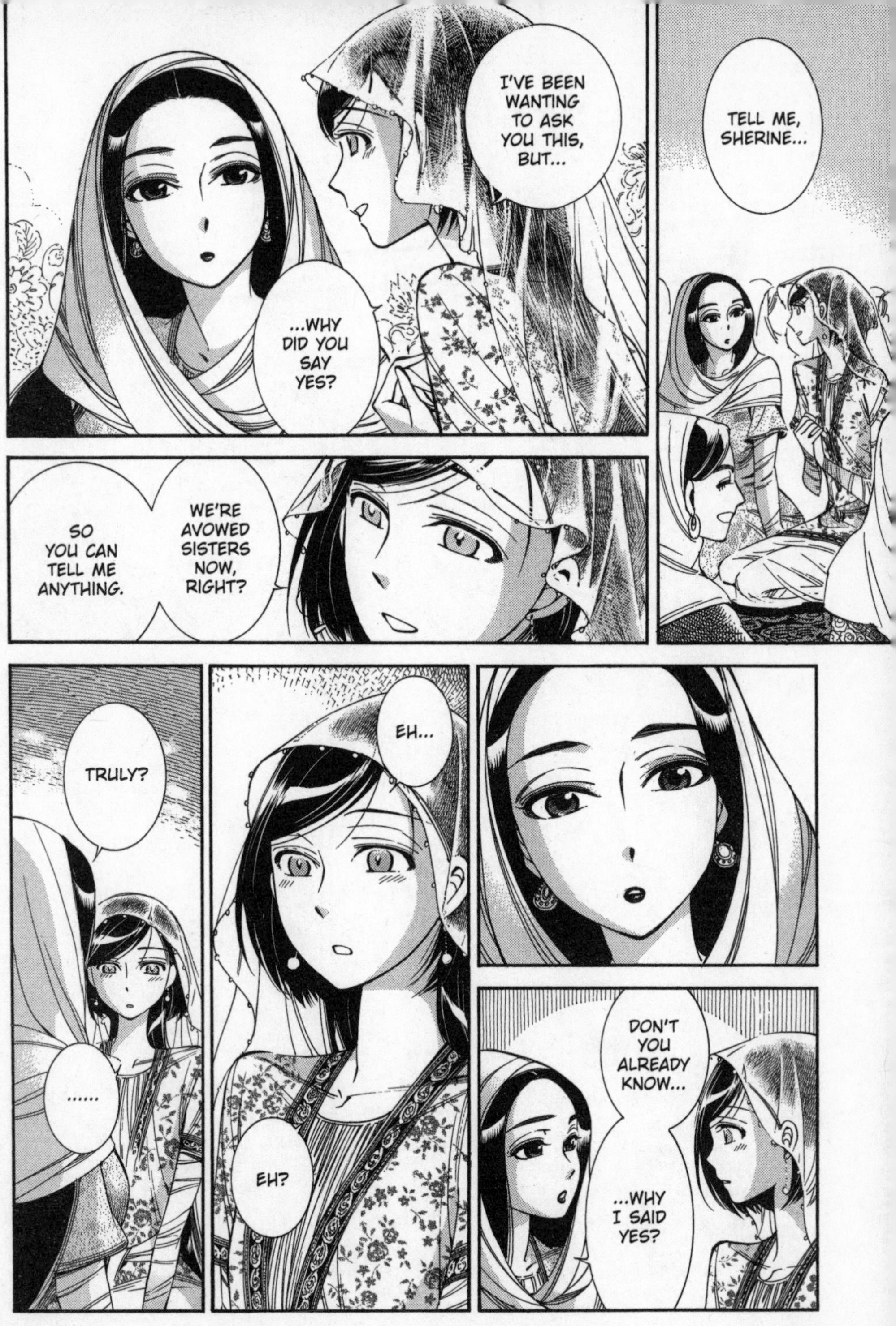
TELL ME, SHERINE...
I'VE BEEN WANTING TO ASK YOU THIS, BUT...
...WHY DID YOU SAY YES?
WE'RE AVOWED SISTERS NOW, RIGHT?
SO YOU CAN TELL ME ANYTHING.
DON'T YOU ALREADY KNOW...
...WHY I SAID YES?
EH...
EH?
TRULY?
......

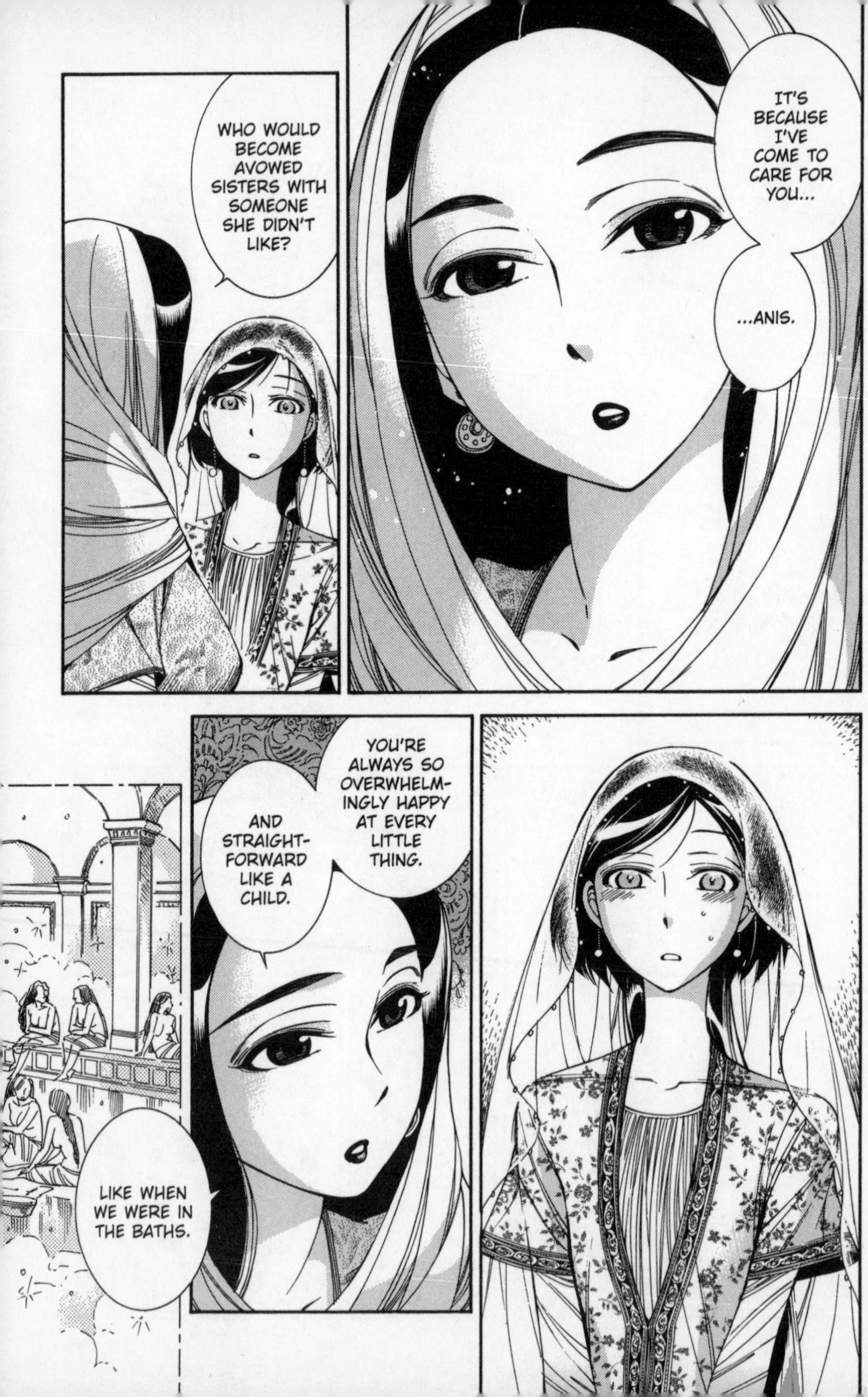
IT'S BECAUSE I'VE COME TO CARE FOR YOU...
...ANIS.
WHO WOULD BECOME AVOWED SISTERS WITH SOMEONE SHE DIDN'T LIKE?
YOU'RE ALWAYS SO OVERWHELMINGLY HAPPY AT EVERY LITTLE THING.
AND STRAIGHTFORWARD LIKE A CHILD.
LIKE WHEN WE WERE IN THE BATHS.

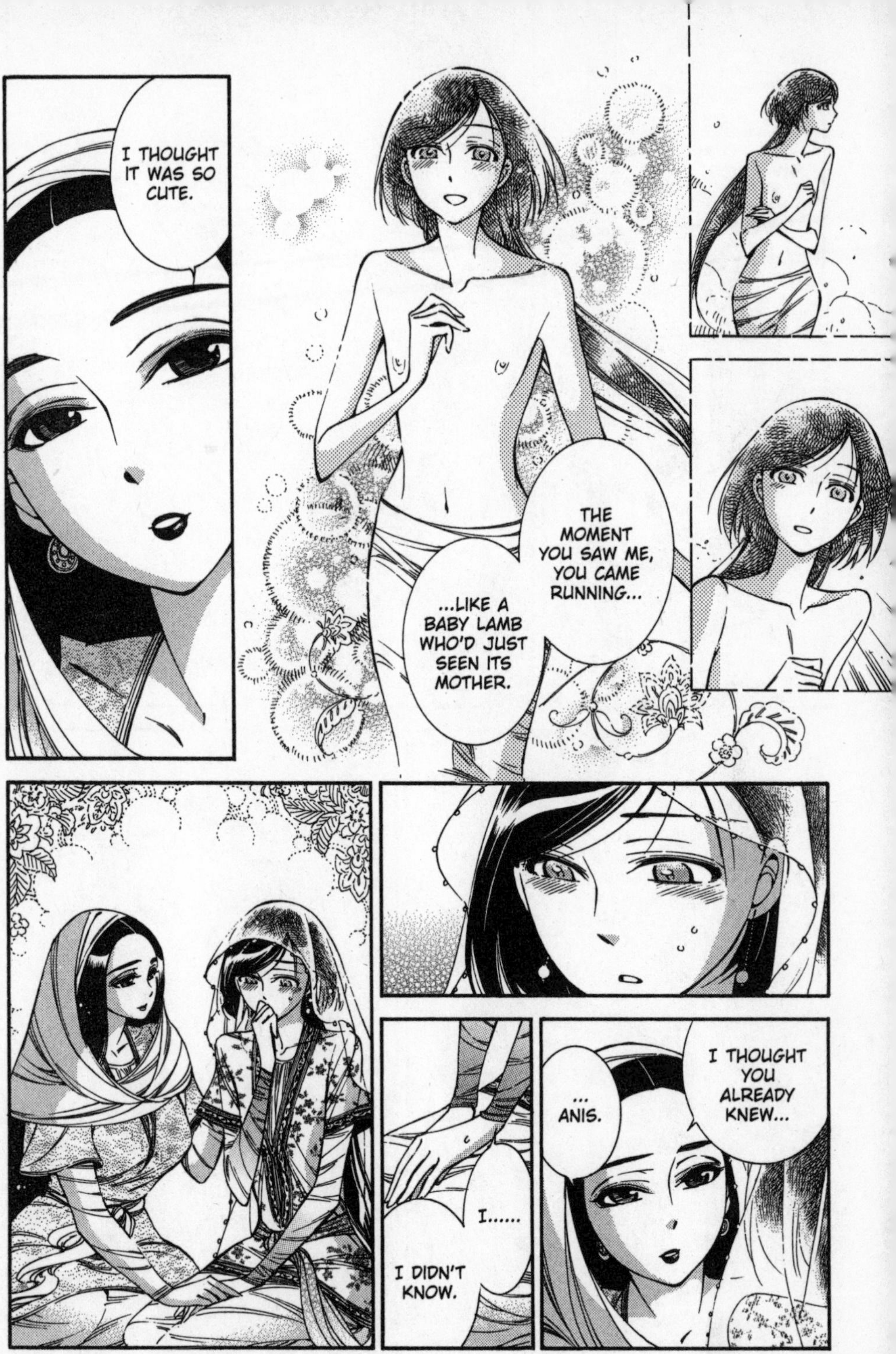
THE MOMENT YOU SAW ME, YOU CAME RUNNING...
...LIKE A BABY LAMB WHO'D JUST SEEN ITS MOTHER.
I THOUGHT IT WAS SO CUTE.
I THOUGHT YOU ALREADY KNEW...
... ANIS.
I......
I DIDN'T KNOW.

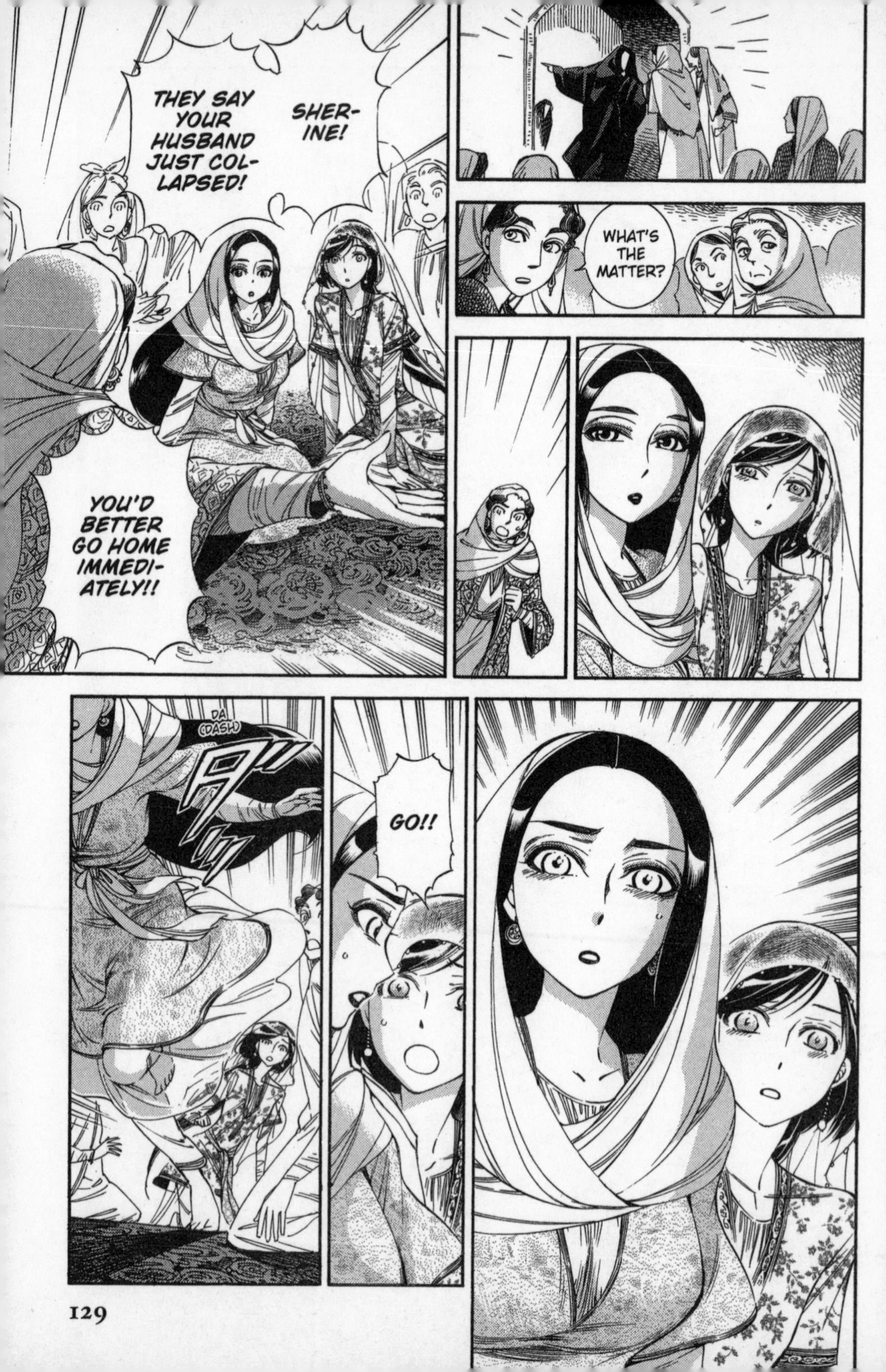
WHAT'S THE MATTER?
SHER-INE!
THEY SAY YOUR HUSBAND JUST COL-LAPSED!
YOU'D BETTER GO HOME IMMEDI-ATELY!!
GO!!
DA (DASH)

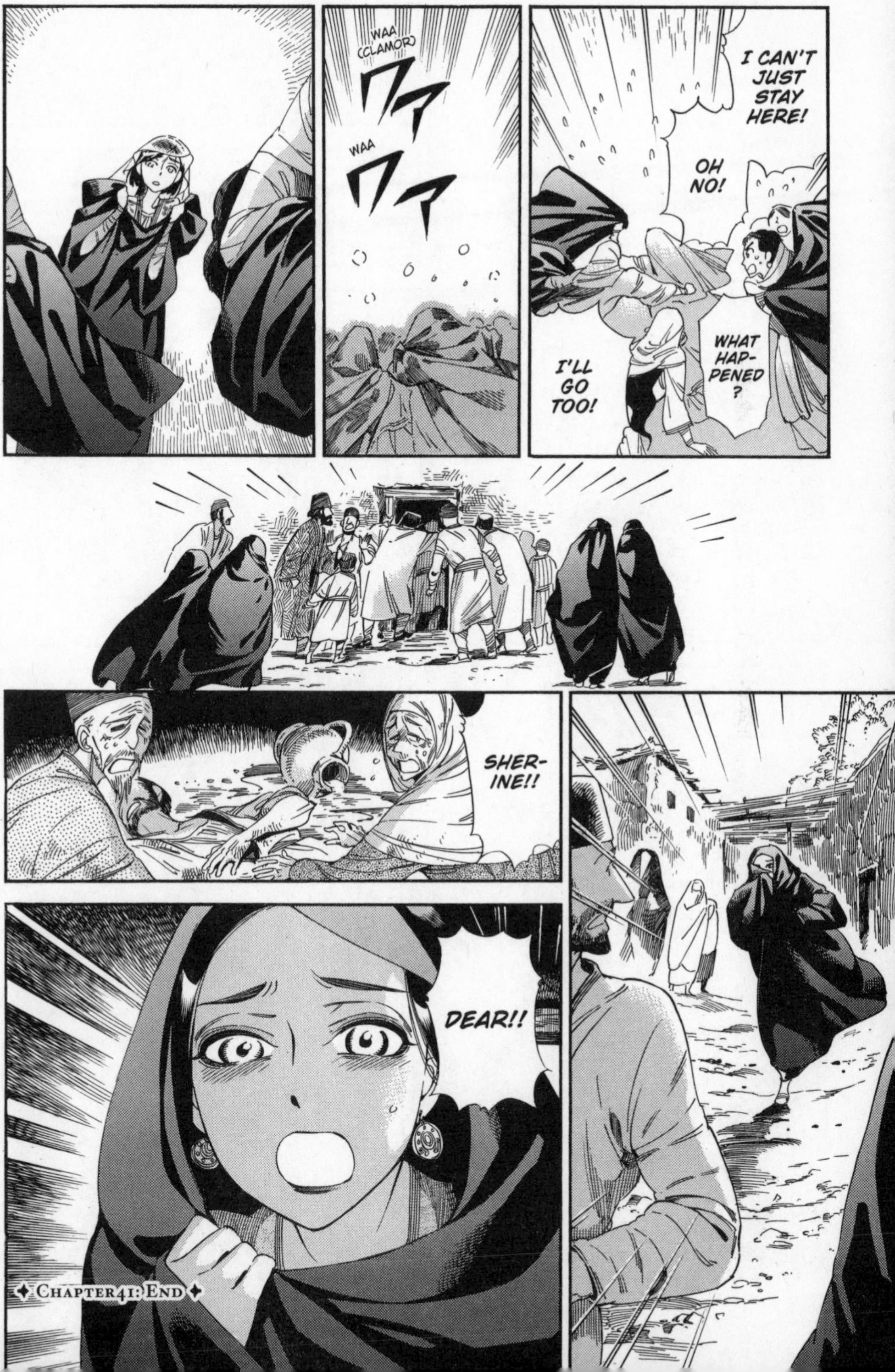
I CAN'T JUST STAY HERE!
OH NO!
WHAT HAP-PENED?
I'LL GO TOO!
WAA (CLAMOR)
ワア
WAA
ワア
SHER-INE!!
DEAR!!
Chapter 41: End

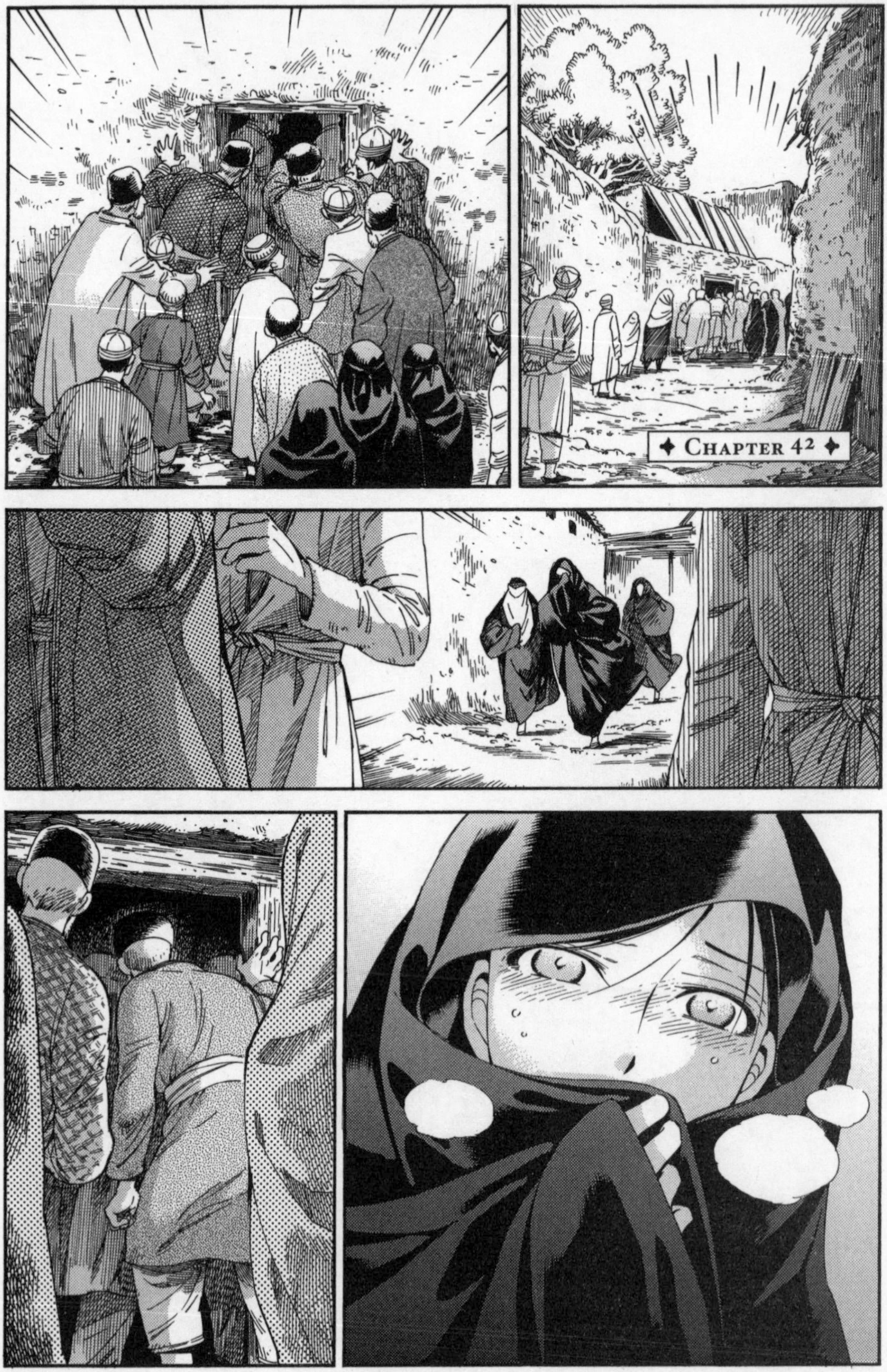
✦ Chapter 42 ✦

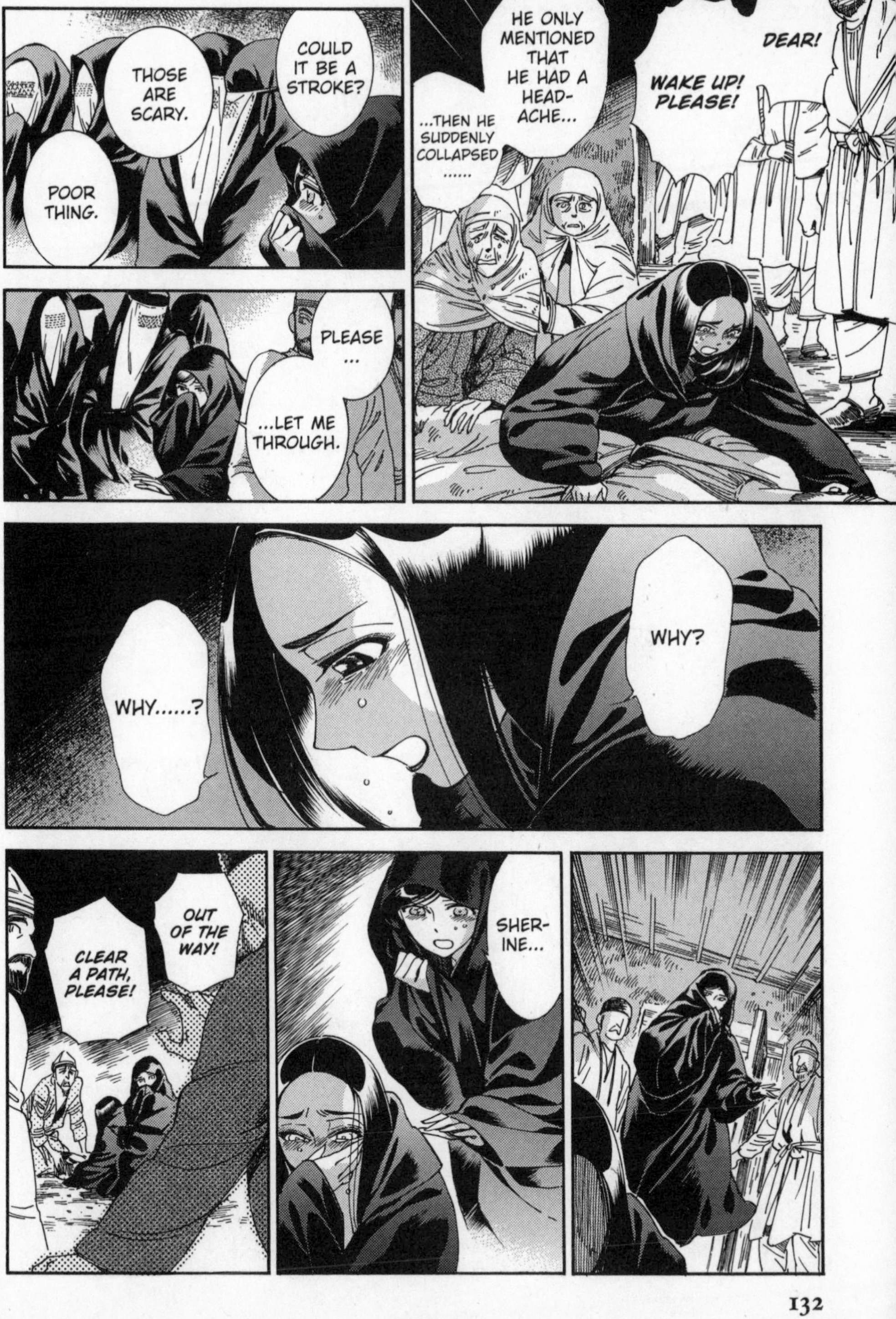
DEAR!
WAKE UP! PLEASE!
HE ONLY MENTIONED THAT HE HAD A HEAD-ACHE...
...THEN HE SUDDENLY COLLAPSED ......
COULD IT BE A STROKE?
THOSE ARE SCARY.
POOR THING.
PLEASE ...
...LET ME THROUGH.
WHY?
WHY......?
SHER-INE...
OUT OF THE WAY!
CLEAR A PATH, PLEASE!

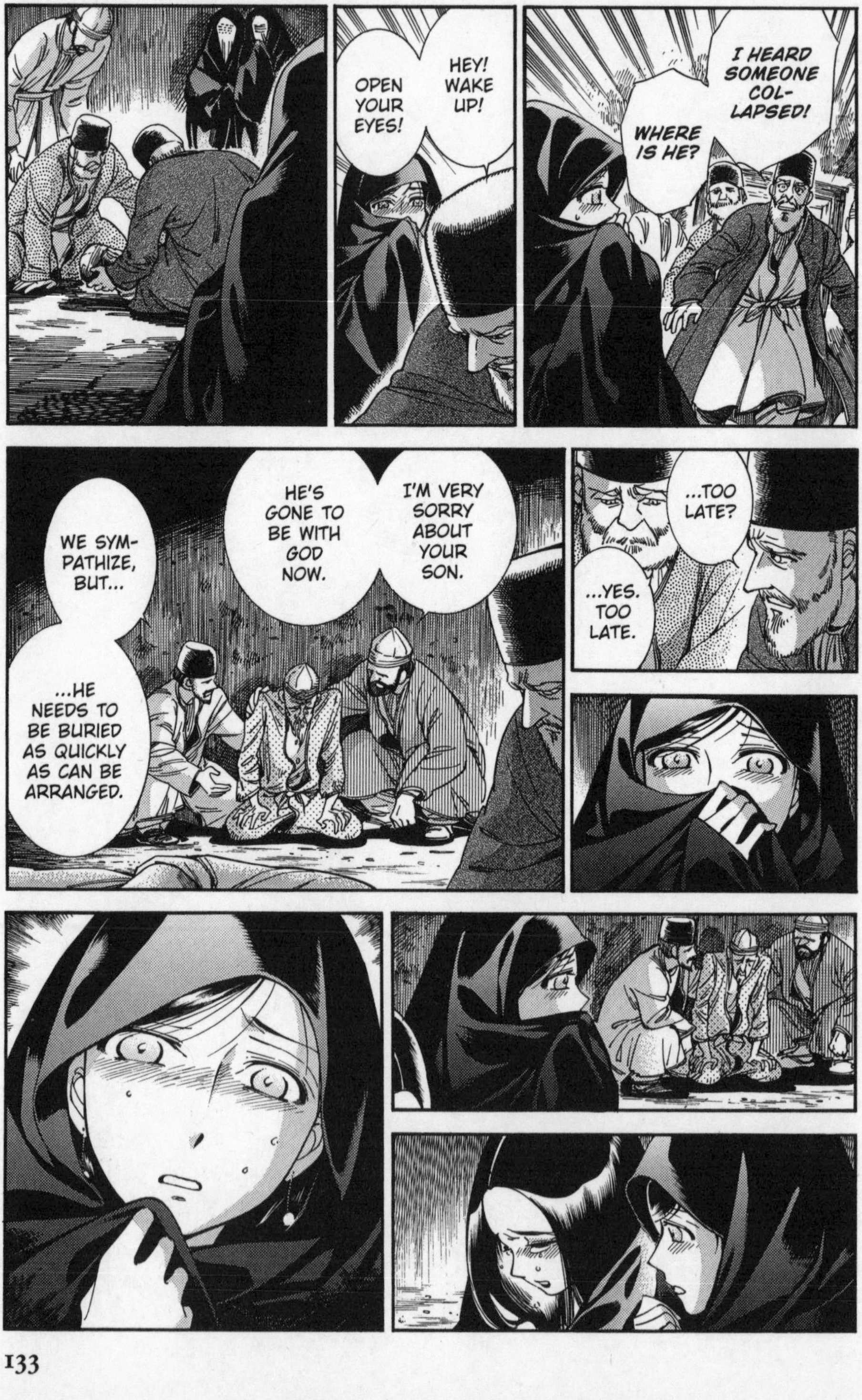
I HEARD SOMEONE COL-LAPSED!
WHERE IS HE?
HEY! WAKE UP!
OPEN YOUR EYES!
...TOO LATE?
...YES. TOO LATE.
I'M VERY SORRY ABOUT YOUR SON.
HE'S GONE TO BE WITH GOD NOW.
WE SYM-PATHIZE, BUT...
...HE NEEDS TO BE BURIED AS QUICKLY AS CAN BE ARRANGED.

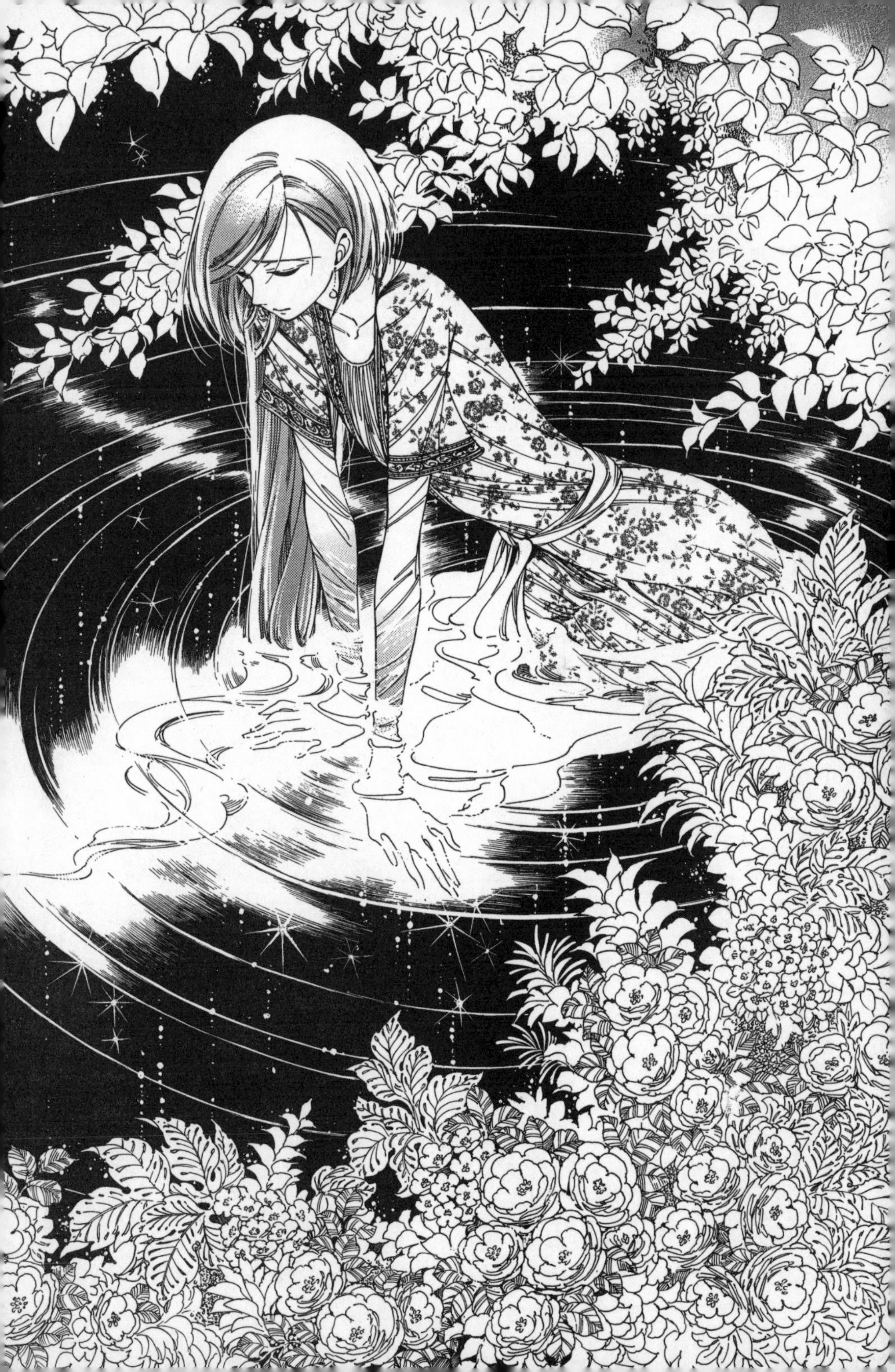

Chapter 42
If It's You

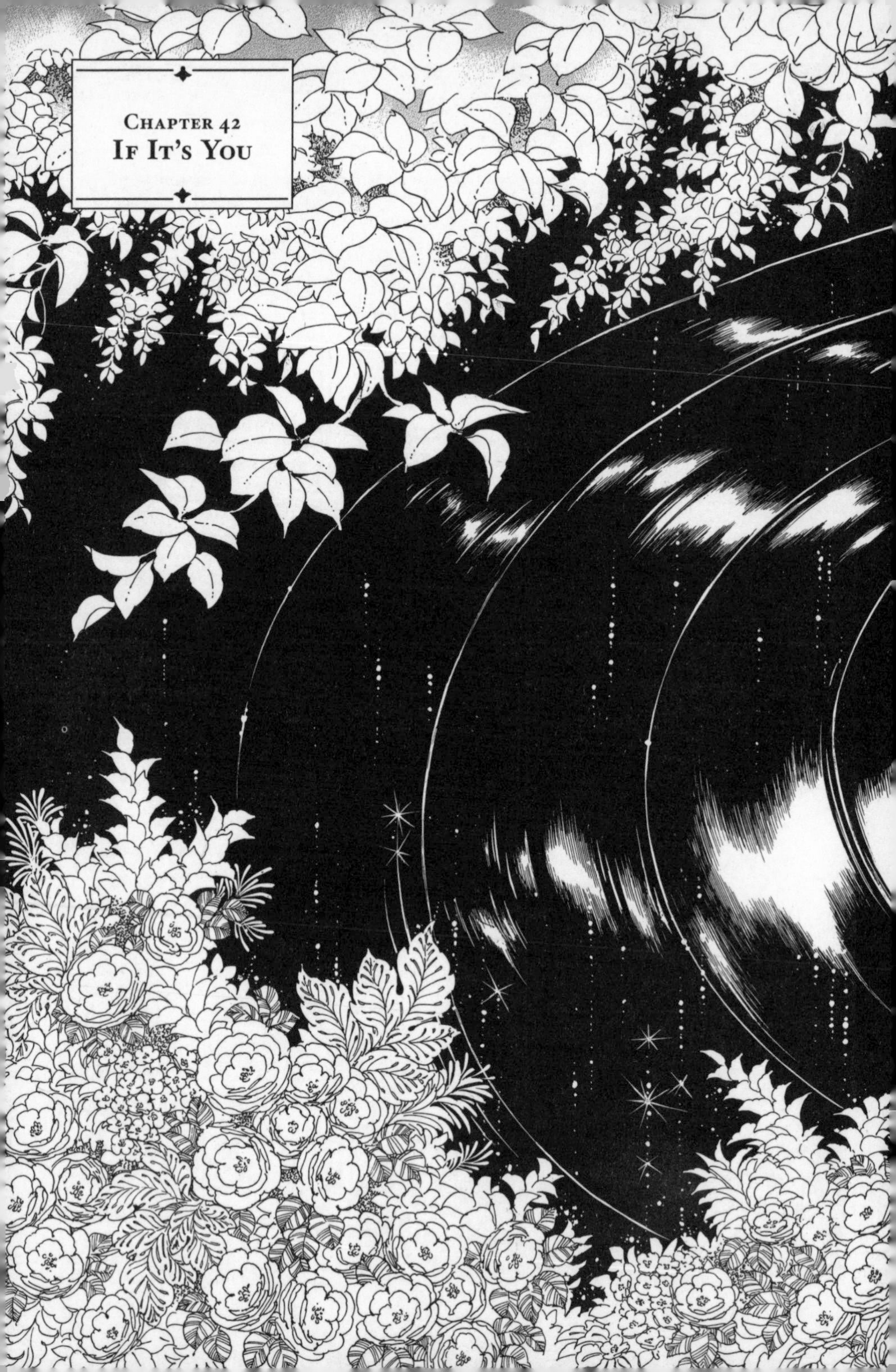

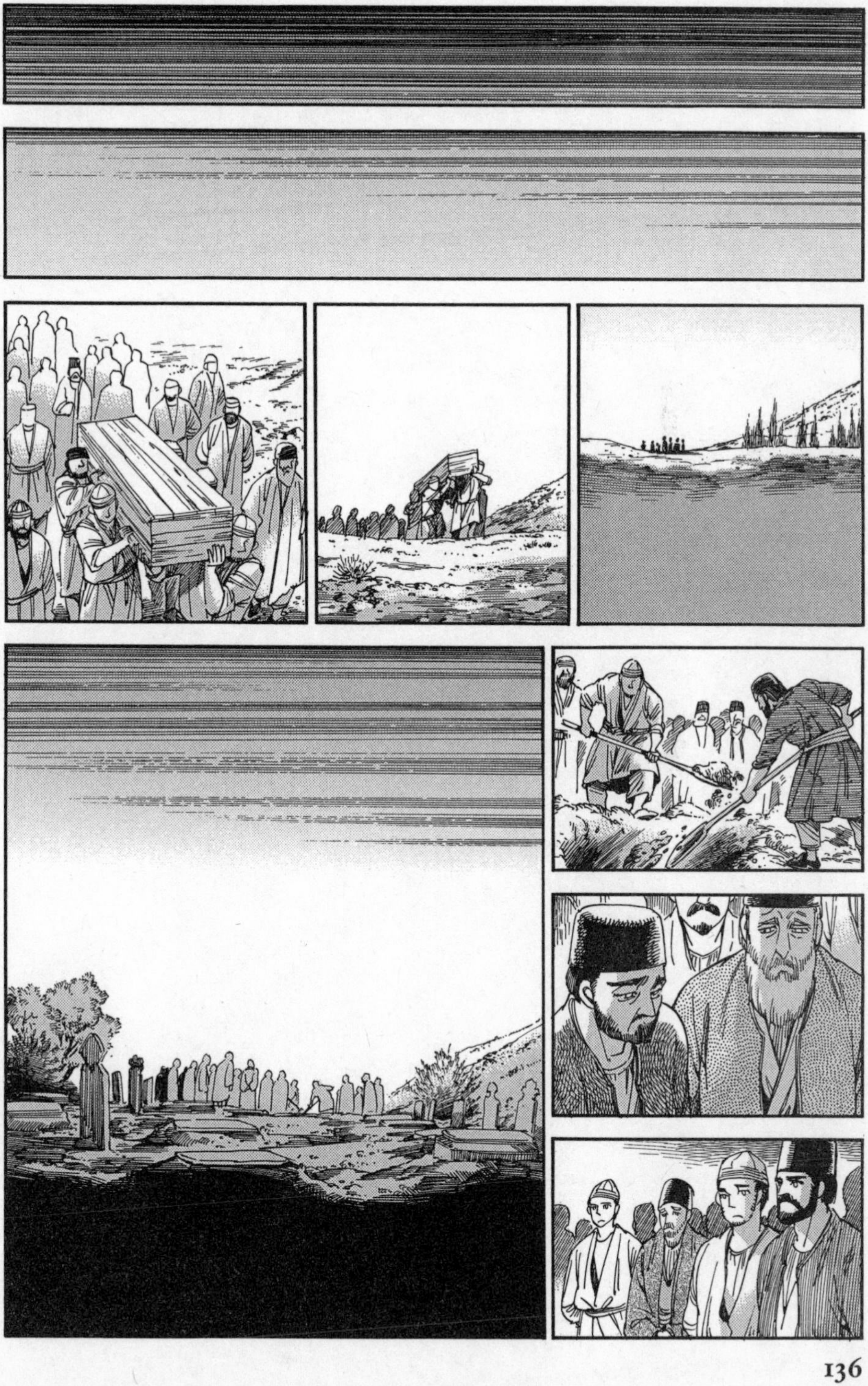

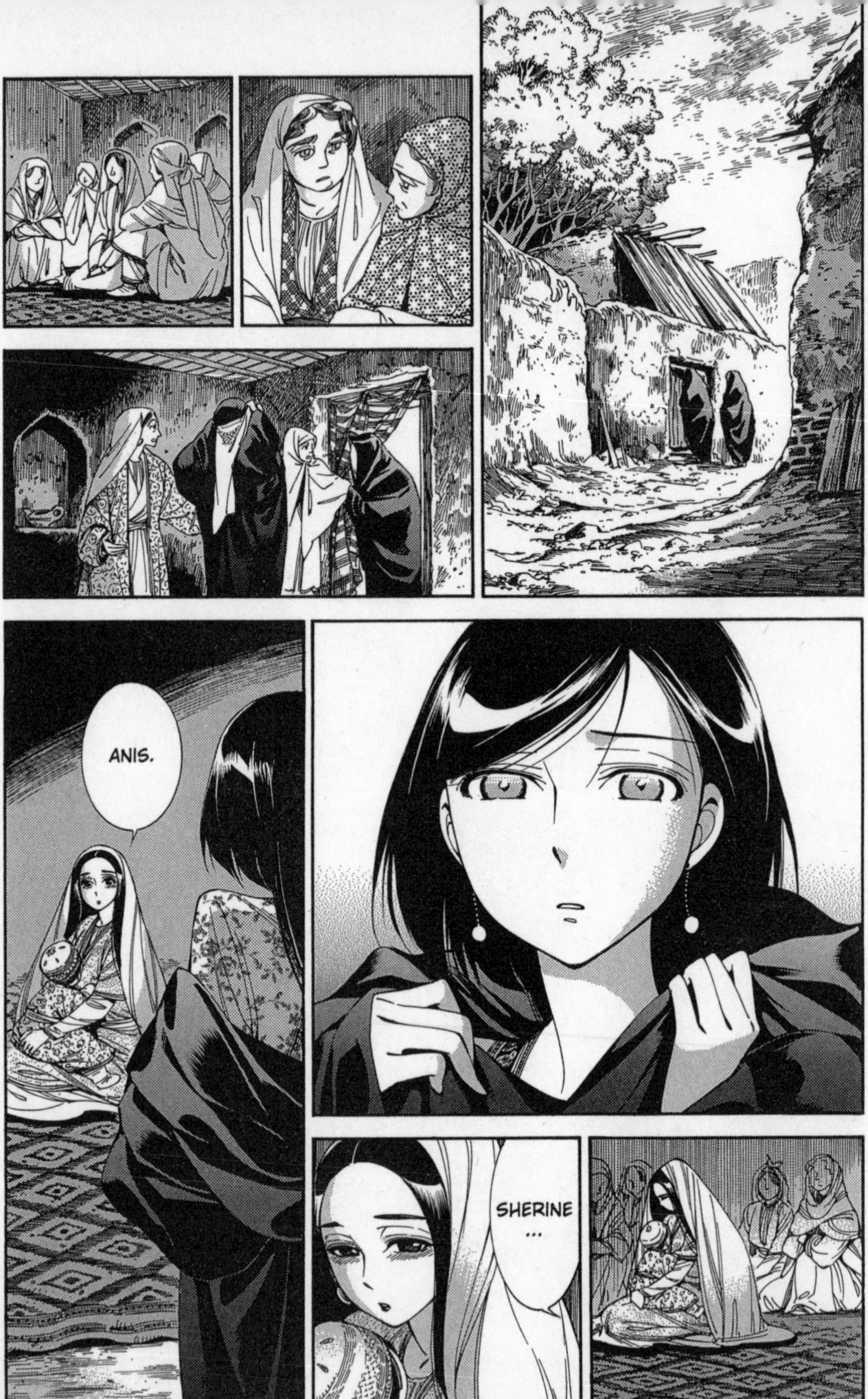
SHERINE
...
ANIS.

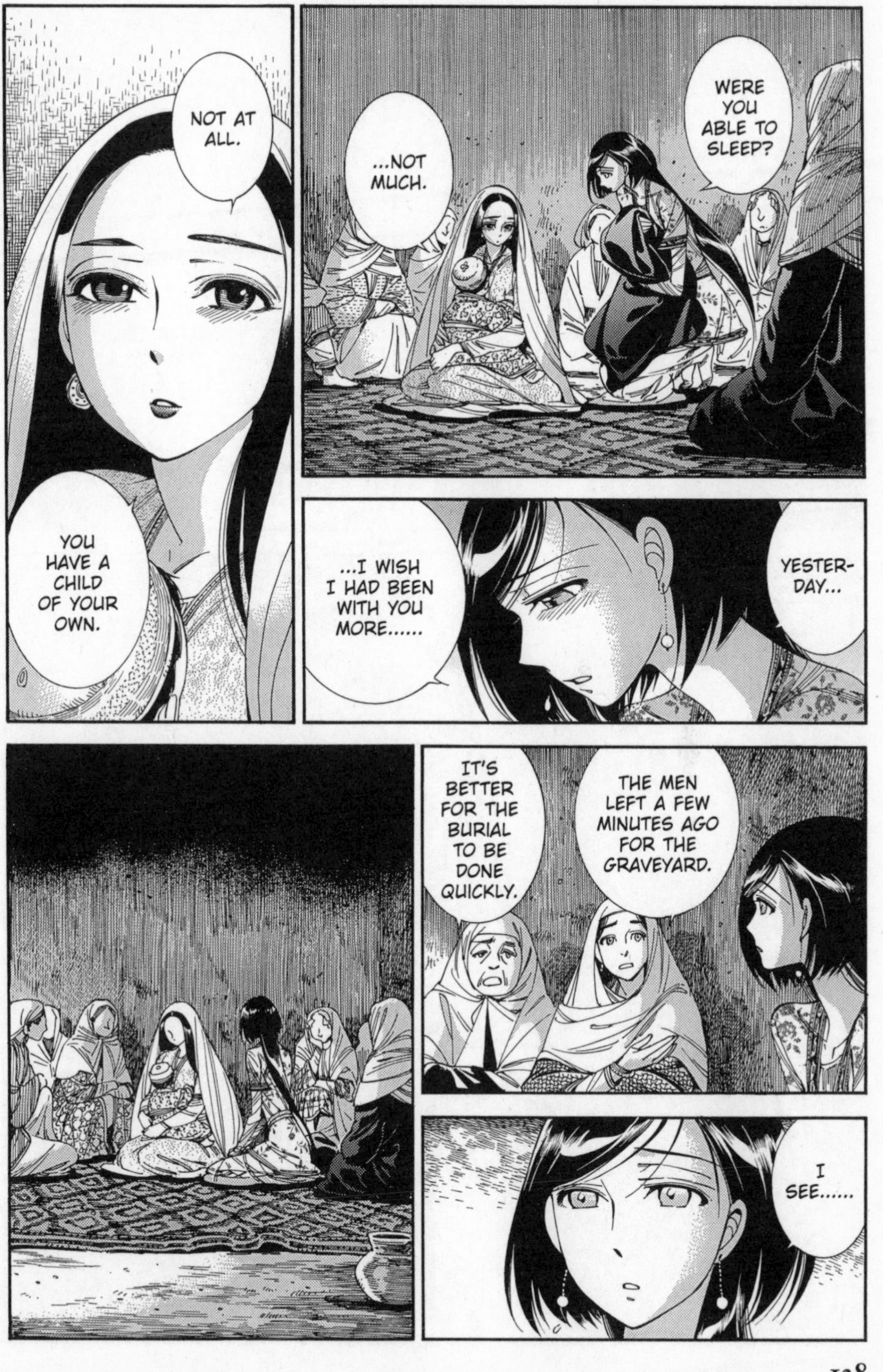
WERE YOU ABLE TO SLEEP?
...NOT MUCH.
YESTER-DAY...
...I WISH I HAD BEEN WITH YOU MORE......
NOT AT ALL.
YOU HAVE A CHILD OF YOUR OWN.
THE MEN LEFT A FEW MINUTES AGO FOR THE GRAVEYARD.
IT'S BETTER FOR THE BURIAL TO BE DONE QUICKLY.
I SEE......

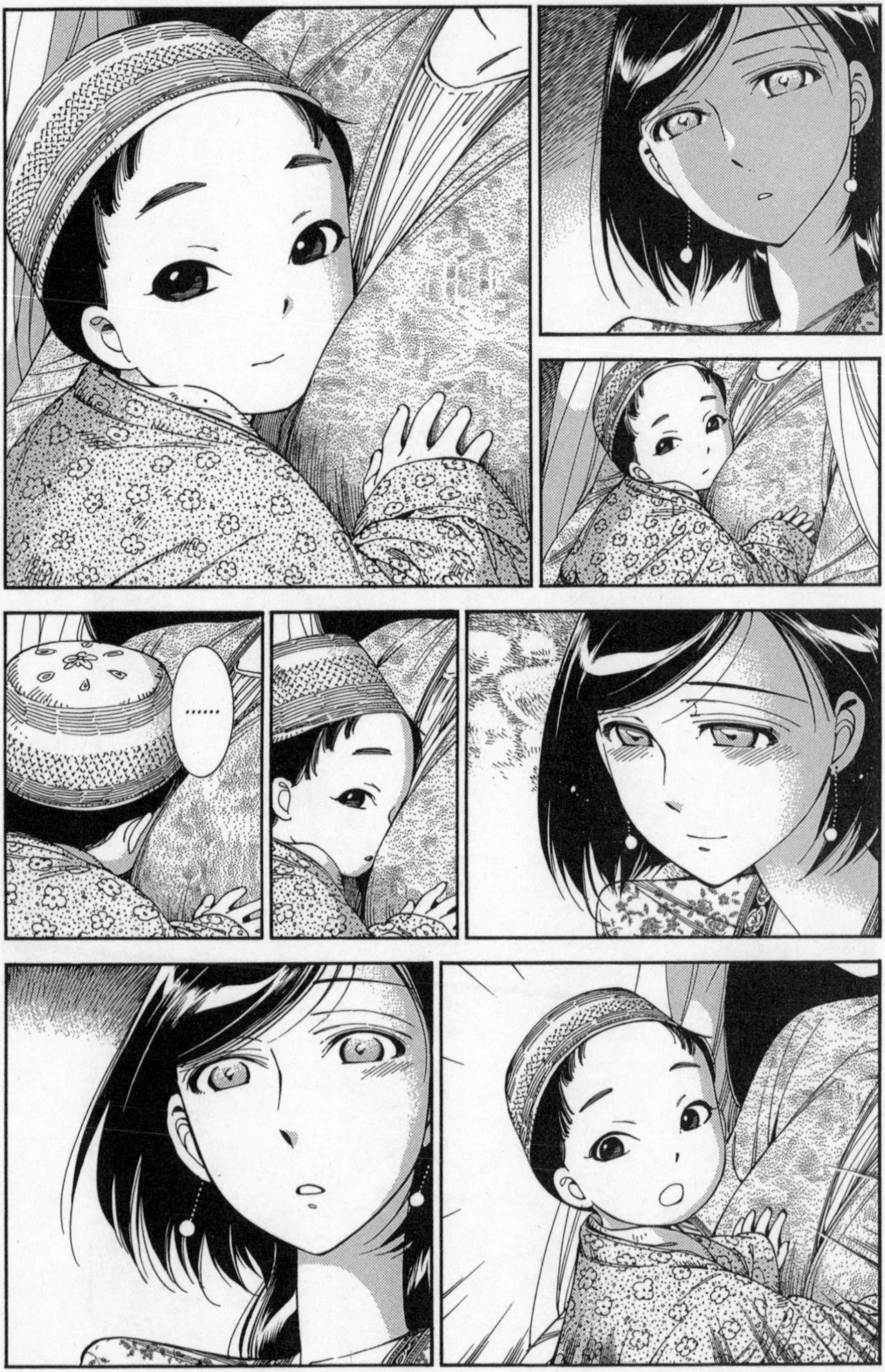
......

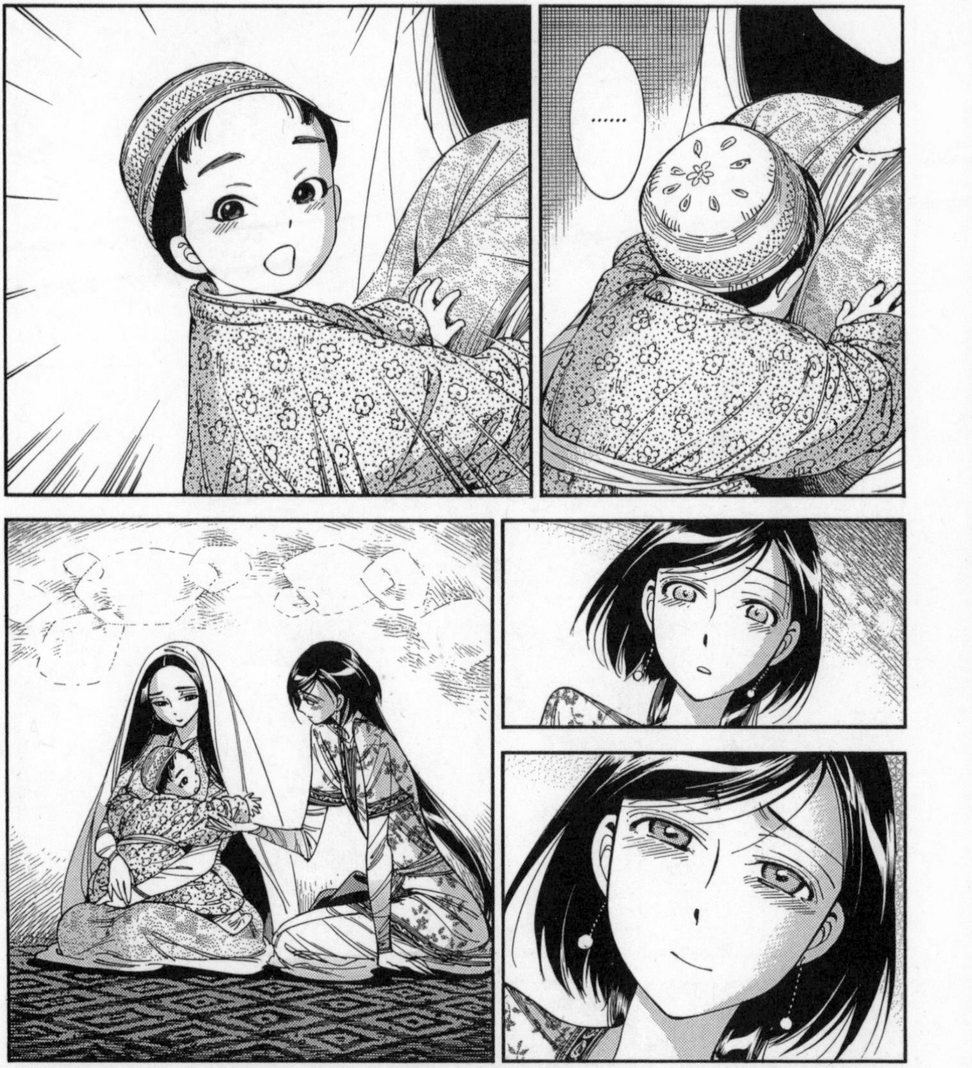
......
WHAT WILL HAPPEN TO YOU NOW?
CAN YOU MANAGE?

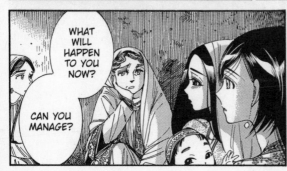

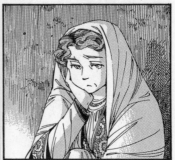

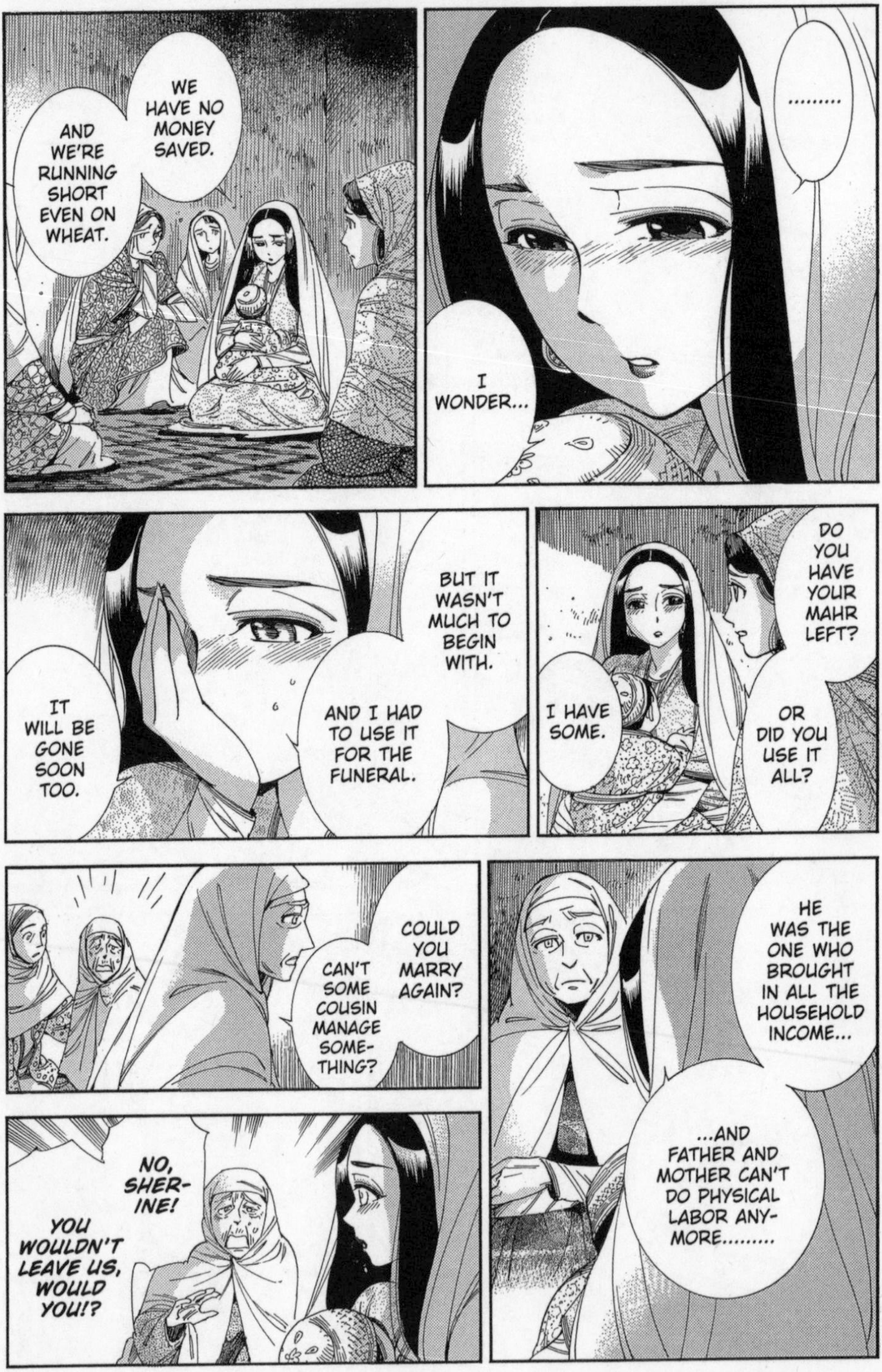
....
I WONDER...
WE HAVE NO MONEY SAVED.
AND WE'RE RUNNING SHORT EVEN ON WHEAT.
DO YOU HAVE YOUR MAHR LEFT?
OR DID YOU USE IT ALL?
I HAVE SOME.
BUT IT WASN'T MUCH TO BEGIN WITH.
AND I HAD TO USE IT FOR THE FUNERAL.
IT WILL BE GONE SOON TOO.
HE WAS THE ONE WHO BROUGHT IN ALL THE HOUSEHOLD INCOME...
...AND FATHER AND MOTHER CAN'T DO PHYSICAL LABOR ANY-MORE.........
COULD YOU MARRY AGAIN?
CAN'T SOME COUSIN MANAGE SOME-THING?
NO, SHER-INE!
YOU WOULDN'T LEAVE US, WOULD YOU!?

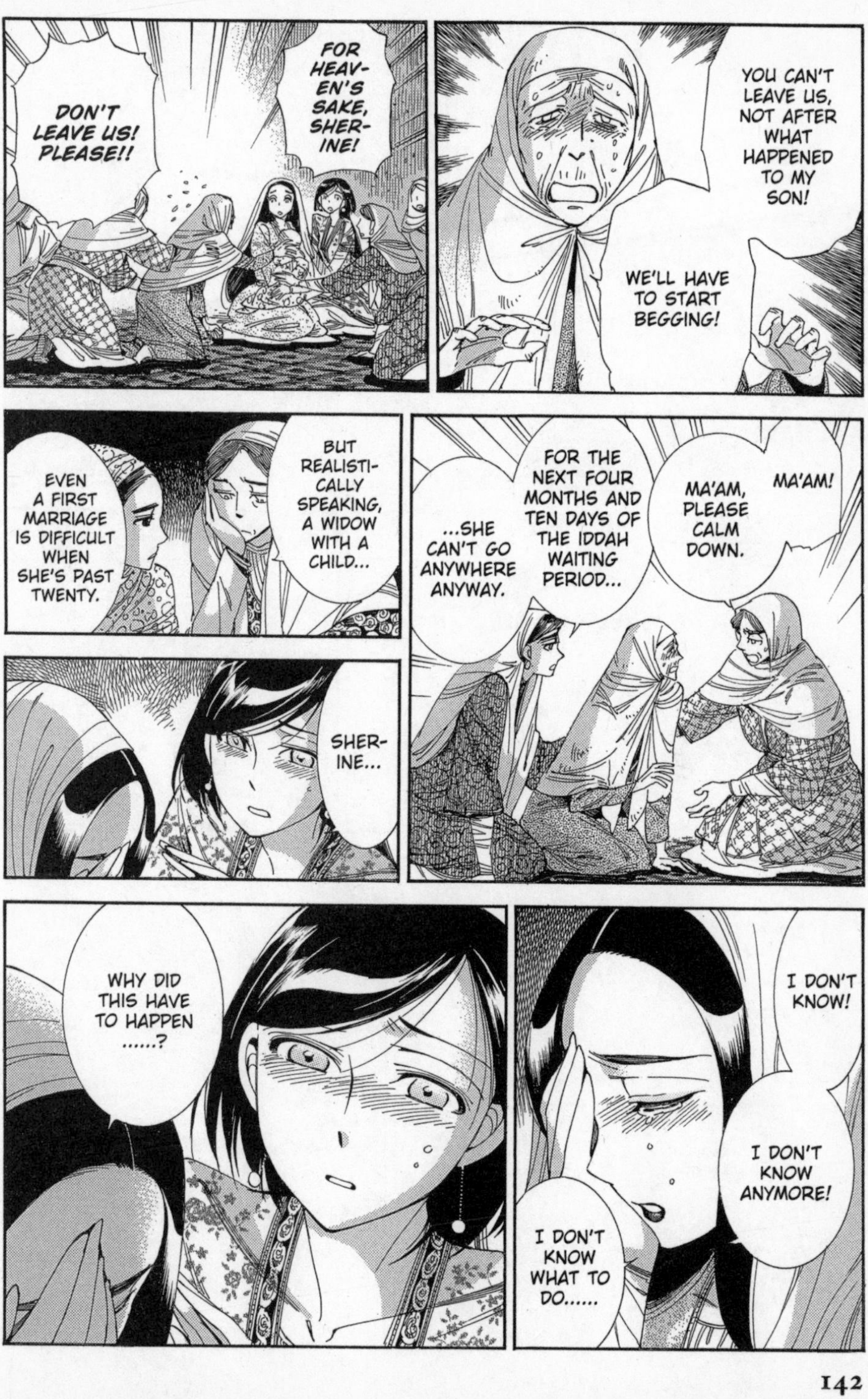
YOU CAN'T LEAVE US, NOT AFTER WHAT HAPPENED TO MY SON!
WE'LL HAVE TO START BEGGING!
FOR HEAVEN'S SAKE, SHERINE!
DON'T LEAVE US! PLEASE!!
MA'AM!
MA'AM, PLEASE CALM DOWN.
FOR THE NEXT FOUR MONTHS AND TEN DAYS OF THE IDDAH WAITING PERIOD...
...SHE CAN'T GO ANYWHERE ANYWAY.
BUT REALISTICALLY SPEAKING, A WIDOW WITH A CHILD...
EVEN A FIRST MARRIAGE IS DIFFICULT WHEN SHE'S PAST TWENTY.
SHERINE...
I DON'T KNOW!
I DON'T KNOW ANYMORE!
I DON'T KNOW WHAT TO DO......
WHY DID THIS HAVE TO HAPPEN ......?

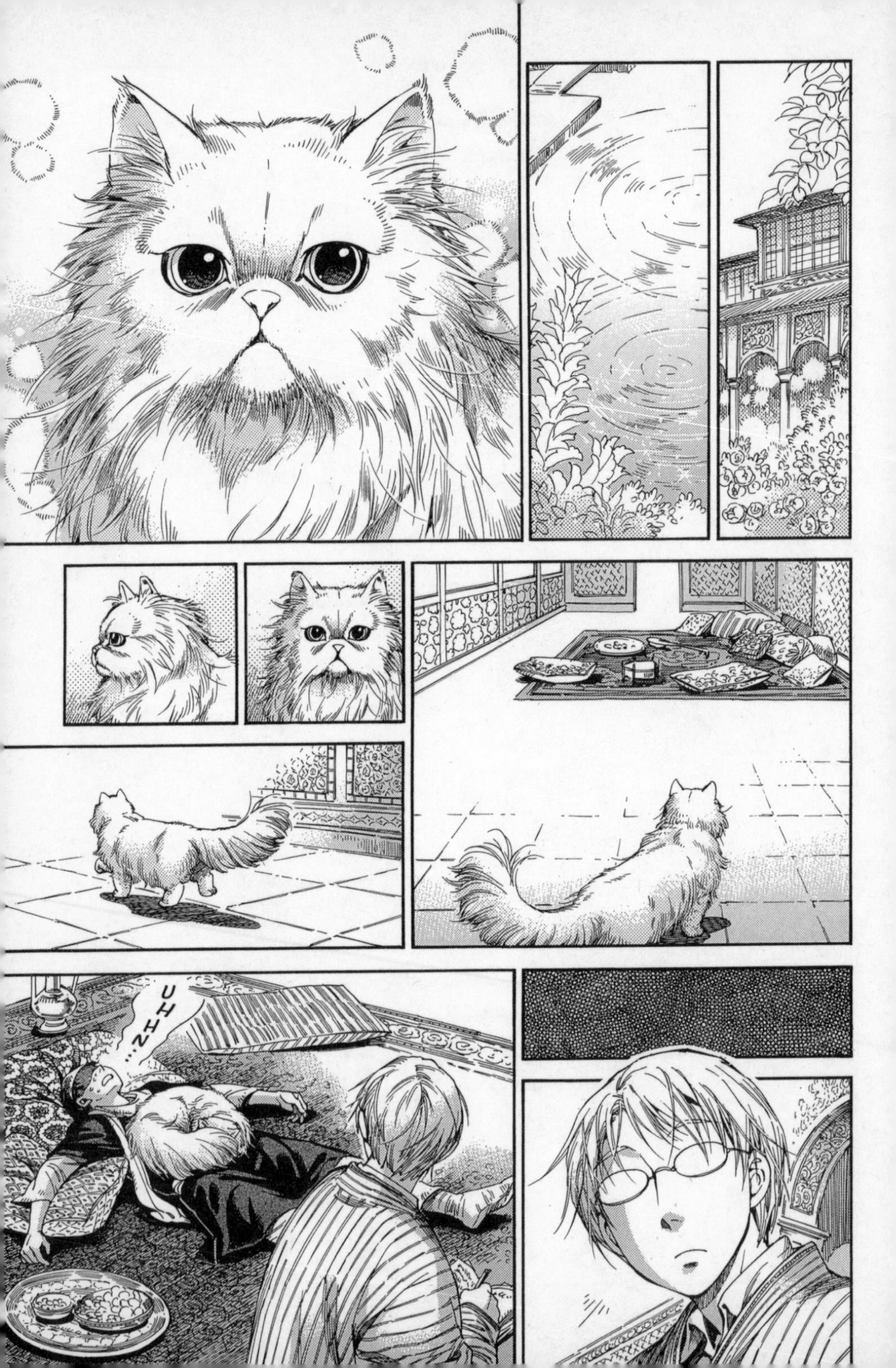
UHHN...

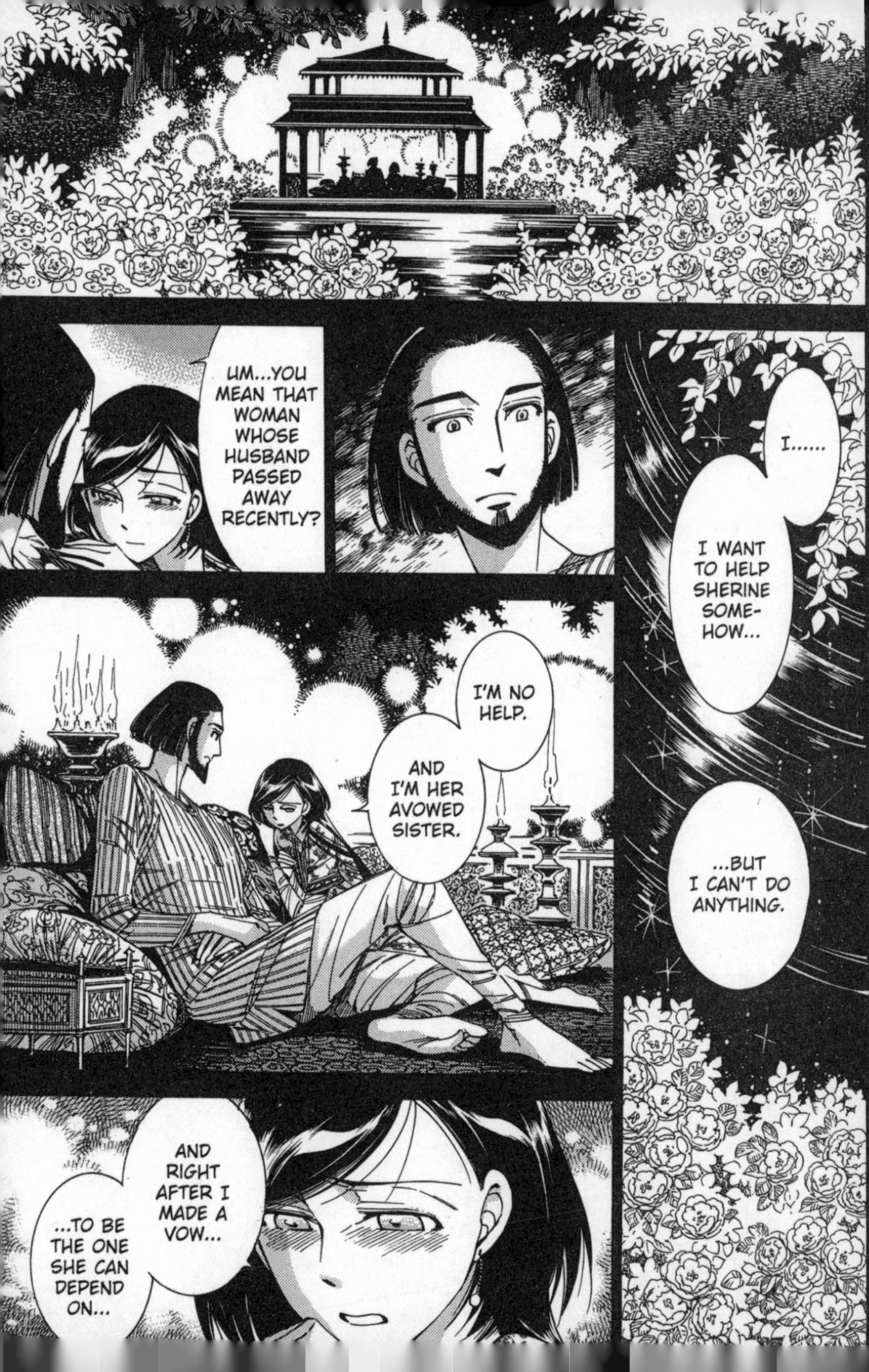
I......
I WANT TO HELP SHERINE SOME-HOW...
...BUT I CAN'T DO ANYTHING.
UM...YOU MEAN THAT WOMAN WHOSE HUSBAND PASSED AWAY RECENTLY?
I'M NO HELP.
AND I'M HER AVOWED SISTER.
AND RIGHT AFTER I MADE A VOW...
...TO BE THE ONE SHE CAN DEPEND ON...

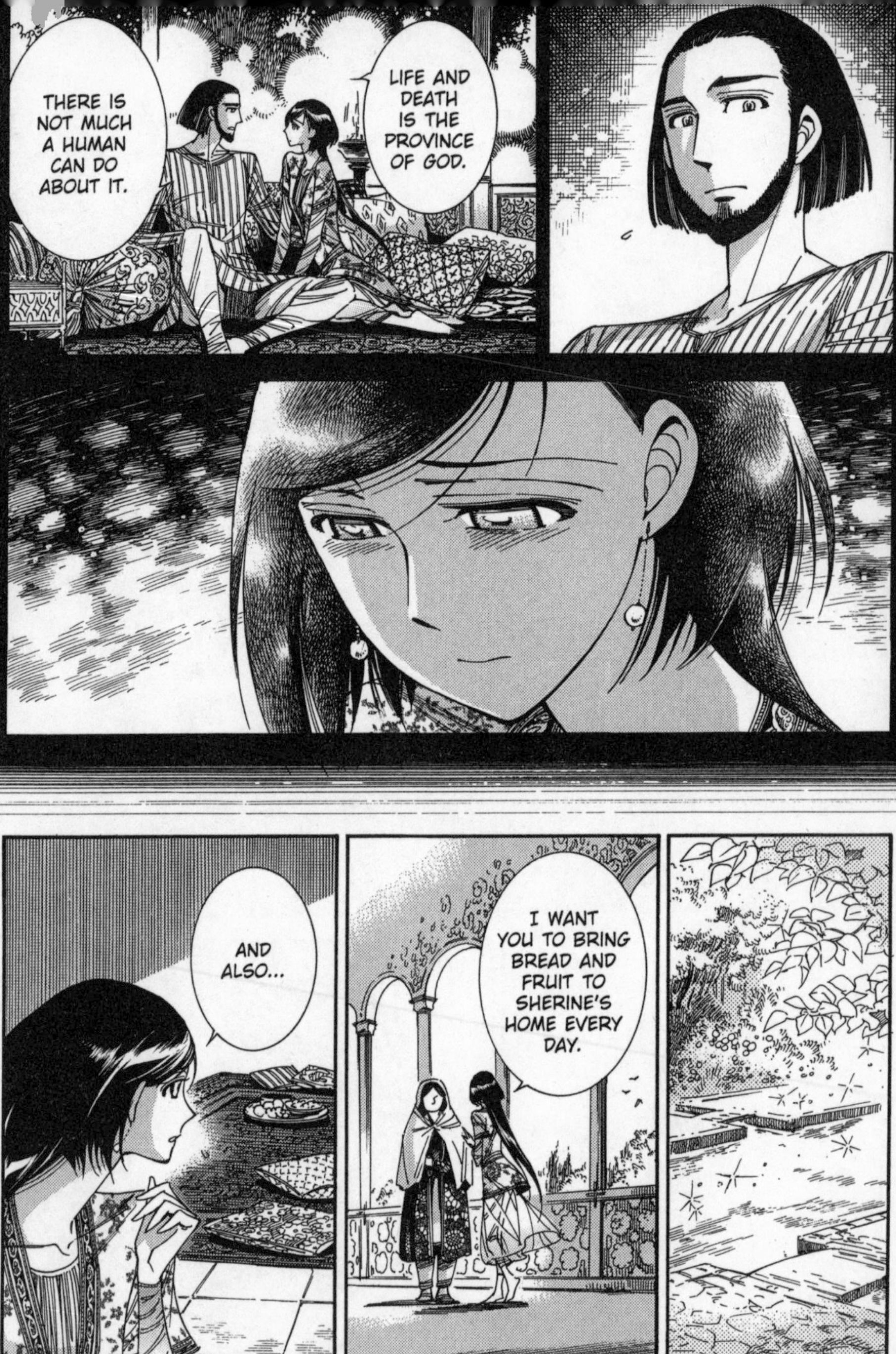
LIFE AND DEATH IS THE PROVINCE OF GOD.
THERE IS NOT MUCH A HUMAN CAN DO ABOUT IT.
I WANT YOU TO BRING BREAD AND FRUIT TO SHERINE'S HOME EVERY DAY.
AND ALSO...

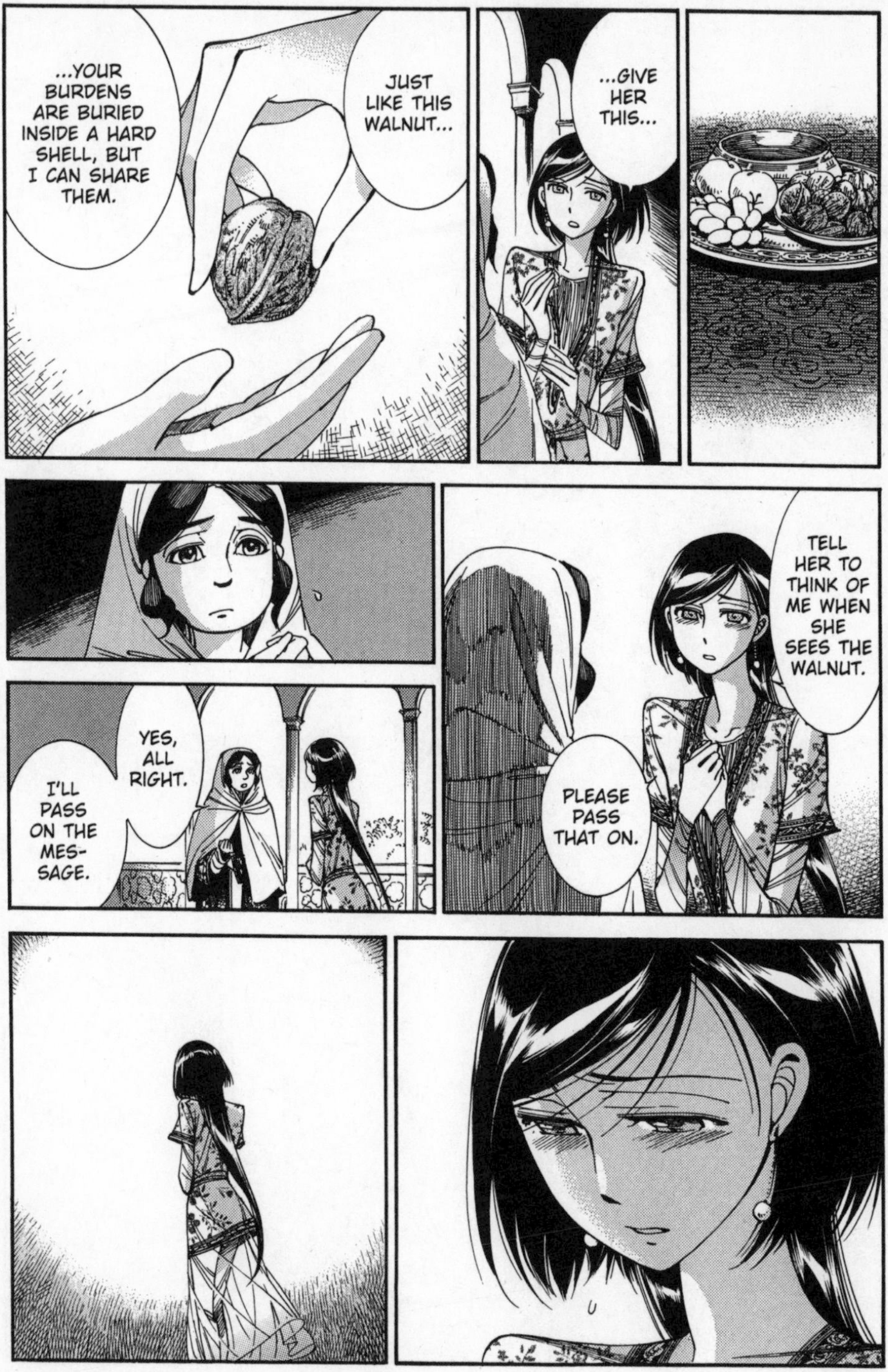
...GIVE HER THIS...
JUST LIKE THIS WALNUT...
...YOUR BURDENS ARE BURIED INSIDE A HARD SHELL, BUT I CAN SHARE THEM.
TELL HER TO THINK OF ME WHEN SHE SEES THE WALNUT.
PLEASE PASS THAT ON.
YES, ALL RIGHT.
I'LL PASS ON THE MES-SAGE.

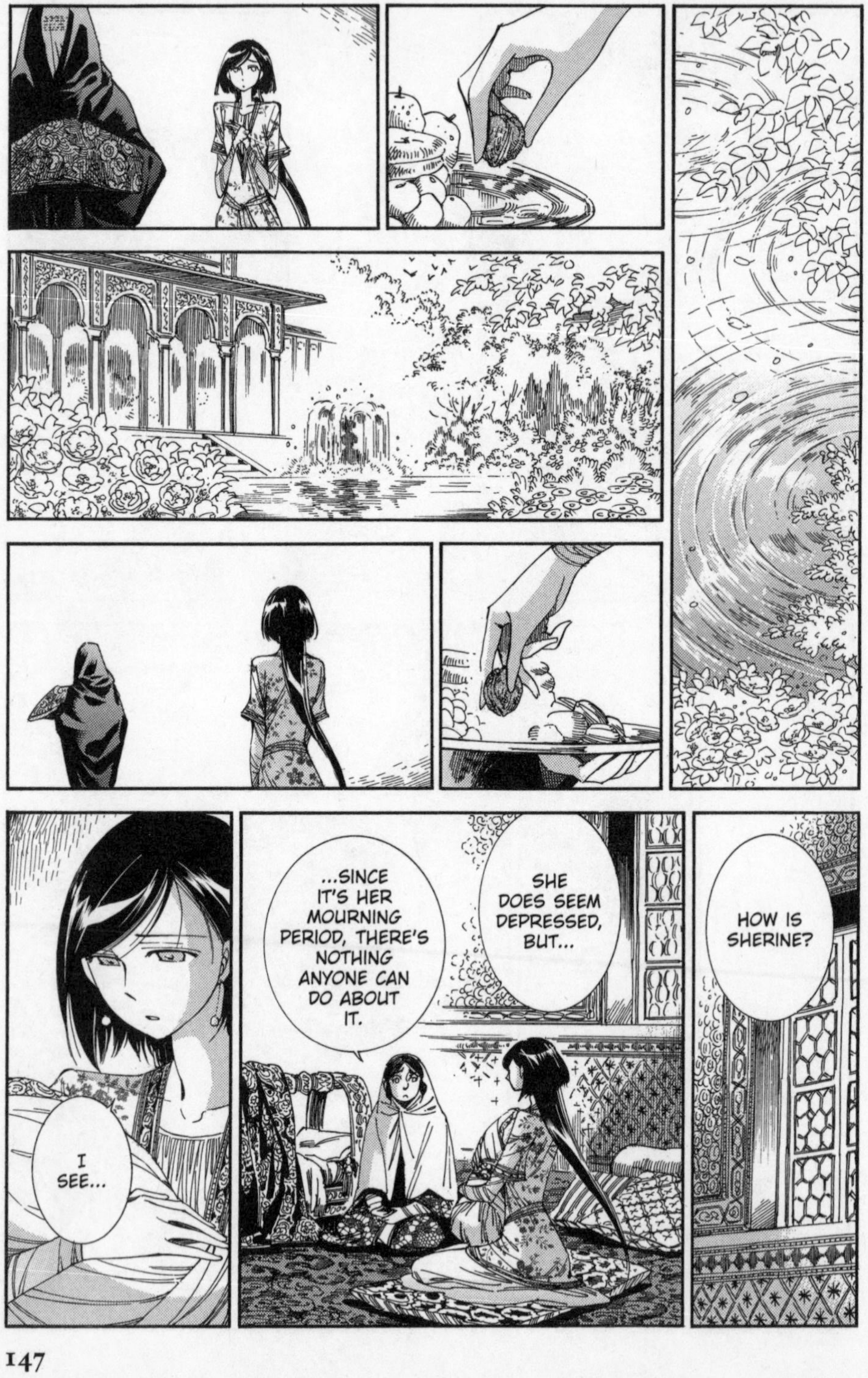
HOW IS SHERINE?
SHE DOES SEEM DEPRESSED, BUT...
...SINCE IT'S HER MOURNING PERIOD, THERE'S NOTHING ANYONE CAN DO ABOUT IT.
I SEE...

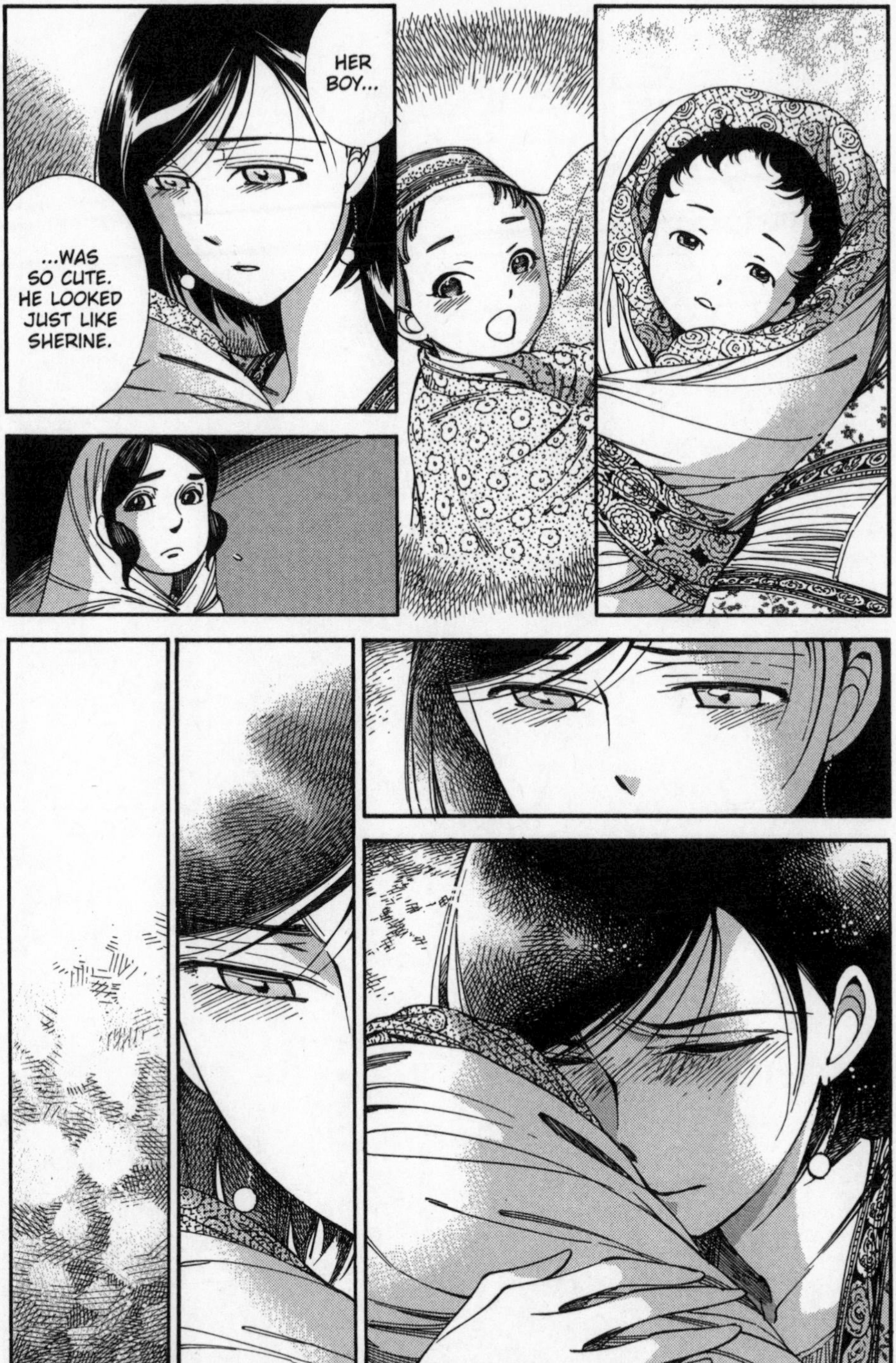
HER BOY...
...WAS SO CUTE. HE LOOKED JUST LIKE SHERINE.

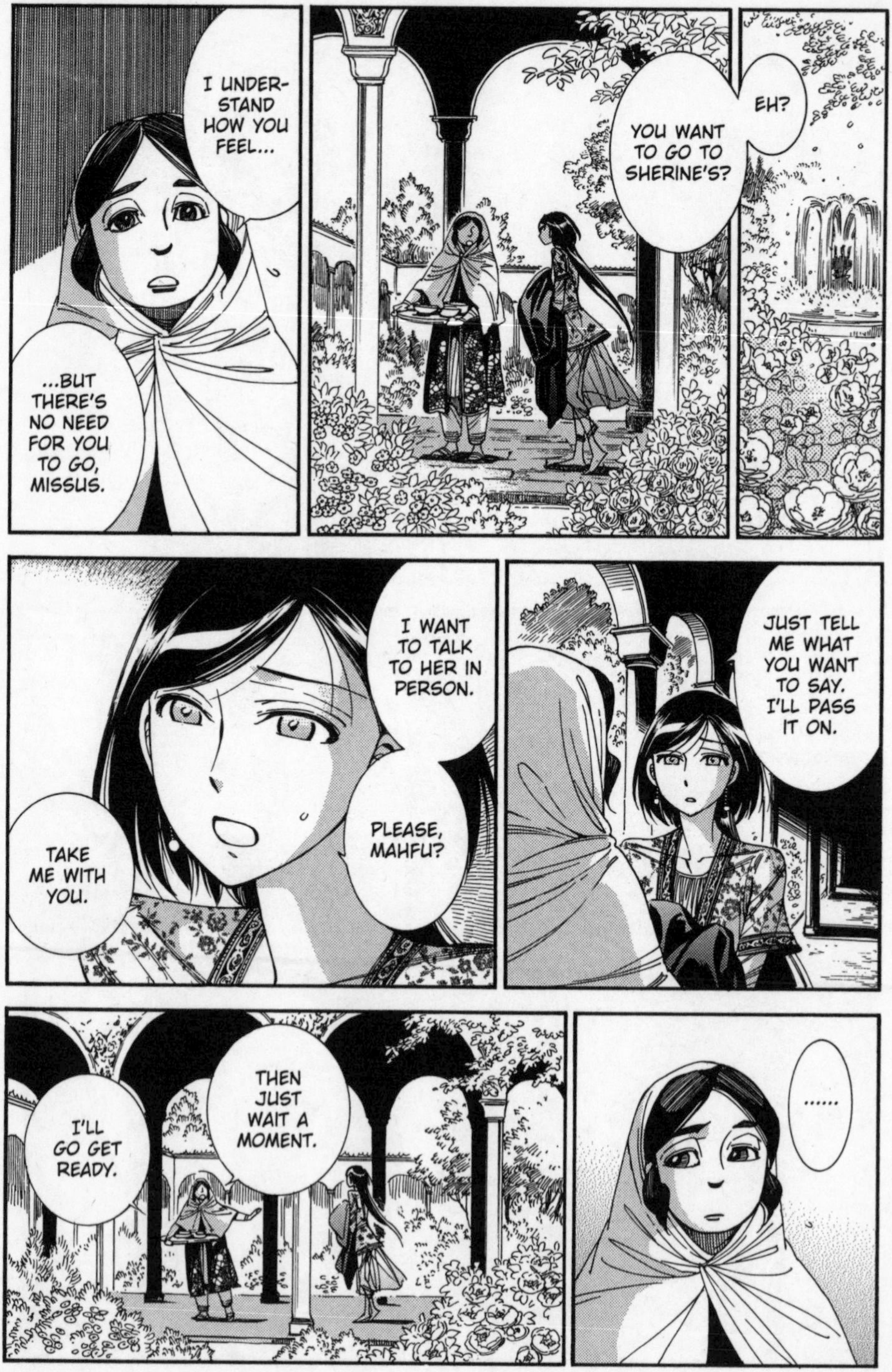
EH?
YOU WANT TO GO TO SHERINE'S?
I UNDER-STAND HOW YOU FEEL...
...BUT THERE'S NO NEED FOR YOU TO GO, MISSUS.
JUST TELL ME WHAT YOU WANT TO SAY. I'LL PASS IT ON.
I WANT TO TALK TO HER IN PERSON.
PLEASE, MAHFU?
TAKE ME WITH YOU.
......
THEN JUST WAIT A MOMENT.
I'LL GO GET READY.

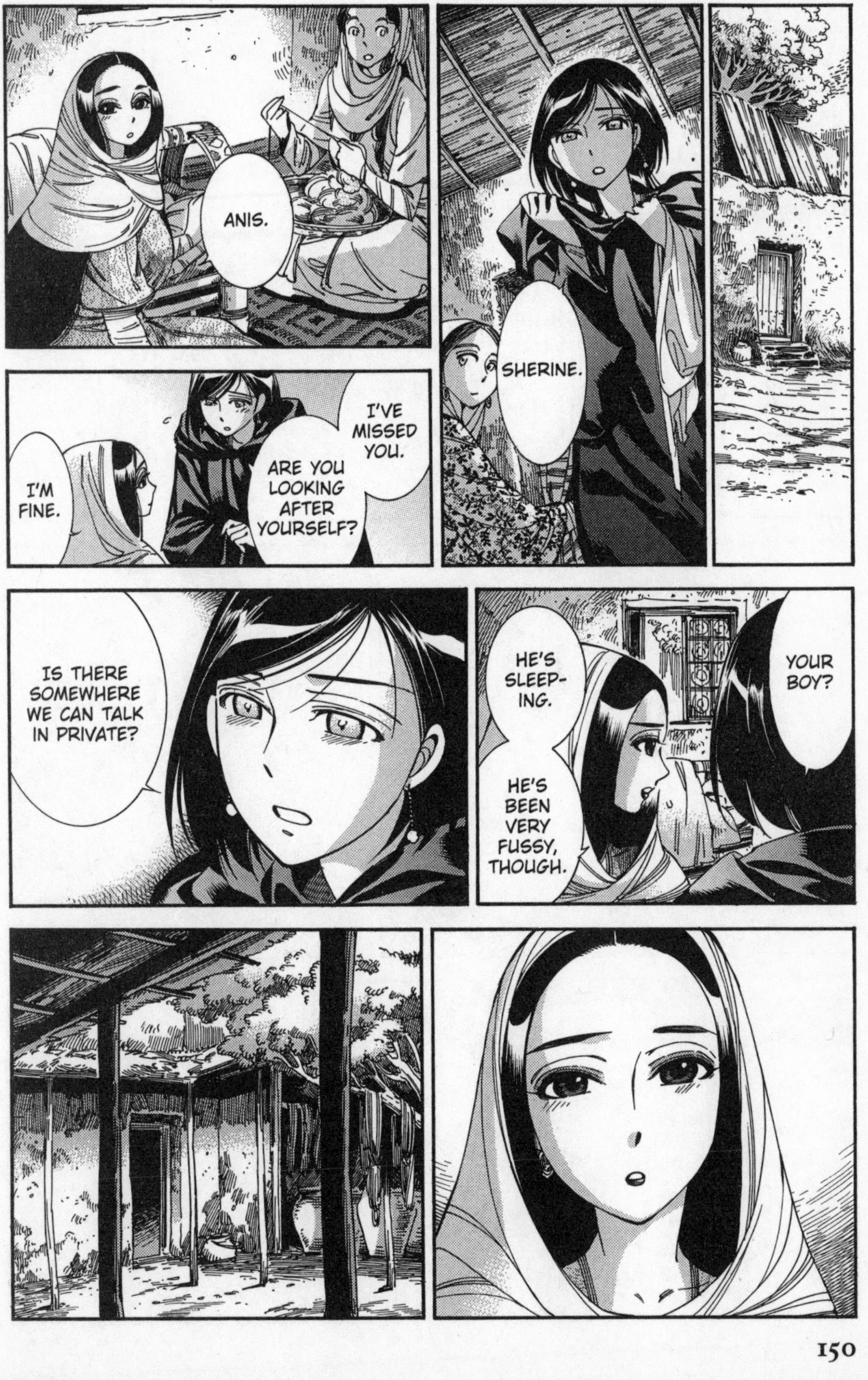
SHERINE.
ANIS.
I'VE MISSED YOU.
ARE YOU LOOKING AFTER YOURSELF?
I'M FINE.
YOUR BOY?
HE'S SLEEPING.
HE'S BEEN VERY FUSSY, THOUGH.
IS THERE SOMEWHERE WE CAN TALK IN PRIVATE?

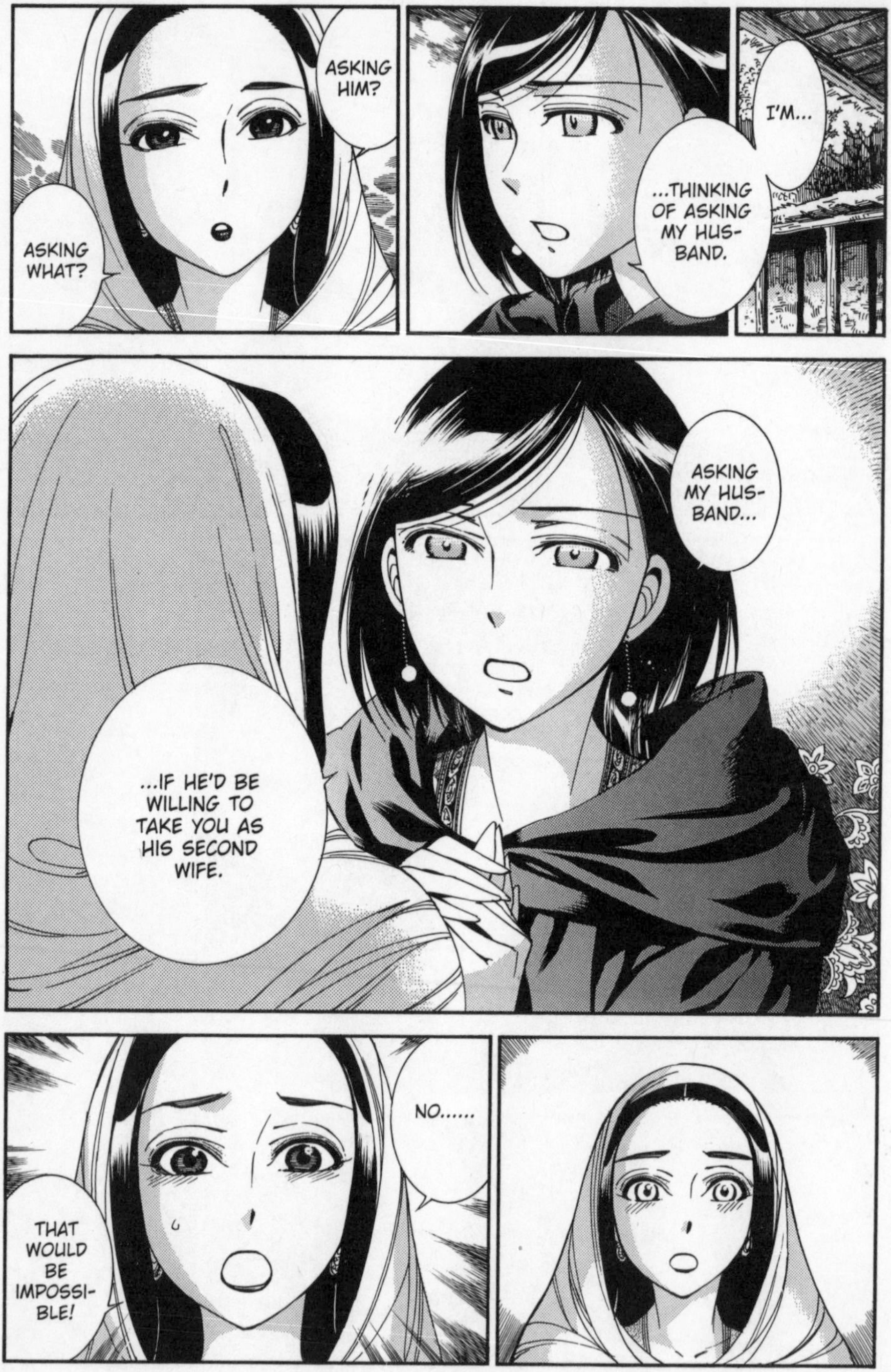
I'M...
...THINKING OF ASKING MY HUSBAND.
ASKING HIM?
ASKING WHAT?
ASKING MY HUSBAND...
...IF HE'D BE WILLING TO TAKE YOU AS HIS SECOND WIFE.
NO......
THAT WOULD BE IMPOSSIBLE!

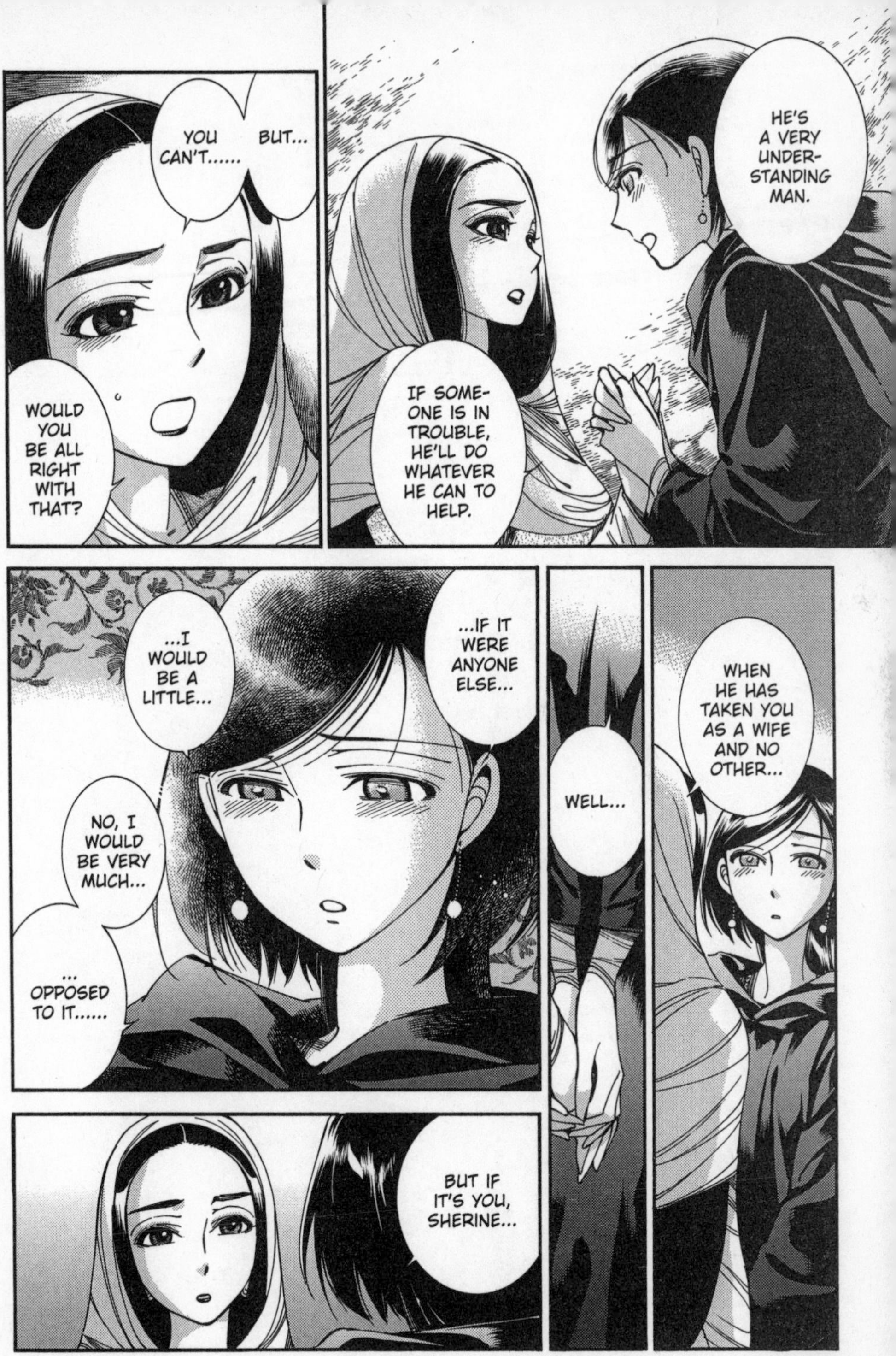
HE'S A VERY UNDER-STANDING MAN.
IF SOME-ONE IS IN TROUBLE, HE'LL DO WHATEVER HE CAN TO HELP.
BUT...
YOU CAN'T......
WOULD YOU BE ALL RIGHT WITH THAT?
WHEN HE HAS TAKEN YOU AS A WIFE AND NO OTHER...
WELL...
...IF IT WERE ANYONE ELSE...
...I WOULD BE A LITTLE...
NO, I WOULD BE VERY MUCH...
... OPPOSED TO IT......
BUT IF IT'S YOU, SHERINE...

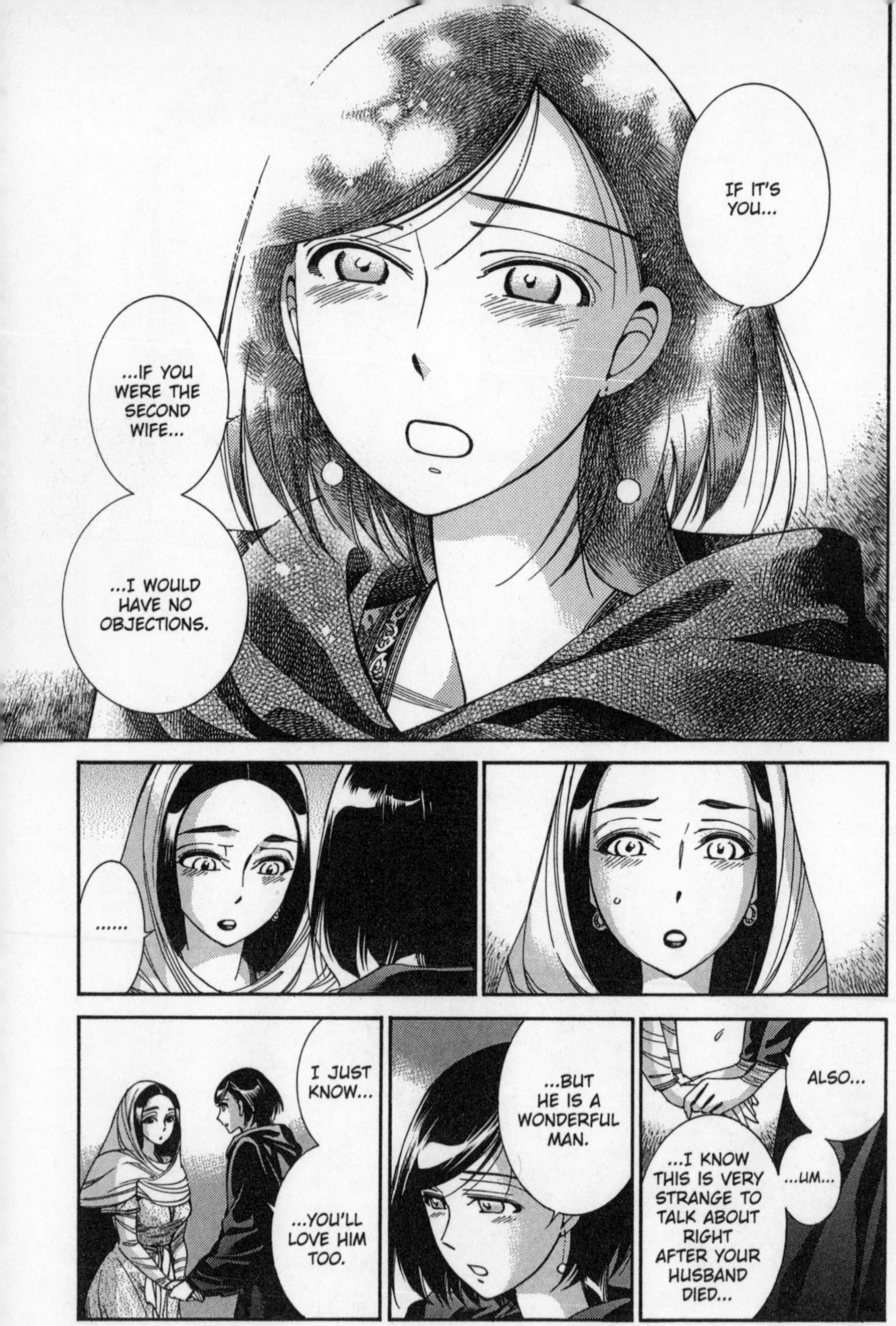
IF IT'S YOU...
...IF YOU WERE THE SECOND WIFE...
...I WOULD HAVE NO OBJECTIONS.
......
ALSO...
...UM...
...I KNOW THIS IS VERY STRANGE TO TALK ABOUT RIGHT AFTER YOUR HUSBAND DIED...
...BUT HE IS A WONDERFUL MAN.
I JUST KNOW...
...YOU'LL LOVE HIM TOO.

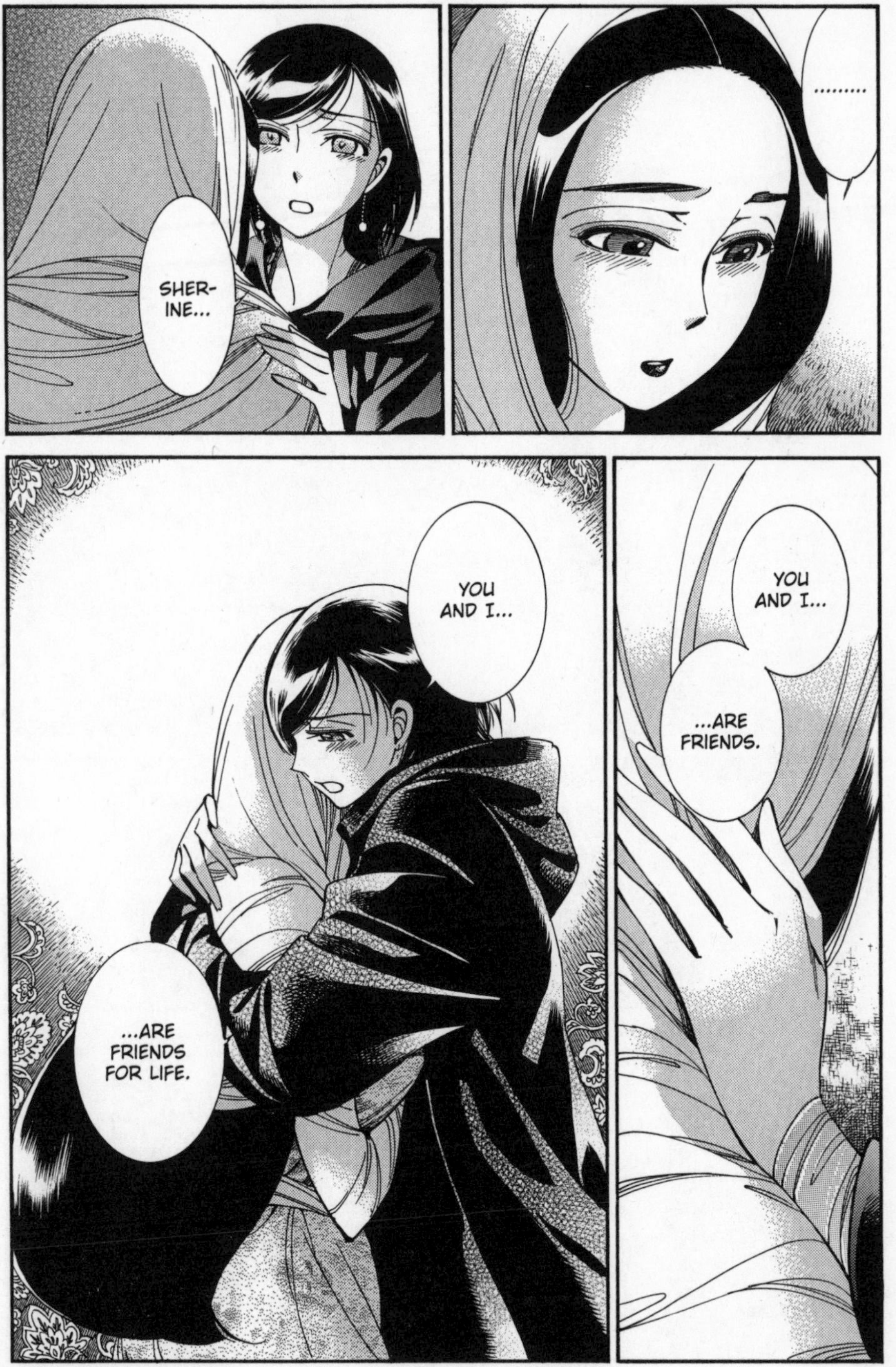
....
SHER-INE...
YOU AND I...
...ARE FRIENDS.
YOU AND I...
...ARE FRIENDS FOR LIFE.

✦ CHAPTER 42: END ✦

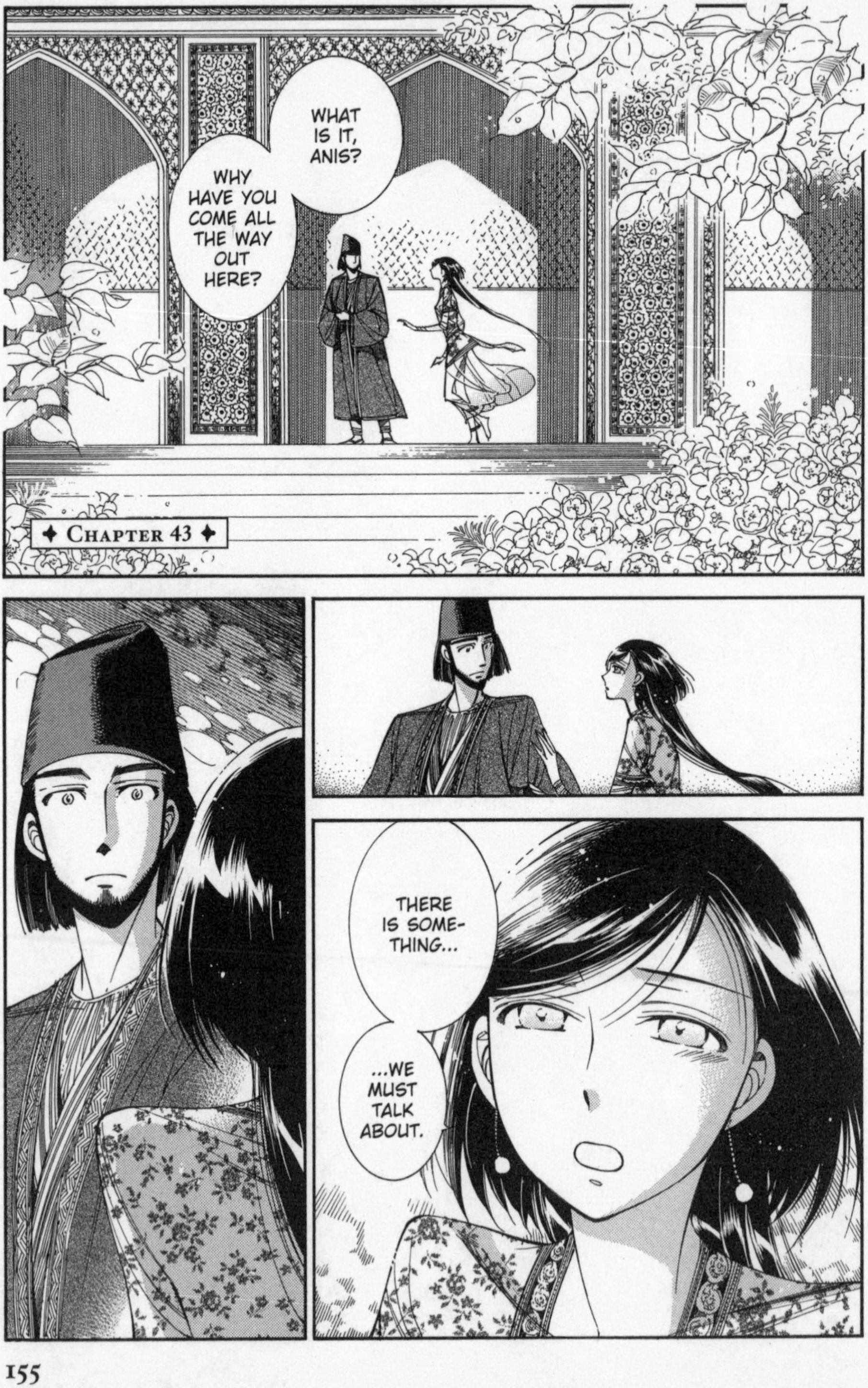
WHAT IS IT, ANIS?
WHY HAVE YOU COME ALL THE WAY OUT HERE?
✦ CHAPTER 43 ✦
THERE IS SOME-THING...
...WE MUST TALK ABOUT.

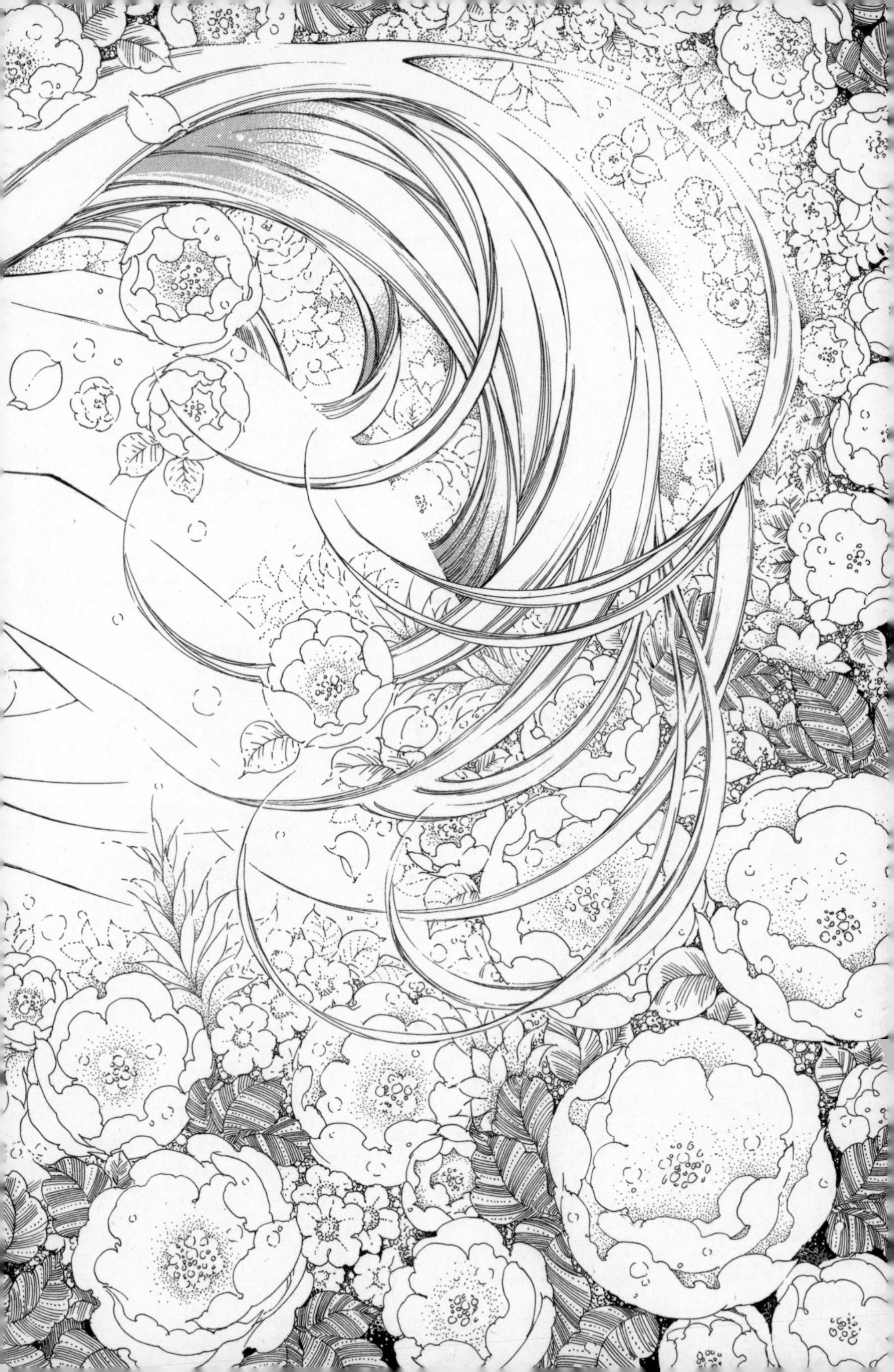

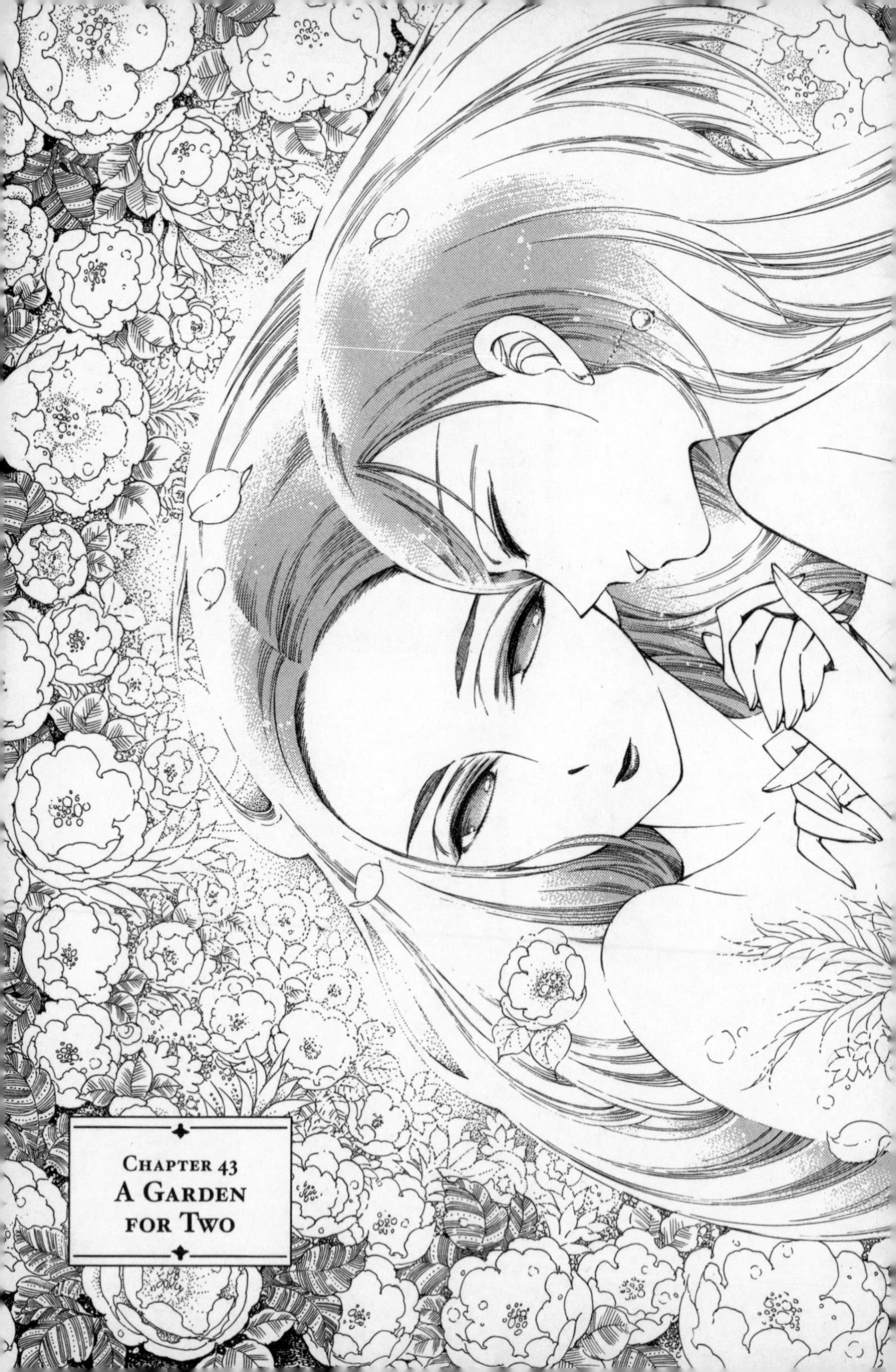
Chapter 43
A Garden
for Two

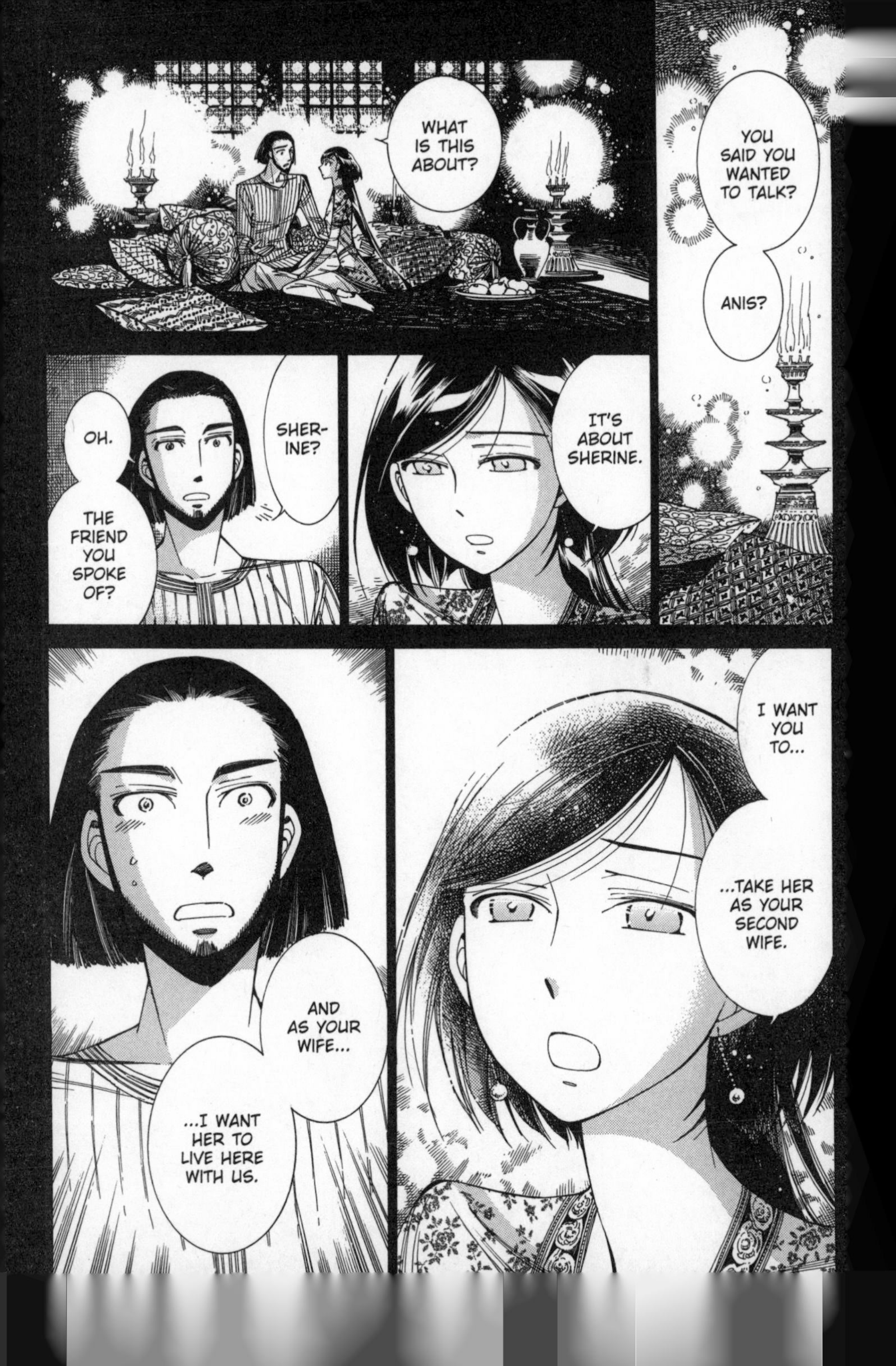
YOU SAID YOU WANTED TO TALK?
ANIS?
WHAT IS THIS ABOUT?
IT'S ABOUT SHERINE.
SHER-INE?
OH.
THE FRIEND YOU SPOKE OF?
I WANT YOU TO...
...TAKE HER AS YOUR SECOND WIFE.
AND AS YOUR WIFE...
...I WANT HER TO LIVE HERE WITH US.

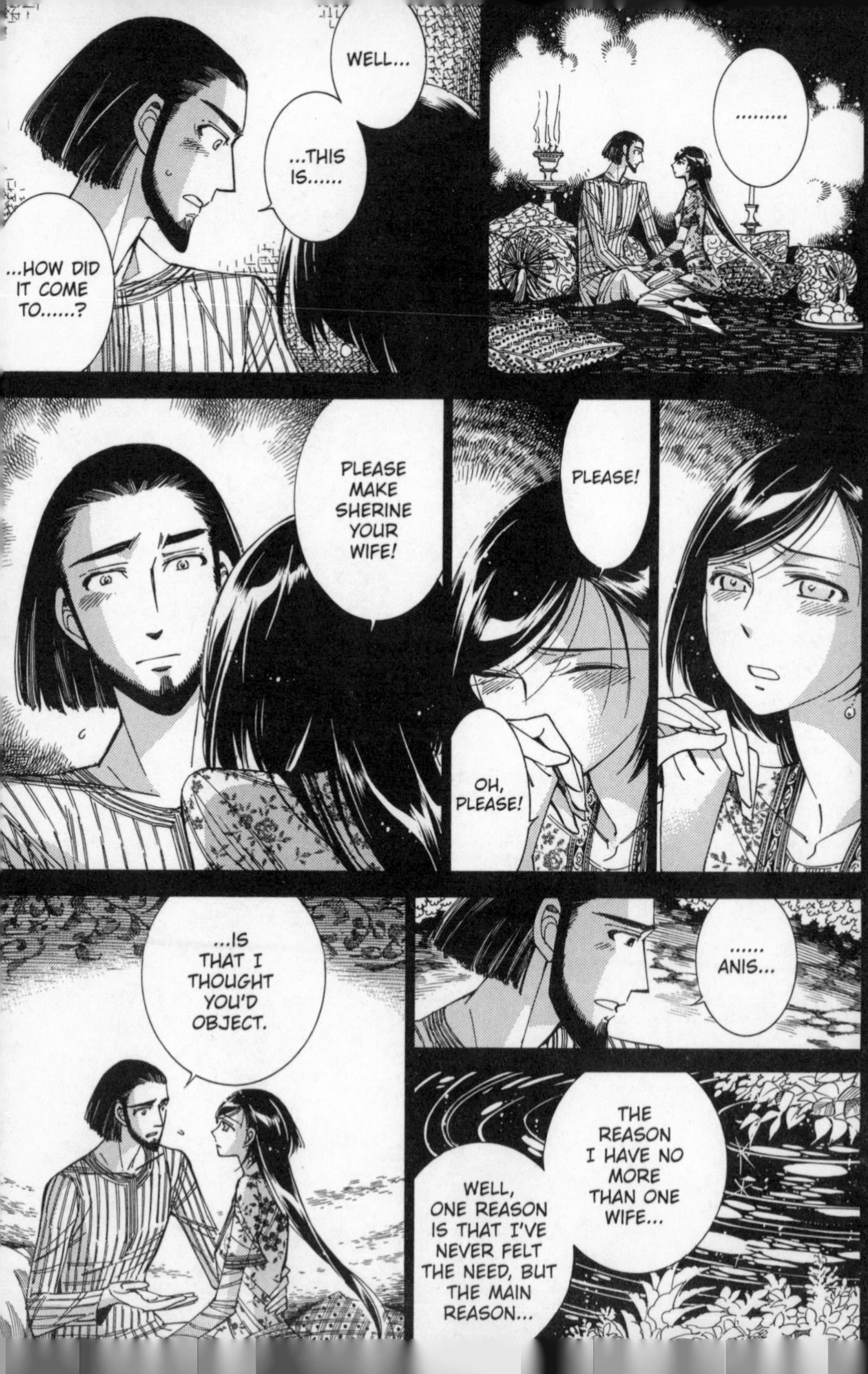
....
WELL...
...THIS IS......
...HOW DID IT COME TO......?
PLEASE!
OH, PLEASE!
PLEASE MAKE SHERINE YOUR WIFE!
...... ANIS...
THE REASON I HAVE NO MORE THAN ONE WIFE...
WELL, ONE REASON IS THAT I'VE NEVER FELT THE NEED, BUT THE MAIN REASON...
...IS THAT I THOUGHT YOU'D OBJECT.

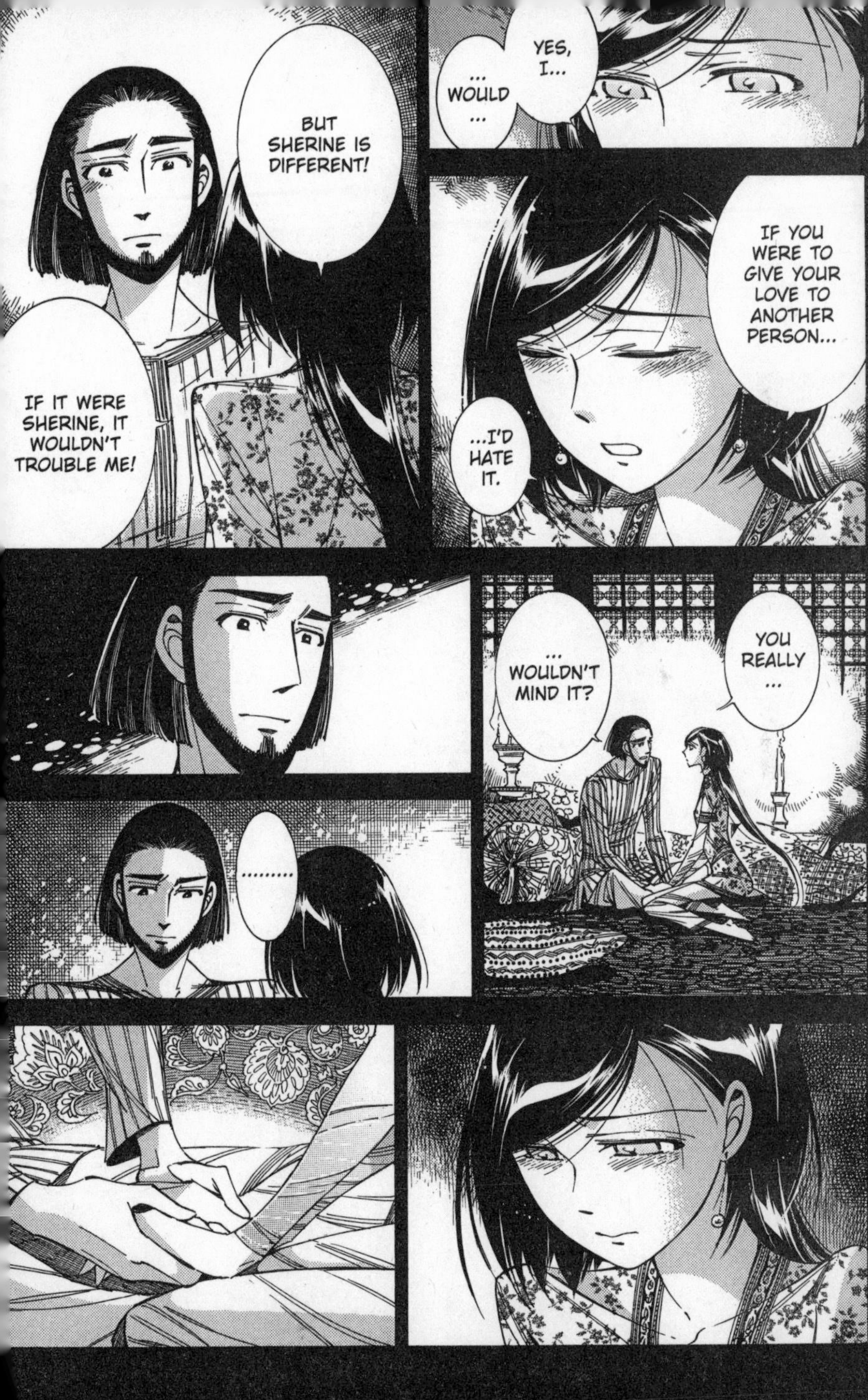
YES, I...
...WOULD...
IF YOU WERE TO GIVE YOUR LOVE TO ANOTHER PERSON...
...I'D HATE IT.
BUT SHERINE IS DIFFERENT!
IF IT WERE SHERINE, IT WOULDN'T TROUBLE ME!
YOU REALLY...
...WOULDN'T MIND IT?
....

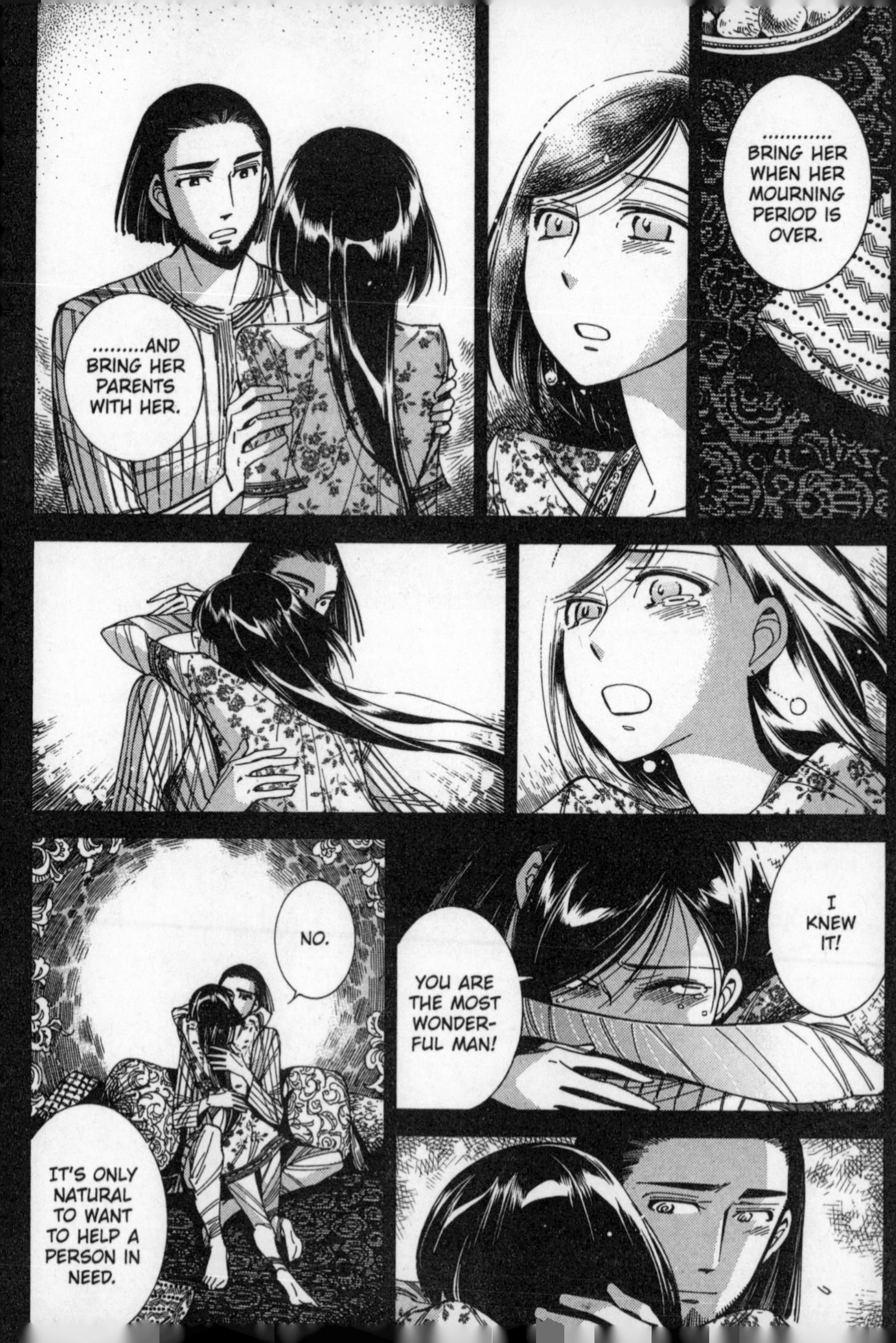
.... BRING HER WHEN HER MOURNING PERIOD IS OVER.
.........AND BRING HER PARENTS WITH HER.
I KNEW IT!
YOU ARE THE MOST WONDER-FUL MAN!
NO.
IT'S ONLY NATURAL TO WANT TO HELP A PERSON IN NEED.

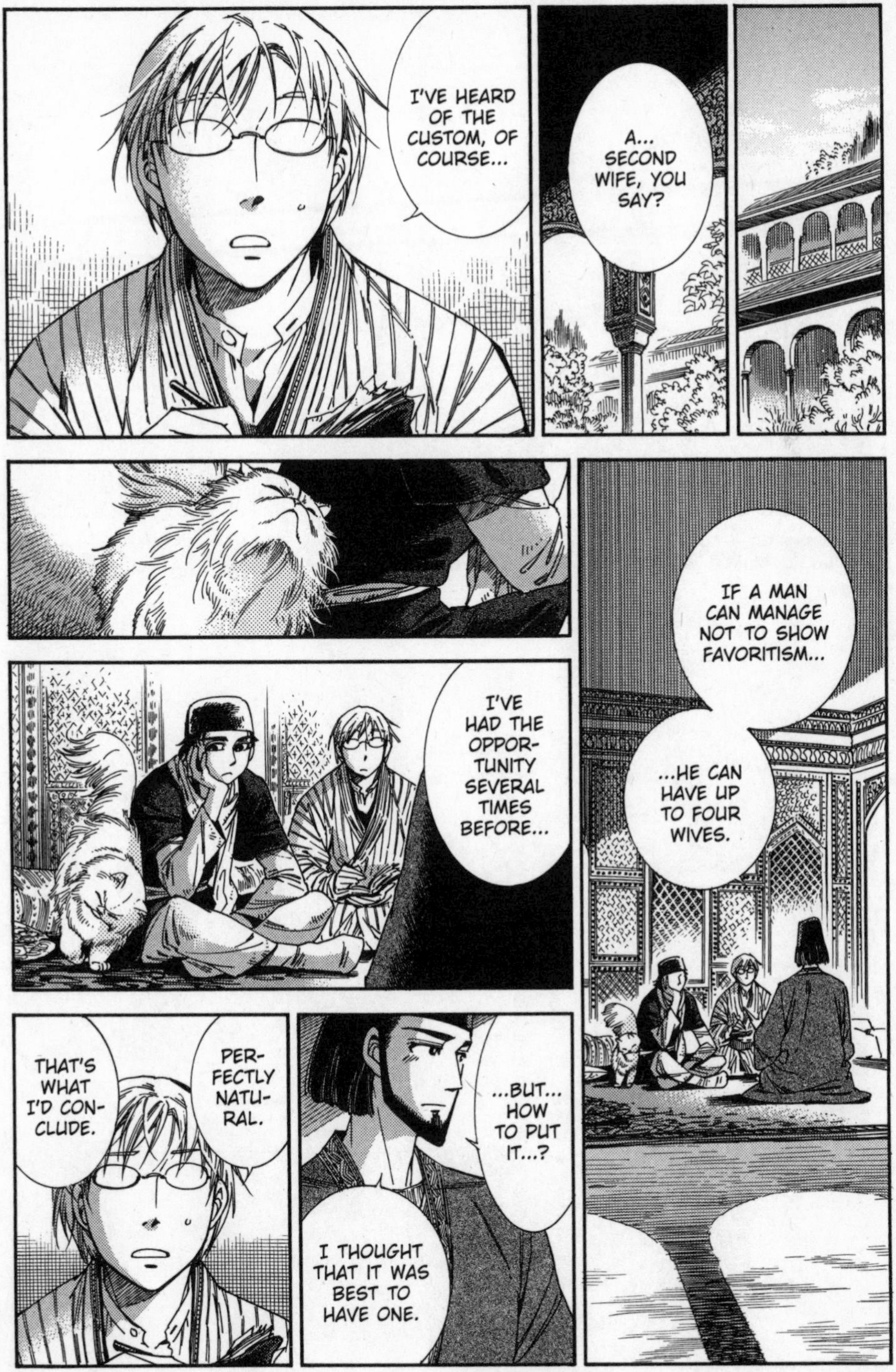
A... SECOND WIFE, YOU SAY?
I'VE HEARD OF THE CUSTOM, OF COURSE...
IF A MAN CAN MANAGE NOT TO SHOW FAVORITISM...
...HE CAN HAVE UP TO FOUR WIVES.
I'VE HAD THE OPPORTUNITY SEVERAL TIMES BEFORE...
...BUT... HOW TO PUT IT...?
I THOUGHT THAT IT WAS BEST TO HAVE ONE.
PERFECTLY NATURAL.
THAT'S WHAT I'D CONCLUDE.

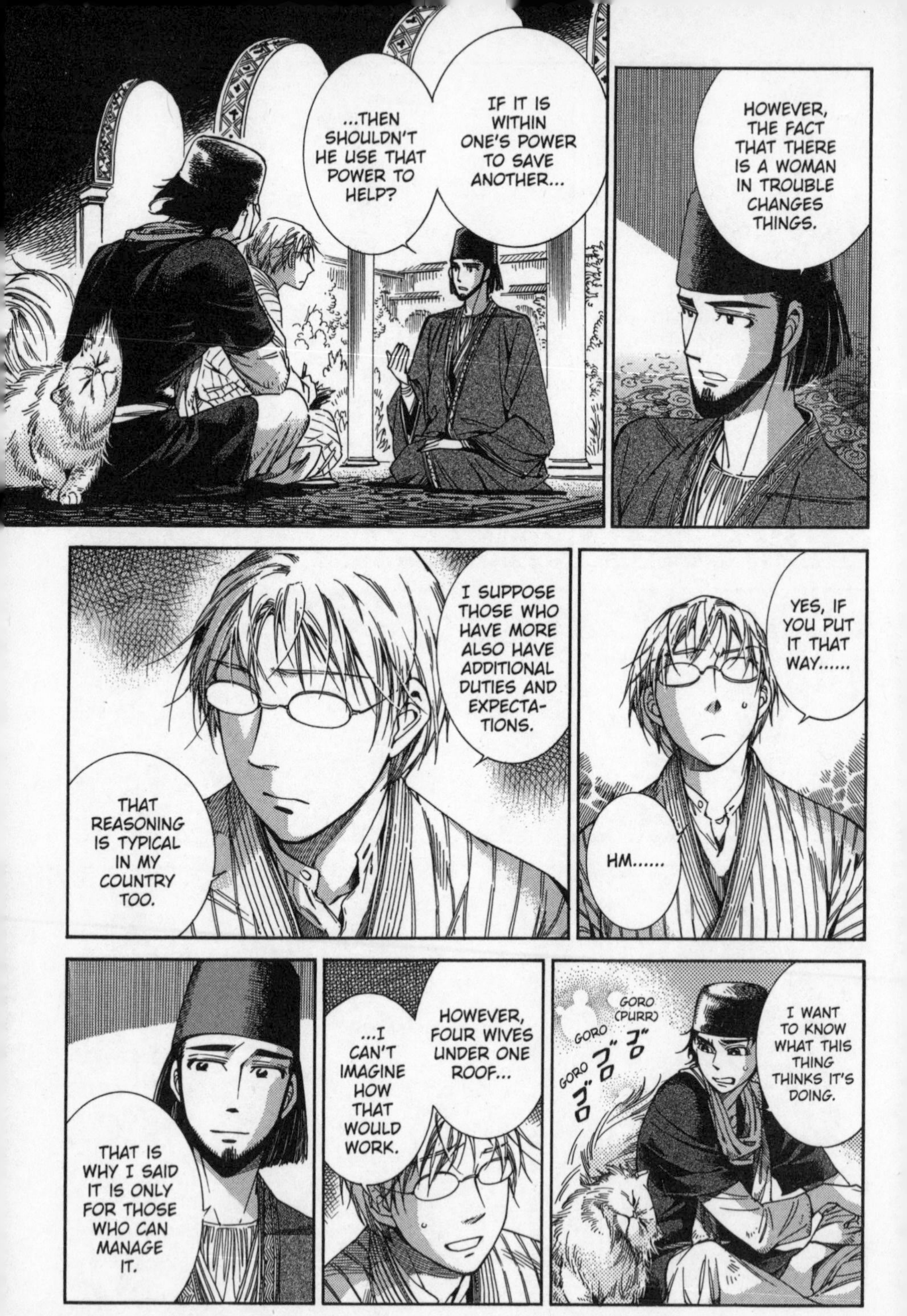
HOWEVER, THE FACT THAT THERE IS A WOMAN IN TROUBLE CHANGES THINGS.
IF IT IS WITHIN ONE'S POWER TO SAVE ANOTHER...
...THEN SHOULDN'T HE USE THAT POWER TO HELP?
YES, IF YOU PUT IT THAT WAY......
HM......
I SUPPOSE THOSE WHO HAVE MORE ALSO HAVE ADDITIONAL DUTIES AND EXPECTA-TIONS.
THAT REASONING IS TYPICAL IN MY COUNTRY TOO.
I WANT TO KNOW WHAT THIS THING THINKS IT'S DOING.
GORO (PURR)
ゴロ
GORO
ゴロ
GORO
ゴロ
HOWEVER, FOUR WIVES UNDER ONE ROOF...
...I CAN'T IMAGINE HOW THAT WOULD WORK.
THAT IS WHY I SAID IT IS ONLY FOR THOSE WHO CAN MANAGE IT.

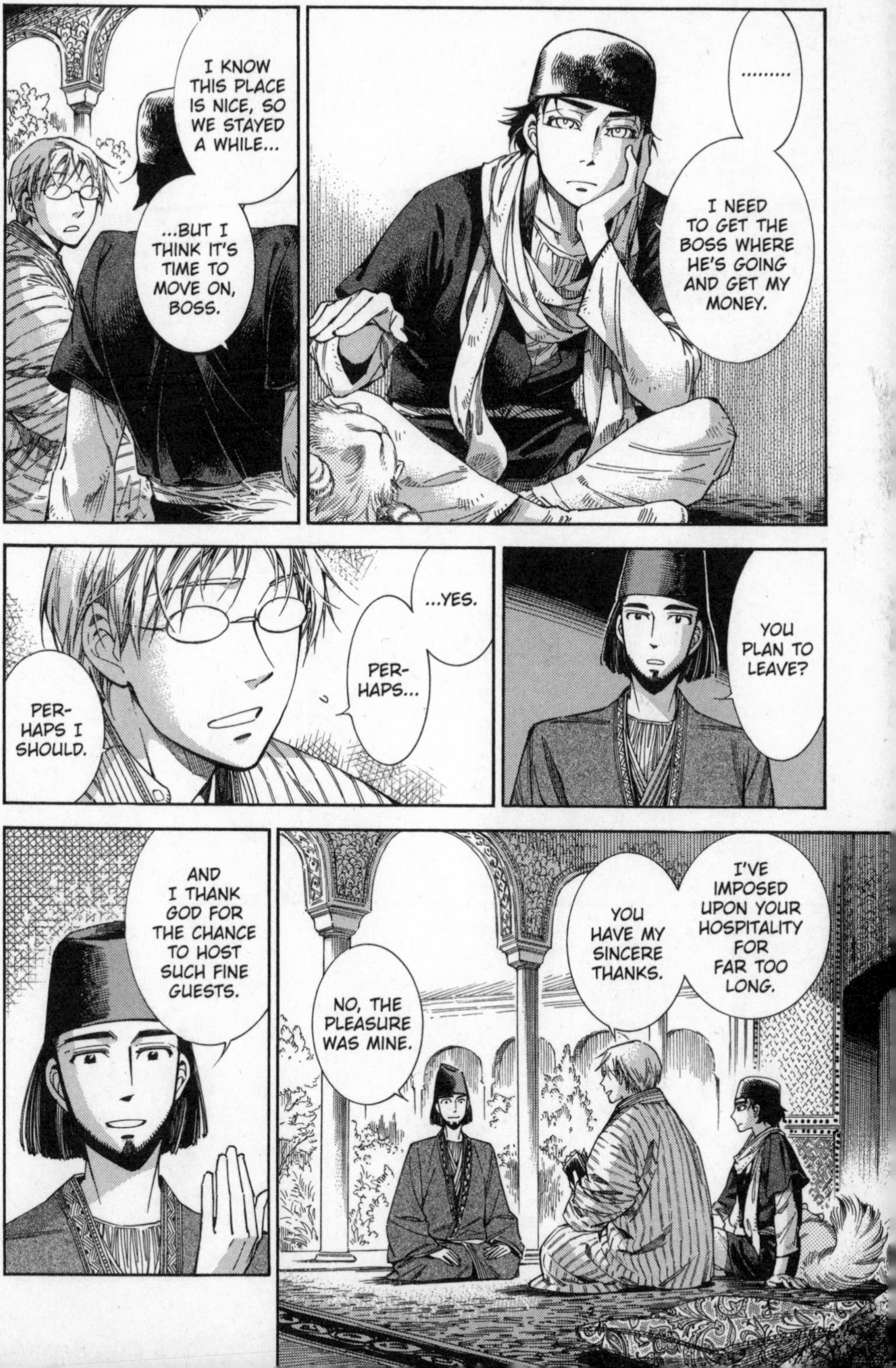
....
I NEED TO GET THE BOSS WHERE HE'S GOING AND GET MY MONEY.
I KNOW THIS PLACE IS NICE, SO WE STAYED A WHILE...
...BUT I THINK IT'S TIME TO MOVE ON, BOSS.
YOU PLAN TO LEAVE?
...YES.
PER-HAPS...
PER-HAPS I SHOULD.
I'VE IMPOSED UPON YOUR HOSPITALITY FOR FAR TOO LONG.
YOU HAVE MY SINCERE THANKS.
NO, THE PLEASURE WAS MINE.
AND I THANK GOD FOR THE CHANCE TO HOST SUCH FINE GUESTS.

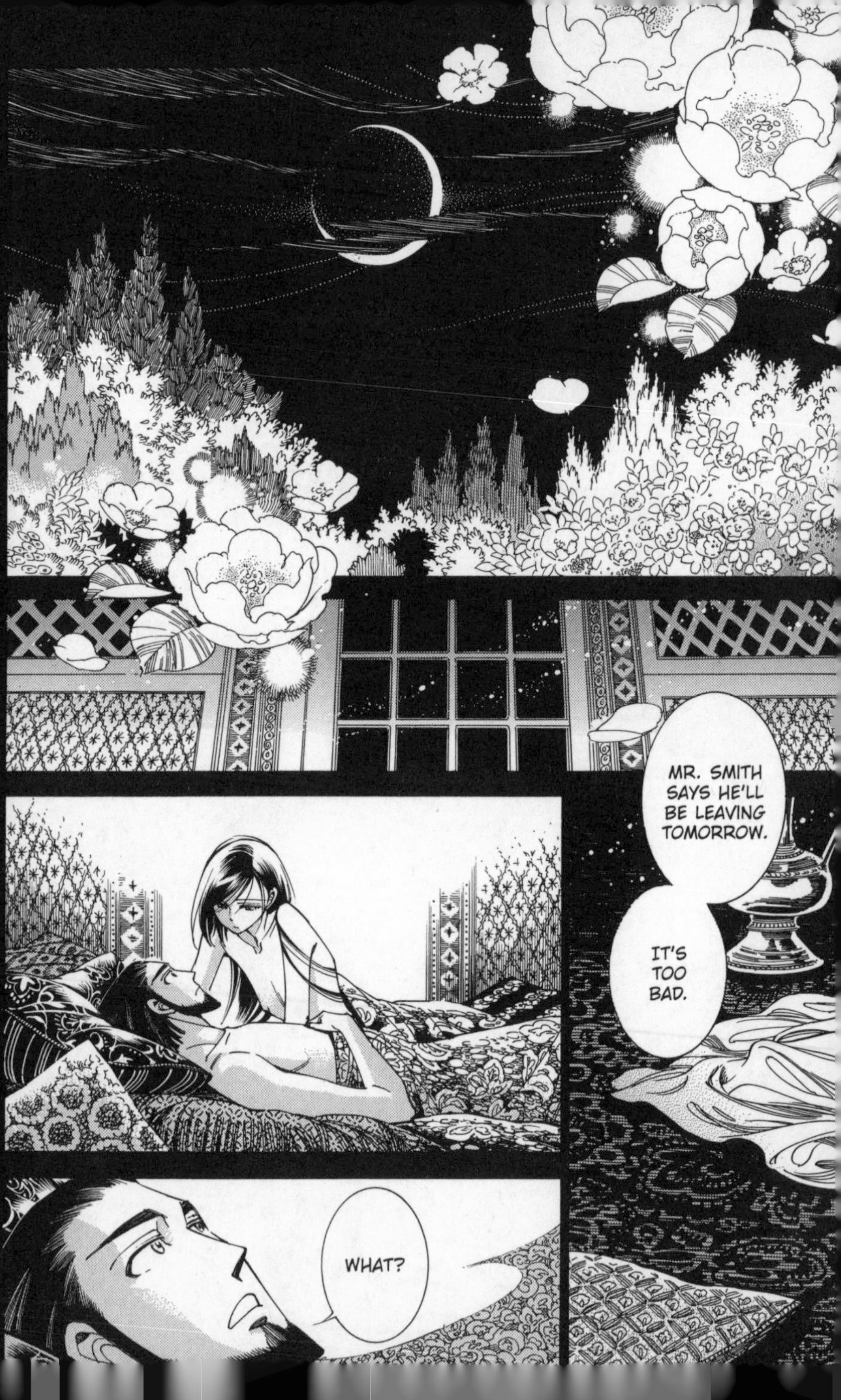
MR. SMITH SAYS HE'LL BE LEAVING TOMORROW.
IT'S TOO BAD.
WHAT?

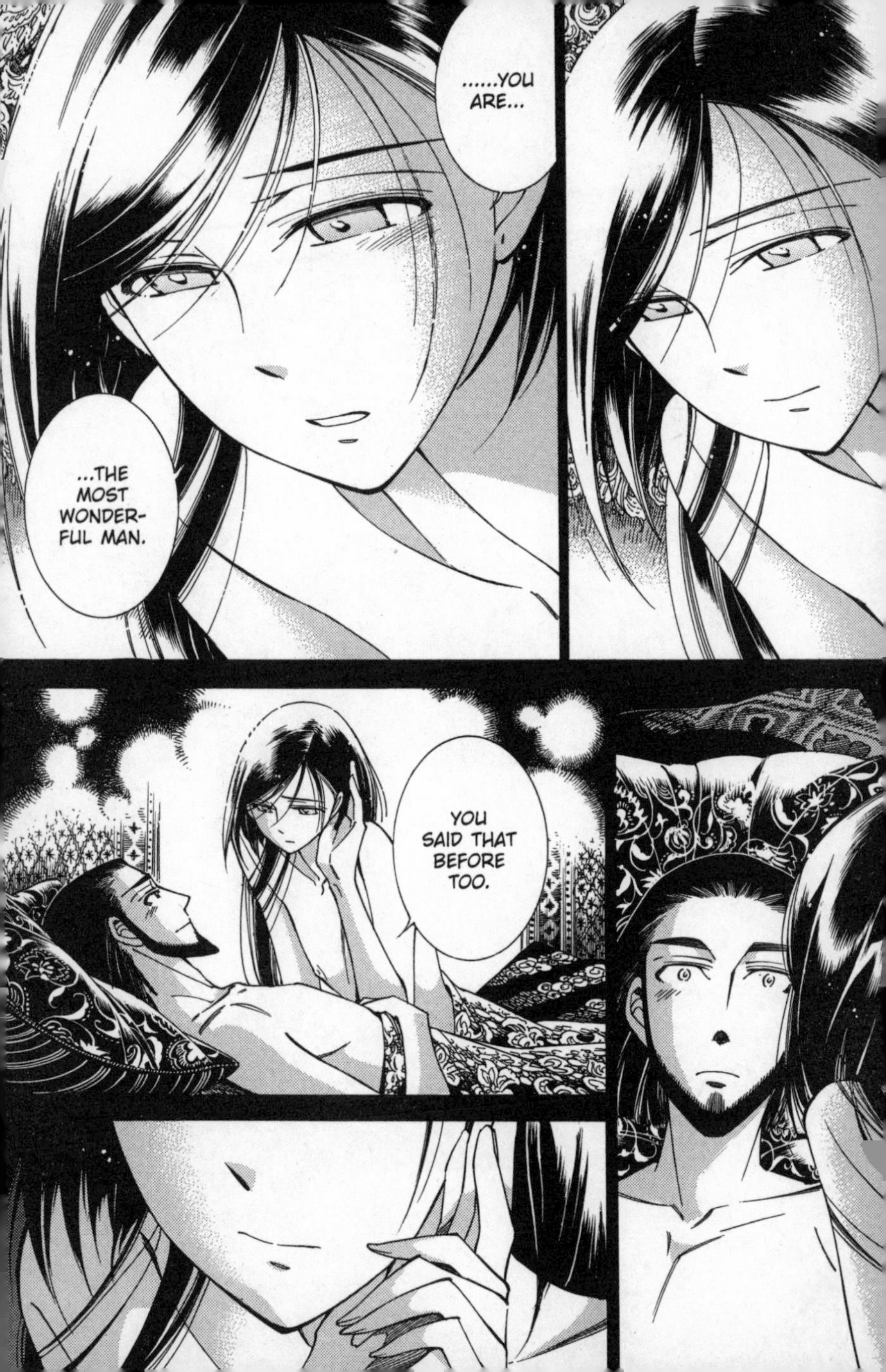
......YOU ARE...
...THE MOST WONDER-FUL MAN.
YOU SAID THAT BEFORE TOO.

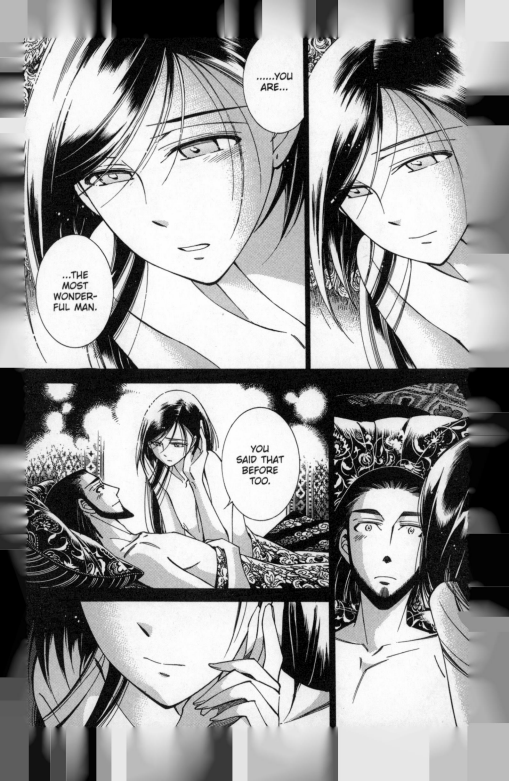

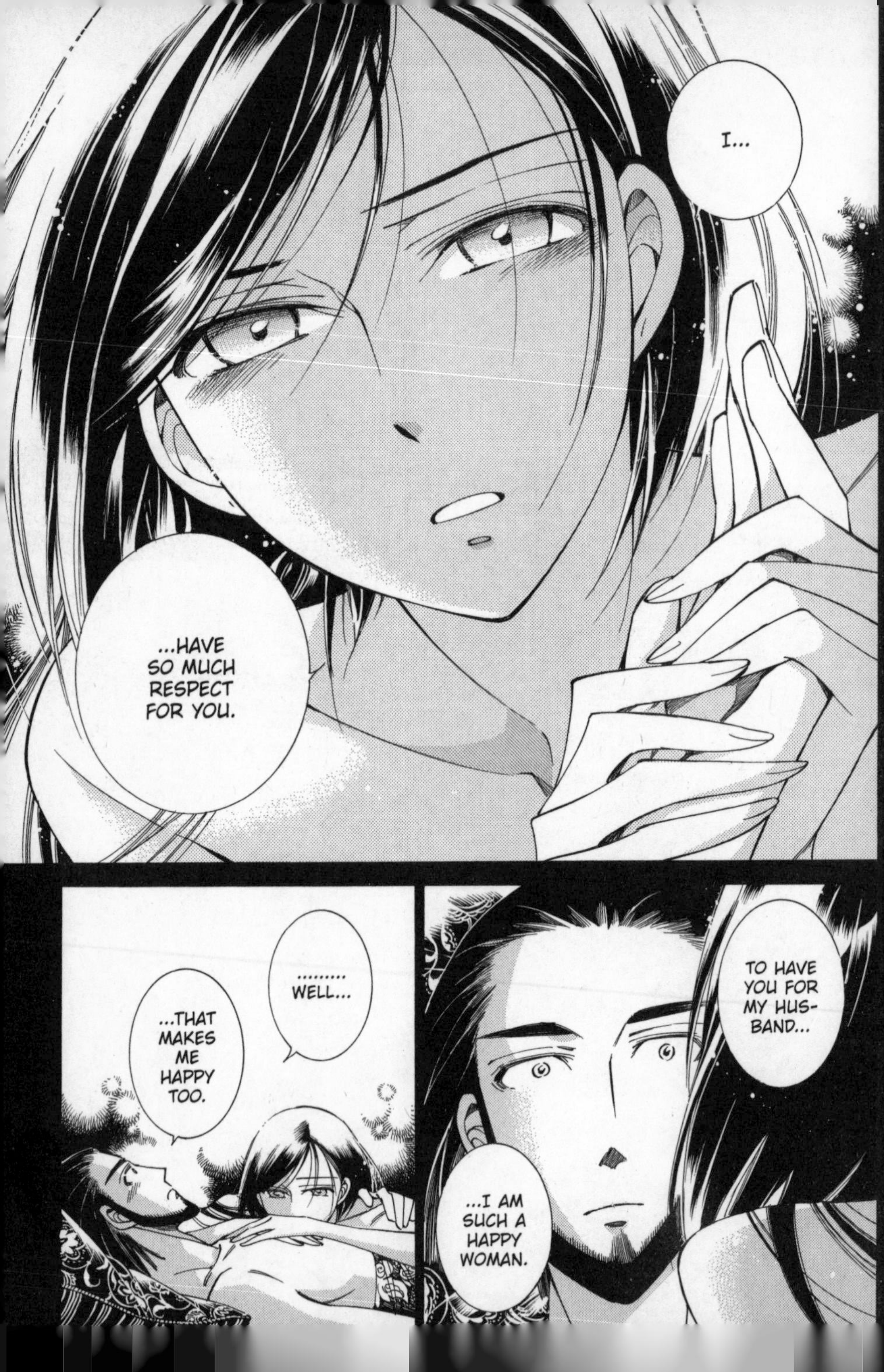
I...
...HAVE SO MUCH RESPECT FOR YOU.
TO HAVE YOU FOR MY HUS-BAND...
...I AM SUCH A HAPPY WOMAN.
....
WELL...
...THAT MAKES ME HAPPY TOO.

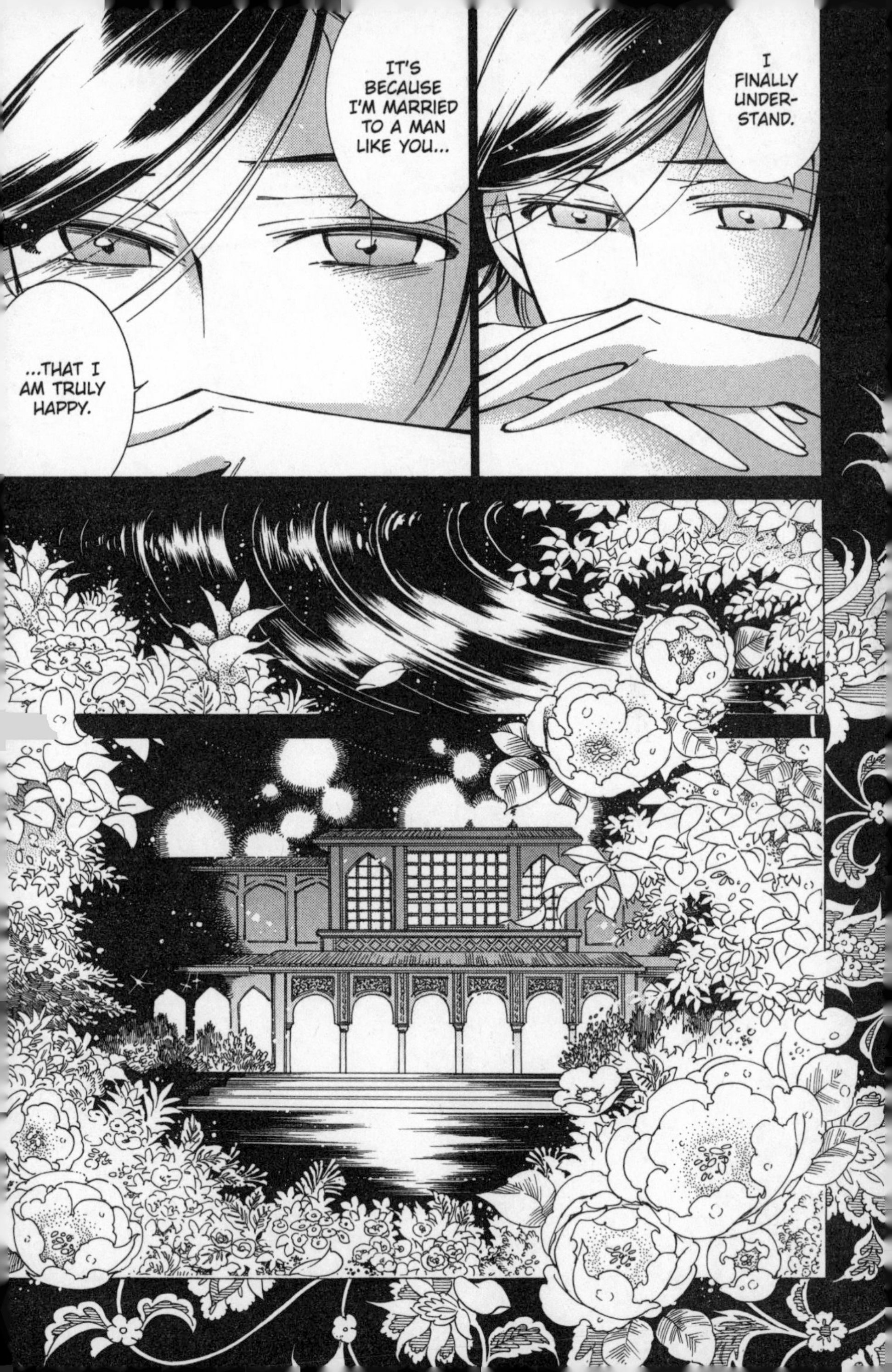
I FINALLY UNDER-STAND.
IT'S BECAUSE I'M MARRIED TO A MAN LIKE YOU...
...THAT I AM TRULY HAPPY.

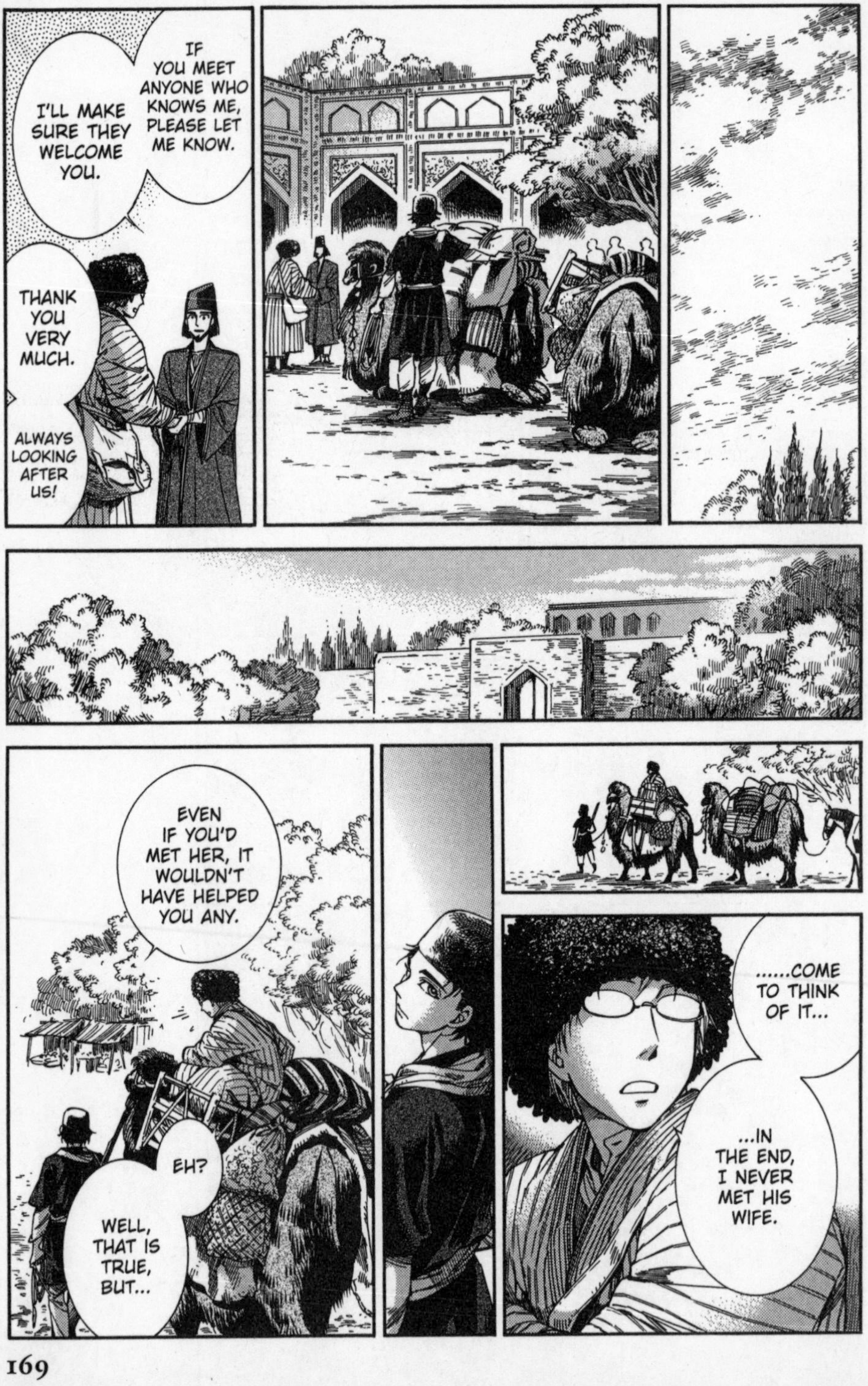
IF YOU MEET ANYONE WHO KNOWS ME, PLEASE LET ME KNOW.
I'LL MAKE SURE THEY WELCOME YOU.
THANK YOU VERY MUCH.
ALWAYS LOOKING AFTER US!
......COME TO THINK OF IT...
...IN THE END, I NEVER MET HIS WIFE.
EVEN IF YOU'D MET HER, IT WOULDN'T HAVE HELPED YOU ANY.
EH?
WELL, THAT IS TRUE, BUT...

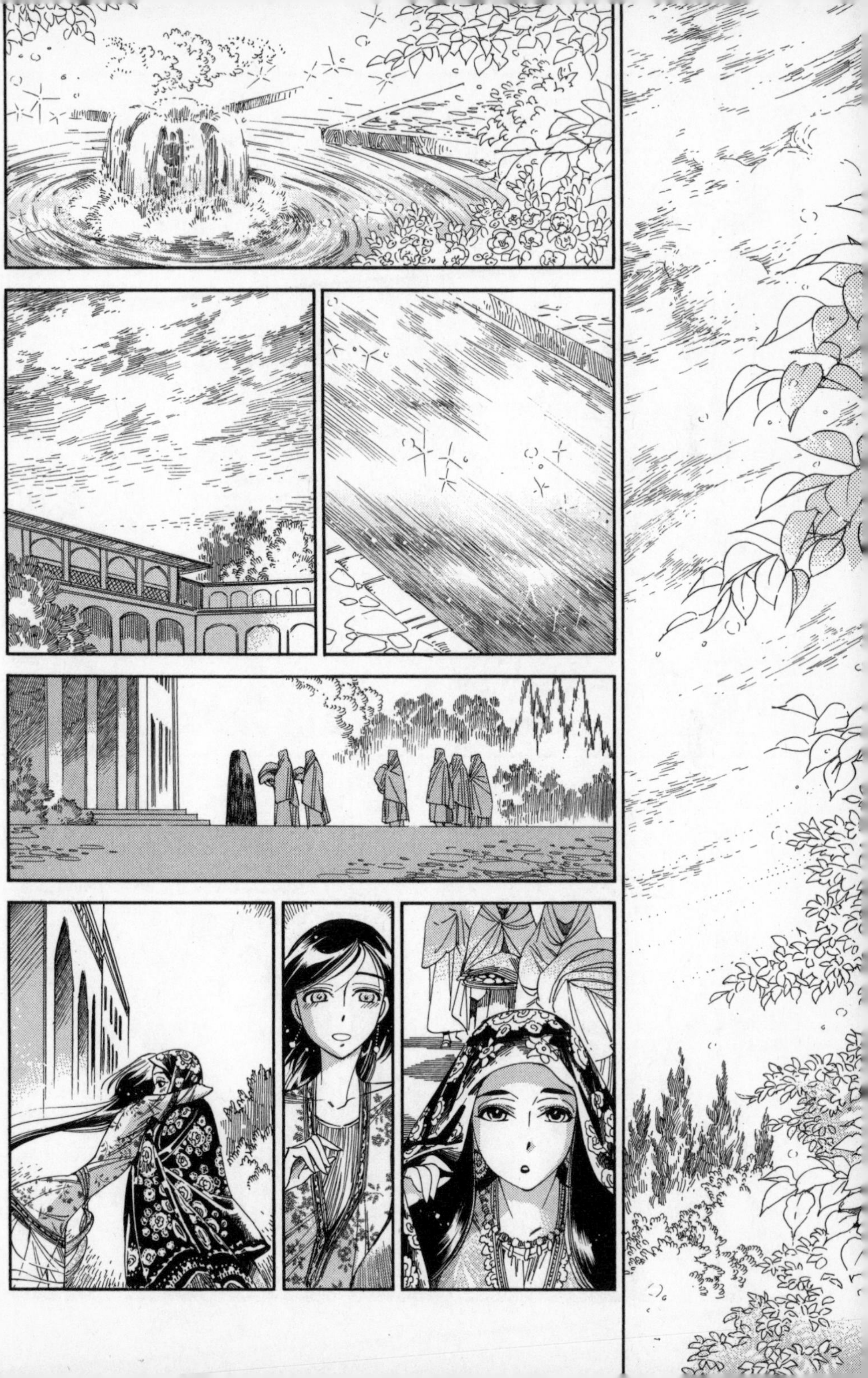

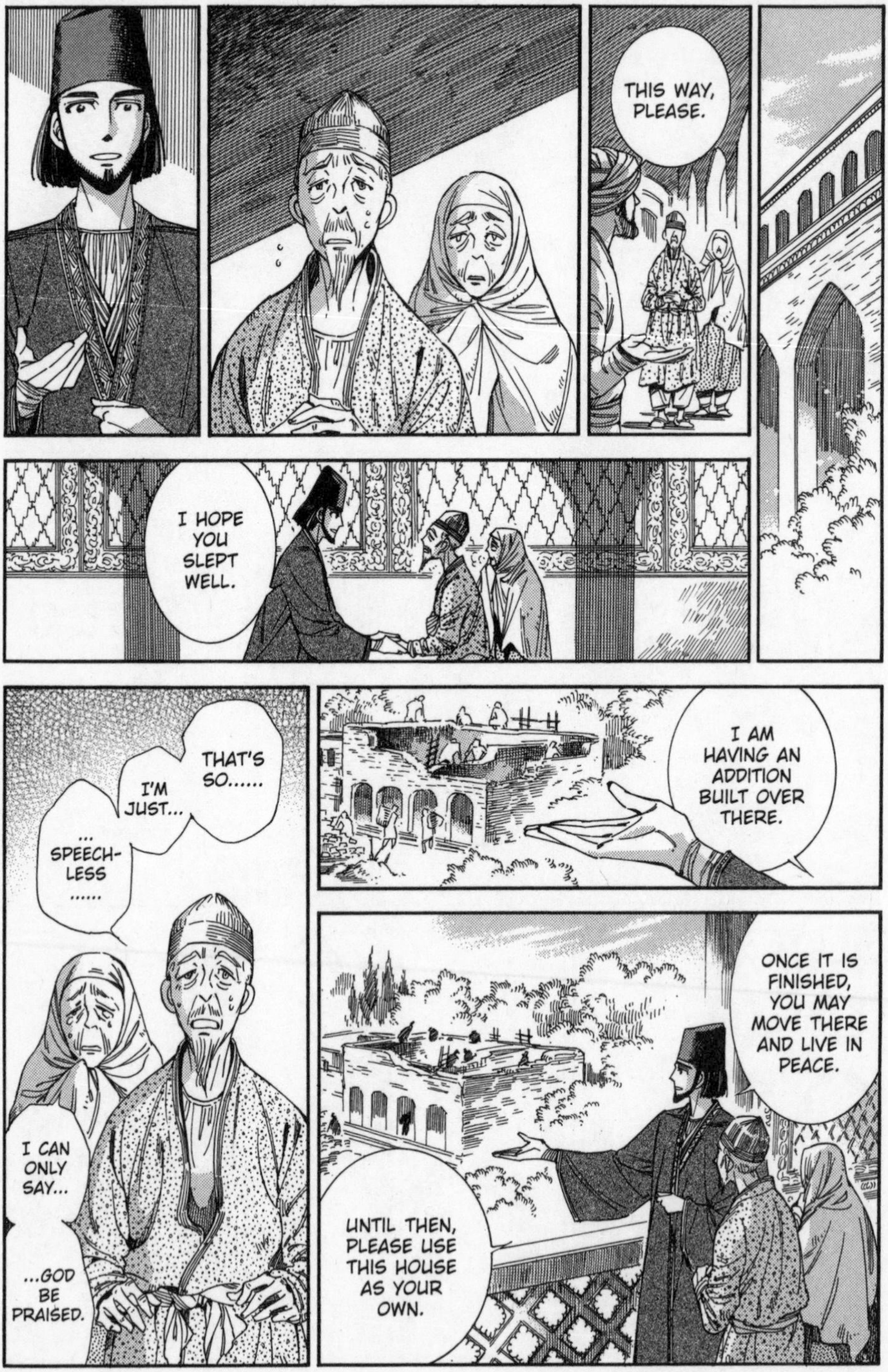
THIS WAY, PLEASE.
I HOPE YOU SLEPT WELL.
I AM HAVING AN ADDITION BUILT OVER THERE.
ONCE IT IS FINISHED, YOU MAY MOVE THERE AND LIVE IN PEACE.
UNTIL THEN, PLEASE USE THIS HOUSE AS YOUR OWN.
THAT'S SO......
I'M JUST...
...SPEECHLESS......
I CAN ONLY SAY...
...GOD BE PRAISED.

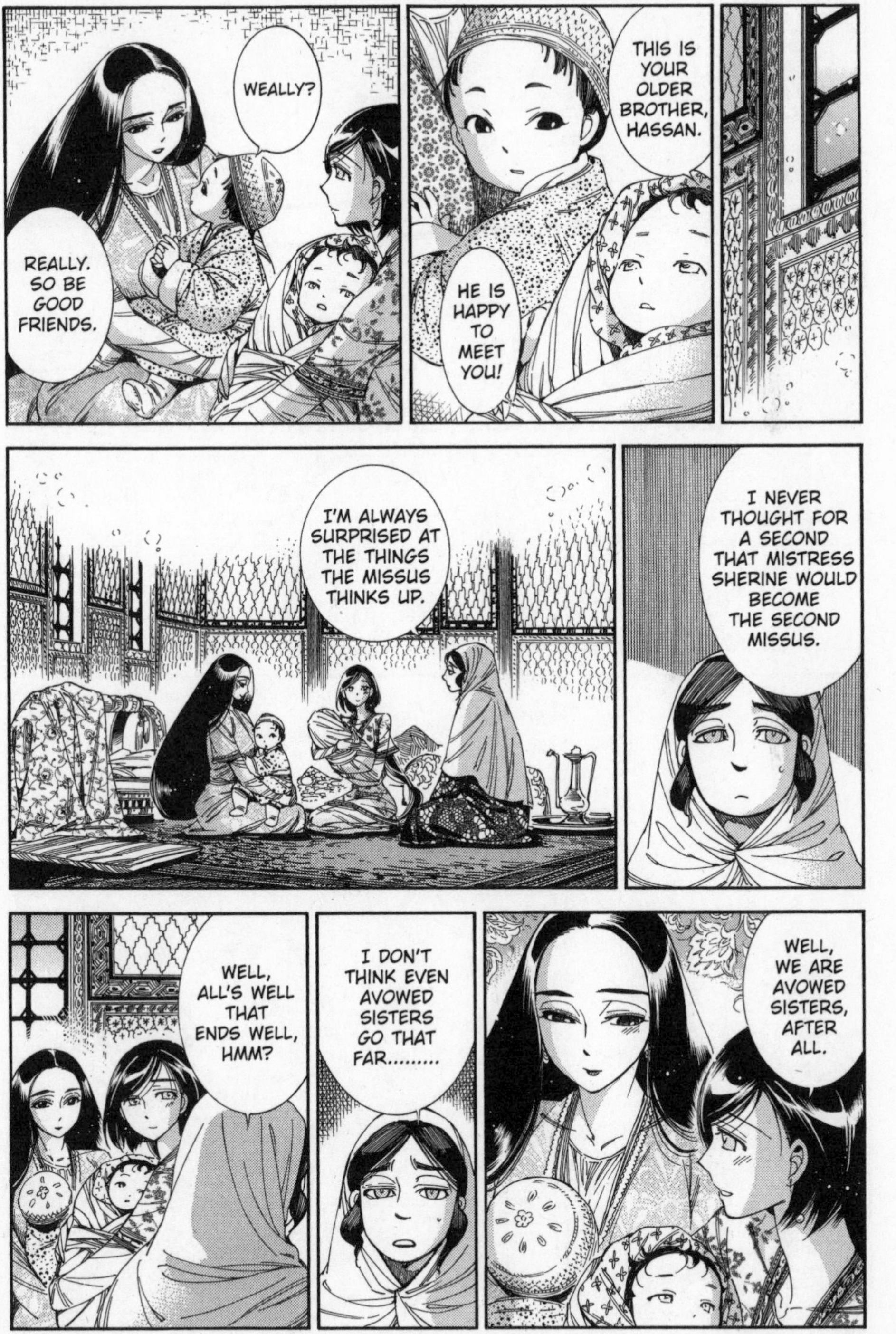
THIS IS YOUR OLDER BROTHER, HASSAN.
HE IS HAPPY TO MEET YOU!
WEALLY?
REALLY. SO BE GOOD FRIENDS.
I NEVER THOUGHT FOR A SECOND THAT MISTRESS SHERINE WOULD BECOME THE SECOND MISSUS.
I'M ALWAYS SURPRISED AT THE THINGS THE MISSUS THINKS UP.
WELL, WE ARE AVOWED SISTERS, AFTER ALL.
I DON'T THINK EVEN AVOWED SISTERS GO THAT FAR.........
WELL, ALL'S WELL THAT ENDS WELL, HMM?

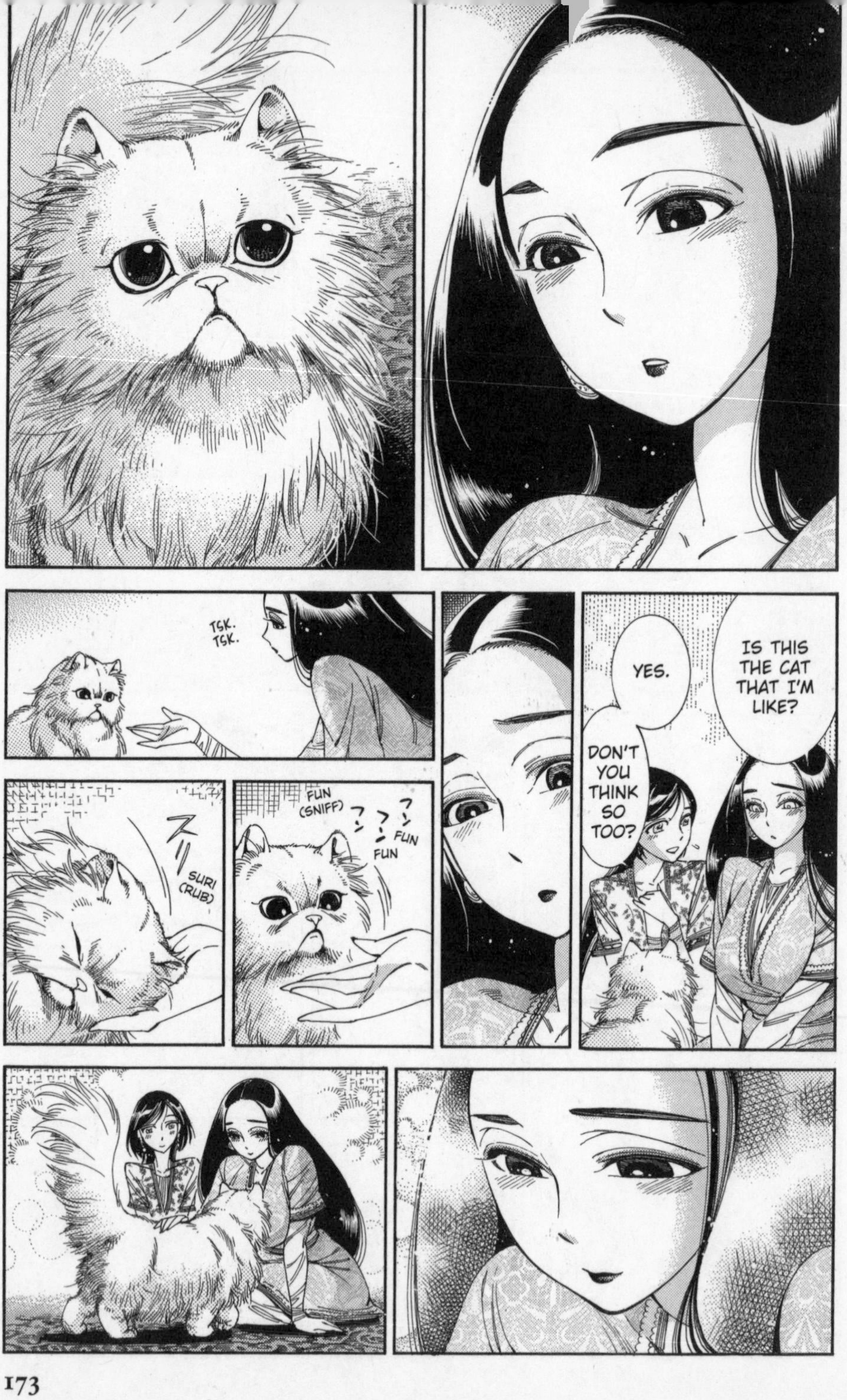
IS THIS THE CAT THAT I'M LIKE?
YES.
DON'T YOU THINK SO TOO?
TSK. TSK.
FUN (SNIFF)
FUN
FUN
SURI (RUB)

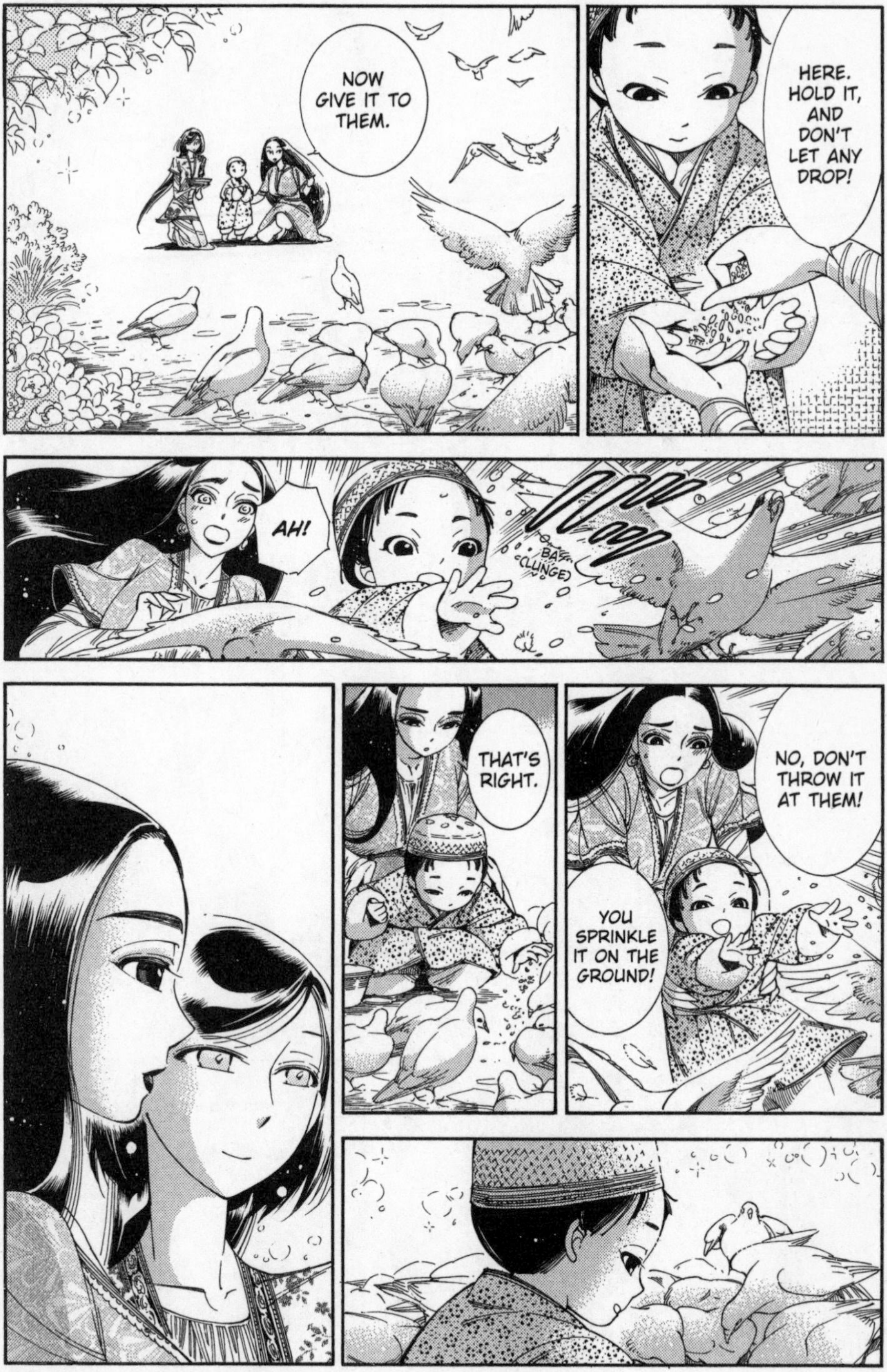
HERE. HOLD IT, AND DON'T LET ANY DROP!
NOW GIVE IT TO THEM.
BA (LUNGE)
AH!
NO, DON'T THROW IT AT THEM!
YOU SPRINKLE IT ON THE GROUND!
THAT'S RIGHT.

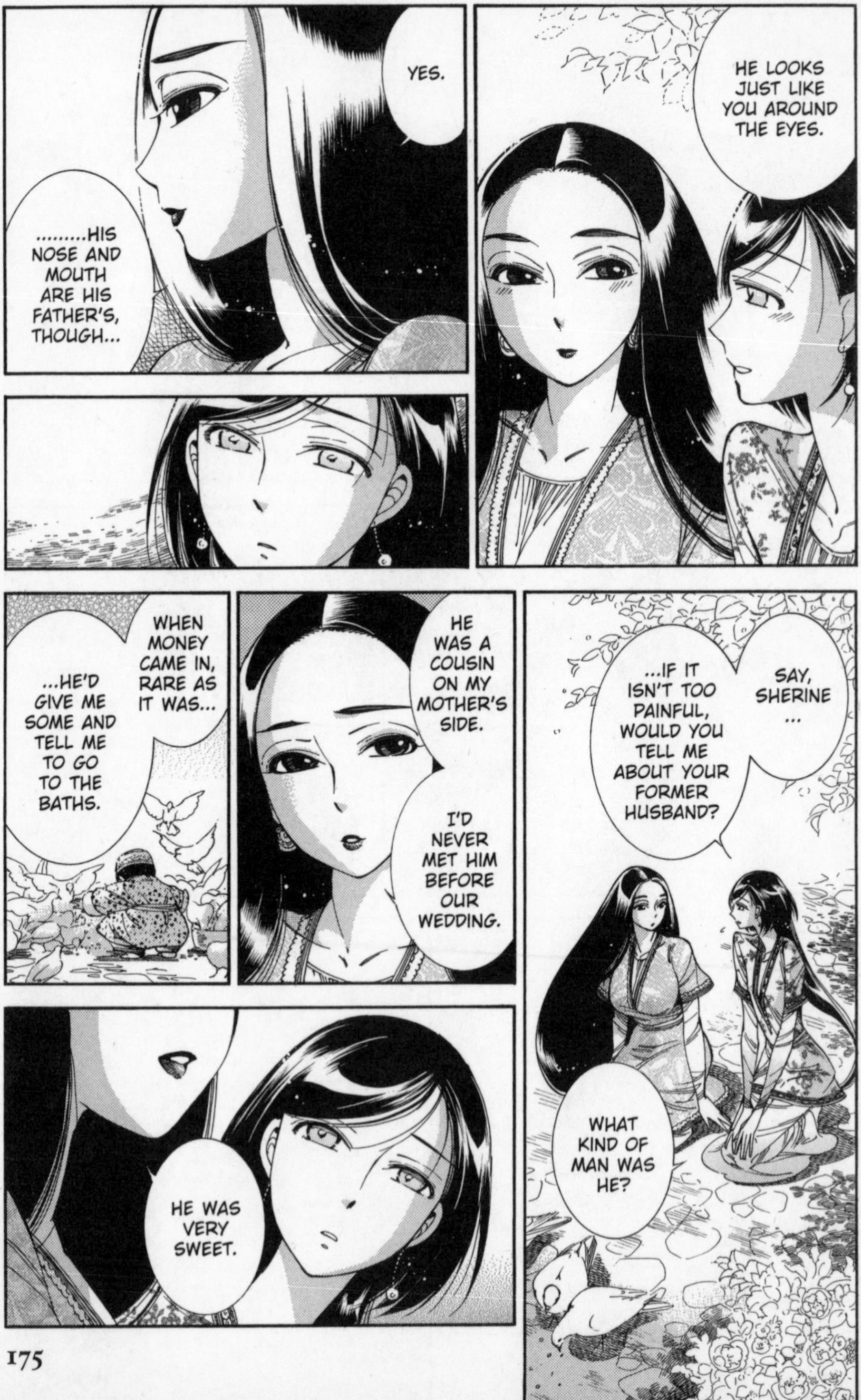
HE LOOKS JUST LIKE YOU AROUND THE EYES.
YES.
.........HIS NOSE AND MOUTH ARE HIS FATHER'S, THOUGH...
SAY, SHERINE ...
...IF IT ISN'T TOO PAINFUL, WOULD YOU TELL ME ABOUT YOUR FORMER HUSBAND?
WHAT KIND OF MAN WAS HE?
HE WAS A COUSIN ON MY MOTHER'S SIDE.
I'D NEVER MET HIM BEFORE OUR WEDDING.
WHEN MONEY CAME IN, RARE AS IT WAS...
...HE'D GIVE ME SOME AND TELL ME TO GO TO THE BATHS.
HE WAS VERY SWEET.

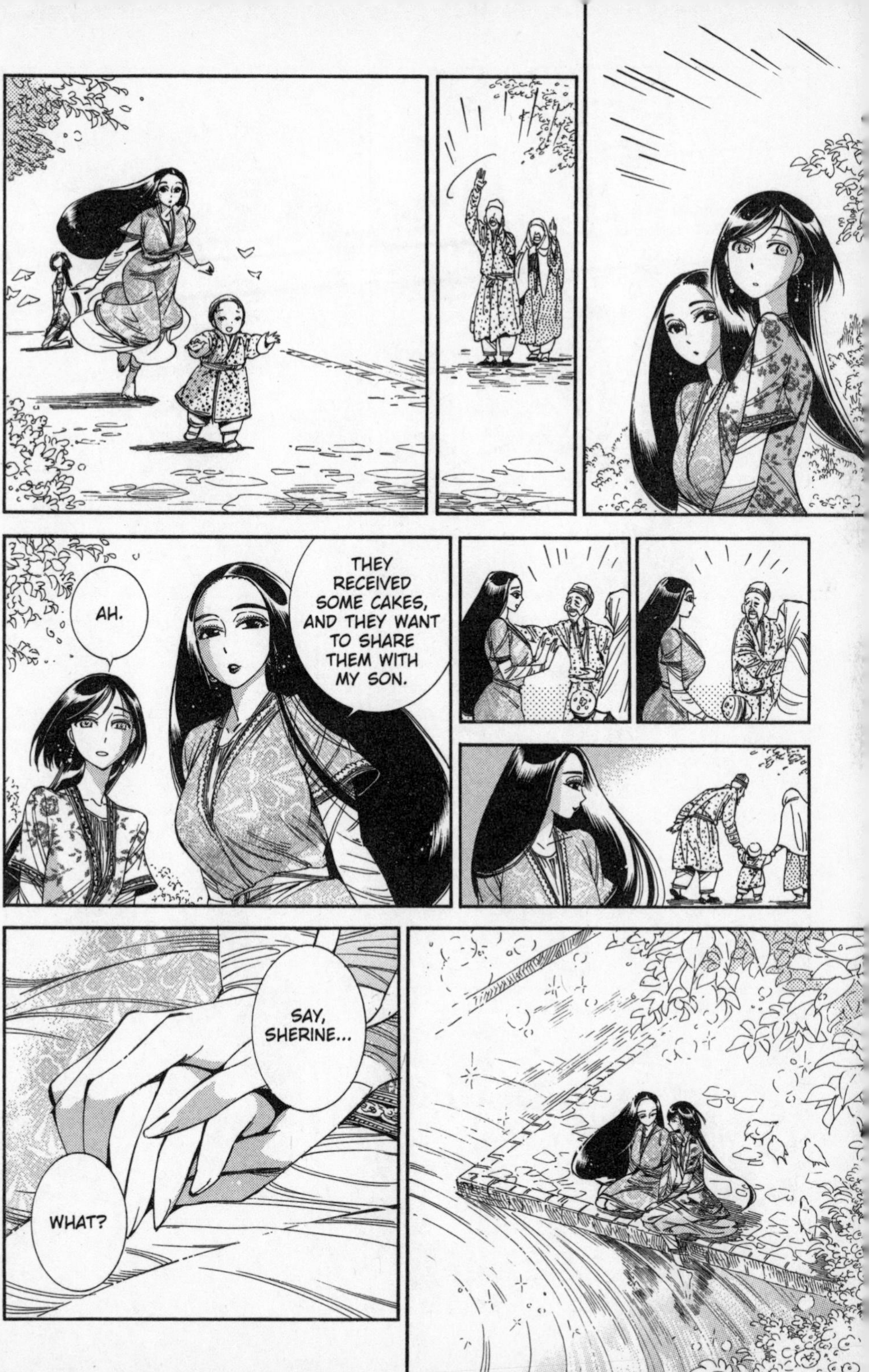
THEY RECEIVED SOME CAKES, AND THEY WANT TO SHARE THEM WITH MY SON.
AH.
SAY, SHERINE...
WHAT?

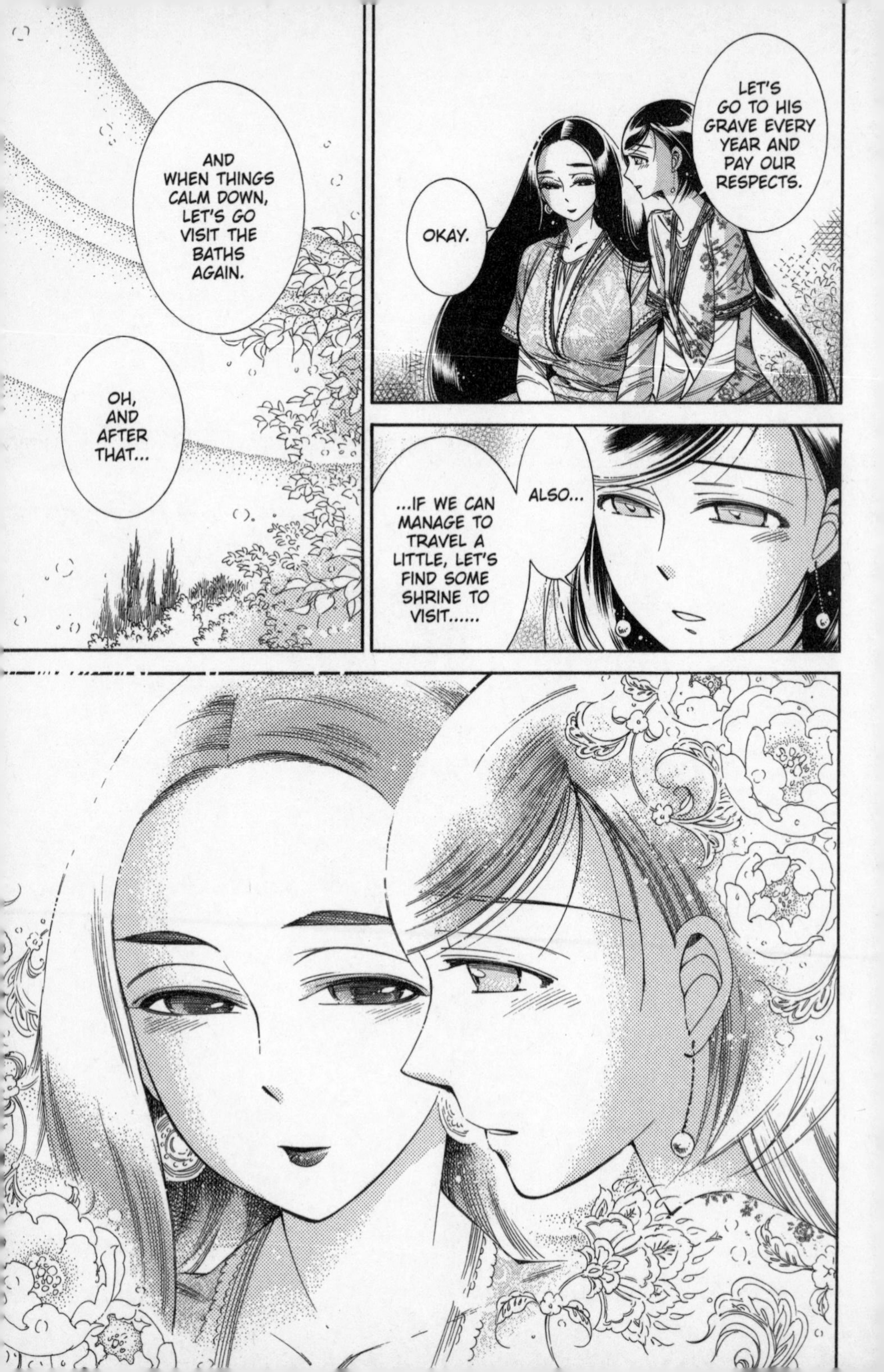
LET'S GO TO HIS GRAVE EVERY YEAR AND PAY OUR RESPECTS.
OKAY.
ALSO...
...IF WE CAN MANAGE TO TRAVEL A LITTLE, LET'S FIND SOME SHRINE TO VISIT......
AND WHEN THINGS CALM DOWN, LET'S GO VISIT THE BATHS AGAIN.
OH, AND AFTER THAT...

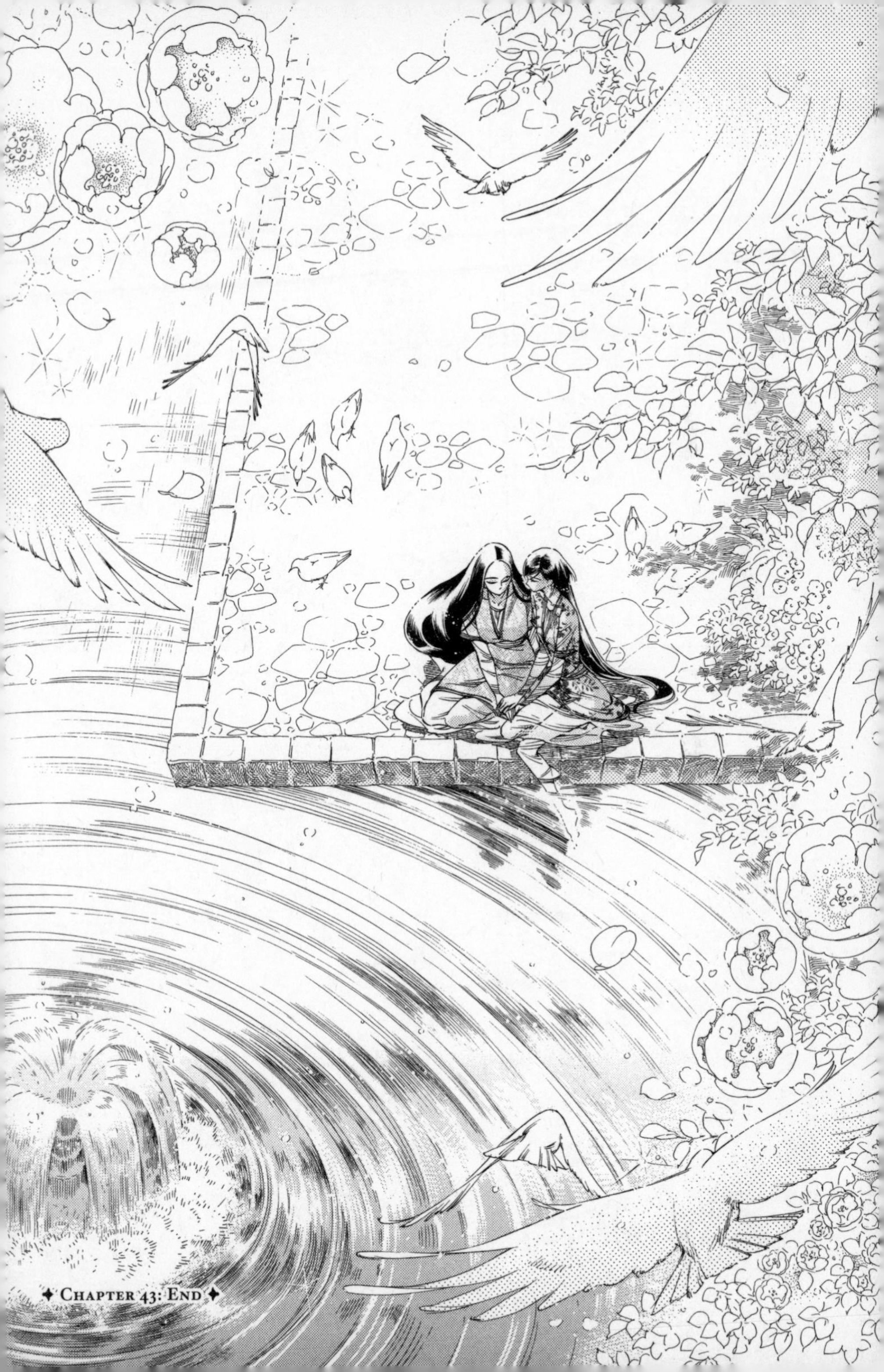
✦ Chapter 43: End ✦

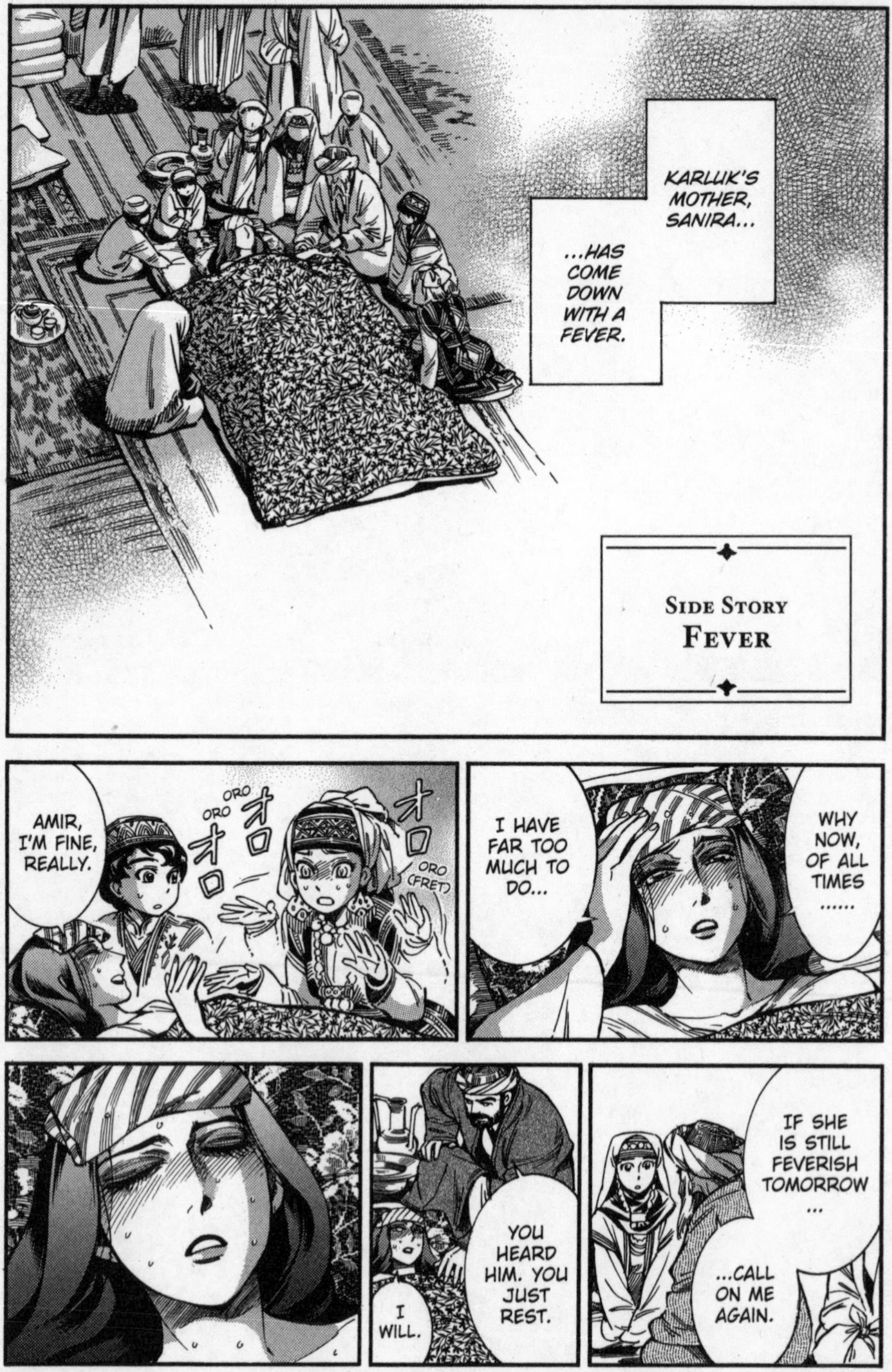
KARLUK'S MOTHER, SANIRA...
...HAS COME DOWN WITH A FEVER.
SIDE STORY
FEVER
WHY NOW, OF ALL TIMES ......
I HAVE FAR TOO MUCH TO DO...
ORO (FRET)
オロ
ORO
オロ
ORO
ORO
AMIR, I'M FINE, REALLY.
IF SHE IS STILL FEVERISH TOMORROW ...
...CALL ON ME AGAIN.
YOU HEARD HIM. YOU JUST REST.
I WILL.

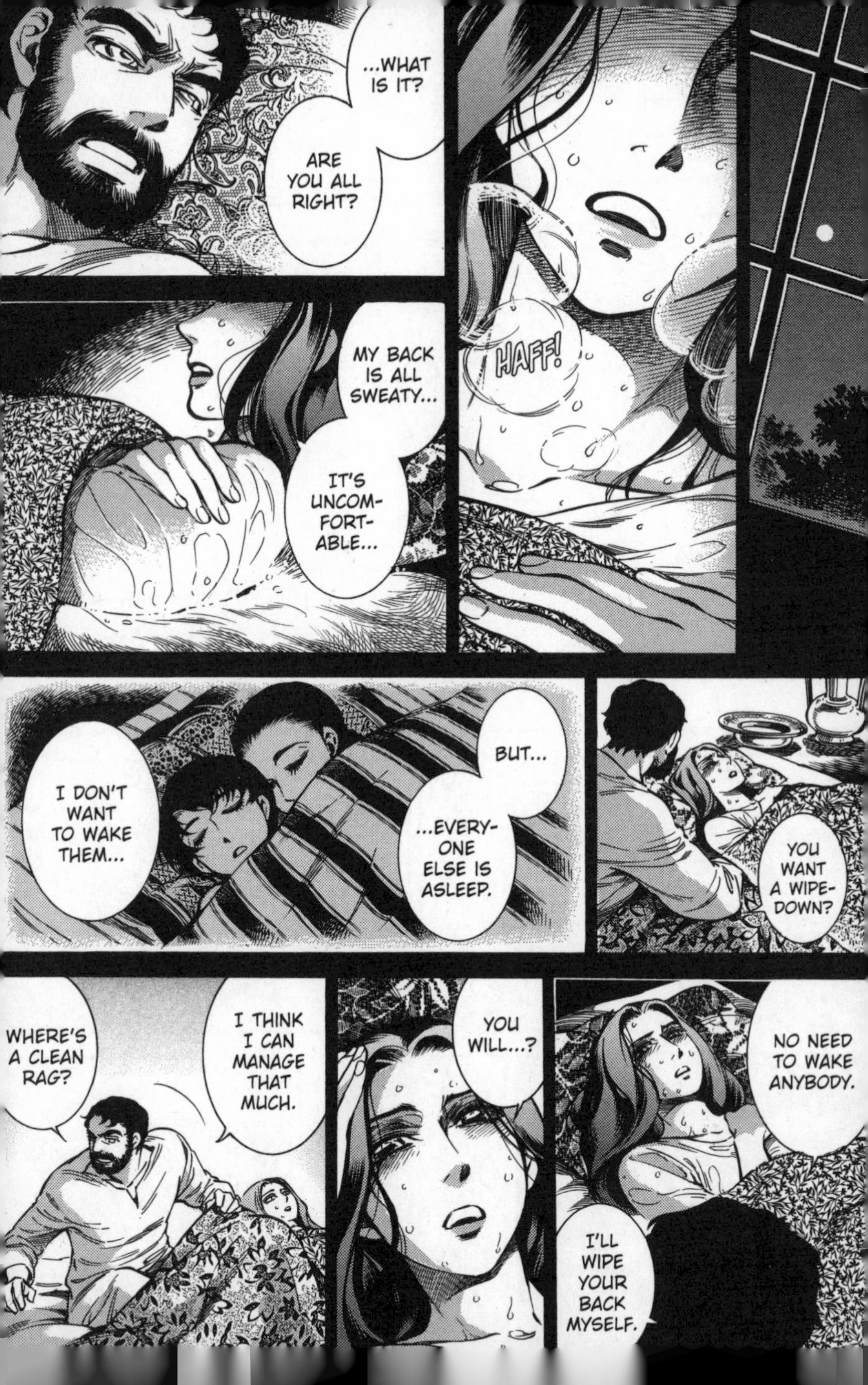
HAFF!
...WHAT IS IT?
ARE YOU ALL RIGHT?
MY BACK IS ALL SWEATY...
IT'S UNCOM-FORT-ABLE...
YOU WANT A WIPE-DOWN?
BUT...
...EVERY-ONE ELSE IS ASLEEP.
I DON'T WANT TO WAKE THEM...
NO NEED TO WAKE ANYBODY.
I'LL WIPE YOUR BACK MYSELF.
YOU WILL...?
I THINK I CAN MANAGE THAT MUCH.
WHERE'S A CLEAN RAG?

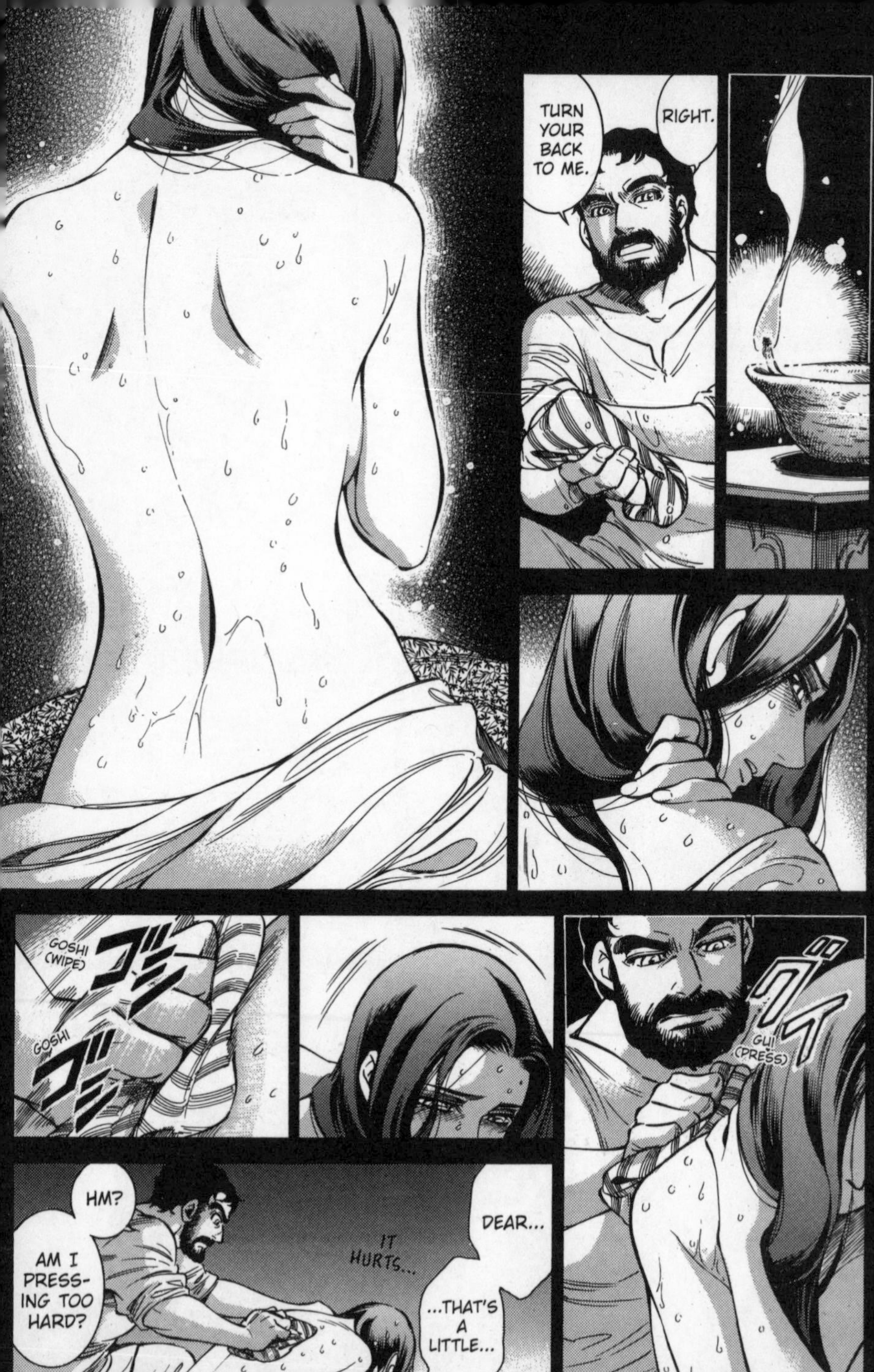
RIGHT.
TURN YOUR BACK TO ME.
GUI (PRESS)
GOSHI (WIPE)
GOSHI
DEAR...
IT HURTS...
...THAT'S A LITTLE...
HM?
AM I PRESSING TOO HARD?

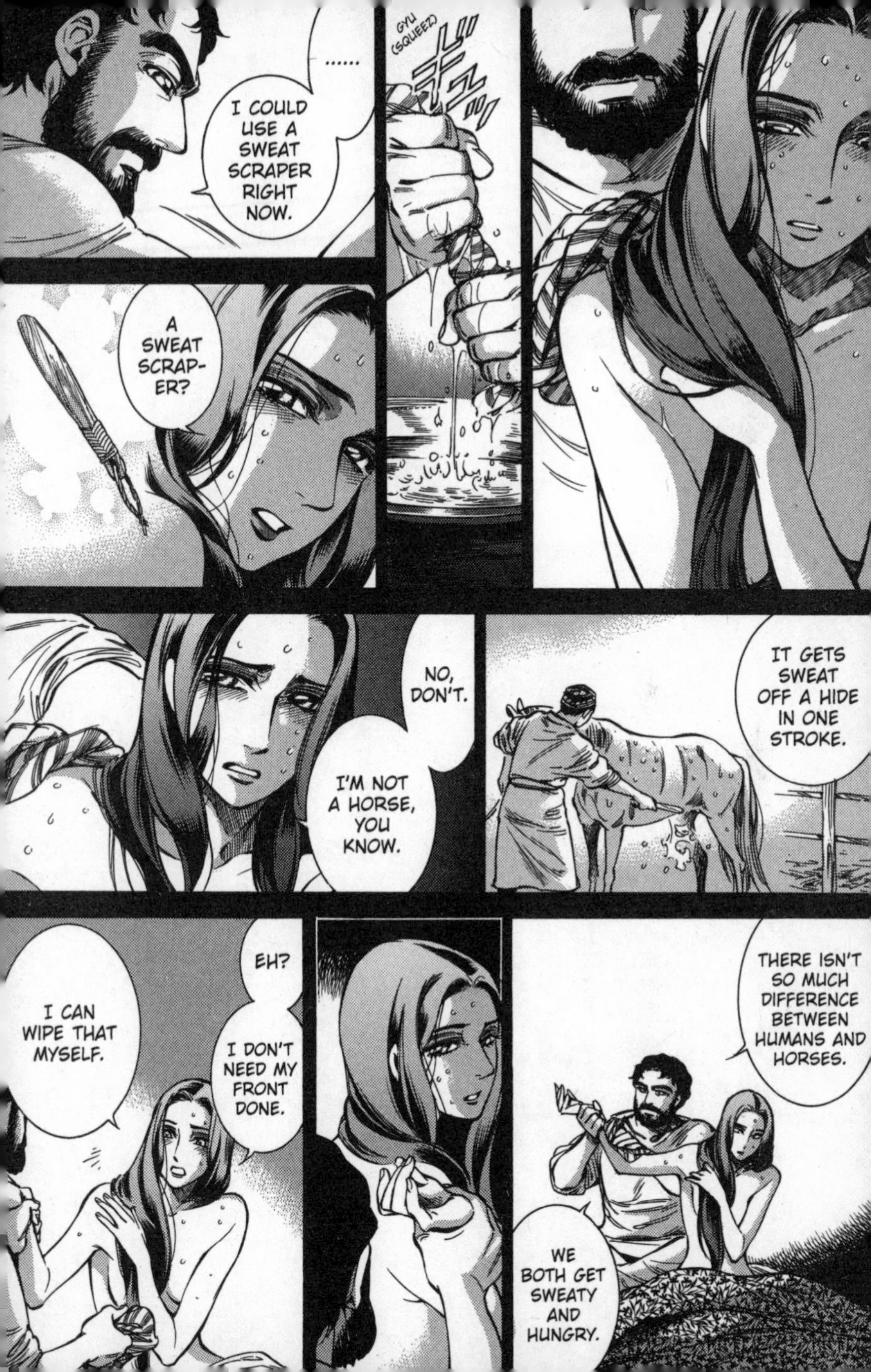
GYU (SQUEEZ)
......
I COULD USE A SWEAT SCRAPER RIGHT NOW.
A SWEAT SCRAPER?
IT GETS SWEAT OFF A HIDE IN ONE STROKE.
NO, DON'T.
I'M NOT A HORSE, YOU KNOW.
THERE ISN'T SO MUCH DIFFERENCE BETWEEN HUMANS AND HORSES.
WE BOTH GET SWEATY AND HUNGRY.
EH?
I CAN WIPE THAT MYSELF.
I DON'T NEED MY FRONT DONE.

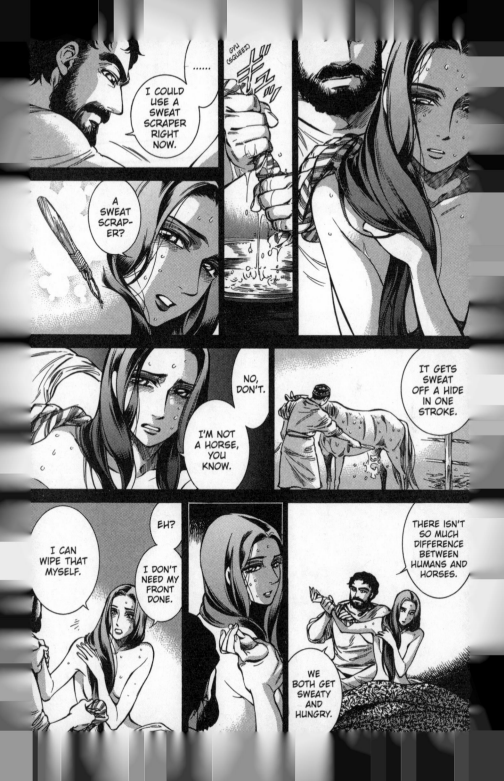

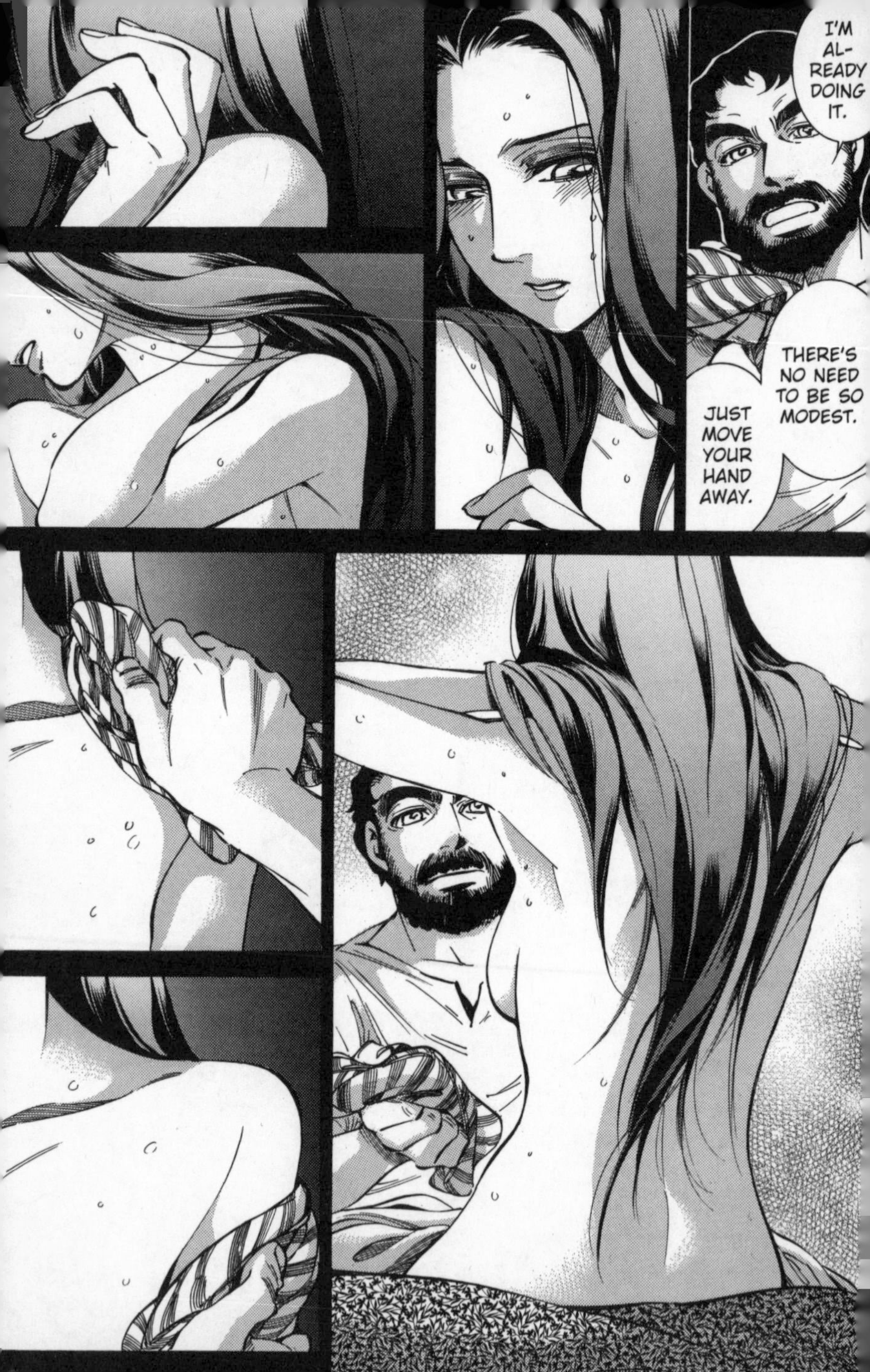
I'M AL-READY DOING IT.
THERE'S NO NEED TO BE SO MODEST.
JUST MOVE YOUR HAND AWAY.

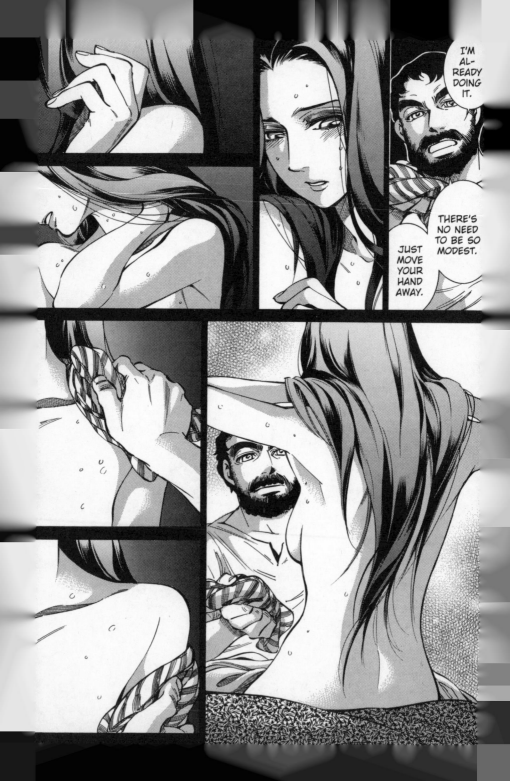

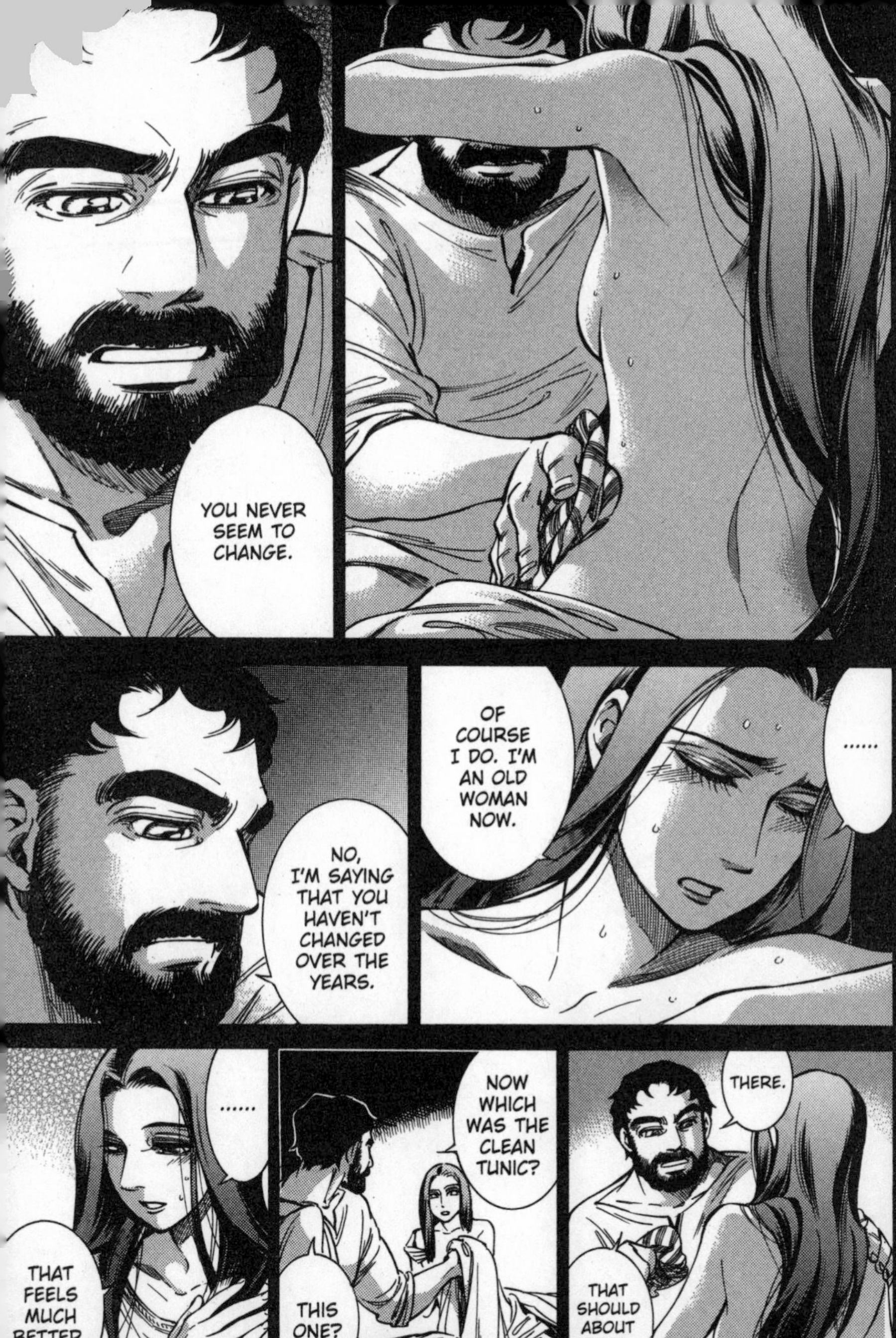
YOU NEVER SEEM TO CHANGE.
......
OF COURSE I DO. I'M AN OLD WOMAN NOW.
NO, I'M SAYING THAT YOU HAVEN'T CHANGED OVER THE YEARS.
THERE.
THAT SHOULD ABOUT DO IT.
NOW WHICH WAS THE CLEAN TUNIC?
THIS ONE?
......
THAT FEELS MUCH BETTER.

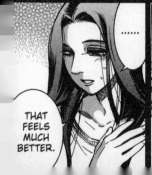

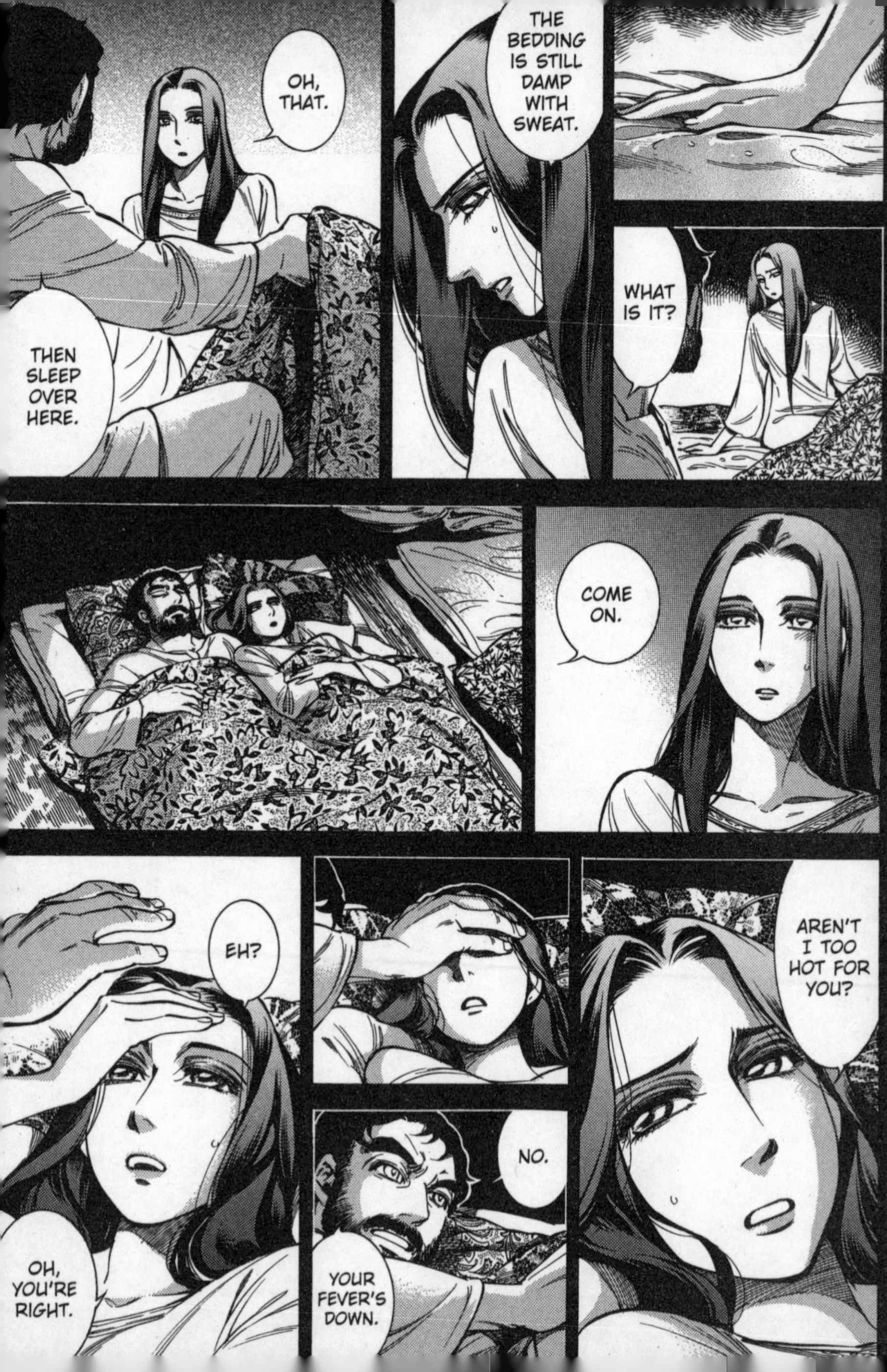
WHAT IS IT?
THE BEDDING IS STILL DAMP WITH SWEAT.
OH, THAT.
THEN SLEEP OVER HERE.
COME ON.
AREN'T I TOO HOT FOR YOU?
NO.
YOUR FEVER'S DOWN.
EH?
OH, YOU'RE RIGHT.

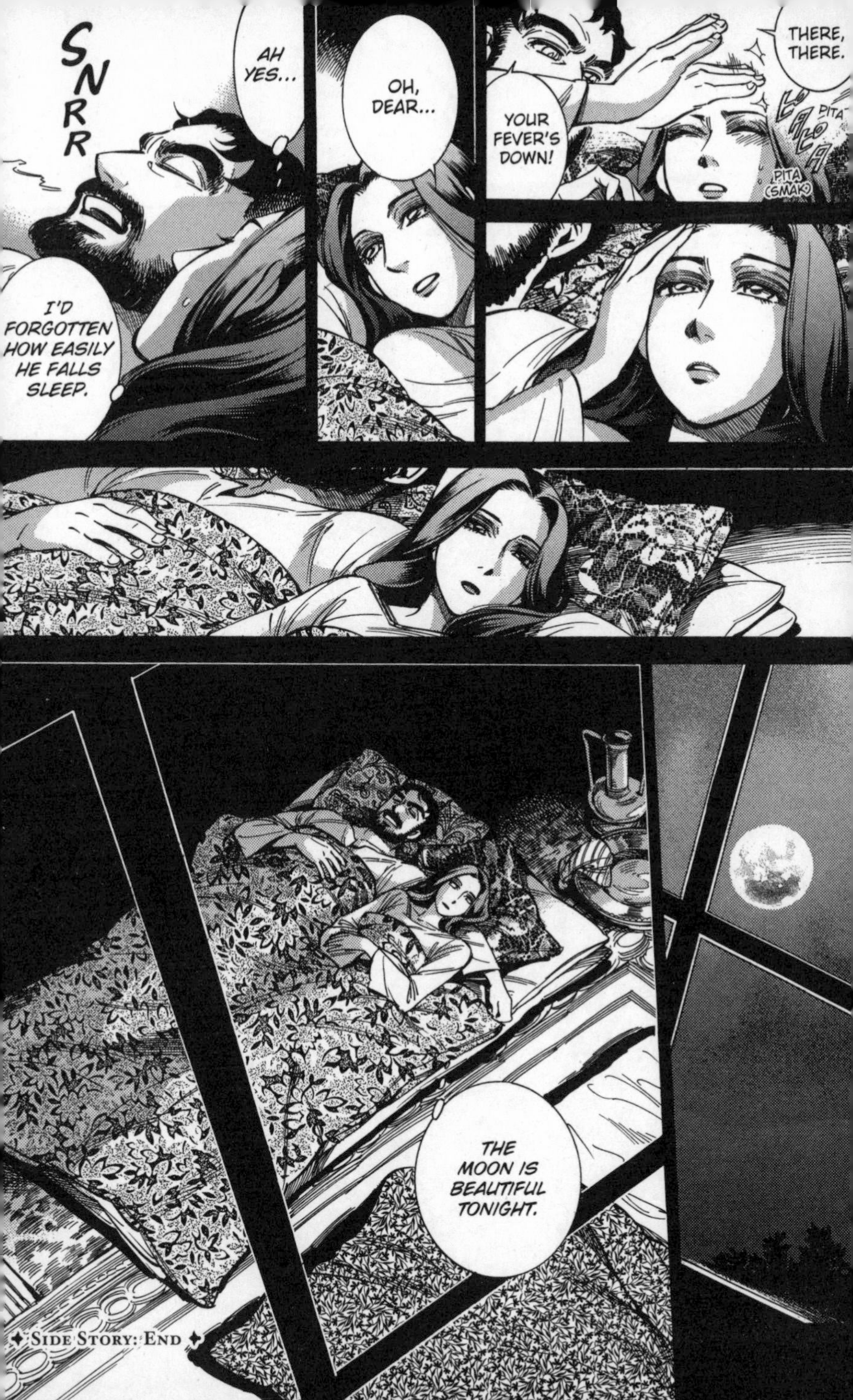
THERE, THERE.
YOUR FEVER'S DOWN!
PITA
PITA (SMAK)
OH, DEAR...
AH YES...
SNRR
I'D FORGOTTEN HOW EASILY HE FALLS SLEEP.
THE MOON IS BEAUTIFUL TONIGHT.
✦ SIDE STORY: END ✦

AFTERWORD

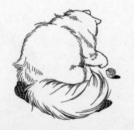

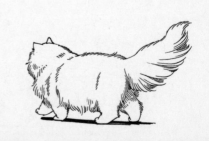

AFTERWORD TAN-TA-DAHH! MANGA!! ♡

"COO-COO-COO, PIGEON, COO-COO"

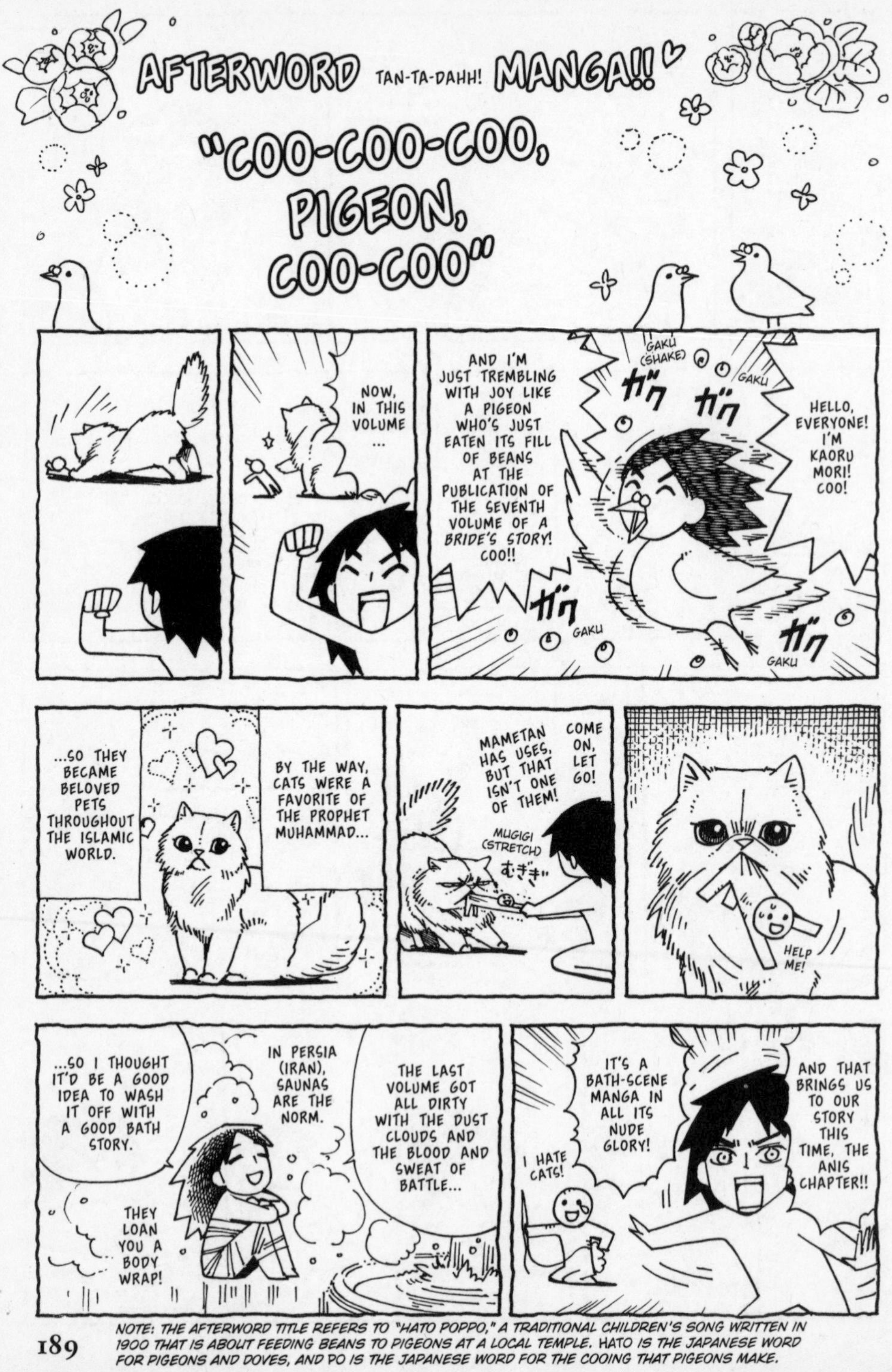
HELLO, EVERYONE! I'M KAORU MORI! COO!
AND I'M JUST TREMBLING WITH JOY LIKE A PIGEON WHO'S JUST EATEN ITS FILL OF BEANS AT THE PUBLICATION OF THE SEVENTH VOLUME OF A BRIDE'S STORY! COO!!
ガク GAKU (SHAKE)
ガク GAKU
ガク GAKU
ガク GAKU
NOW, IN THIS VOLUME ...
HELP ME!
COME ON, LET GO!
MAMETAN HAS USES, BUT THAT ISN'T ONE OF THEM!
むぎぎ MUGIGI (STRETCH)
BY THE WAY, CATS WERE A FAVORITE OF THE PROPHET MUHAMMAD...
...SO THEY BECAME BELOVED PETS THROUGHOUT THE ISLAMIC WORLD.
AND THAT BRINGS US TO OUR STORY THIS TIME, THE ANIS CHAPTER!!
IT'S A BATH-SCENE MANGA IN ALL ITS NUDE GLORY!
I HATE CATS!
THE LAST VOLUME GOT ALL DIRTY WITH THE DUST CLOUDS AND THE BLOOD AND SWEAT OF BATTLE...
IN PERSIA (IRAN), SAUNAS ARE THE NORM.
...SO I THOUGHT IT'D BE A GOOD IDEA TO WASH IT OFF WITH A GOOD BATH STORY.
THEY LOAN YOU A BODY WRAP!

NOTE: THE AFTERWORD TITLE REFERS TO "HATO POPPO," A TRADITIONAL CHILDREN'S SONG WRITTEN IN 1900 THAT IS ABOUT FEEDING BEANS TO PIGEONS AT A LOCAL TEMPLE. HATO IS THE JAPANESE WORD FOR PIGEONS AND DOVES, AND PO IS THE JAPANESE WORD FOR THE COOING THAT PIGEONS MAKE.

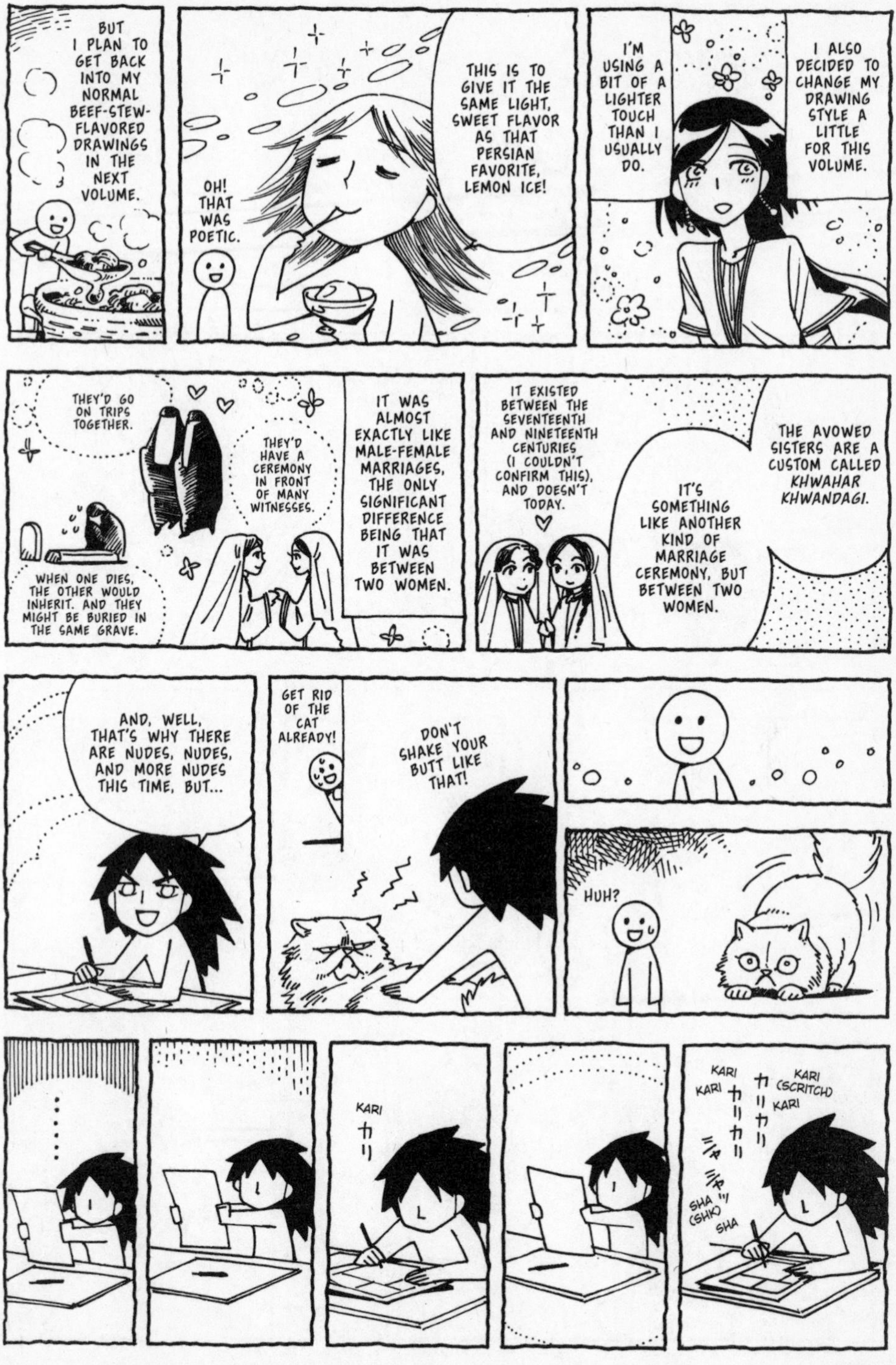

I ALSO DECIDED TO CHANGE MY DRAWING STYLE A LITTLE FOR THIS VOLUME.
I'M USING A BIT OF A LIGHTER TOUCH THAN I USUALLY DO.
THIS IS TO GIVE IT THE SAME LIGHT, SWEET FLAVOR AS THAT PERSIAN FAVORITE, LEMON ICE!
OH! THAT WAS POETIC.
BUT I PLAN TO GET BACK INTO MY NORMAL BEEF-STEW-FLAVORED DRAWINGS IN THE NEXT VOLUME.
THE AVOWED SISTERS ARE A CUSTOM CALLED KHWAHAR KHWANDAGI.
IT'S SOMETHING LIKE ANOTHER KIND OF MARRIAGE CEREMONY, BUT BETWEEN TWO WOMEN.
IT EXISTED BETWEEN THE SEVENTEENTH AND NINETEENTH CENTURIES (I COULDN'T CONFIRM THIS), AND DOESN'T TODAY.
IT WAS ALMOST EXACTLY LIKE MALE-FEMALE MARRIAGES, THE ONLY SIGNIFICANT DIFFERENCE BEING THAT IT WAS BETWEEN TWO WOMEN.
THEY'D HAVE A CEREMONY IN FRONT OF MANY WITNESSES.
THEY'D GO ON TRIPS TOGETHER.
WHEN ONE DIES, THE OTHER WOULD INHERIT. AND THEY MIGHT BE BURIED IN THE SAME GRAVE.
HUH?
DON'T SHAKE YOUR BUTT LIKE THAT!
GET RID OF THE CAT ALREADY!
AND, WELL, THAT'S WHY THERE ARE NUDES, NUDES, AND MORE NUDES THIS TIME, BUT...
KARI (SCRITCH) カリ KARI
KARI カリカリ KARI
シャ シャ
SHA (SHK) SHA
KARI カリ
......

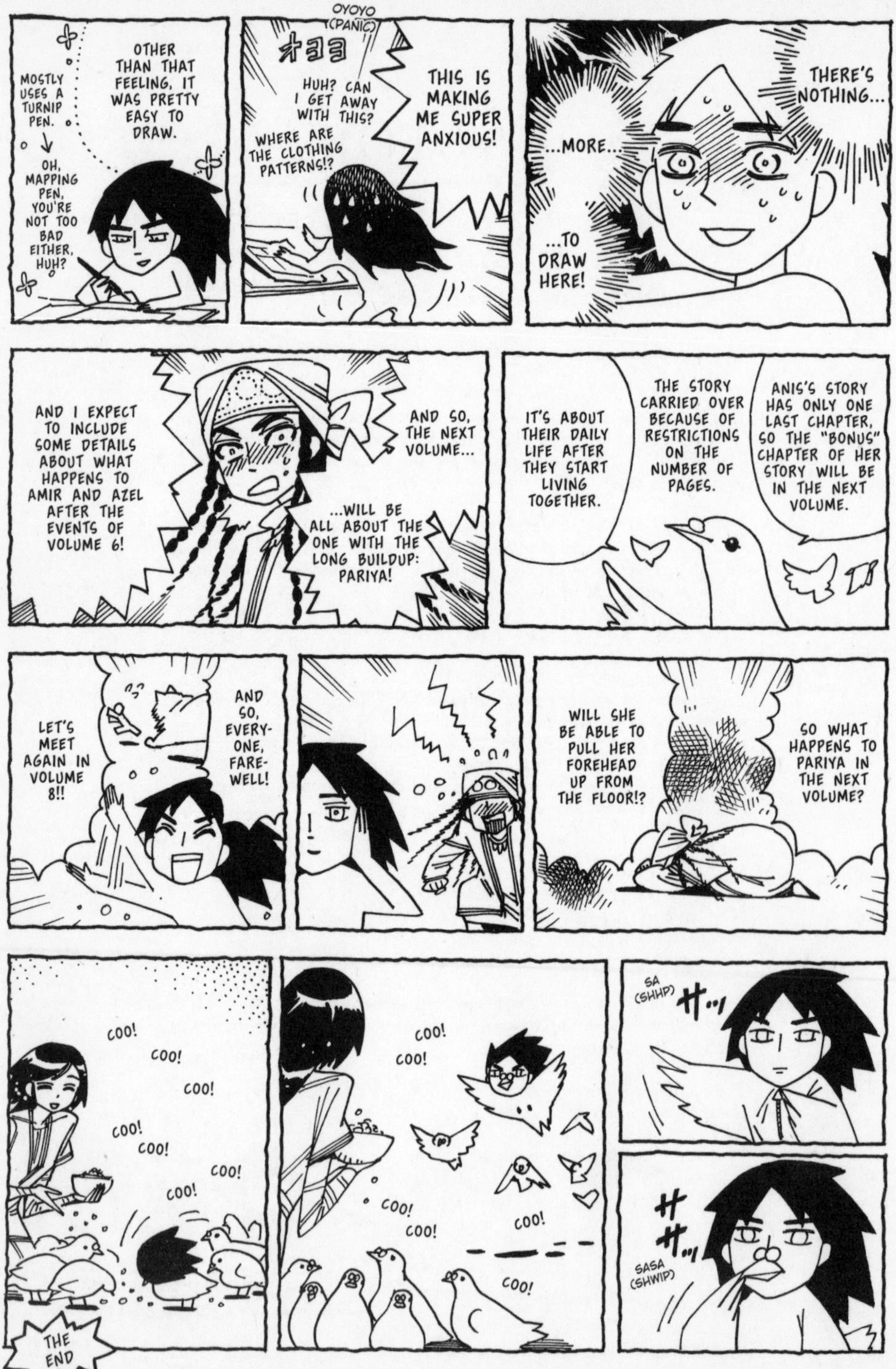
THERE'S NOTHING...
...MORE...
...TO DRAW HERE!
OYOYO (PANIC)
オヨヨ
THIS IS MAKING ME SUPER ANXIOUS!
HUH? CAN I GET AWAY WITH THIS?
WHERE ARE THE CLOTHING PATTERNS!?
OTHER THAN THAT FEELING, IT WAS PRETTY EASY TO DRAW.
MOSTLY USES A TURNIP PEN.
OH, MAPPING PEN, YOU'RE NOT TOO BAD EITHER, HUH?
ANIS'S STORY HAS ONLY ONE LAST CHAPTER, SO THE "BONUS" CHAPTER OF HER STORY WILL BE IN THE NEXT VOLUME.
THE STORY CARRIED OVER BECAUSE OF RESTRICTIONS ON THE NUMBER OF PAGES.
IT'S ABOUT THEIR DAILY LIFE AFTER THEY START LIVING TOGETHER.
AND SO, THE NEXT VOLUME...
...WILL BE ALL ABOUT THE ONE WITH THE LONG BUILDUP: PARIYA!
AND I EXPECT TO INCLUDE SOME DETAILS ABOUT WHAT HAPPENS TO AMIR AND AZEL AFTER THE EVENTS OF VOLUME 6!
SO WHAT HAPPENS TO PARIYA IN THE NEXT VOLUME?
WILL SHE BE ABLE TO PULL HER FOREHEAD UP FROM THE FLOOR!?
AND SO, EVERYONE, FAREWELL!
LET'S MEET AGAIN IN VOLUME 8!!
SA (SHHP)
SASA (SHWIP)
COO!
COO!
COO!
COO!
COO!
COO!
COO!
COO!
COO!
COO!
COO!
COO!
COO!
THE END

A BRIDE'S STORY ⑦

KAORU MORI

TRANSLATION: WILLIAM FLANAGAN

LETTERING: ABIGAIL BLACKMAN

A BRIDE'S STORY Volume 7 © 2015 Kaoru Mori All rights reserved. First published in Japan in 2015 by ENTERBRAIN, INC., Tokyo. English translation rights arranged with ENTERBRAIN, INC. through Tuttle-Mori Agency, Inc., Tokyo.

Translation © 2015 by Hachette Book Group

Yen Press
Hachette Book Group
1290 Avenue of the Americas
New York, NY 10104
www.hachettebookgroup.com
www.yenpress.com

Yen Press is an imprint of Hachette Book Group, Inc. The Yen Press name and logo are trademarks of Hachette Book Group, Inc.

First Yen Press Edition: November 2015

ISBN: 978-0-316-34893-5

10 9 8 7 6 5 4 3 2 1

BVG

Printed in the
United States of America

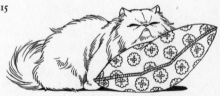

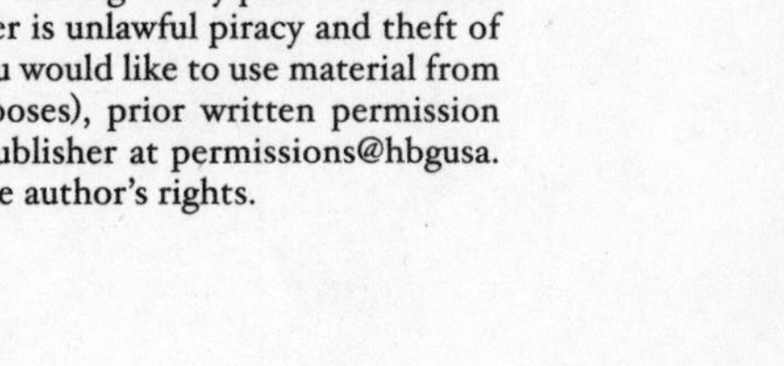

DI

from